PELAGI CITY LIBRARY
RED F

The Granary,
Michael Street,
Limerick.

By the same author

The Winter Queen
Leviathan
Turkish Gambit
The Death of Achilles
Special Assignments
The State Counsellor
Pelagia and the White Bulldog
Pelagia and the Black Monk

PELAGIA & THE RED ROOSTER

BORIS AKUNIN

Translated by Andrew Bromfield

Weidenfeld & Nicolson

LONDON

First published in Great Britain in 2008
by Weidenfeld & Nicolson.

First published in Russian as Pelagiya i krasny petukh by
AST Publishers, Moscow, Russia and Edizioni Frassinelli, Milan, Italy. All rights reserved.

Published by arrangement with Linda Michaels Limited, International Literary Agents.

© Boris Akunin 2003
Translation © Andrew Bromfield 2008

1 3 5 7 9 10 8 6 4 2

A CIP catalogue record for this book is available
from the British Library.

ISBN 978 0 297 85087 8 (hardback)
ISBN 978 0 297 85297 1 (trade paperback)

Typeset by Input Data Services Ltd, Bridgwater, Somerset

Printed in Great Britain by
Clays Ltd, St Ives plc

Weidenfeld & Nicolson
An imprint of the Orion Publishing Group
Orion House, 5 Upper St Martin's Lane, London WC2H 9EA

The Orion Publishing Group's policy is to use papers that are natural,
renewable and recyclable products and made from wood grown in sustainable
forests. The logging and manufacturing processes are expected to
conform to the environmental regulations of the country of origin.

www.orionbooks.co.uk

The true realist, if he is a non-believer, will always discover within himself the strength and ability not to believe even in a miracle . . .

F.M. Dostoyevsky, *The Brothers Karamazov*

PART ONE

Here

I

On the *Sturgeon*

About Muffin

Muffin rolled on board the steamer *Sturgeon* as roundly and gently as the little loaf he was named after. He waited for a thick scrap of fog to creep across on to the quayside, then shrank and shrivelled and made himself just like a little grey cloud too. A sudden dart to the very edge, then a hop and a skip up on to the cast-iron bollard. He tripped lightly along the mooring line stretched as taut as a bowstring (this was no great trick for Muffin – he had once danced a jig on a cable for a bet). Nobody spotted a thing; and there you are now: welcome the new passenger on board!

Of course, it wouldn't have broken him to buy a deck ticket. Only thirty-five kopecks as far as the next mooring, the town of Ust-Sviyazhsk. But for a 'razin' buying a ticket would be an insult to his profession. Buying tickets was for the 'geese' and the 'carp'.

Muffin had got his nickname because he was small and nimble and he walked with short, springy steps, as if he were rolling along. And he had a round head, cropped close. With ears that stuck out at the sides like little shovels, but were remarkably keen of hearing.

What is known about the 'razins'? A small group of river folk, inconspicuous, but without it the River would not be the River, like a swamp without mosquitoes. There are experts at cleaning out other people's pockets on shore as well – 'pinchers' they're called – but those folk are petty, ragged riff-raff and for the most part homeless strays, so they aren't paid much respect, but the razins are, because they've been around since time out of mind. As for the question of where the name came from, some claim that it must have come from the word 'razor', since the razins are so very sharp; but the razins themselves claim it comes from Ataman Stenka Razin, the river bandit, who also plucked fat 'geese' on the great River-Mother. The philistines, of course, claim that this is mere wishful thinking.

It was good work, and Muffin liked it exceptionally well.

Get on the steamer without anyone noticing you, rub shoulders with the passengers until the next mooring and then get off. What you've taken is yours; what you couldn't take can go sailing on.

So what are the trump cards in this game?

Sailing airily down the river is good for the health. That's the first thing. And then you see all different kinds of people; sometimes they'll start telling you something so amusing you clean forget about the job. That's the second thing. But the most important thing of all is: you won't do any time in jail or hard labour. Muffin had been working on the River for twenty years, and he had no idea what a prison even looked like, he'd never laid eyes on one. Just you try catching him with the swag. The slightest hitch, and It's gone: 'The rope ends are under the water.' And by the way, that old Russian saying was invented about the razins, only other folk never bother to think about it. 'Ends' is what whey call their booty. And as for the water, there it is, splashing about just over the side. Get spotted, and you just chuck the ends in the water, and there's no way they can prove a thing. The River-Mother will hide it all. Well, they'll give you a thrashing, of course – that's just the way of things. Only they won't beat you really hard, because the public that sails on steamers is mostly cultured and delicate, not like in the villages by the river, where the peasants are so wild and ignorant they can easily flog a thief to death.

The razins call themselves 'pike' as well, and they call the passengers 'geese' and 'carp'. As well as 'The rope ends are under the water,' there's another saying that everyone repeats all the time, but they don't understand the real meaning: 'The pike's in the river to stop the carp dozing.'

The most important festival of all for a razin is the first steamer of spring, better than any saint's day. During the winter you can turn as dull as lead for lack of work, and sometimes you can find yourself hungry too. Just sitting there, doing nothing, cursing tedious old winter, waiting for the spring, your young bride. Sometimes your dear-heart will play hard to get for a long time and there'll be no steamers sailing almost until June, but this year spring had come calling on Muffin when she was still a young thing, cute and pretty, and not been obstinate at all. So passionate and affectionate she was, the way she'd clung to him – he'd never known the like. Would you believe it, only the first of April and all the ice was gone already, and the shipping season had begun.

The River's floodwaters spread out so far and wide, you could scarcely even see the banks, but the *Sturgeon* was sticking strictly to the fairway, moving at her slowest speed. Because of the fog, the captain was being extremely cautious, and every two or three minutes he gave a hoarse blast on the whistle: 'Ooohdooo! Get out of it – I'm coming!'

The fog was a nuisance to the captain, but it was Muffin's trustiest comrade. If he could only have cut a deal, he would have given it half the loot, just as long as it kept rolling in thick and heavy.

He certainly had nothing to complain about today; the fog had made a really first-rate effort, spreading itself thickest just above the river, so that the lower deck, where the cabins were, was as good as smothered. The boat deck, where the lifeboats lay and the folks with sacks and bundles sat along the edge, was sometimes released from the fog's grip and sometimes covered over: it was like in a fairy tale: the people were there, then suddenly they all disappeared and there was nothing left but white murk. Only the tall black funnel and the bridge were above the fog. Up there, the captain probably felt like he wasn't a captain sailing on the *Sturgeon* at all, but more like the Lord God Sabaoth himself, floating on the clouds.

All the vessels in the river fleet of the Nord shipping line were called after some kind of fish; it was one of the owner's whims – from the flagship, the triple-decked *Great Sturgeon*, with first-class cabins that cost ten roubles each, to the last little panting, puffing tug, the *Gudgeon* or the *Blay*.

The *Sturgeon* was not one of the biggest steamers in the line, but it was a good one, lucrative. It sailed from Moscow to Tsaritsyn. The passengers were mostly long-distance travellers, on their way to the Holy Land, some even going all the way to America. Many of them were travelling on special concessionary tickets from the Palestinian Society. Muffin himself had never sailed the seas, because there was no point to it, but he knew the whole business backwards.

On the Nord Line's tickets they travelled as follows: from Moscow along the Oka to Nizhni, and after that along the River to Tsaritsyn, then by train to Taganrog, and from there by steamer again, only this time it was a seagoing vessel, and they carried on to wherever it was they wanted to go to. Sailing third class to the Holy Land cost only 46 roubles and 50 kopecks. Of course, if you went to America, then it was more expensive.

Muffin hadn't fleeced anyone yet; he was keeping his hands in his pockets, only his eyes and his ears were at work. And his feet too – that goes without saying. The moment the fog thickened a bit, he shuffled along on his soft felt soles from one group to another, keeping his eyes peeled and his ears pricked. What kind of people are you? How good a watch are you keeping?

That was how it was done: first take a good look around, get the feel of things, and then, closer to the mooring, do the job, neat and clean. And the most important thing was to sniff out the 'dashers'. They were bound to be hanging about, they'd been waiting for the shipping season too. Horses of altogether a different colour from Muffin, they were. They didn't often do any jobs on board; in their trade there was no point. The only thing the dashers did on the water was select their goose; they plucked and fleeced him later, on shore.

Well let them – it's no skin off our nose. The only trouble is that the dashers don't wander around with a Finnish knife clutched in their teeth, they keep themselves hidden, and you could make a mistake. Vasya Rybinsky, a well-respected razin, went and lifted a gold watch off a certain estate manager, and the manager turned out not to be a manager at all – he was a dasher, from the Kazan set. They found Vasya afterwards and, of course, they broke his bonce for him, even though it wasn't Vasya's fault. That's the way it is with the dashers: they simply can't bear for anyone to filch anything from them. And they can't show their faces in their own crowd again until they've got even for the shame of it.

Muffin started with the boat deck. There were deck passengers there, mostly poor; but, in the first place, a chicken pecks one grain at a time and, in the second place, it was in Muffin's nature to leave the daintiest morsels to last. He ate his food the same way. For instance, if it was buckwheat with crackling, then first he would gather the grain together with his spoon and for the time being arrange the fatty bacon prettily around the edge of his plate. If it was cabbage soup with a marrow bone, first he would sup the broth, then gobble up the cabbage and carrot, scrape up the meat, and only after that suck the marrow out of the bone.

Anyway, he gave the boat deck a thorough working over: from poop to waist to forecastle. Muffin knew all the shipboard words and fine details better than any sailor, because the sailor doesn't love the steamer. Hard-drinking soul that he is, he can't wait to get back ashore and into the tavern; but for a razin everything on a ship is useful, everything is interesting.

Sitting huddled together in the bow were people journeying to the Lord's Sepulchre, about a dozen and a half men and women, each with a knotty stick – pilgrim's staff – proudly displayed beside himself or herself. The pilgrims were eating bread with salt, washing it down with hot water from tin kettles, and glancing haughtily at the other travellers.

Now, don't you go putting on such airs, Muffin told them, speaking to himself. There's others more pious than you. They say as some pilgrims don't make their way to Palestine on steamships – they use their own two feet. And once they reach the border of the Promised Land, they crawl the rest of the way on their knees. Now that's genuine holiness for you.

But anyway, he left the godly travellers alone and moved on. What could you get from them anyway? Of course, each of them had five roubles tucked away, and getting it was an absolute cinch, but you had to be completely shameless to do that. And a man couldn't live without a conscience, even in the thieving trade. Maybe you needed it even more in the thieving trade than in any other – otherwise you could go to the Devil completely.

Muffin had long ago drawn up a rule for himself, so he could keep his peace of mind: if you can see someone's a good person or in misfortune, don't take any ends from him, even if his wallet is sticking out and just begging to be pinched. It didn't make sense. You might end up thirty roubles richer, or even three hundred, but you'd lose your self-respect. Muffin had seen plenty of thieves who had lowered themselves like that. Human garbage who had sold their souls for crumpled banknotes. Is the price of self-respect three hundred roubles? You've got to be joking! There probably isn't enough money in the entire world for that.

He hung around some German colonisers, eyeing them keenly. These ones had to be on their way to Argentina, that was the fashion among the Germans now. Supposedly they were given as much land as they wanted there, and not taken for soldiers. Your German was like your Yid: he didn't like to serve our tsar.

And they'd taken deck tickets, the cheapskates. The sausage-eaters had plenty of money, but they were too tight-fisted.

Muffin sat down under a lifeboat and listened to the German conversation for a while, but it just made him spit. They spoke just like they were deliberately playing the fool: *Guk-mal-di-da*.

One of them, with a red face, finished smoking his pipe and put it down on the deck, real close. Well, Muffin couldn't resist it and he picked up the nice little thing, didn't put it off. It was foggy now, but who knew how things would turn out later?

He inspected the pipe (porcelain, with little figures – a real sight for sore eyes) and stuck it in his swag-bag, a small canvas sack with a string for hanging it under his arm.

A good start.

Sitting further on were some Dukhobors, reading a godly book out loud. Muffin left them alone. He knew they were travelling to Canada. Quiet people, they never gave offence to anyone; they suffered for the truth. The writer Count Tolstoy was for them. Muffin had read one of his stories – 'How Much Land Does a Man Need?' It was funny, about what fools the peasants were.

All right then, Dukhobors, sail on and God be with you.

From the waist deck all the way to the poop deck it was nothing but Yids, but they weren't in a crowd either, they were in groups. That was no surprise to Muffin. He knew what this nation was like, always squabbling with each other.

It was the same as with the Russians, the ones most highly thought of were the ones sailing to Palestine. Muffin stood there for a while and listened to a 'Palestinian' Yid boasting to an

'American' one. 'No offence intended,' he said, 'but we're travelling for the sake of our souls, not our bellies.' And the 'American' swallowed it; he didn't try to talk back at all, just hung his head.

Muffin took a folding ruler – a tailor's rule, that is – out of the 'Palestinian's' pocket. It wasn't a really fat prize, but he could give it to the widow Glasha; she sewed skirts for women, and she'd say thank you. He took the 'American's' watch. A rubbish watch it was too – brass, worth maybe a rouble and a half.

He stashed the loot in his sack and slipped into a little group of young lads with sidelocks, some of them gabbling away in their own tongue, but most of them talking Russian – all skinny, with sharp Adam's apples and squeaky voices.

They were making a din because a rabbi, a Yiddish priest, had come up from the cabin deck to see them and they'd gone dashing over to him.

The priest was distinguished-looking, in a cap with fur trim and a jacket right down to his knees. A huge, long, grey beard and sidelocks like another two beards, and thick eyebrows like another two absolutely tiny little beards. The little Yids had crowded round him and were complaining. Muffin was there in a flash – the more crowded it got, the easier it made things for him.

'Rabbi, you told us we would go sailing like Noah's chosen ones on the ark! But this is some kind of *hoishek*!' a freckle-faced little Jew squeaked. 'There's everyone you can think of here! Never mind the *Amerikaners*, there are *apikoires** too, Zionists and goys eating pig fat' – he meant the Germans, Muffin guessed – 'and even – pah! – *goys* pretending to be Jews!'

'Yes, yes, the *"foundlings"*! And they say their prophet himself is with them! The one you said such terrible things about!' said the others, taking up the theme.

'Manuila?' The rabb's eyes flashed. 'He's here? That tail of Satan! You listen to me! Don't go anywhere near him! Or the *"foundlings"* either!'

One of the complainers leaned down to an ear overgrown

* *apikoires* (Yiddish): atheists

9

with fine grey hairs and whispered, but not exactly quietly – Muffin could hear every word.

'And they say *they're* here – the Oprichniks of Christ.' The words were uttered in a fearful, hissing whisper and all the others immediately fell silent. 'They want to kill us! Rabbi, they won't let us get away alive! We ought to have stayed at home!'

Muffin had read about the Oprichniks of Christ in the news-paper. Everybody knew that in some cities, where the people didn't have enough to keep them busy, they just went rushing off to beat the Jews at the slightest excuse. Why not beat them and rob them, if the authorities permitted it? But in addition to the usual plunderers, a while ago the so-called 'Oprichniks' had appeared, serious people who had sworn to give the Yids and those who indulged them no quarter. And supposedly they had already killed someone – some barrister and a student. Never mind the barrister – they were all shameless hucksters; but what did they have against the student? He must have had a father and mother too.

Anyway, all that business was a long way off. On the River-Mother, praise be to Thee, O Lord, there weren't any Oprichniks, and there had never been any pogroms.

While the little Yids kicked up their din, Muffin went through the pockets of one-two-three, but all the gelt he got for his pains was a five-kopeck piece and a twenty-kopeck coin.

Meanwhile the Jewish priest listened and listened, then sud-denly stamped his foot down real hard.

'Silence!'

It went quiet. The distinguished-looking old man jerked his spectacles off his nose and stuck them in his pocket (the frames glinted – could they be gold?) He took a fat little book bound in leather out of another pocket and opened it. He cackled something menacing in his own language and then repeated it in Russian – clearly there were some Yids there who didn't understand much of their own talk.

'And the Lord said unto Moses: "How long shall this wicked company murmur against Me? The murmurs of the sons of Israel, which they do murmur against Me, I do hear. Say unto them: I live, and all you who have murmured against me shall not enter into the land on which I have sworn to settle you." Have you heeded what was said by Moses, ye of little faith?'

With his white beard and one finger raised in the air, he himself looked like Moses in a picture that Muffin had seen in the Bible.

They all bowed. Muffin also leaned over and stuck his arm between the two standing in front of him. His arm was special, with almost no bones at all, it worked on cartilage. It could bend all manner of ways and when necessary it even stretched out much further than was humanly possible. With this remarkable arm of his, Muffin reached as far as the rabbi's pocket, hooked out the spectacles with the end of his little finger and squatted down on his haunches. Then he just slipped back into the fog.

He tested the spectacles with his tooth. Sweet Lord, they were gold!

And the Jewish priest rumbled on behind the bent backs: 'If I don't banish anyone who grumbles and is faint-hearted, my name's not Aron Shefarevich! Take a look at yourselves, you shrivelled tapeworms! What would the Oprichniks want with you? Who has any interest in you . . . ?'

Muffin didn't bother to listen to any more; he went while the going was good.

The fog turned really thick, you could barely even see the railings. The razin started slipping along them.

'Ood-ooo!' came the deafening hoot from above. So the deckhouse was here.

And when the steamer finished hooting, strange words were borne to Muffin's ears.

Up ahead someone was chanting:

> 'Breath to my lips she did provide,
> And then upon her flaming torch did breathe,
> And in that momen's madness did divide
> Into the Here and There the whole world's breadth
> She left – and all was cold around . . .'

'Stop that howling, Coliseum,' another voice interrupted, a sharp, mocking voice. 'Try strengthening those muscles of yours instead. What did I give you that rubber ball for?'

There was a breath of wind from the left bank and the shroud of white instantly thinned, becoming more transparent. Muffin saw an entire assembly under the stairway of the wheelhouse: young lads sitting there, about twenty of them, and two girls with them as well.

It was an odd sort of group, not the kind you saw very often.

Among the young men there were many with spectacles and curly hair, and some with big noses too – they looked as if they were young Jews too, but at the same time they didn't. They were far too jolly, with smiles that reached back to their ears. One was a bit older, with broad shoulders; he had a singlet under his open blouse and a pipe clenched in his teeth. He had to be a seagoing man, with that beard and no moustache – that was the way sailors shaved, so as not to singe themselves with the embers in their pipes.

The girls were even odder. Or rather, not girls: young ladies.

The first was slim, with white skin and huge eyes that took up half her face, but for some reason the little fool had cut her hair short like a boy's. And it was grand hair, too – thick, with a golden shimmer to it.

The second was short and round and the way she was dressed was a real fright: on her head she had a white canvas cap with a narrow brim; instead of a skirt she was wearing a pair of short green trousers, so that her legs were all open to view, and on her feet she had white socks and flimsy slippers with leather straps.

Muffin blinked his eyes at this unusual sight. Well, did you ever! – you could see her ankles, and her fat thighs, covered in goose pimples from the cold.

And it wasn't just the legs he found interesting.

What sort of people were they? Where were they going and what for? And what was a 'rabberboll'?

It was the one with the beard who had pronounced the incomprehensible word. The one who had been reciting verse laughed at his reproach and started jerking his hand about. Muffin looked more closely – the young lad had a small black sphere grasped between his fingers and he was squeezing it, over and over. But what for?

'Feeling chilly, Malka?' the one with the beard asked the fat girl (he looked at her goose-bumps too). 'Never mind, you'll look back on this journey as heaven. It's cool, and there's all the water you could want. Why did I set Nizhni as the place to meet?

To say goodbye to Russia. Look around, breathe. Soon there won't be anything to breathe. You still don't know what real heat's like. But I do. One time we were anchored in Port Said, we had to patch up the plating. I asked the captain for a week's leave; I wanted to taste the desert for myself, take a close look.'

'And did you get a close look?' the delicate young lady asked.

'I did, Rokhele, I did,' the man with the beard chuckled. 'My skin's not as white as yours, but by the evening my face was covered with blisters. My lips were all cracked and bloody. My throat felt like it had been scraped out with a file. And I couldn't go drinking water, I had to lick salt.'

'Why salt, Magellan?' one of the young lads asked in surprise.

'Because when you sweat, the body loses salt, and that's more terrible than dehydration. You can croak like that. So I was sweating, and licking salt, but I kept moving on. I'd made my mind up: two hundred versts to Gaza, a day there, and back again.' Magellan blew out a stream of smoke. 'Only I never got to Gaza, I lost the way. I relied on the sun and didn't take a compass, like a fool. On the third day the desert started swimming and swaying about – Moving in waves: to the left, to the right, left, right. I saw a birch grove in the distance, then a lake. Aha, I thought, I've sweated myself into seeing mirages now. And in the evening, when the shadows ran down in long stripes from the sand dunes, the Bedouins attacked from behind a hill. At first I thought it was just another mirage. Just picture it: triangular shadows rushing along at supernatural speed, getting bigger and bigger all the time. They'd set their camels to a gallop. And everything happening in total silence. Not a sound, only the sand rustling, as quiet as quiet. I'd been warned about bandits, so I had a Winchester with me, and a revolver. But I froze in the saddle, like a total idiot, and watched death come rushing towards me. Such a beautiful sight, I couldn't tear my eyes away. What's the most dangerous thing in the desert, after all? The sun and the heat blunt the instinct of self-preservation, that's what.'

Everyone was listening to the speaker with bated breath. Muffin was interested too, but it's not good to forget about work. Fat-rumped Malka's purse was sticking temptingly out of the pocket of her funny trousers. Muffin even took it out, but then he put it back. He felt sorry for the great fool.

'Not like that! I showed you!' Magellan cried, interrupting his tale. 'Why are you jerking your wrist about! Use your fingers, your fingers! Give it here!'

He took the ball away from Coliseum and started squeezing it repeatedly. 'With rhythm, with rhythm. A thousand times, ten thousand! How are you going to hold an Arabian horse by the bridle with fingers like that? Here, catch. Now work.' He threw the ball back, but the versifying dunce didn't catch it.

The ball struck the deck and suddenly bounced back up mischievously, and with such a solid sound – Muffin really liked that. And then the ball went rolling across the decking, bouncing all the way; but the fog crept across again from the right and drowned the entire honest company in thick white curds.

'Butterfingers!' said Magellan's voice. 'All right, you can get it later.'

But Muffin already had his sights set on the miraculous little ball. To give to Parkhomka the newspaper boy – let the little kid have a bit of fun.

If only it didn't go over the side. Muffin quickened his step.

It must have been a funny sight – two round loaves rolling along. A little one and a big one.

Stop now, you won't get away from me!

The little ball ran up against something dark, stopped and was grabbed up immediately. Muffin was so absorbed in the chase that he almost crashed into the man sitting on the deck (the one who had brought the rubber ball to a halt).

'I beg your pardon,' Muffin announced in a cultured voice. 'That's mine.'

'Take it, if it's yours,' the seated man replied amiably. And he turned back to his companions (there were two others there with him) and continued the conversation.

Muffin's jaw simply dropped. They seemed even odder to him than the previous group.

Two men and a woman, but all dressed exactly the same, in loose white robes down to their heels, with a blue stripe round the middle – the woman's was a ribbon sewn on to her robe, the men's were daubed on with paint.

They're 'foundlings' Muffin twigged – the ones the Jews were swearing about. He'd never seen them before, but he'd read about them – these people who imitated the Yids – and about

14

that Manuila of theirs too. You could read about absolutely anything in the newspaper.

The 'foundlings' were Russian people, but they had forsaken Christ and turned to the faith of the Yids. Muffin had forgotten why they wanted to be Yids and why they were called 'foundlings', but he did remember that the newspaper had been very abusive about the apostates and written bad things about Manuila. He had deceived many people into turning away from Orthodoxy, and who could possibly like that?

So Muffin took an immediate dislike to these three and started thinking what he could filch from them – not for his own gain, but to teach them not to go betraying Christ.

He settled down to one side, hiding away behind a cable locker.

The one the ball had run into was really old already, with a crumpled face. He looked like a drunken clerk, except that he was sober. He was speaking gently and courteously.

'Verily I say unto you: He is the Messiah. Christ was the false prophet, but He is the absolutely genuine one. And evil people will not be able to crucify Him, because Manuila is immortal, God protects him. You know yourselves that He has been killed already, but He rose again, only He didn't ascend into heaven, He remained among the people, because His coming is the final one.'

'Ieguda, I have doubts about circumcision,' a huge man boomed in a deep bass. From his massive hands and the black spots on his face Muffin could tell he was a blacksmith. 'How much are you supposed to cut? A finger length? Half a finger?'

'I can't tell you that, Iezekia, I'm not sure myself. They told me in Moscow that one cobbler cut off his willy with scissors and afterwards he almost died. I myself am thinking of abstaining for the time being. Let's get to the Holy Land first, then we'll see. They do say Manuila said we shouldn't circumcise ourselves. The way I heard, He hasn't given the foundlings His blessing to do it.'

'They're raving,' the blacksmith sighed. 'We should be circumcised, Ieguda, we should. A real Jew is always circumcised. Otherwise we'll be ashamed to go to the bathhouse in the Holy Land. They'll laugh at us.'

'You're right, Iezekia,' Ieguda agreed. 'Even if we're frightened, we ought to, it's clear.'

At that the woman piped up. Her voice had a rotten, snuffling sound, which was not surprising, since there was no nose to be seen on her face – it had completely collapsed. 'Frightening you say? Call yourself Jews? A pity I'm not a man; I wouldn't be frightened.'

What can I nick from these monsters, Muffin was thinking – maybe the blacksmith's sack? And he began creeping stealthily towards the sack; but just then the three seated people were joined by a fourth, wearing the same kind of robe, only the blue stripe wasn't daubed on with paint but sewn on with white thread.

This man seemed even more repulsive to Muffin: little screwed-up eyes in a flat, oily face, greasy hair down to his shoulders, a mangy little beard. He had to be a tavern-keeper.

The other three all turned on him: 'What are you doing, Solomosha; have you left him all alone?'

The elderly man who was called Ieguda looked around (but he didn't see Muffin – how could he?) and said in a quiet voice: 'It was agreed: there should always be two of us with the treasury!'

Muffin thought he must have misheard. But flat-faced Solomosha gestured with one hand and said: 'What can happen to the treasury? He's asleep, and the chest's under his pillow, and he's got it grabbed in his paws too. It's stuffy in that room.'

He sat down, took off one boot and started rewinding his foot wrapping.

Muffin rubbed his eyes in case he was dreaming.

A treasury! A chest!

Heigh-ho for the first sailing! Heigh-ho for the *Sturgeon*!

Those gold specs he had were a worthless trinket, not to mention the other things. In a cabin, under the prophet Manuila's pillow, there was a treasury in a chest, waiting for Muffin. There was his marrowbone!

And you say your prophet's gone to sleep?

The razin was out from behind the cable locker in a flash. Down, down the ramp Muffin flew to the lower deck, where you couldn't see anybody or anything, except yellow patches through the whiteness – that was the cabin windows glowing.

Muffin asked the yellow patches: Right then, which one of you are they carrying the treasury in?

There were curtains on the windows, but not all the way up

to the top. If you stood on a chair (and there were chairs on the deck, as if they'd been put there deliberately for Muffin to use) you could glance in over the top.

In the first window Muffin saw a touching scene: a family drinking tea.

Papa – very respectable-looking, with a thick beard – was sipping his tea from a large glass. His wife was sitting facing him on a small sofa, doing her embroidery in her house cap – she was a rather mannish creature, but her face was extremely kind and gentle. And sitting on both sides of Papa, nestling against his broad shoulders, were the children, a grammar-school-boy son and a daughter about the same age. They weren't twins, though: the little lad was dark, but the girl had golden hair.

The little daughter was singing – quietly, so Muffin couldn't hear the words through the glass, only a kind of angelic vibration in the air. The young lady's expression was pensive, her pink little lips sometimes opened wide, sometimes pursed up and stretched out forward.

Muffin admired this heavenly vision. He would never, ever have filched anything from such lovely people.

The little son said something and stood up. He kissed his papa – and so very tenderly, full on the lips. He took his peaked cap and went out into the corridor. No doubt he had decided to go for a walk and get a breath of air. His dear papa blew a kiss after him.

Muffin was very touched. After all, Papa was such a very fearsome-looking man. No doubt in his office at the bank or the ministry he set all his subordinates trembling, but in his family, in domestic surroundings, he was a perfect lamb. And Muffin sighed, of course, at his own lonely life. Where could a razin ever get himself a family?

The very next window turned out to be the right one: Manuila's. Muffin was lucky again.

There was no need to stand on a chair this time, the curtains weren't closed tightly. Through the gap Muffin saw a gaunt peasant with a light-brown beard, lying on a velvet divan. And he thought: There's a fine prophet; he's driven his flock out on deck and he's living it up in first class. And how sweetly he's sleeping, with that slobber dangling out of his mouth.

What was that glittering there under the pillow? A lacquered casket, for sure.

Well then, sleep, and make sure you sleep soundly!

Muffin started squirming in his impatience, but he told himself not to start getting agitated. This was a serious job that had turned up, he didn't want to botch it.

Should he go in from the corridor, pick the lock?

No, what if someone saw him? It was simpler from where he was. His friendly protector, the fog, would help him out.

The closed window was a doddle. Every razin had a special tool for dealing with that, a 'hack'. You used it to catch hold of the screws keeping the window frame in (only first you mustn't forget a few drops of oil from the oilcan, so it wouldn't squeak), a jerk to the left, a jerk to the right, and it was almost done. Now a more generous dose of the same oil on the sides, in the slots. And lift it out nice and easy.

The window slid upwards without the slightest sound, just as it ought to.

After that it was simple. Climb inside and tiptoe across to the bed. Pull the casket out from under the pillow and put a rolled-up towel there instead.

To make sure the sleeper didn't wake up, you had to listen to his breathing – that would always warn you. But you mustn't look at his face – everybody can feel somebody staring at him when he's sleeping.

Muffin gathered himself up tight to climb in the window and he had already stuck his head through, but suddenly, right there beside him, a window frame squeaked and a loud woman's voice said testily: 'You just stop that.'

Muffin's heart fell: disaster, he'd been spotted!

He pulled his head back out, turned round – and the sense of alarm passed.

They'd opened the window in the next cabin. It must have been too stuffy for them.

The same voice went on angrily. 'There, take a breath of fresh air, Your Eminence! God only knows what you're saying now! At least leave me my sins!'

A rich bass voice, also angry, replied: 'It's my sin, mine! I condoned, I set you the work of penance, I should answer for it! But not to the procurator in St Petersburg – to the Lord God!'

Ai-ai, this is bad. They'll wake the prophet with all their shouting.

Muffin went down on all fours and crawled across to the open window. He peeped in cautiously, with just one eye.

At first he thought there were two people in the cabin: a grey-haired Bishop with a fancy cross on his chest and a nun. Then he spotted a third person in the corner, a monk. But he was sitting there mute, with nothing to say for himself.

What's all this yelling about, people of God? Why don't you act like Christians, meek and mild? You'll wake all the passengers.

The nun seemed to have heard Muffin's wish. She sighed and hung her head. 'Your Reverence, I swear to you: I'll never give way to temptation again. And I won't tempt you either. Only don't punish yourself.'

The Bishop wiggled his thick eyebrows (one was already almost grey, the other still mostly black) and patted the nun on the head. 'Never mind, Pelagia, God is merciful. Perhaps we can beat off the attack. And we'll atone for our sins in prayer together.'

A colourful pair, all right. In his own mind Muffin had already found names for them: Little Sister Fox (that was because of the lock of ginger hair that had escaped from under her wimple) and Ataman Kudeyar (the priest had a far too tough, bellicose look about him). It was like in the song:

> His comrades true were left behind,
> His plundering ways were now ignored,
> Bold Kudeyar went for a monk
> To serve the people and the Lord!

At any other time Muffin would have been very interested to hear about a sin committed together by a Bishop and a nun. But what time did he have for that now? They'd made up and stopped shouting, and praise be to Thee, Lord, for that.

Down on his knees again, he crawled back under the prophet's window.

He took hold of the frame and lifted himself up a little bit.

Still dozing, the darling. He hasn't woken up.

At the very last moment, when there was nothing he could

do about it, Muffin heard a rustling sound behind him. He tried to turn round, but it was too late.

Something crunched and exploded inside Muffin's head. And for him there was no more spring evening or river mist – there was nothing at all.

Two strong hands grabbed hold of the limp body by the feet and dragged it across to the edge of the deck – quickly, before a lot of blood could flow. The swag-bag, that little underarm sack for Muffin's loot, snagged on the leg of a table. A jerk, the string snapped, and the movement was continued.

And then Muffin went flying through the air, sent up a fountain of spray in a final farewell to God's world, and was united with the River-Mother.

She welcomed her ne'er-do-well son into her loving embrace, rocked him a little, lulled him a little and laid him down to sleep in her deepest, darkest little bedroom, on a soft downy mattress of silt.

Troubles in the capital

'But it's still amazing how Konstantin Petrovich could have found out,' His Eminence Mitrofanii repeated yet again, with a brief glance in the direction of a muffled sound from outside the window – as if someone had dropped a bundle or a bolt of cloth on the deck. 'He truly does sit high and see far.'

'That is what His Excellency's duty of service requires of him,' Father Serafim Userdov put in from his corner. The conversation between His Eminence, his spiritual daughter Pelagia and the Bishop's secretary, always about one and the same subject, was already in its third day. It had begun in St Petersburg, following an unpleasant interview with the Chief Procurator of the Holy Synod, Konstantin Petrovich Pobedin. This unpleasantness had been spoken of in the train, and in the Moscow hotel, and now on the steamer that was carrying the provincial prelate and his companions to their native Zavolzhsk.

The Chief Procurator's disagreements with the Bishop were of long standing, but hitherto they had not reached the stage of direct confrontation. Konstantin Petrovich had seemed to be taking a close look, respectfully measuring up his venerable opponent, according his strength and truth due respect, for he himself was a powerful man and he had his own truth, although it was clear that sooner or later these two truths would clash, for they were too different from each other.

Mitrofanii had been prepared for absolutely anything after the summons to appear before the Chief Procurator in the capital city; he had been ready for any pressure, but not on the flank from which the blow came.

Konstantin Petrovich had begun in his customary manner – quietly, as if he were treading cautiously. He praised his guest from Zavolzhsk for his good relations with the temporal authorities, and especially for the fact that the Governor took Mitrofanii's advice and went to him for confession. 'This is an example of the inseparability of the State and the Church, on which alone the edifice of the social order can stand secure,' Pobedin had said, raising one finger for greater effect.

Then he had delivered a mild rebuke for the Bishop's spineless and insipid approach in dealings with members of different creeds and faiths, of whom there were very many in Zavolzhie: there were Protestant colonists there, and Catholics descended from the old Poles in exile, and Moslems, and even pagans.

His Excellency had a distinctive manner of speaking – as if he were reading a report from a written text. A smooth and fluent manner, but somehow dry and wearisome for his listeners. 'The state Church is a system under which the authorities recognise one confession as the true faith and exclusively support and patronise one church, to the greater or lesser diminution of the honours, rights and privileges of other churches,' Konstantin Petrovich had pontificated. 'Otherwise the State would lose its spiritual unity with the people, of whom the overwhelming majority adhere to Orthodoxy. A state without a faith is nothing other than a Utopia that is impossible to realise, since the absence of faith is the direct negation of the State. What trust can the Orthodox masses have in the authorities if the people and the authorities have different faiths, or if the authorities have no faith at all?'

Mitrofanii tolerated this lecture for as long as he could (which was not for very long, since patience was definitely not one of the Bishop's strong points) and eventually interrupted the exalted orator.

'Konstantin Petrovich, I am convinced that the Orthodox confession is the truest and most beneficent of all faiths, and I am so convinced not for reasons of state, but by the acceptance of my soul. However, as your Excellency is aware from our previous conversations, I consider it harmful and even criminal to convert those of other faiths to our religion by means of force.'

Pobedin nodded – not in agreement, but in condemnation, as if he had expected nothing else from the Bishop but impolite interruptions and obduracy.

'Yes, I am aware that your Zavolzhsk *faction*' – Pobedin emphasised this unpleasant, even *ominous*, word in his intonation – 'is opposed to all violence . . .'

At this point the Chief Procurator paused before striking a crushing blow that had, beyond the slightest doubt, been prepared in advance.

Violence and *criminality*' – again that emphatic intonation. 'But I had never before suspected just how far your zealousness in eradicating the latter extended.' After waiting for an expression of caution to appear on Mitrofanii's face following these strange words, Pobedin asked in a menacingly ingratiating tone: 'Just who do you and your entourage imagine you are, Bishop? The new Vidoques? Or Sherlock Holmses?'

At this point Sister Pelagia, who was present at the conversation, turned pale and could not suppress a quiet exclamation. Only now had she realised why His Eminence had been ordered to bring her, a lowly nun, to the audience.

The Chief Procurator immediately confirmed her dark surmise: 'It was not by accident that I asked you to bring with you the head of your famous convent school. No doubt, Sister, you thought that we would be discussing education?'

That really was what Pelagia had thought. It was only six months since the Bishop had given his blessing for her to take over as head of the Zavolzhsk school for young girls, following the death of Sister Christina, but during that brief period Pelagia had managed to introduce more than enough reforms to draw down on her head the displeasure of the head of the Holy Synod. She was prepared to defend every one of her innovations and had armed herself for this with numerous highly convincing arguments, but on hearing mention of Vidoque and some unknown Sherlock (he must be a detective too, like the famous Frenchman), she was completely taken aback.

Meanwhile Konstantin Petrovich was already drawing a sheet of paper out of a calico-bound file. He searched for something on it and jabbed a dry, white finger at one of the lines of writing.

'Tell me, Sister, have you ever heard of a certain Polina Andreevna Lisitsyna? – a highly intelligent individual, so they say. And extremely brave. A month ago she rendered the police invaluable assistance in the investigation into the heinous murder of the arch-priest Nektarii Zachatievsky.' And he fixed Pelagia with his owlish stare.

She blushed as she babbled: 'She's my sister . . .'

The Chief Procurator shook his head reproachfully: 'Sister? That's not the information I have.'

He knows everything, the nun realised. How shameful! And the most shameful thing of all was that she had lied.

'You even lie about it. A fine bride of Christ,' said Pobedin pricking her on her most painful spot. 'A detective in a nun's habit. Well, what can I make of that?'

However, the powerful man's gaze was curious, rather than wrathful. How could this be – a nun investigating criminal cases?

Pelagia no longer attempted to deny anything. She lowered her head and tried to explain. 'You see, sir, when I see evil-doing triumph, and especially when someone innocent is accused, as happened in the case you mentioned . . . Or if someone is threatened by mortal danger . . .' She broke off and her voice began to tremble. 'It feels here' – the nun pressed one hand to her heart – 'as if a little ember catches fire. And it burns, it will not let me be until truth and justice are restored. In keeping with my vocation, I ought to pray, but I cannot. Surely, what God requires from us is not inaction and futile lamenting, but help – such as each of us is capable of. And he only intervenes in earthly matters when human powers are exhausted in the struggle with Evil . . .'

'It burns, here?' Konstantin Petrovich echoed. 'And you cannot pray? Ai-ai-ai. Why that's a devil sitting in you, Sister. All the signs are there. You have no business being a nun.'

At these words Pelagia went numb and Mitrofanii dashed to her aid. 'Your Excellency, she is not to blame. I ordered her to do it. With my blessing.'

That was apparently just what the leader of the Synod was waiting for. Or rather, his response seemed to indicate that this was the last thing he had been expecting and he threw his hands up in the air in great astonishment as if to say: I don't believe it, I don't believe it! You? You? The provincial arch-pastor?

He seemed to have been struck dumb. His face darkened and he knitted his brows together in a frown. After a pause, he said wearily: 'Go now, Bishop. I shall pray to God for enlightenment as to what to do with you . . .'

Such was the conversation that had taken place in St Petersburg. And it was still uncertain what it would lead to, what intuition concerning the Zavolzhsk 'faction' would be vouchsafed to the Chief Procurator by the Almighty.

'The right thing would be to apologise to Konstantin Petrovich,' Userdov said, interrupting a pause. 'With a man like that, there's no shame in yielding to humility . . .'

That was probably right. Konstantin Petrovich was a special kind of man. As a character in one of Ostrovsky's plays remarked, for him there was 'little that is impossible' in the entire Russian Empire. The Zavolzhians had been presented with evidence of that at the very beginning of the audience in St Petersburg.

One of the telephones on His Excellency's desk had rung – the most beautiful one: mahogany with gleaming mouth- and earpieces. Pobedin had broken off in mid-word and raised a finger to his lips while he used his other hand to turn the handle and press the earpiece to his ear.

Secretary Userdov, sitting on the very edge of his chair with a briefcase containing a report on the affairs of the diocese, was the first to guess who was calling – he had jumped to his feet and stood to attention like a soldier.

In the whole of Russia there was only one person for whom Konstantin Petrovich would have interrupted himself. And it was well known that a special line had been installed from the Palace to the Chief Procurator's office.

The visitors could not, of course, hear the monarch's voice, but even so they had been greatly impressed, especially by the strict paternal tone in which Pobedin addressed God's anointed: 'Yes, Your Majesty, the text of the decree as received from you did not strike me as satisfactory. I shall draft a new one. And clemency for a state criminal is also absolutely out of the question. Some of your advisers have become so perverted in their thinking that they consider it possible to do away with capital punishment. I am a Russian and I live among Russians, I know what the people feels and what it demands. Let not the voice of flattery and dreams insinuate itself into your heart.'

At that moment Father Userdov's expression was a sight to behold: a compound of fright and awe, mingled with an awareness of complicity in the great mystery of the Supreme Power.

His Eminence's secretary was fine in almost every respect, in fact, as far as industry and efficiency were concerned, he was above reproach, but in his heart Mitrofanii was not truly fond of him. Evidently this was the very reason why the Bishop was especially charitable to Father Seraphim, employing an affectionate attitude to subdue the sin of groundless irritation. But sometimes, nonetheless, he would burst out, and once he had even flung a *kamelaukion* at Userdov, but afterwards he would always apologise. The mild-mannered secretary would take fright, and for a long time be unable to find the courage to pronounce the words of forgiveness, but eventually he would babble: 'I forgive you, forgive me too,' following which peace would be restored.

With her restless mind, Pelagia once expressed to Mitrofanii a seditious idea concerning Father Seraphim – that the world has real, live people in it, but there are also other creatures who only try to be like people, as if they have been planted among us from a different world or, perhaps, from a different planet, in order to observe us. Some of them are better at their pretence, so that you can hardly tell them apart from genuine people; others are not so skilful, and you can spot them straight away. Userdov, now, was one of the less successful examples. If you took a look under his skin you were bound to find nuts, bolts and gearwheels.

The Bishop had roundly abused the nun for this 'Theory'. However, Pelagia was not infrequently visited by foolish thoughts, and His Reverence was accustomed to this: he rebuked her largely as a matter of form.

As for Father Seraphim, the Bishop knew that the secretary dreamed of a high clerical position. And why not? He was learned, of good conduct and quite charmingly handsome. The secretary kept his hair and beard clean and well groomed, anointing them with sweet fragrances. He polished his nails with a brush. He wore only cassocks of fine woollen cloth.

There didn't really seem to be anything reprehensible in all this. Mitrofanii himself appealed to the clergy to keep themselves neat and presentable, but even so he found his assistant irritating – especially on this journey, when the heavenly spheres had rained down bolts of fiery lightning on His Reverence. He was unable to talk heart to heart with his spiritual daughter or to express his most intimate thoughts while this six-winged angel sat there, tending his thin little moustache with a small comb. He said nothing for ages, and then he would put in something entirely out of place and ruin the entire conversation – like now, for instance.

In response to the appeal to apologise to the Chief Procurator, Pelagia said hastily: 'I would, gladly. I would even swear on a holy icon: Never again, not for anything, will I ever stick my nose into a criminal investigation. Not even if it is absolutely the most mysterious mystery possible. I won't even give it a sideways glance.'

But Mitrofanii merely cast a sideways glance at his secretary, without saying a word.

'Come, Pelagiushka, let us take a stroll around the ship. To stretch our legs ... No-no, Seraphim, you stay here. Get those documents on the consistory ready for me. I'll read through them when I get back.' And the two of them left the cabin with a sigh of relief, leaving Userdov alone with his briefcase.

Of every kind a pair

They didn't walk on the lower deck, because the fog made it quite impossible to distinguish the River or the sky (or even the deck). They went up higher, where the passengers of the very cheapest category were sitting around in small groups.

Glancing around through the semi-transparent gloom at all this human variety, Mitrofanii said in a low voice: 'Of the pure cattle, and of the impure cattle, and of all the reptiles that crawl upon the earth, of every kind a pair ...'

He blessed the peasant pilgrims and let them kiss his hand, merely casting a sad glance over the others, who were leaving Russia for ever and had no need of an Orthodox pastor's blessing.

Speaking to his companion in a quiet voice, he said: 'Behold, such a highly intelligent man, who truly wishes his fatherland well, and yet he is in such a state of spiritual error. Just look how much harm he causes.' He did not mention any name, but it was quite clear whom he had in mind: Konstantin Petrovich.

'Feast your eyes on the fruits of his struggle for good,' His Reverence continued bitterly as he walked past the members of dissenting sects and different faiths. 'If anyone is not like the majority, if they are strange – out of the state with them! No need to drive them out by force, they will leave of their own accord, fleeing oppression and the hostile attitude of the state. He imagines that as a result Russia will be more firmly united, stronger. That may be so, but her colours will be the poorer for it, she will be impoverished. Our procurator is convinced that he alone knows how the fatherland should be organised in order to save it. In the times we live in, prophets have become a fashion. We are surrounded by them. Some are laughable, like our next-door neighbour Manuila. Others are more serious, like Count Tolstoy or Karl Marx. And even Konstantin Petrovich imagines that he is a messiah. Not on a global scale, though – a strictly local messiah, such as they had in Old Testament times, when a prophet was sent not to the whole of mankind, but only to a single people . . .'

The Bishop's dour complaints were interrupted by a respectable family who had also come up to the boat deck for a stroll: a thickset gentleman, a lady with her knitting and two juveniles – a cute grammar-school boy and a pretty young lady with light hair.

The grammar-school boy pulled off his cap and bowed, asking for a blessing.

'What is your name, young man?' Mitrofanii asked the darling lad, making the sign of the cross over the entire family.

'Antinous, Your Reverence.'

'That is a pagan name, for domestic use only. What is your baptismal name?'

'Antip, Your Reverence.'

'A fine name, a name of the people,' the Bishop said approvingly.

The boy gently pressed his lips against his hand, and Mitrofanii, touched, patted Antip-Antinous on the back of the head.

The Bishop walked on unhurriedly, but Pelagia hung back – the pious grammar-school boy's mother was knitting her stitches in such a very skilful manner. The nun was an enthusiastic knitter herself; she always carried a little bag with her handiwork hanging round her neck, but her fingers were so stupid that she was always getting her rows confused and making a mess of her knots.

'Tell me, madam, how do you manage to cast on so cleanly?' she was about to ask, but instead she suddenly blinked and pressed her spectacles back against the bridge of her nose.

The skilful knitter had strange hands: broad, with little hairs on the fingers.

Pelagia raised her eyes, saw an unfeminine face and a neck with a protruding Adam's apple above the lace collar, and gasped out loud.

Catching the nun's gaze, the remarkable lady stopped and suddenly winked.

Her family continued on its way, leaving the two knitting enthusiasts alone together.

'Are you a man?' Pelagia asked in a whisper, opening her eyes wide in amazement.

The other woman nodded and raised a finger to her lips: Sh-sh-sh.

'But . . . who are they?' the nun asked, with a confused nod in the direction of the broad-shouldered gentleman and his charming offspring.

'My family.' The voice of the man in women's clothes was high, with a slightly squeaky note, almost indistinguishable from a woman's. 'My husband, Lev Ivanovich. And our children, Antinous and Salome. We are Sodomites.'

The final phrase was pronounced in a perfectly normal tone of voice, as if the speaker had said, 'We are Oddesites,' or 'We are Mennonites.'

'S-Sodomites? You mean . . . You mean pederasts?' Pelagia asked, stumbling over the shameful word. 'But what about the young lady? And then . . . surely you can't have children?'

'Salome is no young lady; he used to work in a men's bath-house. That was where Lyova picked him up. So delicate, so delicate! And the way he sings! Antinous is a jolly one, naughty; he likes to get up to mischief sometimes, but little Salomeia is simply an angel. All three of us love Lev Ivanovich,' declared Pelagia's amazing companion. 'He's a real man, not like the ordinary ones. Women are not enough for a real man, for him all other men are like women.'

It was shameful to listen to this, but interesting too. Pelagia turned to see how far Mitrofanii had moved on. If only he didn't find out who it was he had blessed so benignly!

His Reverence was not far away. He had stopped beside a group of Jews and was listening to something. That was good.

'And how long have you . . . you know, been living like this?' the nun asked curiously.

'Not long. Only for seven months.'

'And before that?'

'Before that I used to live like everyone else. I had a wife, a daughter. A job. I'm a teacher, from a classical grammar school, you know. Latin, ancient Greek. I reached the age of forty without ever realising who I was or what I was – as if I'd been watching life through the dusty window of a railway carriage, and life just kept rolling on by. But when I met Lev Nikolaevich, the glass suddenly shattered and broke. You can't imagine how happy I am! As if I had risen from the dead!'

'But what about your family? I mean *that* family.'

The classical grammar-school teacher sighed. 'What could I do, when it was a matter of love and resurrection? I left them everything. The money in the bank – all that there was. The house. I feel sorry for my daughter; she's a clever little girl. But she's better off without a father like this. Let her remember me as I used to be.'

Glancing at her resurrected companion's mob cap and silk dress, Pelagia could not find it in herself to dispute this assertion.

'Where are you heading for now?'

'Sodom,' came the reply. 'I told you, we are Sodomites.'

Once again Pelagia completely failed to understand. 'What Sodom? The one laid waste by the Lord together with Gomorrah?'

'It was destroyed. But now it has been reborn. An American

millionaire, Mr George Sairus, the well-known philanthropist, discovered the spot where the biblical Sodom stood. And now a heavenly new city is being built there – for people like us. No persecution from the police, no disdain from society. And no women,' the speaker said with a sly smile. 'You naturals will never make the kind of woman that a man can. Although, of course, you do have something worth looking at.' The former classicist cast an appraising glance over the nun's figure. 'The bust is no great feature, you can stuff that with cotton wool; but the shoulders now, the line of the thigh . . .'

'Irodiada! Where have you disappeared to?' a stentorian voice called out of the fog. 'The children want to go back to the cabin.'

'Coming, darling, coming!' Irodiada called with a start and went hurrying after the call of her beloved.

Is there no end to the variety of the Lord's creatures? Pelagia thought in wonder, and set off after Mitrofanii.

She saw that the His Reverence had already moved from the passive state of listening to others speaking to the active state of wagging his mighty finger and pronouncing on something to a grey-bearded rabbi who was surrounded by a huddle of juveniles.

Sister Pelagia did not see how the argument began. No doubt the Bishop, with his customary curiosity, had started questioning the Jews about where they were going and what their motives were – was it a matter of need, or faith, or were they perhaps fleeing from unjust persecution? – and he had clashed with his Judaic colleague over some point.

'That is precisely why you are persecuted everywhere, because you have so much arrogance!' the Bishop rumbled.

The exponent of the Old Testament responded no less thunderously: 'We do have our pride, it is true! Man cannot live without pride! He is the crown of creation!'

'It is not pride that your people is so full of, but precisely arrogance! You despise all who do not live as you do, you are always afraid of being defiled! If you are so squeamish, then who will love you?'

'It is not people we despise and shun, but people's impurity! And as for love, King David said: "On all sides do they surround me with words of hate, they arm themselves against me without cause; for my love they make war on me, but I pray."'

Provoked by this rebuff, Mitrofanii explained: 'Who is it that you love, apart from those of your own tribe? Even your prophets addressed themselves only to you, the Jews, but our saints feel for the whole of mankind!'

Pelagia thought what a pity it was that the Chief Procurator could not hear the Bishop fulminating against the infidels – how glad he would have been!

The dispute made interesting listening, and even more interesting watching: for all their religious differences, the two opponents were extremely similar in both temperament and appearance.

'We do not turn our backs on mankind!' the rabbi exclaimed, shaking his beard, 'but we remember what a heavy burden has been laid upon us – to demonstrate to other nations an example of constancy and purity. And all who wish to be pure may join us. If you wish, we will accept even you!'

'What you say is not true!' Mitrofanii rumbled triumphantly, and his beard began jerking about. 'Those lost sheep who are called "foundlings"' – he pointed to the three vagabonds sitting a short distance away in their clowns' costumes with the blue stripe – 'have reached out to your faith and abjured Christ. And what has happened? Have you taken them in, reverend rabbi? No, you turn your noses up!'

The rabbi began choking on his indignation. 'Take *them* in? Pah and pah again, a plague on them and their false prophet! It is said in the Law of Moses: "Those who practise wizardry shall be put to death, they must be stoned, let their blood be on them." I know you churchmen have launched an intrigue against us, to hold our faith up to mockery through this marketplace clown Manuila! According to your vile priestly habit!'

One of the accuser's disciples, a little older than the others, grabbed the rabbi by the sleeve and whispered something in Yiddish in an alarmed voice.

Pelagia could only make out one word: 'police'.

But the Jew was not frightened. 'I can see for myself from his cross and cap that he's a Bishop. Let him complain. Tell them, tell them that in your person Aron Shefarevich has insulted the Christian Church!'

These words had a surprising effect on His Reverence. Instead of growing even more heated, he fell silent. No doubt he had recalled that as a provincial Bishop he had the power of the state and the dominant Church behind him. What real dispute could there be?

He had noticed Pelagia too, and he felt ashamed. 'You are too wrathful, rabbi, like your own Judaic God,' the Bishop said after a pause. 'That is why so few hear His voice. But our apostle Paul said: "Let all irritation and fury be far removed from you."' And having fired this final salvo at the enemy, he withdrew with dignity, although Pelagia could see from the excessive straightness of his stance and the tight way he was clenching his fingers behind his back that Mitrofanii was seriously annoyed – not with the insolent rabbi, of course, but with himself, for entering into a pointless and unseemly squabble.

Knowing perfectly well that when His Reverence was in this kind of mood it was best to keep away from him, the nun did not go hurrying after her spiritual father, but chose instead to linger where she was. And in any case, she had to reassure the poor Jews.

'What's your name?' she asked a skinny, hook-nosed juvenile, who was staring after the Bishop in fright.

'Shmulik,' he replied with a shudder, and began staring at the nun with the same fright in his eyes. 'Why?'

How pale he is, thought Pelagia, feeling sorry for the boy. He needs to eat better and spend more time playing outside, but he probably spends all day from morning till night poring over the Talmud.

'You tell your teacher there's no need to be afraid. Bishop Mitrofanii won't complain to anyone.'

Shmulik tugged on the side-lock coiled round his ear and declared triumphantly: 'Rabbi Shefarevich isn't afraid of anything. He's a great man. He's been summoned to *Erushalaim* by the *khakham-bashi* himself, to help fortify the Holy City against vacillation.'

Pelagia had no idea who the *khakham-bashi* was, but she nodded respectfully.

'To fortify *Erushalaim*!' Shmulik's eyes glinted in ecstasy. 'Eh? See how highly they think of our rabbi! He is firm in the faith, like a rock. Do you know who he is? He is the new Shamai, that's who!'

The nun had read about the intransigent Shamai, the founder

of ancient Phariseeism. But of all the Pharisees she preferred a different religious teacher, the uncensorious Gillel – the same Gillel who, when asked about the essential core of God's Law, replied with the single phrase: Do not do unto others what you yourself find hurtful – that is all the law, the rest is mere commentary on it.'

Once again the deck was wreathed in tattered cotton wool and the despondent figures of the Jews quivered and paled and became like ghosts.

This made the sound of singing even more surprising: it came from the centre of the deck, from somewhere below the captain's bridge. The young voices launched into a very harmonious choral rendition of the student song 'Dubinushka'.

Not students, surely? Pelagia wanted to listen, but as she was walking through the milky white soup, the singing came to an end. The voices had just got into their stride, just passionately declared: 'Of all songs, one is engraved in my memory, it is the song of the workers' artel,' but they didn't give the whoop that should have followed. The choir disintegrated, the song choked off and the unison shattered into discordant hubbub.

The nun, however, continued on her way, determined to see what kind of young people these were.

No, they weren't students, although at first glance they were similar: from their faces and clothes and the words that reached her ears, Pelagia could tell that they were settlers moving to Jewish Palestine.

'You're wrong, Magellan!' a youthful voice exclaimed. 'Aryan civilisation seeks to make the world beautiful, and Jewish civilisation to make it moral, that's where the main difference lies. Both tasks are important, but it's difficult to combine them, and that's why we need to build our state far away from Europe. We shall learn beauty from them, and they shall learn morals from us. We shall have neither exploitation nor repression of the female sex by the male, nor any vulgar bourgeois family! We shall become an example for the whole world!'

Ah, how interesting, thought Pelagia, and she stood unobtrusively at one side. These must be the Zionists that everybody was writing and talking about. How likeable they were, how young and how fragile, especially the young ladies.

33

But then, that young man with the skipper's beard (the Magellan whom the rhapsodic speaker was addressing) could hardly be called fragile. He was older than the others as well – probably about twenty-five. His calm blue eyes gazed at the passionate orator in a mocking sneer.

'We'll do well in Palestine if we don't starve to death, or turn into snivelling ninnies, or end up squabbling among ourselves,' he said coolly. 'We can think about moral ideals afterwards.'

Pelagia leaned towards a sweet girl in a pair of children's trousers (she thought they were called 'shorts', after the British manner) and asked in a whisper: 'You are all in a commune, are you?'

The girl lifted up her round face and smiled. 'Oi, a nun! Yes, we're members of the Megiddo-Khadash commune.'

'What does that mean?' asked the curious nun, squatting down on her haunches.

'"New Megiddo". In ancient Hebrew "Megiddo" means "City of Happiness". There really was a city called that, in the Isreel Valley, but it was destroyed, either by the Assyrians or the Egyptians, I've forgotten which. But we're going to rebuild Megiddo; we've already bought the land from the Arabs.'

'Is he your leader?' Pelagia asked, pointing at the bearded young man.

'Who, Magellan? We don't have any leaders, we're all equal. It's just that he has experience. He's been to Palestine, and he's sailed round the world – that's why we call him Magellan. You know what he's like?' the bare-legged young lady asked in a voice full of unfeigned admiration. 'With him, you're not afraid of anything! The Oprichniks in Poltava tried to kill him – because he organised self-defence for the Jews. He fired back at them and got away! And now the police are looking for him! Oi!' Afraid that she had let too much slip, the young lady pressed her fingers to her lips, but Pelagia pretended that she hadn't heard or hadn't understood – after all, everyone knew that nuns were not very bright and not really of this world.

The girl immediately calmed down and carried on chattering rapidly, as if nothing had happened. 'It was Magellan's idea about the City of Happiness. And he gathered us all together, and got the money from somewhere. Thirty thousand! Can you imagine? He transferred it to Jaffa, to the bank, and all he left us for the journey was eight kopecks each a day!'

'Why only eight? That's very little!'

'Coliseum (he's a student in the history faculty)' – the girl pointed to one of the young men, who was incredibly emaciated and stooped – 'calculated that that was the precise sum – if you translated it into today's money, of course – that a simple farmer had to live on in King Solomon's times. So it has to be enough for us. We're farmers now too. And we'll need the money in Palestine. We have to buy livestock, drain swamps, build houses.'

Pelagia looked at the starveling Coliseum. How would someone like that be able to swing a mattock or walk behind a plough?

'But why is he Coliseum? He's not really very big.'

'He's called Fira Glusky really. But Magellan nicknamed him Coliseum. Well, It's because everyone's always saying "the ruins of the Coliseum", "the ruins of the Coliseum". Fira isn't a real person at all, he's a walking ruin – he has every sickness in the world: a curved spine, and fallen arches, and sinusitis. But see, he's coming too.'

The subject of discussion caught the nun's compassionate gaze on himself and cried out merrily: 'Hey, Sister, come along to Palestine with us!'

'I'm not a Jew,' Pelagia said, embarrassed to see that the entire company was looking at her. 'And it's hardly likely that I ever shall be.'

'No need,' laughed one of the communards. 'There are enough fake Jews without you. Just look at those over there!'

Everyone turned their heads and started laughing as well. A little distance away the three 'foundlings' had covered their heads with prayer shawls and were bowing repeatedly right down to the ground. The fervent, resounding thumping of heads against the deck was clearly audible.

'Nothing funny about that, you fools,' Magellan hissed through his teeth. 'You can smell the Okhranka off them a mile away. That Manuila of theirs draws his pay on Gorokhovaya Street – I've a keen nose for that. I'd like to take the rotten bastard by the feet and smash his brains out against the mooring post . . .'

The Zionists fell silent, and Pelagia felt sorry for the 'foundlings'. The poor things: nobody loved them, everybody had a bad word for them. They weren't really foundlings at all, they were more like orphans. And anyway, she wondered, where did they get such a strange name?

She went across to ask, but suddenly felt shy – the people were praying, after all.

And then she realised that she had spent too long promenading. The Bishop would be displeased. She ought to call into his cabin, show her face and wish him a good evening, and then go to her own berth in the second class – to read a book for a while and prepare a lesson. They would be home tomorrow.

She went down the steps to the cabin deck.

Glass-Eye

Up above the River, above the overflooded banks and the fog, the sunset must be a blaze of colour now – in any case, the gloom ahead was faintly tinged with pink. Drawn towards this magical glow, Pelagia walked to the bow of the steamer. What if, just for an instant, the wind were to blow a breach in the irksome curtain and she could admire the evening colouring of the sky?

At the bow the wind was indeed blowing, but not strongly enough to clear a path for the setting sun. Pelagia was about to turn back when she suddenly noticed that she was not alone.

There was a man sitting on a wickerwork chair in front of her. His long legs were clad in high boots and he had his feet up on the railings. She could see a straight back, broad shoulders, a cap with a humped crown. The man took a pull at his *papyrosa* and blew out a small cloud of smoke, which instantly melted into the mist.

Then suddenly he turned round, with a startling, feline impetuosity. He must have heard her breathing or the rustling of her habit.

The face looking at Pelagia was narrow and triangular, with the pointed ends of a moustache protruding to the sides. It seemed to the nun that there was something odd about the stranger's glance: as if somehow he was looking straight at her, but not quite.

Embarrassed at having intruded on the smoker's solitude, she mumbled: 'I beg your pardon . . .'

She even bowed clumsily, which was quite unnecessary. Especially since the response it drew from the man with the moustache was not courteous. Quite the contrary, in fact – he suddenly played a very strange trick, grinning fiercely so that she could see his gums, raising a hand to his left eye and – oh, horror! – taking it out of its socket!

Pelagia cried out and staggered back when she saw the small gleaming sphere with the little iridescent circle and the black spot of the pupil: and only then did she realise that the eye was glass.

The prankster gave a dry chuckle, pleased with the effect produced. In a rasping, mocking voice he said: 'What a fine dame, and her a nun too! It's a sin, holy Mother to turn your nose up at a wretched cripple.'

What an unpleasant man, the sister thought, turning away and beating a hasty retreat. If he didn't want anyone to interrupt his solitude he could have made it clear in some more delicate way.

She walked along the edge of the deck, fighting a battle against the devil of resentment. She subdued her horned foe quickly, with no great effort – a skill she had acquired in her years as a nun.

Ahead of her, at about the spot where Mitrofanii's cabin ought to be, there was something white fluttering in the air.

When she walked closer, she saw it was curtains flapping about – not in the Bishop's cabin, but the next one, in which the notorious prophet was travelling. He must have opened the window and forgotten about it; and then gone out or fallen asleep.

She really wanted to take a look at the charlatan's quarters. If she simply walked by and peeked sideways just a tiny bit, surely that was all right?

To be on the safe side, she looked round and made sure there was nobody anywhere nearby, then started walking more slowly, so that there would be time to take a more thorough peek.

Manuila's lamp was lit – that was very opportune.

Pelagia proceeded decorously as far as the small window,

directed her peripheral vision to the right and almost tripped over her own feet.

The prophet was in, and he seemed to be asleep, only not on the divan but on the floor, with his arms extended in the form of a cross. Was that one of the practices these 'foundlings' had? Or did Manuila have a special dispensation?

The nun took another little step towards the window and stood up on tiptoe.

That was very strange, now – there were two white eggs lying on the sleeper's face, in the hollows of his eyes. Pelagia pressed the bridge of her spectacles back against her nose and then screwed her eyes up to get a better look at this oddity.

A second later her vision adjusted to the dim light in the cabin and she saw that the objects weren't eggs at all, but something so terrible that Pelagia's mouth simply dropped open of its own accord, with the intention of uttering a brief exclamation appropriate for a nun: 'Oh, Lord!' but giving vent instead to a shameful, womanish screech.

II

Solving Puzzles

The correct way to photograph corpses

'The right hand in close-up,' Investigator Dolinin ordered the police photographer, at the same time beckoning to Pelagia with one finger. 'Look, Sister, how do you like our modern-day prophets? The soul was already out of his body, but he still clung on to the money.'

Pelagia walked over to him and crossed herself.

Manuila's death could not possibly have been more hideous. Someone had stove in the back of the pitiful prophet's head with a blow of such extreme force that it had jolted his eyeballs out of their sockets. They were what the nun had seen in the semi-darkness and taken for chicken's eggs. There were particles of brain and crumbs of bone on the pillow and on the carpet. And another thing that made it a torment for her to look at the body was the fact that the dead man's nightshirt had ridden up, revealing a pale, hairy stomach and private parts, but the nun tried not to let her gaze wander that far. Clutched tight in Manuila's clenched fingers was a fragment of a hundred-rouble note.

There was a blinding flash of magnesium, but the investigator was still not satisfied.

'No, no, my dear fellow. You have to spread the magnesium on both sides of the camera, or you'll get shadows. And not in a heap, not in a heap – in a line. It will burn longer that way. I suppose you don't have a tripod for taking vertical shots? Oh, the wonderful Russian provinces . . .'

The forensic doctor twisted the lifeless head, holding it by the hair. 'What a blow!' he said, poking his finger into a neat hole the size of a silver rouble. 'Such strength, such crisp impact! Like the hole made by a shrapnel bullet. Penetration almost as far as the third ventricle, and the outline is a regular oval, with smooth edges. I've never seen a wound like it, not even in a textbook.'

'Yes, it's certainly unusual,' Dolinin agreed, bending down. 'A hammer, perhaps? Only the force is immense, almost satanic. To make the eyeballs jump out of their sockets – I tell you, that takes . . .'

The cabin was filled with the dank smell of drying blood. Pelagia felt slightly sick. The worst thing of all was the way the disgusting smell mingled with the aroma of the eau de cologne that the *Sturgeon*'s captain was wearing. He was obliged to be present at the inspection of the scene by virtue of his position, but he stood modestly at one side and didn't get under the specialists' feet.

The sister closed her eyes, struggling with her nausea. Nothing in the world is more terrible or more oppressive than the mystery of death stripped of its dignity and rendered shameful. And there was that well-thumbed banknote too.

'The male organ bears signs of circumcision, relatively recent,' the doctor announced as he continued his examination. 'The scar is still crimson. Perhaps seven or eight months, unlikely to be more.'

Pelagia waited for the doctor and the photographer to finish their work and move away from the body, then asked the investigator's permission to say a prayer. She went down on her knees and first of all covered the dead man's nakedness. Then she pulled the vain, worldly scrap of paper out of the lifeless hand. She had expected the rigid fingers would be reluctant to part with their property, but the scrap came out remarkably easily.

As she handed the clue to the investigator, Pelagia said: 'Strange. Did he sleep like that, clutching money in his hands? Or after his head was already broken in, did he try to tear it out of the villain's hands?'

Dolinin said nothing for a moment, gazing with interest at the bespectacled holy sister.

Then he sniffed and scratched the bridge of his nose above the arch of his pince-nez. 'Indeed. My thanks for being so observant. According to the testimony of Manuila's travelling companions, the money – or, as they put it, the "treasury" – was in a casket under the pillow . . . The casket, naturally enough, is missing. Hmm. Grab hold of your killer's hands, with your head smashed in right through "to the third ventricle". Miraculous. Let's enter that in the "puzzles" section.' And he made an entry in a little leather-bound book. Pelagia liked that: the man was not being hasty with his conclusions.

She liked Dolinin in general, because he worked sensibly, thoroughly – you could see straight away that the man knew his job as a detective and loved it.

You might even say that Manuila had been lucky with his investigator.

A master at work

Everything had gone quite differently at first.

At the sound of the nun's screams, people came running up and started gasping in horror. The 'foundlings' made even more noise. When they learned that their leader had been killed, they started howling and wailing: 'Oh Lord! Disaster! Azochnvei! Help! Eloim!' But the words repeated most often of all were 'The treasury! The treasury!'

The captain appeared, and instead of restoring order he turned the proceedings into total chaos – perhaps because he was frightened, or perhaps owing to a certain degree of insobriety.

The commander of the steamer was transformed into a Zeus, scattering lightning bolts around him. In front of the ill-fated cabin and beneath its window he installed watches of sailors armed with items of fire-fighting equipment. He ordered first-class and second-class passengers to stay in their cabins and not stick their noses out: he herded all the deck passengers on to the poop deck and put them under the guard of two swarthy stokers with shovels in their hands. He himself donned his white dress-uniform tunic, hung a huge revolver at his side and poured a whole bottle of eau de cologne over himself to eliminate the smell of drink.

In defiance of the schedule, the *Sturgeon* sailed past the mooring at Ust-Svyazhsk without stopping and dropped anchor at the district town, standing at some distance from the dock. The first mate was despatched in a lifeboat to contact the authorities.

An hour later the passengers in the cabins located on the

starboard side saw the boat come gliding out of the evening mist swirling above the River. It was crammed with people, mostly in uniforms, but there were also some civilians.

The person who arrived to conduct the investigation was no mere police officer, not even a superintendent. That is, of course, the new arrivals did include a superintendent and other ranks, including even the commander of the district police force, but they were not the most important individuals; that person was a lean gentleman in civilian garb. His keen, intelligent eyes glinted coldly through his pince-nez, his narrow hand occasionally stroked his wedge-shaped beard. A university badge glinted on the lapel of his frock coat.

The civilian turned out to be a hugely important official, a member of the Council of the Ministry of the Interior. His name was Sergei Sergeevich Dolinin. It was later ascertained from local police officials that His Excellency had been travelling around the province of Kazan on an important tour of inspection. When he heard that a murder had taken place on board a steamship of the Nord Line, he had expressed a desire to head the investigation in person.

Sergei Sergeevich himself, in a conversation with His Reverence Mitrofanii (whom he had felt it his duty to visit immediately upon discovering such an important individual in the passenger list), accounted for his zeal by the exceptional importance of the victim's identity: 'Our Mr Manuila here had a history of serious scandal. I can assure you, Bishop, that this will cause a sensation throughout the whole of Russia. Of course, if . . .' At this point Dolinin paused and appeared to leave something unsaid. What he meant by 'if' remained unclear.

Pelagia, who was with Mitrofanii at the time, had the impression that when the investigator mentioned a sensation throughout the whole of Russia his eyes glinted. But what of it, for a man in state service, ambition was a pardonable sin, and possibly not even a sin at all, for it encouraged zeal.

It seemed very probable that Sergei Sergeevich's visit to the prelate was not paid out of courtesy, but for a completely different reason, one of a practical nature. In any case, no sooner had Dolinin concluded his outpourings of respect than he turned to Pelagia and said briskly: 'You must be the nun who discovered the body? Excellent. With His Reverence's permission' – a brief bow in Mitrofanii's direction – 'I must ask you, Sister, to accompany me to the scene of the crime.'

And that was how Pelagia came to be one of the small number of people in that nauseating cabin that reeked of blood and eau de cologne. If not for that smell, if not for the presence of the mutilated body, observing Sergei Sergeevich's professional work would have been an undiluted pleasure.

He started by rapidly jotting down a plan of the cabin in his notebook, questioning the holy sister all the time as he did so: 'Was the corner of the rug turned up? Are you certain? Was the window raised to exactly this level? Are you certain? Was the bedspread lying on the floor?'

He was pleased with the positive clarity of the answers he received and even praised her: 'You're an exceptional witness. An excellent visual memory.'

Glancing at the investigator's sketch, which looked rather unusual, Pelagia asked in turn: 'What is that?'

'That's called a field sketch,' Dolinin replied, tracing rapid lines with his pencil. 'A diagram of the scene of the crime. This here is the scale, in metres. The letters indicate the points of the compass – that's essential. Since this is a ship, the place of north is taken by the bow (B), and instead of east I have starboard (S), the right side of the ship.'

'You know,' said Pelagia, 'the chair wasn't standing like that. When I glanced into the cabin, it was over there.' She showed how the chair had been standing. 'And the papers on the table were lying in a neat pile, but now they're scattered all around.'

Sergei Sergeevich turned his head to the right and the left and stabbed one finger at the captain: 'Have you been taking liberties, my dear fellow?'

The captain gulped and shrugged guiltily.

The investigator looked through the sheets of paper scattered across the table and picked up one that was covered with crooked capital letters. He read it:

'*Baruch ata Adonoai Elochein melech cha-olam* ...' He put it down. 'It's some kind of Jewish prayer.'

Pelagia, her spirits somewhat restored following the concealment of the dead man's nakedness, carried on looking around.

She herself was surprised at how much she remembered from

43

those brief moments before she had started screeching. 'And this pipe wasn't here, either,' she said, pointing to a meerschaum tobacco pipe lying on the rug. Dolinin had already placed a little card with the number 8 beside the pipe, and for some reason had covered the item of material evidence with an inverted glass jar.

'Are you absolutely certain about that?' he asked, disconcerted.

'Yes, I would have noticed.'

'How annoying. You've cancelled out my most important clue. And like an idiot, I'd already covered it to prevent any microscopic particles from being blown off.'

Sergei Sergeevich called the captain over and asked him about the pipe.

The captain confirmed Pelagia's assertion. 'Yes sir. That's the boatswain Savenka's pipe; he's the one who came in with me and shone the torch in the corners. He must have dropped it.'

'Well done, the little nun,' Dolinin exclaimed in admiration. 'I'm lucky that you're here. I tell you what, my dear, why don't you stay for a while? You never know, you might notice something else, or remember something.'

And after that, as he thought out loud (which was a habit that the investigator had), he addressed his remarks only to Pelagia, paying no attention to the others present, even to the district police commander. Obviously Sergei Sergeevich found it more interesting or, shall we say, exotic, to address his rhetorical questions to the quick-witted nun.

'Well then, Sister, shall we examine the clothes now?' he said, picking through the victim's wardrobe: nankeen trousers, a waistcoat, a white linen mantle with a blue stripe. 'Right, then. There's no label on the trousers. Rubbishy trousers, bought at a flea market. And he was travelling first class, with the "treasury". The little skinflint . . . What do we have on the shirt? Is there a laundry mark? What do you think on that score, sister? . . . You think right: our prophet didn't employ the services of a laundry . . . We'll put the boots aside for the moment, the seams have to be slit open.'

Having finished with the clothing, Dolinin looked around and nodded to himself. 'Well then, that seems to be all for the cabin. Let's examine the periphery. And, of course, the two of us will start, my sweetheart, with the means of entry.'

He fiddled at the door, unscrewing and removing the lock with his own hands, then studying it through a magnifying glass.

'Lit-tle scra-tches,' Sergei Sergeevich purred. 'Fresh. A pick-lock? Or a new key? Let's find out?'

Then he moved on to the window and found something there that interested him. He climbed up and kneeled on the little table, then leaned across.

Reaching one hand back behind him, he clicked his fingers impatiently. 'A light here, a light!'

Two men dashed over to him at the same time: the captain and police commander. The first held out a kerosene lamp, the second an electric torch.

Dolinin chose progress. Shining the electric torch on the slot in the frame, he said slowly: 'Someone used a hack on this. That's clear then. Now, Sister, there you have the answer to our puzzle. Take a look'

Pelagia looked, but she couldn't see anything out of the ordinary.

'Surely you see it?' Sergei Sergeevich asked in surprise. 'The screws have been screwed out. And there are traces of oil. A razin has been at work here – it's their trademark.' And he immediately explained to Pelagia who the razins were. Although she lived by the River, she had never heard anything about these people before.

'The picture is growing clearer,' the investigator declared with a satisfied air. 'There's nothing like doing the job right! Manuila woke up when the thief had already pulled the casket out from under him. There was a fight. The razins don't usually go in for murder, but this one must have lost his head over the big money. Or he got frightened. And so he hit him.'

There was a tap-tap on the door. A head in a peaked cap was thrust into the room. 'Your Excellency, look, they found it on the deck. By the edge.'

Sergei Sergeevich took the canvas sack with a broken string from the policeman and rummaged inside it. He took out a pair of spectacles with gold frames, a porcelain pipe, a tailor's rule and a rubber ball. The investigator's brow furrowed into deep folds of incomprehension, but almost immediately smoothed out again.

'Why, it's a swag-bag!' the master detective exclaimed. 'The sack the razins use for putting their loot in. Here, this is the confirmation of my hypothesis!'

'Then why did the thief abandon it?' asked Pelagia.

Dolinin shrugged. 'Why would a razin want this trash if he'd got his hands on some serious loot? He tore it off his shoulder so that it wouldn't get in his way, and discarded it. And he wasn't really himself after the murder. He wasn't used to it.'

Everything fitted. Pelagia was impressed by the sharp wits of the man from St Petersburg, but her own thoughts were already hurrying on.

'How can you tell which of the passengers is a razin? Do they have any distinctive features?'

Sergei Sergeevich smiled condescendingly. 'If it's a razin – and it definitely *is* a razin – then his trail has been cold for ages.'

'Where could he have gone to? No one has been allowed off the steamer. The *Sturgeon* hasn't moored at the shore.'

'And what of it? Cold water's no problem for a razin, they swim like water rats. He slid down the anchor chain into the water, and he was gone. Or he jumped off earlier on, immediately after the murder. Never mind. Give me time. All the rest is just a matter of time now, Sister. I'll send a request to all the departments along the river. We'll find him all right . . . What's that you're looking at there?'

While listening to Dolinin, Pelagia had gone across the divan and carefully touched the pillow. 'It doesn't fit,' she said, leaning down towards the pillowcase. 'It simply doesn't fit.'

'What doesn't fit?' asked the investigator, walking up to her. 'Come on now, come on, out with it.'

'Your solution to the puzzle won't work. There wasn't any fight, and the victim didn't grab the killer by the hand. He was killed on the bed. Look,' said Pelagia, pointing, 'there's the imprint of a face in the pillow. That means that when the blow was struck, Manuila was lying face down. And there are drops of blood around it, oval ones. So they fell down from above. If he had jerked his head up, the drops would run on a slant.'

Sergei Sergeevich muttered in embarrassment: 'Well now, that's right . . . and the trickles of blood on the face run from the back of the head to the nose. You're right. I repent, I was careless. But then, begging your pardon, how did the body come to be on the floor, and in such a pose?'

'The killer dragged it off the divan. He pulled up his shirt and put the torn piece of a hundred-rouble bill in his hand. That's the only possible explanation. As for why he did it – I'd rather not think about that.'

The investigator fixed the nun with a perplexed stare, paused for a little while and shook his head. 'What crazy nonsense. No, no, Sister, you're mistaken. I think it happened differently. You have no idea how hard these so-called "prophets" and "elders" are to do away with. There's some genuinely diabolical kind of energy smouldering inside them, and killing anyone possessed like that is no easy matter. I remember an instance from the time when I was still a court investigator. I was handling the case of the murder of a certain prophet of the Skoptsy sect. His spiritual sons very nearly took his head clean off him with an axe; it was left hanging by a single scrap of skin. Well, the prophet, just imagine, carried on running around the room and waving his arms for another minute. Blood spurting out of him like a fountain, his head bobbling about behind his shoulders like a rucksack, and he's still running. How do you like that? It must have been the same with our Manuila here. The razin thought he'd killed him and stopped in the middle of the cabin to count the banknotes. But the dead man suddenly came to life and made a dash to get his money back.'

'With a hole like that in his head? With his brain damaged?' the doctor said doubtfully. 'But then, all sorts of strange things do happen. The physiology of pre-mortem convulsions has been too little studied by science.'

Pelagia did not argue – Sergei Sergeevich's explanation appeared more convincing than her own. So it turned out that this 'puzzle' had been solved after all.

But others soon came to light.

The passenger in number thirteen

'As you wish, but even so, he still pulled up the dead man's shirt,' said Pelagia. 'Did you notice the folds? They ran down from the chest in the form of a letter V. If he had fallen they wouldn't have been like that.'

'Really?' Dolinin looked at the dead body, but owing to the

modest nun's good offices the shirt had been pulled down, so that no folds remained.

That did not put the holy sister off her stride. 'You can look afterwards, in the photographs. So it turns out the killer wasn't at all horrified by what he had done; what he wanted was definitely to mock his victim ... It takes a special personality type to act like that.'

Sergei Sergeevich looked into the meticulous witness's eyes with extraordinary intensity. 'I can sense you have some reason for saying that. Do you have any grounds for suspecting anyone?'

The investigator's astuteness made the holy sister lower her eyes. She had no grounds for suspicion, there was no way she could have. But the abominable prank to shame the dead body and, even more so, the eyeballs that had come out of their sockets had reminded her of another trick of a similar character. Should she tell, or would that be wrong?

'Well then,' said Dolinin, pressing her.

'It's not really a suspicion ...' the nun said and hesitated. 'It's just that there is a certain gentleman travelling on board ... Tall, with a long moustache, wearing thigh boots. And he has a glass eye. I'd like to know who that man is ...'

The investigator looked at Pelagia from under his eyebrows, with his head lowered, as if he were trying to read in her face what she had left unsaid.

'Tall, long moustache, in thigh boots, with an artificial eye?' he said, repeating the description and turned to the captain. 'Is there someone like that?'

'There is, sir, in cabin number thirteen. Mr Ostrolyzhensky; he has a ticket from Nizhni to Kazan.'

'In thirteen?'

Dolinin turned rapidly on his heels and went out.

The others exchanged glances, but refrained from any exchange of opinions.

The captain poured some water from a carafe, wiped the edge of the glass with his handkerchief and drank voraciously. Then he poured himself some more. Pelagia, the police commander, the doctor and the photographer watched his Adam's apple twitching above the collar of his white tunic.

'Ah, that was very wrong,' Pelagia thought uneasily. 'I've cast a shadow on someone without any good reason ...'

The captain had barely polished off his second glass of water and set about a third, when the door swung open sharply.

'Did you order all the passengers to stay in their cabins?' Dolinin barked at the captain from the doorway.

'Yes.'

'Then why is thirteen empty?'

'How do you mean, empty? I saw Mr Ostrolyzhensky go in there with my very own eyes! And I warned him not to go anywhere until he was specifically instructed!'

'Warned him! You should have put a sailor in the corridor!'

'But it's absolutely impossible! By your leave, I . . .' The captain dashed towards the door.

'Don't bother,' Sergei Sergeevich said with a frown of distaste. 'I've just come from there. His luggage is all there, but the passenger's gone. I forbid anyone to go in and touch anything. I've put a police constable on the door.'

'I don't understand a thing,' said the captain, shrugging and spreading his hands.

'Search the vessel!' Dolinin ordered with a gloomy, intense expression. 'From the funnel to the coal hole!'

The captain and the police commander ran out into the corridor, and the investigator spoke to the nun in a completely different tone of voice, as an equal to an equal. 'This Glass-Eye of yours has disappeared. So there you have it, Mademoiselle Pelagia, puzzle number two.'

The holy sister was not offended by the ironic 'Mademoiselle', because she realised the free-and-easy form of address was not intended as mockery, but as an expression of liking.

'This man is no razin,' the investigator mused. 'They never take tickets, especially not in first class. He's probably a dasher. It's their style.'

'A dasher – is that a bandit?'

'Yes, from one of the respected gangs on the river. Or else a casual migrant – there are quite a few lone wolves amongst them.'

The suspicious disappearance of the man with one eye freed Pelagia of her sense of guilt and she grew bolder: 'You know, that man really did look like a bandit. Only not some petty predator, not even a wolf, but something like a tiger or a leopard.'

Once she had said it, she felt ashamed of her excessively flowery turn of phrase, and so she switched to a dry, businesslike tone of voice. 'What I don't understand is this. If the murder was committed by a high-class bandit, then what do we make of the sack, that what was it called – a swag-bag? What would a man like that want with petty theft?'

'A puzzle,' Dolinin admitted. 'A definite puzzle.' And he made an entry in his notebook.

He leafed through the small pages covered in writing and sketches, and began summing up.

'That would seem to be all for the initial investigation. And so, thanks to you, dear Sister, we have acquired a prime suspect. We have his description (I'll take it down from your words in more detail later), and also his name. Although the name is most likely false. Now we need to examine the victim.'

Dolinin leaned down over the corpse and frowned in annoyance. 'Just look at how distorted his face is. Identification's going to be a problem.'

'Why does he have to be identified?' the nun asked in surprise. 'After all, he wasn't travelling alone, he had companions. They'll identify him.'

Sergei Sergeevich glanced at the doctor and the photographer, who were listening to the conversation, and said: 'Doctor, go to the captain's office and write your report. Keep it brief, but don't leave anything essential out. And as for you' – this was to the photographer – 'would you please go to the boatswain and bring me a reel of string. And ask for a knife too – a cable knife, the boatswain knows.'

Only when he was left alone with Pelagia did he answer the question, and he lowered his voice to a confidential undertone to do so: 'Do you know, mademoiselle, why I came dashing to investigate this murder myself?'

The question was clearly rhetorical and, after maintaining a pause for the period required by the laws of the stage, Dolinin would certainly have answered it himself. However, the nun, who was beginning to like this intelligent investigator more and more, permitted herself to take a liberty (since she was no longer 'Sister', but 'mademoiselle').

'I assume you found your tour of inspection boring and wanted to get back to real live work.'

Sergei Sergeevich gave a short laugh, which softened the lines of his dry, bilious face and made it look younger.

'Let's assume that is correct, and it makes me admire your shrewdness yet again. You know, I really cannot get used to administrative work. My colleagues envy me. Such a rapid advance in my career, a general's rank at the age of forty, a member of the council of a ministry, but I'm constantly tormented by nostalgia for my old job. Only a year ago I was still an investigator, for especially important cases. And not a bad investigator either, I assure you.'

'I can see that. No doubt your superiors singled you out for promotion for distinguished service?'

'If only.' Dolinin chuckled. 'An investigator can be as wise as Solomon, he can wear out the knees of a thousand pairs of trousers and the elbows of a thousand frock coats, but he'll never be elevated to such dizzy heights. That's not the way great careers are made.'

'How then?'

'With paper, dear Sister. Paper is the only magic carpet on which you can soar up to the mountain peaks in our mighty state. When I took up the pen, to be honest I wasn't thinking about my career at all. Quite the opposite: I thought they would probably send me packing for such audacity. But I couldn't carry on watching the sheer Asiatic chaos in our investigative work. I wrote a project of reform and sent it to the individuals in high state positions who are charged with managing the protection of the rule of law. I decided to do it, come what may. I had already started looking for another job, as a lawyer. And suddenly this humble servant of God was summoned to Mount Olympus itself. Well done, they said. We've been waiting for someone like you for a long time.' Dolinin raised his arms in a comical gesture, as if he were capitulating in the face of the unpredictable caprice of destiny. 'I was instructed to prepare a reform designed to regulate the interaction between police investigative agencies and court investigations. Well, I asked for it, as they say. And now I'm like the Eternal Jew, wandering round the cities and the provinces. At this stage I've done so much regulating, I could just sit down and howl, like a wolf. However, Mademoiselle Pelagia, you must not think that Dolinin has simply run away from a boring lesson, like some grammar-school boy. No, I am a responsible man, not given to puerile impulsiveness. You see, the case of the prophet Manuila is special. This is the second time he has been murdered.'

'How can that be?' gasped Pelagia.

Magical Manuila

'It's a fact. There are many people who cannot bear this particular individual.'

The holy sister nodded: 'I've already realised that.'

'The first time Manuila was murdered was three weeks ago, in the province of Tver.'

'I'm sorry, but I don't quite—'

Dolinin waved his hand, as if to say: Please don't interrupt, listen.

'The dead man turned out to be a commoner by the name of Petrov or Mikhailov, I don't remember now. A "foundling", a follower of Manuila and similar to him in appearance. Hence the rumours of Manuila's immortality.'

'What if this isn't him either?' asked Pelagia, pointing at the dead man.

'A reasonable question. I'd like very much to find out. The appearance fits, as far as I can recall. It's just a pity that we don't have a photograph of the prophet. Manuila had no criminal record, so our department had no excuse for recording his charming features. And his travelling companions are nothing more than that. I've ordered them to be locked in a storeroom for the time being, but what sense can I get out of unbalanced creatures like them? They might even lie. Or they themselves could be confused about the dead man's identity.'

'What an amazing story!'

'It certainly is . . . Not only is it amazing, even more importantly, it's political.' Sergei Sergeevich became more serious. 'The murder of a prophet, especially an immortal one, is a matter of state importance. It will be a huge sensation in all the newspapers, and not only in Russia. Which makes it all the more essential to determine for certain if this is Manuila or another double.'

At this point the photographer returned with the string and a short, extremely sharp knife.

The investigator called the police constables in from the corridor and gave them strange, indeed blasphemous instructions. 'Dress him' – a nod in the direction of the dead man – 'sit him on the chair and tie him on with string. Quickly now!' Dolinin shouted at the suddenly timid men, and explained to the nun: 'We have to get the corpse into an identifiable condition. It's a new method, my own personal invention.'

While the policemen grunted as they inserted the still flexible limbs of the dead man into his trouser legs and sleeves, Dolinin very deftly ripped the soles off the prophet's boots, with the knife and slit open the tops. 'There now,' he said in a satisfied voice, extracting some papers from the ripped leather. He gave them a quick glance and shrugged slightly. He didn't show them to his confidante, and Pelagia felt awkward about asking, although she was really very curious.

'Have you got him sitting up?' Sergei Sergeevich asked, turning to the policemen. 'The eyes, the eyes. Ah, damn it.'

The holy sister took a cautious peep – and immediately squeezed her own eyes shut. The eyeballs were hanging out on to the dead man's cheeks, and the sight was beyond all human bearing.

'The rubber glove from my bag,' the investigator's brisk voice said. 'That's the way. Excellent, the peepers are back in. Cotton wool. No, no. Two small pieces and roll them out a bit. Under the eyelids it goes, under the eyelids. Now they're open, very good . . . Ah, the cornea has dried out, it's dull. I've got a bottle of nitroglycerine and a syringe in there, give them here . . . Into the right . . . Into the left . . . Ughu. Now we'll comb his hair . . . And now the wet towel . . . all done. Open your eyes, mademoiselle, don't be afraid.'

Wincing before she even started, Pelagia took a cautious look and was stupefied.

Sitting there on the chair – admittedly in a rather forced pose, with his head hanging to one side – was a gaunt, bearded peasant who looked absolutely alive, watching her with intense, gleaming eyes. He was wearing a shirt, waistcoat and trousers. His beard and long hair were neatly combed,

This sudden resurrection of the departed was so unexpected that the holy sister took a step back.

Sergei Sergeevich laughed contentedly. 'There, now we can even photograph Mr Shelukhin.'

'What did you call him?' Pelagia asked.

'That's the name in his passport.' The investigator read from the document he had extracted from the top of the boot: 'Pyotr Saveliev Shelukhin, 38 years of age, religion Orthodox, peasant of the village of Stroganovka, Staritskaya Rural Territory of the Gorodets district in the province of Zavolzhie.'

'Why, that's our province!' the holy sister gasped.

'But I'd heard that Manuila was born in the province of Vyatka. In any case, that was where he began preaching. The "found-lings", by the way, are convinced that their prophet was born in the Holy Land and will soon set out to go back. And actually, Shelukhin did have a ticket to Jaffa . . .'

The magnesium hissed and flared.

'One more full-face. Then three-quarter profiles from the right and the left. And both full profiles,' Dolinin instructed. He gave the tidied-up corpse a sceptical look and sighed. 'Height above average, facial features ordinary, light-brown hair, blue eyes, slight build, no distinguishing features. No, gentlemen, this is simply not good enough. I need a hundred per cent clarity . . .' He wrinkled up his brow as he figured something out. Tugged on his wedge of beard. Shook his head decisively.

'Sister, from here to Zavolzhsk is twelve hours' sailing, right? And how long from there to Gorodetsk?'

'Two days along the rivers. But the Gorodets district extends a long way, and Stroganovka is right over by the Ural Mountains. You have to travel through the forest to get there, through a remote wilderness. It's a difficult journey, and a long one. I've been in those parts once, with the Bishop. We travelled round the schismatics' hermitages, trying to persuade the local monks not to be afraid of the authorities . . .'

'I'm going,' Sergei Sergeevich declared, and his eyes glinted fervently. 'This really is a case of public importance. Once Dolinin finds himself at the scene of a crime, he has to get right to the bottom of it! He can't just let it go. I'll send the minister a telegram: the tour of inspection is being interrupted owing to exceptional circumstances. He'll only be glad that I happened to be at the right place at the right time.'

III

Struk

Only herself to blame

On the third day of the journey they disembarked from the barge and stopped for the night in the large Old Believer village of Gorodets, where the women in white shawls spat over their left shoulders when they saw Pelagia in her habit. And after that they set off by land, through the Forest.

It didn't have any name – just 'the Forest', that was all. At first deciduous, then mixed, then almost entirely coniferous, the Forest extended for a hundred versts as far as the Urals Crest, crept over the mountains and, on emerging into the wide open space beyond them, swept all the way to the Pacific Ocean across an unimaginably vast expanse of land, its immense mass seamed with dark, broad rivers, many of which also had no name, for how could anyone think up such a great number of names, and who was there to do it?

At its western extremity, in Zavolzhie, the Forest was still far from mature, but even its shallows differed from its European counterparts in the same way as an ocean wave differs from a wave in a lake – by virtue of the distinctive leisurely might of its breath, and also an absolute contempt for any human presence.

On first acquaintance the road posed as a decent country track, but by the tenth verst it had already abandoned any pretence at carrying regular traffic and shrivelled to the dimensions of an ordinary forest path.

After an hour or two of rattling and shaking along a rutted surface on which black water gleamed dully through an overgrowth of spring grass, it was hard to believe that cities, broad steppes, deserts, open sky and bright sunlight really existed in the world. Out there, in the realm of freedom, warmth reigned supreme, the meadows were full of yellow dandelions and the buzzing of bees as yet only half-awake; but in here patches of grey snow lay in the hollows, an equal mixture of meltwater and ice pellets frothed in the ravines, and the deciduous trees still stood in their mournful winter nakedness.

When the birches and aspens were replaced by fir trees, it became even darker and more forbidding. The space closed in, the light faded, new smells appeared in the air, setting your skin creeping and prickling. There was the scent of absolutely wild animal life lurking in the thickets, and in addition a certain vague, damp terror. As night approached, the alarming scent became stronger, and the horses crowded close round the camp-fire, whinnying fearfully and flicking their ears.

Pelagia could not help recalling the Zavolzhian tales about all sorts of evil spirits in the Forest: about the bear Babai, who took girls for his brides, about the fox Lizukha, who appeared in the form of a fair maiden and lured young lads and even family men away for ever. According to the Zavolzhian legends, the most terrible creature of all was man-wolf Struk, with eyes of fire and huge teeth of iron: people frightened their children with him, so that they wouldn't wander far into the Forest. Struk's jaws belched fire and smoke and he didn't run at all, he hopped across the treetops like a lynx, and if he fell and hit the ground, he turned into a dashing young fellow in a grey caftan. God forbid that you should ever meet a mouse-grey man like that in the forest.

In the town these ancient legends seemed to be the naïve and endearing creations of the national spirit, or – as people said more and more often nowadays – folklore, but in the Forest, with an owl hooting funereally and a pack of wolves howling in the distance, it was easy to believe in both Babai and Struk.

There could be absolutely no doubt at all that the Forest was alive, that it was listening to you, watching you, and that this glance was unfriendly, even hostile. Pelagia sensed the oppressive gaze of the Forest on her back and the nape of her neck. Sometimes, indeed, she sensed it so keenly that she glanced round and furtively crossed herself. It must be truly terrifying to be all alone in the forest thickets.

Fortunately, she was not alone in the Forest.

The expedition fitted out by Sergei Sergeevich looked as follows.

Striding along at the front, tapping vigorously with his staff, was the guide – the district sergeant major; behind him came Dolinin himself, riding on a sturdy light bay relinquished to the important visitor by the district police officer; then the body, packed round with straw and lumps of ice, lying in a box on a cart accompanied by two guards; the small caravan was concluded by a wagon covered with tarpaulin, carrying the provisions and the baggage. The Zytyak driver sat on his box, with Pelagia sitting beside him, stoically enduring the jolting over the potholes, and the monotonous chanting of her broad-faced neighbour, and the acrid smoke of his birch-bark pipe.

The holy sister glanced around fearfully, all the while feeling amazed at herself. How had it happened that she, a quiet nun and the headmistress of a convent school, came to find herself in this remote wilderness, among strangers, accompanying the body of a scandalous false prophet? Truly wondrous are Thy ways, O Lord. Or it could, perhaps, be put differently: the nun had been afflicted by temporary insanity. The energetic investigator from St Petersburg had turned her head and bewitched her.

They had disembarked from the steamer *Sturgeon* in Zavolzhsk.

Sergei Sergeevich had not detained any of the passengers, not even the 'foundlings', since he had a definite suspect – the passenger from cabin thirteen.

Pelagia had been astounded that Manuila's followers expressed no desire to accompany their adored prophet's body on its final journey, but continued on along their own way, to the Holy Land. Dolinin's comment concerning this was as follows: 'Being a prophet's a thankless kind of job. Croak, and no one gives a damn for you any more.'

'But it seems to me, on the contrary, that this man, whoever he might be, has done his job,' said the holy sister, interceding for Manuila and his mangy flock. 'The word has outlived the prophet, as it rightly should. Manuila is gone, but the "foundlings" have not been diverted from their path. And, by the way, I don't know why they call themselves that.'

'They say that Manuila "sought them out" among men,' Dolinin explained. 'He found them, picked them up out of the stinking filth, swaddled them in white garments and bestowed the blue stripe on them as a sign that the Kingdom of Heaven is near at hand. There's an entire philosophy to it, although, mark you, it's rather primitive in nature. A few distorted quotations from the Old Testament. They reject Christ and the Gospel, since they wish to be Jews. But let me repeat, this is all extremely vague and indefinite. As far as I am aware, Manuila didn't concern himself overmuch with ministering to his new "Jews". Once he turned some simple soul's head, he moved on, and these poor wretches try to think for themselves what they should do now and how they should live. As far as that goes, you're probably right. Manuila's death won't change very much . . . Ah, Sister . . .' The investigator's face hardened. 'That's the way times are. The fishers of souls have embarked on a really big hunt. The longer it continues, the more numerous they will become, the more abundant their harvest will be. Remember what it says in Matthew: "And false prophets shall abound, and they shall deceive many."'

'"And from the multiplication of lawlessness love shall grow cold in many,"' said Pelagia, continuing the apostolic citation.

Dolinin started and gave the nun a strange look, as if he had just heard those words for the first time or, perhaps, had never really thought about their meaning before.

'Never mind about love,' he said dourly. 'The thing is to save the souls from the fishers.'

'Without love?' Pelagia almost asked, but she didn't, because the moment was not appropriate for abstract discussions. However, she did take note of one thing: apparently in the sphere of love all was not well with the judicial reformer's life. She wondered if he was married.

But aloud she asked about something different: 'Is it all right for you to let them all go?'

'Let them sail on. At the very first port of call several agents of the criminal police will go on board the *Sturgeon* – I forwarded instructions by telegraph. I can't exclude the possibility that Mr Ostrolyzhensky might yet surface out of some nook or cranny. A steamer's not a shed, you can't examine every little corner. And if our explanation is mistaken and Mr Glass-Eye is not involved . . .'

'How can he not be involved?' Pelagia retorted. 'Then where has he gone?'

'Let's suppose he was killed. And thrown into the water. Perhaps he saw too much. Such cases are not rare ... Well then, if the killer is not Ostrolyzhensky, but someone else, after my departure this individual will relax and let his guard down a bit. The agents have been instructed to pay special attention to anyone who disembarks sooner than he should according to his ticket. And to anything else that is even in the slightest degree suspicious. They still have a long journey ahead of them to Tsaritsyn. If the killer's on the steamer, we have plenty of time to arrest him.'

Pelagia said nothing, impressed by the investigator's judicious prudence.

'And in the meantime I'll take a ride to Stroganovka and back again,' Sergei Sergeevich continued. 'I'll check this Shelukhin's identity. And perhaps at the same time there might be some kind of trail to be picked up there.' Then suddenly, without the slightest pause or transition, he continued in the same businesslike tone of voice: 'Dear Sister, I have a request to put to you. An unusual request, absurd in fact. But somehow I feel that you won't resent it and, if I am lucky, you might even agree ...' He coughed and blurted out: 'Will you agree to accompany me?'

'How do you mean?' the nun asked, confused.

'I mean, will you join me on the journey to Stroganovka?' Dolinin said, and before the nun could say no, he continued quickly: 'Although this Manuila foreswore the faith of his fatherland, he was still a baptised soul. It doesn't seem right to transport the body without a member of the clergy. They'll give me some sour monk as an escort. It would be incomparably more agreeable with you ...' At this point Sergei Sergeevich realised that this final remark sounded too frivolous and he hastily corrected himself. 'And, more importantly, more logical. You told me yourself that you've been in this remote neck of the woods before. You can help me find a common language with the local inhabitants ...'

'I haven't been in Stroganovka. Only in Staritsa, and that's fifty versts away.'

'That's not important, in any case you're familiar with the local customs. And the locals will be less afraid of a nun than of a visiting dignitary ... and again, I have the impression that you are not entirely indifferent to this pitiful prophet's fate. At least you can say a prayer for his lost soul along the way ... Well, what do you say?'

Pelagia was already choosing the words for a polite refusal, but the way he looked into her eyes made her falter. The important thing was that she realised the devil of pride was tempting her. The real reason for Sergei Sergeevich's 'absurd request' was absolutely clear: the master detective had appreciated her perspicacity and her keen eye, and he was hoping for help in the investigation.

As a member of the clergy, Pelagia did not allow herself even to suspect any other possible grounds of a sinful, worldly nature. But in any case the devil of pride proved to be quite sufficient. Weak soul that she was, she could not resist the temptation.

It's my own fault, Pelagia told herself, blushing with pleasure. I ought to have kept my peace and not butted in with my deductions. And now it would be rather strange to abandon Sergei Sergeevich in the middle of the investigation.

'You just tell me you agree,' Dolinin appealed to her in a low voice, noticing her hesitation. 'I'll have a word with His Eminence myself.'

'No,' sighed Pelagia. 'I'd better do it.'

On the Heavenly Bridegroom

She prepared thoroughly for the difficult conversation, trying to structure the discussion after Mitrofanii's much beloved masculine manner – that is, without any appeal to emotion, on the basis of pure logic. She made no mention at all of the arguments concerning the benefit to the investigation and laid the greatest emphasis on the danger that the expedition undertaken by Dolinin represented.

'If it is confirmed that the sectarian prophet is a native of our diocese, think what a gift that will be for Konstantin Petrovich,' the holy sister said. 'They'll write about it in all the newspapers, and they are certain to mention the province of Zavolzhie. And in the Synod they'll say: A fine bishop they have in Zavolzhie, hatching out an adder like this in his nest. Your position is already insecure enough in any case.'

'I have no attachment to my see,' Mitrofanii said with a frown.

'I know. It is not a matter of you, but of us. Who will the procurator send us to replace you? It is sure to be some favourite of his own. One of those ardent inquisitors. And that will be the end of quiet times in Zavolzhsk.' And then she demonstrated at length how important it was that she, one of Mitrofanii's own people, should be there at the identification beside the important official from St Petersburg – in the very worst case, to warn the Bishop in good time if events were to take a bad turn; but perhaps not only for that since she and Mr Dolinin had formed a very friendly relationship and it was quite possible that she would be able to influence the content and the tone of the report that the investigator would send to St Petersburg.

His Eminence heard his spiritual daughter out attentively, nodding in acknowledgement of the reasonableness of her arguments. But when he parted his lips, it was to speak of something quite different. 'Perhaps Pobedin is right, and you ought not to be a nun?' Mitrofanii said thoughtfully. 'Just wait a moment, don't get excited. You and I have reasoned a great deal about the significance of earthly life and we are both seemingly in agreement that the main duty owed to God by every individual is to find himself and his own path, to live out his own life, and not someone else's. You yourself have said that the most of humanity's woes result from the fact that nine hundred and ninety-nine people out of every thousand simply live until they die, without ever having understood themselves, having filled their entire lives with business that was not their own. I also think that God requires nothing else of us, except that each one should seek out his own road and follow it to the end. Take yourself, for instance. It is quite clear to me and you that your mission is to solve human mysteries. But you, Pelagia, spend your time on something quite different. The business of being of a nun may indeed be supremely worthy – praying to the Lord for sinners – but does it not mean that you take sin upon yourself? By living a life that is not *your own*, denying your talent, disdaining this God-given gift – a most heinous sin, the most grievous of all crimes that a person can commit against himself and the Lord. Do you understand what I am speaking about?'

'I do,' the holy sister replied in a trembling voice. 'You mean to say that I have no talent for service as a nun and my place is not in the cloister but in the world. Where I shall be of the greatest use to people and the Lord.' She lowered her head, so that the Bishop would not see the tears that had sprung to her eyes. The conversation was warping out of shape, shifting from the male manner to the female in a presentiment of weeping and emotional entreaty.

'It is very possible, Your Eminence, that this really is so. But surely you have not forgotten' – at this point Pelagia raised her face and looked at Mitrofanii with her brightly gleaming eyes – 'that I did not come to the monastic life out of piety or out of spiritual strength, but from the edge of the abyss? Not even from the edge, but from out of the very abyss itself, into which I was falling inexorably and was already on the point—'

The nun's voice broke off; she was unable to complete the phrase.

Alas, the logical discussion had been an inglorious failure.

'I remember,' said the prelate. 'You were in a state of grief, of self-destructive despair.'

'But I was fortunate. The Lord sent me you. And you said: "Your only salvation, if you would not destroy your soul for all eternity, is to hold tight to the Heavenly Bridegroom, who will never abandon you, because he is immortal."'

'I remember that too.'

'I listened to you. I took a vow too be faithful. To Him. What am I to do now – break it? Simply because I have a knack for the investigation of earthly secrets?'

'Jesus will understand and forgive.'

'Of course He will understand. Only I cannot treat Him like that. I am Christ's bride; I must serve him.'

'You can serve Christ in the world no worse than in a convent. Even better, in fact.'

'You can, but not with all your strength. Because you will have to divide yourself between earthly matters and Eternal Love.' Pelagia wiped her eyes with a handkerchief and finished in a firm voice, without any tearful trembling. 'I promised you, and I repeat it again: there will be no more investigations. And my ingenuity will not be needed here anyway. Mr Dolinin is a born detective; I am no match for him.'

Mitrofanii looked distrustfully at his red-headed confidante and heaved a heavy sigh, but raised no more objections.

He let her go.

The cuckold's tale

The news that His Reverence had given Pelagia his blessing for the journey had failed to inspire the anticipated enthusiasm in Dolinin. He had merely nodded, as if taking note of the information, and said nothing, and also twitched the corner of his mouth nervously. This gentleman was certainly not without his eccentricities. And on the way his behaviour had been emphatically distant. He had not joked or entered into conversation, limiting himself to the most essential civility. Sergei Sergeevich was like a changed man.

At first the nun was perplexed and alarmed that she might have offended him in some unknown fashion, but then she resigned herself to the investigator's gloominess and attributed it to a hypochondriacal temperament.

While they were travelling on the barge – first along a tributary of the River, then along a tributary of the tributary – Dolinin kept looking through his notebook and writing letters or reports. Pelagia did not pester him. She knitted a waistcoat of dog's hair for Mitrofanii, read the book she had brought for the journey, *Lives of the Female Saints of Modern Times*, or simply gazed at the river banks drifting past. But when she moved from the barge to the wagon, the first two of these occupations was rendered impossible by the jolting and the third was rendered meaningless by the restricted view: whichever way you looked, there was nothing but trees.

For the first half-day after they entered the Forest Sergei Sergeevich behaved in the same way, maintaining his distance. Every now and then, it's true, he turned round in the saddle and looked back, as if he were checking that the nun was still there and had not disappeared from the driving box.

During the halt for lunch Pelagia approached the crudely knocked-together crate in which the murdered man lay and began whispering a prayer. She thought: What is the significance of the tragic event known as 'sudden death', when a man is parted from his soul in the very prime of life, with no preparation or warning? Why would the Lord want this? Could it really only be as an example and a lesson to others? But what then of the one who has died? Is it worthy of a man to be no more than an edifying example for others?

She became so engrossed in her complicated meditations that she did not hear the footsteps and started at the sound of Dolinin's voice speaking right beside her ear.

As if nothing untoward had happened, as if the two and a half days of silence had never been, the investigator asked: 'Well now, Sister, what do you think about the whole thing?'

'About what?'

'You understand me perfectly well.' Sergei Sergeevich's face quivered in an impatient nervous tic. 'You must surely have constructed your own picture of the crime. Who, how, to what end. You are a perceptive woman, with a keen intelligence and superb intuition. The help you gave me at the preliminary stage of the investigation was invaluable. So don't stop halfway. Tell me. Hypotheses, surmises, the most fantastic assumptions – I shall be grateful for everything.'

If the question had been posed earlier, before the tearful interview with Mitrofanii and not now, then Pelagia would definitely have shared all of her reasoning with Sergei Sergeevich. However, the conversation with the Bishop and the promise she had given had worked a decisive change in the nun's attitude. Having frankly admitted to herself that the most important factors in her agreement to make the journey to Stroganovka had been reckless vanity and sinful curiosity, the nun had strictly forbidden herself to think about where Glass-Eye had got to, whether he had killed the 'prophet' and if so, why – out of hatred or greed or other motives?

She answered the investigator meekly, with her eyes lowered. 'I have not even thought about it. It is none of my concern. No doubt you must have formed the impression that I think of myself as a detective in a nun's habit. I assure you, sir, that that is not the case. Is it seemly for a nun to meddle in worldly affairs, especially of such a sinful nature? If I said too much on that day, it was owing to my shock at the sight of the dead body. You, sir, have your job to do, and I have mine. May God assist you, and I shall pray for the success of your efforts.'

He gave her a keen, searching look.

Then suddenly he smiled – a bright, friendly smile: 'That's a shame. We could have made our deductions together. And it is even more of a shame, my little Sister, that you do not work in the detective department. We don't have many women agents, but every one of them is worth ten men. With your abilities you would be worth a hundred. Very well, I'll leave you in peace. I believe you were saying a prayer?'

He walked away to the campfire, and from that moment his behaviour changed, he became the old Sergei Sergeevich – an intelligent conversation partner whose mildly sardonic matter made the time pass faster and more pleasantly.

Now Dolinin preferred to ride beside the wagon, rather than up ahead. Sometimes he drove the Zytyak off the box and took the reins himself. There were times when he even dismounted and walked, leading the horse by the reins. Once he actually suggested that Pelagia should take a ride on the horse, but she refused, citing her calling as a nun, although she wanted very much to sit in the saddle like a man, the way she used to do in times long before, press her knees against the horse's strong, hot flanks, half-stand up in the stirrups and go flying across the soft, squelchy ground . . .

The nun found Sergei Sergeevich's sardonic tone impressive, rather than irritating, because it was absolutely free of the cynicism that was so widespread in the educated sections of society. She sensed that not only was he a man with convictions and ideals, but also – something altogether amazing for the present times – a man of profound faith, untainted by superstition.

In the presence of their dismal cargo, the conversation at first centred on the victim. The nun learned certain details of the sinful life of the 'fisher of souls' from Dolinin.

The latter-day messiah had apparently only begun preaching quite recently – two years earlier, in fact – although he had managed to make his way on foot round almost half the provinces in the country and had acquired a substantial number of followers, for the most part of the very lowest social standing. No crowds of 'foundlings' had gathered, no mass demonstrations had been organised, yet even so they had drawn a lot of attention to themselves with their white-and-blue robes and their emphatic rejection of Christianity, together with the Orthodox Church. At the same time, as is usually the case with perturbers of souls who have risen up out of the darkest depths of the people, the meaning of Manuila's preaching was obscure and resistant to logical exposition. Vague imprecations against Sunday, priests, icons, the chiming of bells, military service, the eating of pork and an incomprehensible glorification of Jewishness (although Manuila, if he really had come from a remote corner of the province of Zavolzhie, could not possible have seen any actual Jews there), together with all sorts of other nonsense.

Eventually, as Dolinin related, the wandering preacher had come to the attention of Chief Procurator Pobedin, whose professional duty included keeping a watchful eye on heresy of all kinds. The high official had summoned the uncouth peasant and engaged him in spiritual discussion. ('Konstantin Petrovich loves spiritual combat with heretics, simply for the sake of his own inevitable victory,' Dolinin laughed as he narrated this incident in a comical tone, but without the slightest trace of acrimony.) And Manuila, always ready to take his chance, had waited until the Chief Procurator turned towards an image of the Saviour in order to cross himself, and then pinched a gold and diamond clock – a present to Pobedin from the sovereign himself – off the desk. He had been caught in the act and led away to the police station. Konstantin Petrovich, however, had taken pity on the vagabond and set him free to go on his way. 'They didn't even have time to photograph him or carry out a bertillonage, and that would have made my job so much easier now!' the narrator sighed regretfully and concluded with the following words: 'It would have been better if he hadn't let him go in his misguided generosity. Manuila would be in the lock-up now, and still alive.'

'A sad story,' said Pelagia, when she had heard it all. 'And the saddest thing of all is that the Orthodox religion, supposedly our natural faith, fails to give many Russian people spiritual comfort. There is something lacking in it for the simple heart. Or perhaps just the opposite: there is some kind of impurity in it, something untruthful – otherwise people would not abandon our Church for all sorts of absurd heresies.'

'There is nothing lacking. Our faith has everything,' Dolinin snapped with an unshakeable certainty that Pelagia had not expected from this sceptic.

For some reason the nun's words had agitated the investigator. He hesitated for a moment and then blushed as he said: 'Let me tell you ... a little story about a certain man ...' He pulled off his pince-nez and rubbed the bridge of his nose agitatedly. 'Well, never mind "a certain man" – the story is about me. You're intelligent – you will guess in any case. You, sister, are only the second individual in the entire world to whom I have told it . . . I don't know why . . . No, that's a lie, I do know. But I won't say – it's not important. I feel I want to, that's all.'

There was something happening to Sergei Sergeevich: he was growing more and more agitated. Pelagia was familiar with this condition in people: someone carries inside himself something that is burning his very soul, he bears it for as long as he can, sometimes for years, and then all of a sudden he simply pours out his great pain to a person he just happens to meet, some chance travelling companion. It has to be a chance acquaintance, that is the whole point.

'It s an ordinary story – banal, in fact,' Dolinin began with a crooked grin. 'There are plenty of stories like it all around. It's not really a tragedy, more a brief scenario for a dirty joke about a cuckolded husband and an unfaithful wife . . . A certain man (whom you see here before you, but I'd better use the third person, it's more proper that way) had a young and lovely wife. Of course, he adored her, he was happy and he assumed that she was happy too, that they would live together until the end of their lives and, as they say, die on the same day. No, I won't make a meal of it, it's well-worn material . . . And then suddenly – thunder out of a clear blue sky. He looked in her handbag for some unimportant trifle . . . No, I'd better be precise, because that will emphasise the banal and comical nature of the event . . . The poor fool wanted her powder compact, to conceal a pimple, since he had an important court appearance coming up and he had this pimple on his nose – you understand, it was embarrassing. In other words, in those days I used to think that a statement at a trial was a very important thing,' said Sergei Sergeevich, abandoning his third person narrative after all. 'Until the moment when I found the note in that handbag. A note of the most savoury character imaginable.'

Pelagia gasped.

'I told you, this is an extremely banal story,' Dolinin said, smiling fiercely.

'No, no, It's not banal!' the nun exclaimed. 'It is the very worst of misfortunes! And as for it happening frequently, death itself is no rarity, but no one calls it banal. When the one person who means the whole world betrays you, it is even worse than if he had died . . . No. I have said something sinful. It is not worse, it is not.' Pelagia turned pale and shook her head sharply twice, as if driving away some memory or vision, but Sergei Sergeevich was not looking at her and seemed not even to have heard her objection.

He continued his interrupted story: 'I went dashing to her to demand an explanation, but instead of asking my forgiveness or at least lying, she said: "I love him, I have for a long time, I love him more than life itself. I couldn't bring myself to tell you, because I respect you and feel sorry for you, but since it has turned out like this . . . " It turned out to be an old acquaintance of ours, a family friend and frequent visitor to the house . . . Rich, good looking, and an "Excellency"to boot. Anyway, to keep it short, she moved in with him. I completely lost my head. To hell with the job and the important trials, if the world's collapsing around me . . . I would never have thought I was capable of imploring abjectly, sobbing and all the rest. But I was, I was perfectly capable! Only it was all in vain. My wife is a kind creature, she is compassionate; when I sobbed, she shed tears with me. I went down on my knees, and she immediately plumped down on hers too. There we were crawling about in front of each other. "Forgive me"– "No, you forgive me!" etc., etc. But for all her compassionate feelings she's a resolute lady. She won't be shifted when it comes to anything important – I already knew that about her. And I respected her for it. Of course, she wouldn't be shifted this time either, I was simply tormenting her and myself pointlessly. And one day she took advantage of my miserable sniveling' – at this point a note of undisguised bitterness appeared in Dolinin's voice for the first time – 'and she asked me to let her have our son. And I did. I was hoping to impress her with my nobility and self-sacrifice. I did impress her. But even so she didn't come back to me . . . and that was when I wrote the famous project, the project of reform. With a secret, almost insane purpose in mind. I contravened all the rules of subordination, adopted a highly insolent tone. I thought, if they throw me out of my job, let them, it's all the same to me. But what if I rise high, make a career? After all, these ideas are far from stupid; they are ideas of national importance, the product of long experience . . . At first I was removed from my post, but I didn't flinch, I even felt a certain satisfaction. Well then, that's the way it's going to be,

I thought. You see, at that time I conceived a certain plan.'

'What plan?' Pelagia asked, guessing from his tone of voice that this plan would be something very wicked.

'A most excellent one,' Dolinin chuckled. 'Actually quite unique in its own way. The point is that the happy lovers had set the date for a wedding. Well, of course, not an entirely legitimate one, because there couldn't be any marriage, but nonetheless something in the nature of a wedding feast. After all, morals in the capital are different from in the provinces – even a wedding with someone else's wife is no great rarity there. "Civil marriage" is what they call it. They had planned for everything on a grand scale. In the modern style, with no hypocrisy. If there's to be a feast, let the whole world come – Meaning that true love is higher than human laws and scandal. And I pretended that I had reconciled myself to the inevitable. Several well-wishers had long been trying to persuade me to "take a broader view of things", and so I did.' Sergei Sergeevich gave a dry laugh, more like a cough. 'I made myself out to be such a gentle lamb, such a Tolstoyan, that I was even – believe it or not – honoured with an invitation to this festival of love, along with the other members of the select company. That was when the plan came to me ... First I thought I would follow the example of the inhabitants of the Land of the Rising Sun, by slitting my belly open with a knife in public and spilling my insides out straight on to the wedding table – help yourselves to that, so to speak. But then I thought of something even better.'

Pelagia gaped at him and put her hand over her mouth.

The narrator continued implacably with his agonising tale: 'I'll arrive, I thought, with a bouquet of flowers and a bottle of her very favourite white wine, the one I could previously only afford to buy twice a year – on her saint's day and on our wedding anniversary. At the very height of the feasting I was going to request the floor, saying that I wished to make a toast. Of course, everyone would prick up their ears and fix their eyes at me. How poignant: the abandoned husband congratulating the young couple. Some would be touched, others would grin maliciously to themselves. And I would make a speech, a very short one. I would say: "Love is a force that conquers all. May its smile always shine on you as mine does now." I would open the bottle, fill a goblet to the very brim, raise it above my head and hold it there for a while – that was to be specially for my son who, of course, would also be present at the feast. So that he would remember everything clearly. And then I would pour the contents of the goblet here.' Dolinin jabbed one finger against his forehead. 'Only my bottle would not contain wine, but sulphuric acid.'

Pelagia cried out, but once again Sergei Sergeevich appeared not to hear.

'Not long before that I had been investigating a case – a crime of passion. A certain street woman splashed acid in her "cat's" face out of jealousy. I saw his corpse in the morgue: the skin had all come off, the lips were completely eaten away, and the bare teeth were set in an evil grin ... So my idea was to show the young couple exactly the same "smile of all-conquering love". I wasn't afraid of the pain, I even yearned for the gratification of it. Only that kind of pain could possibly compare with the fire that had been consuming me from the inside all those months ... I would have expired on the spot, of course, because the shock is too much for the heart when a large area of the skin is burned away. And then let them carry on with their lives and revel in their happiness. Let them dream at night ... and let my son remember for the rest of his life ... That is the broad outline of the plan that took shape in my head.'

'And what prevented you from putting it into effect?' the nun asked in a whisper.

This time Dolinin heard her – he nodded.

'On the very eve of the red-letter day, I suddenly received a summons to the very pinnacle of power. A miracle had occurred; somewhere up on high, individuals capable of thinking like statesmen had been found. They treated me kindly, exalted me, gave a new meaning to my life. And I, of course, still not being right in the head, took this as a sign. Here, as it were, was the chance to prove to my wife that I was a great man, bigger than her little count. I was going to have a position, and wealth, and power. I was going to exceed him in every respect. Then she would be sorry, and she would repent. (Of course, she would never have repented of anything, because she is not that kind of woman, but as I told you – I was not in my right mind.)'

After saying nothing for a while, Sergei Sergeevich went on to conclude his story in an entirely different tone of voice, without any trace of bitterness: 'That, however, was not the meaning of the sign at all. A certain individual explained it to me later – it doesn't matter who, you don't know him. He said: "God took pity on you. He took pity on you and saved your soul." As simple as that. God took pity on me. And when I understood that, I began to believe. With no sophistry or speculation. I simply began to believe, and that's all. And my real life began from that moment.'

'Verily, that is the truth!' Pelagia exclaimed and then, surrendering to an unaccountable impulse, she blurted out: 'You know what, let me tell you about myself too . . .' But the investigator tugged on his reins, halting his bay, and the wagon rolled on forwards.

The nun jumped down to the ground and went back to Dolinin. No longer in order to tell him about herself (she realised that Sergei Sergeevich was in no mood for other people's intimate outpourings just at the moment), but in order to finish saying the most important thing of all. 'God saved your life and your soul. And He will not limit Himself to these mercies. Time will pass, the wound will heal, and you will stop feeling angry with your former wife. Understand – she is not to blame. She is simply not the one whom the Lord intended for you. And perhaps you will still meet your true match.'

Dolinin's smile seemed derisive, but there was no sarcasm in it. 'No, begging your pardon. I've had enough. Unless perhaps I should meet someone else like you? But I suspect there is no one else in the world like you, and unfortunately there is no way in the world to marry a nun.'

He lashed at the horse with his heels and galloped off to the head of the caravan, leaving Pelagia in a state of total confusion.

Forest horrors

For a long time after that the holy sister rode on in silence. God only knows where the nun's thoughts were straying, but her expression was strange – both sad and dreamy at the same time. Pelagia smiled several times, and the tears ran down her cheeks and she wiped them away, unawares, with her open hand.

Then suddenly the mood was gone, her thoughts were scattered. Pelagia did not immediately understand what was hindering and distracting her.

Then she realised: it was the same thing again. She could quite distinctly feel someone's intent gaze on her neck and the back of her head.

It was not the first time this had happened. Only a short time before, during the afternoon halt, it had been exactly the same: Pelagia had swung round sharply and seen – actually seen – a branch sway at the far edge of the clearing.

This time too the nun could not restrain herself, and she looked round. She clutched at her heart: there was a large, grey bird sitting on a fir tree and staring at the nun with round yellow eyes.

The holy sister laughed quietly. Lord, Lord, an eagle owl! Nothing but an eagle owl . . .

But that evening when they set up camp to spend the night, something happened that she could not laugh away.

While the men were building the huts and collecting brushwood, the nun walked off to answer the call of nature. In her shyness of the men, she went quite a long way; since the twilight had not fully condensed into darkness, she wouldn't get lost.

Suddenly she caught the faint odour of smoke from somewhere – not from the clearing, but from the opposite direction. Immediately she remembered stories about forest fires. The great Forest burned only rarely – the swamps rescued it. But if it once began to blaze, then there was no escape for anything or anyone from the fiery inferno.

Drawing the smoke in through her nose, Pelagia walked towards the suspicious smell. Up ahead there really was a flickering light. Perhaps it was touchwood?

When she was already very close to the light, she heard a sudden crack. The sound was not really all that loud, but it was clearly made by some living thing, and the nun froze.

Something moved behind the fir tree.

Not something – someone!

Frozen in fear, the nun noticed something swaying rhythmically. On looking more closely, she saw that it was a tail – a wolf's tail! And the most incredible thing was that the tail was not dangling close to the ground, but quite high up, as if the beast were sitting on a branch!

Pelagia made the sign of the cross and began walking backwards, muttering: 'God is our refuge and our strength . . .'

From out of the twilight there came a low growling with a strange sound like someone smacking their lips, not so much ferocious, more – or so it seemed to the poor nun – sneering.

Recovering her wits, she turned and ran back as fast as her legs would carry her.

She ran so hard that she stumbled over a tree stump, fell over, tore her habit and didn't even notice: she jumped up straight away and set off even faster.

She ran out into the clearing as white as a sheet, with her lower lip bitten between her teeth in terror.

'What is it? A bear?' said Dolinin, snatching his revolver out of its holster as he dashed towards her. The policemen reached for their rifles.

'No . . . no,' Pelagia babbled, grasping at the air with her lips. 'It's nothing.'

The sight of her travelling companions sitting having a peaceful smoke round the campfire made her feel ashamed. A wolf sitting on a branch, and smacking his lips too? You could imagine seeing anything in the Forest.

'Come on now, come on,' Sergei Sergeevich said in a quiet voice, leading her aside. 'You're not a timid sort of woman, but right now you look absolutely terrible. What's happened?'

'There's a wolf there . . . a strange one . . . It's like it's sitting in a tree. And there's a little light shining . . . I remembered about Struk. You know, the Forest monster,' Pelagia admitted, somehow managing to force a smile.

But Dolinin did not even smile. He looked over his shoulder into the blue evening thickets. 'Well then, let's go and see if it is Struk or not. Will you show me?'

He went ahead, lighting the way with a torch. He walked confidently, without trying to hide, the branches crunching loudly under his feet and her fear shrank and released her.

'Over there,' said the nun, pointing as she led the investigator up to the terrible spot. 'That's it, the fir tree.'

Sergei Sergeevich parted the prickly green branches intrepidly and leaned down.

'A twig, broken,' he said. 'Someone stepped on it, and only just recently. A pity about the moss, or there would be tracks.'

'He ... It growled,' Pelagia complained. 'And it was mocking somehow, not like an animal. And the most important thing – the tail was at this level, here.' She went up on tiptoe to point. 'Honest to God! But the light disappeared. And it doesn't smell of smoke any more ...' She suddenly felt ashamed of talking such rubbish.

But even at this point Dolinin did not think of making fun of her. He sniffed at the air. 'No, no, there's still a slight smell ... you know, mademoiselle, I am a man of a rational inclinations, I subscribe to a scientific view of the world. But I am by no means of the opinion that science knows all the secrets of the earth, let alone those of the heavens. It would be naïve to assume that the nature of things is exhausted by the laws of of physics and chemistry. Only very limited people can be materialists. You're not a materialist, are you?'

'No.'

'Then why are you so surprised? Well, you got a fright – that's understandable; but what is there to be surprised at? You can see for yourself what kind of place this is.' He gestured around at the gloom in which the Forest had swathed itself with the approach of night. 'Where should evil spirits dwell, if not in deep waters and forest thickets?'

'Are you joking?' Pelagia asked in a quiet voice.

Sergei Sergeevich sighed. 'Tell me, nun, do God and angels exist?'

'Yes.'

'That means, so do the Devil and his cohorts. That is the only possible logical conclusion. If white exists, then black must exist too,' the astonishing investigator snapped. 'All right, let's go and have some tea.'

IV

Was it a Dream?

The wild Tartar

They reached Stroganovka early in the evening of the fourth day.

The village's plain little houses were scattered across a broad meadow that must have been won from the Forest in an age long past.

Two or three hundred years earlier, as the name of the village testified, the Stroganov family of merchants – the very same ones who conquered Siberia – had held land here. These old times were represented by a rectangle of rotten timber beams – the remnants of a small fortress – and several dozen pits, mementos of the salt factory that once existed here.

The peasants who lived in these parts were rough men with long beards, descendants of the Stroganovs' wild ragamuffins, the wandering rabble that had been drawn to the free life here from all over Russia. The absence of any plough land, the small, sentry-box windows of the huts and the animal skins drying on wattle fences immediately made it clear that these settlers had not come from peaceful, farming stock. The villagers of Stroganovka did not plough the land. They lived by harvesting the Forest and scraping rock salt out of the long-exhausted pits. It was foul and grey, and only the peasants from the neighbouring districts took it, for a cheap price.

But beyond the pine trees, on the other side of a small, rapid river strewn with rocks, there were craggy cliffs – the first spurs of the Urals Mountains.

The village elder who talked things over with Dolinin was a morose old man who looked like a wood sprite, completely covered in grey hair with a greenish tinge to it. Present in the communal hut with the old man were two other men, also not young, who never opened their mouths but only gaped warily at the uninvited guests.

If it were not for the district sergeant major, who happened to be godfather to one of the village elder's children, probably no conversation at all would have taken place.

The most important thing – the reason why they had come – was established almost immediately.

Glancing into the open wooden crate, the village elder crossed himself and said the body was definitely Petka Shelukhin, a native son of Stroganovka. He had left three years earlier, and since then no one there had seen any sign of him.

'Under what circumstances did he leave his place of residence?' Dolinin asked.

'How be that?' said the elder, gaping at him. He spoke in the local dialect, which was rather difficult to understand if you weren't used to it. 'What's that un say?'

'Well, why did he go?'

'He just went, thar'n all. Year gone as we wrote his house over to commune,' said the old man, gesturing round the room which, it should be said, was absolutely wretched, its low ceiling covered in the corners by grey cobwebs.

'"Year gone" means "last year",' Pelagia translated. 'They've turned Shelukhin's house into their communal hut.'

'Merci. I'm not asking him about the hut. What sort of man was he, this Shelukhin? Why did he leave the village?'

'Runty little man,' said the elder, pronouncing the ugly phrase distinctly, and making the nun wince. 'Dawdling braghead. Gyp-handed swiper. Hent more'n once.'

'Eh?' Dolinin asked Pelagia.

She explained: 'A boaster and idler. He lied. And he had been caught stealing.'

'Sounds like our man,' Sergei Sergeevich remarked. 'The habits match. What suddenly made Shelukhin leave these glorious parts? You'd better ask, Sister – this Methuselah and I don't seem to understand each other too well.'

Pelagia asked.

The elder exchanged glances with the taciturn peasants and answered that Petka 'went off with the wild Tartar'.

'With who?' Sergei Sergeevich and the nun asked in a single voice.

'There been this man as weren't ourn. Come from yon, bain't known where.'

'What's this "from yon"?' Dolinin asked, glancing nervously at Pelagia. 'And what does "bain't" mean?'

'Just wait, will you?' said Pelagia, impolitely brushing the investigator aside. 'But tell me, granddad, where did the Tartar come from?'

'No place. Yon Tartar, twere Durka as brung un.'

At this point even the nun began feeling lost.

'What?'

In the course of a long cross-examination abounding in every possible kind of misunderstanding, it was established that Durka was what they called a feeble-minded dumb girl who lived in Stroganovka.

The question of what Durka's real name was provoked a quarrel among the natives.

One man believed it was Steshka, another that it was Fimka. The elder was unable to say anything about the witless little girl's name, but he did inform them that she lived with her granny Bobrikha, who had been lying paralysed for over six years. Durka looked after the sick woman as best she could, and the commune helped them out a little bit.

One day in spring, three years earlier, this Durochka had brought an 'awtogether wild' man, an outsider, from God only knew where.

'Why do you say he was wild?' Pelagia asked.

'That's as he were, wild. Swinging uns head all around and gawking, talking as sounded human, and no sense to it. "Hey, fuani, hey fuani." Freak he was, such as begs on Christ by the churches in towns.'

'A freak? You mean he was a cripple?' put in Sergei Sergeevich, who was listening intently.

'No,' replied the nun. 'Freak is fool, as in "holy fool". Tell me, grandad, how was this man dressed?'

'Not dressed at all, nigh on. No pants on him, nought but a sack, and it belted round with blass string.'

'What sort of string was that, Sister?'

'Blass – that means blue . . .'

Dolinin whistled. 'Well, that's a fine turn up all right. So it isn't Manuila we've got in the coffin . . . *Quod erat demonstrandum*.'

'Wait, wait,' said Pelagia, turning back to the elder. 'But why did you decide he was a Tartar?'

The old man squinted at the nun, but didn't answer her directly – he ordered one of the men to do it: 'You tell un, Donka, that's low of my place.'

'We took un to bathhouse for to wash un, and his willy were lopped,' Donka explained. 'Like yon Tartars.'

'What's that?'

'That I understood,' Sergei Sergeevich remarked. 'The wild Tartar was circumcised. There's no doubt about it, he's Manuila. He really is immortal, the scoundrel . . .'

The subsequent conversation yielded a few more details.

For some reason Petka Shelukhin, the most idle, dishonest peasant in the whole of Stroganovka, had become attached to the 'wild man', let him live in his but and followed him around everywhere like his own brother. According to the elder, they really were alike – the same height, similar faces. Petka actually called the stranger his 'elder brother', and the stranger named his mentor Shelukhai.

'Naah, not Shelukhai. Sheluyak – that be how the Tartar called un,' Donka corrected the old man.

'That be it,' confirmed the second man. 'Sheluyak. And Petka answered to un.'

The investigator ordered the girl who had brought the 'Tartar' to be called.

They brought her, but she was absolutely no help at all. Durka must have been about fourteen, but she was so small and stunted that she looked ten. She didn't understand what they were asking about – she only mumbled, raked her dirty fingers through her tangled hair and sniffed.

Eventually Dolinin gave up on her.

'So, you say Shelukhin became friends with this new arrival?' he asked, turning to the elder. 'On what grounds?'

Pelagia heaved a sigh at Sergei Sergeevich's sheer hopelessness and prepared to translate his question into the language of Stroganovka – in order to avoid a repetition of the conversation between the Prince of Denmark and the gravedigger: 'Why, here in Denmark, sire.' And then, purely by chance, she happened to

78

glance at Durka, who was huddling by the door. Now that the grown-ups had stopped paying any attention to the little girl, her face had changed: her eyes were lit up by a bright spark and the expression of stupidity had disappeared. The girl was listening to the conversation, and very eagerly too!

'Step on! Step on! [Go away! Go away!]' the elder shouted at her.

The girl reluctantly left the room.

The conversation about the 'wild man' was continued.

'How did the Tartar win Petka's friendship?' Pelagia asked.

'Petka fibbed as the wild man told him about the Holy Land. And living in truth.'

'Why was Petka lying?'

'Well, how could yon Tartar speak on the Holy Land, if he had none of our tongue?'

'You mean, he couldn't talk at all?'

'Aha.'

One of the men (not Donka, but the other one) said: 'Wussn't him'n Durka grand though, eh, Dad? Her mooing, him cooing. Hilarious. Remember Okhrim joking on it? "Durka's got herself a bridegroom," he says. "That'll be a right family – Noddle and Noodle."' And he stroked his beard, which must have been considered the height of frivolity in Stroganovka, because the elder pulled the bright spark up short.

'Give over that grinning. Or has you forgot as what happened after?'

'What did happen afterwards?' Dolinin immediately enquired.

The Stroganovka men glanced at each other.

'We flung'un Tartar out,' said the elder. 'That's what we done, gimma right threshing, stuck his head down the catch and lashed him out of bounds.'

'What did they do?' Sergeevich asked, looking round help-lessly at the nun.

'Beat him within an inch of his life, ducked him in the cesspit and drove him out of the village with their whips,' she explained.

'Ought to have beaten the filthy beast to death, we ought,' the elder commented sternly, 'and ripped off that Tartar willy of his. That Durka, poor witless orphan, she runs round after him like a chicken, and he wants to befoul her. There be bastards in the world all right. Two days after Durka were sleepsick.'

Sergei Sergeevich frowned.

'And what did Shelukhin do?'

'Ran off into the forest after the Tartar. Moment as we set in beating the filthy beast, Petka come flailing at the lads, wouldn't let them teach his "big brother" a lesson. So we smashed Petka's mug in too. Then when we flung the Tartar out into the forest, Petka tied up his bundle and went after. "He'll die in the forest!" he was yelling. "He's a godly man!" And we saw nowt of Petka again till today.'

'Tell me, granddad, then what direction did the Tartar go in when he left you? Toward sunset, sunrise, north or midnight?' Dolinin asked.

Pelagia quietly got up and went towards the door.

There were two reasons for this. The first was that Sergei Sergeevich seemed gradually to be getting to grips with the local idiom. The second concerned the door itself, which was behaving in a most mysterious fashion – first opening slightly, and then closing again, although there was no draught at all. Turning her head as she slipped out into the dark hallway, the nun spotted a shadow over in the corner, behind a trunk.

She walked over and squatted down. 'Don't be afraid, come out.'

A tousled head poked up from behind the trunk. Two wide-open eyes glinted in the darkness.

'Well, why did you hide?' Pelagia asked the little simpleton affectionately. 'Why were you listening?'

The little girl straightened up to her full height and looked up at the seated nun.

Surely she can't really be a complete simpleton? Pelagia thought doubtfully, looking the little savage straight in the eyes.

'Do you want to ask about something? Or ask for something? You explain, with signs, or any way you like. I'll understand. And I won't tell anyone.'

Durka jabbed her finger against the holy sister's chest, where the little copper cross was hanging.

'You want me to swear?' Pelagia guessed. 'I swear to you on Christ the Lord that I'll never tell anyone anything.' And she readied herself for the difficult task of deciphering the imbecile's grunts and gesticulations.

There was the sound of footsteps from inside the room – someone was coming towards the door.

'Come to the mill,' the dumb girl suddenly said. Then she darted out of the hallway on to the porch like a little mouse.

That very second – or perhaps the next – the door swung open to reveal Sergei Sergeevich.

Pelagia had no time to wipe the look of astonishment off her face, but the investigator interpreted her raised eyebrows in his own fashion.

'What a scoundrel, eh?' he said angrily. 'That's the secret of his immortality for you. The good shepherd takes good care of himself, and he puts others in his place. Now we know why the "foundlings" on the steamship didn't bother to accompany the body of their prophet. They knew, the scoundrels, that it wasn't the prophet at all, but a substitute.'

'And it was the treasury they shouted about most of all when the murder was discovered,' Pelagia recalled. 'I should have noticed that at the time.'

'Shall we sum up?' Dolinin suggested when they went out on to the porch. 'The picture we have is as follows. Manuila entrusted the "treasury" to his "younger brother" Pyotr Shelukhin to carry. Obviously he expected that someone might come after the money. He didn't want to risk his own precious person.'

'But I think they weren't after the money; they were after Manuila himself.'

'Reasoning?' the investigator asked quickly, screwing up his eyes and peering at Pelagia.

After the trick that Durka had just played, the nun was feeling rather distracted, and therefore failed to recall the oath that she had sworn not to get drawn into deductive reasoning about the case.

'Well, after all, you told me yourself that that there had already been an attempt on the prophet's life. Did they steal any money that time?'

'No, I don't recall anything of the kind.'

'There, you see. It's Manuila they want. It wasn't a razin at work on the steamer, and the murder was not committed by accident. This adventurer Manuila has annoyed someone very badly.'

'Who?'

Dolinin's frown kept growing sterner and sterner, and as for Pelagia – why conceal the fact? – she found this intense attention from him flattering.

'There are only a few possible explanations. In the first place –' she began, but then bit her tongue, having finally remembered her promise. And she became flustered. 'No, no! I'm not going to talk about it. Don't even try to persuade me. I swore not to. You're clever enough, you can work everything out for yourself.'

Sergei Sergeevich laughed. 'You can't forbid the intellect to work, whether you swear to or not – especially an intellect as sharp as yours. All right, if you think it over, you can expound your "possible explanation" on the way back. There's nothing else for us to do here. The prophet's alive and kicking, so we'll have to issue a denial to the newspapers. What fine publicity for Manuila! First he's killed, then he rises from the dead again.' And he spat in annoyance. That is, he didn't actually spit, of course, because he was a cultured man; he did it the symbolic Russian way, by exclaiming 'Tphoo!'

'No point in dithering about; we'll set off back straight away.'

'With the night coming on?' Pelagia exclaimed in alarm, glancing round at Stroganovka in the moonlight. Which way was the mill from here?

'Never mind, we won't get lost. And we've wasted so much time here. I thought this was a case of state importance and it's turned out to be a damp squib.'

I think that must be where she's hiding, the nun thought, spotting a square structure by the river. She even thought she could hear the millwheel creaking.

'I can't just leave like that,' said the holy sister. 'The elder doesn't want to send to Staritsa for a priest. He says there are no horses to spare and they'd have to pay. So now is a man to be buried like a dog? I can't actually read the funeral service – it's not permitted – but at least I will read a prayer over his grave. It's my duty. And don't you distress yourself, my good sir. It would be far worse if you had not come here. You would have reported to your superiors that Manuila had been killed, and then it would have turned out that nothing of the sort had happened. Then you would have found yourself in an awkward situation.'

'That's true enough, of course . . .' Sergei Sergeevich growled, apparently seriously upset by the failure of the expedition. No doubt the ambitious reformer really had wanted to flaunt his success in front of the newspaper correspondents. 'All right. You bury Shelukhin tomorrow morning. Only please, make it early. Damn, how I hate to lose the time!'

The first mention of the rooster

Having wished the investigator goodnight and told him that she would find her own lodging for the night, Pelagia hurried in the direction of the little river.

She walked along the street, past the wattle fence, behind which the Stroganovka dogs, who were actually more like wolves, growled quietly. Outside the village boundary fence, in the meadow, the sound of water became louder. When the nun had hardly any distance left to go to the mill, a frail little figure detached itself from the log-built structure and came toward her.

The little girl ran up impatiently to the holy sister, grabbed hold of her hand with a tenacious, rough little paw and asked: 'Is he alive? Is he?'

'Who?' asked Pelagia, astonished.

'Emmanuel.'

'You mean Manuila?'

'Emmanuel,' Durka repeated. 'His name's Emmanuel.'

'How do you know?'

'I know. He pointed to hisself so like' – the girl jabbed a finger against her own chest – 'and he said "Emmanuel, Emmanuel". He said lots of all sorts too, only I didn't understand then. I was too little and stupid.'

It must have been the Russian name Manuil, Pelagia realised. And the folk version. Manuila had appeared later, when the mysterious 'Tartar' began preaching his message round the villages.

'Your Manuil is alive, all right,' she reassured Durka. 'Nothing has happened to him. You know what: why don't you tell me where you found him?'

'It weren't me as found him, it were Belyanka.' And then Durka told Pelagia a quite incredible story, to which the nun listened very carefully indeed, right to the very end. She was also astounded by how coherently the supposed deaf-mute could speak – far more spryly and colourfully than the village elder.

And this was the story.

It all started when Belyanka, an extremely 'ockerd' – that is, cantankerous – laying hen escaped from the commune's poultry house, which Durka kept watch over. The poultry house was located on the far side of the little river, so the fugitive fowl had to be sought either in the low bushes or further off, beside the 'rocks' (cliffs).

Durka had beaten through all the bushes but failed to find Belyanka. The problem was that the laying hen belonged to the elder's oldest son, Donka, a quarrelsome and sharp-tongued man, whom Durka was terribly afraid of.

There was nothing else for it so she went to look beside the 'rocks'. She shouted, and begged in chicken language, and wept, but all in vain.

And so she came to Devil's Rock, a place where she would never have wandered of her own free will, especially not alone.

'Why?' asked Pelagia. 'What sort of place is this Devil's Rock?'

'A very unclean place.'

'Why is it unclean?'

'Because of the gentleman.' And Durka told Pelagia that long, long ago, a visiting gentleman had disappeared in the area of the Devil's Rock. Her granny had told her about it, before she was struck dumb by the lying sickness. And her granny had been told by her own grandfather.

It might have been a hundred years earlier, or perhaps even earlier than that, but in any case a gentleman had come to Stroganovka. He had been looking for a treasure – gold and precious stones. He had climbed all over the hills, in places the locals had never even glanced into in their lives, because they had no reason to. He had dug up the earth and gone down into the 'hollows' (caves). He had gone into the Devil's Rock hollow too, and taken a rooster with him.

'What for?' the nun asked, bemused.

'If as you lose the way in a hollow, you need to set a rooster free, and he'll find the way out for sure.'

But the rooster had not helped the gentleman. They had both disappeared; neither the man nor the bird came back out of the cave. Then the bolder villagers had gone in to look for them.

And they'd found the gentleman's cloth cap and a tail feather from his rooster. That was all. The Devil had carried them away, because everyone knew that it was his rock.

Durka had been terribly afraid to go into such a place, but she couldn't go back without Belyanka.

She walked 'longward of' (around) the cursed cliff, she 'plainted' (cried) and trembled all over. Suddenly she heard something like a rooster crowing: a dull, muffled sound, as if it were coming from under the ground. She looked behind a large boulder and gasped. There, under a bush, was a gaping black hole, and that was where the crowing was coming from.

Durka realised that this was the gentleman's cave. For a long time she couldn't bring herself to go in. What was a cockerel doing in there? Could it really be the same one that the Devil had carried away? Perhaps the gentleman who had disappeared was there too? She was terribly afraid!

She wanted to run, and get out of harm's way, but suddenly she heard a familiar clucking. It was Belyanka! That meant she was there, in the cave!

Crossing herself (she couldn't say a prayer, she was tongueless'), she went in to get Belyanka.

At first she couldn't make anything out – it was dark. Then she got a bit more used to it. She saw a white spot – that was Belyanka. She dashed towards it and saw there was a rooster there too: a lively one – he kept jumping up on the hen. Then suddenly she saw a man with a beard, wearing a long white shirt, lying on one side, snoring. If the man hadn't been asleep, she'd have darted out of that place as fast as she could and never gone back. But why be afraid of a sleeping man? That is, she felt afraid, of course, for a little while, but when she looked closer, she could see he wasn't frightening at all and she woke him up and took him to the village, together with the rooster.

The red-feathered bird became Durka's, because the man from the cave told her: You take it. It turned out to be a fine rooster, far better than the ones in the village. Durka and her old granny let it cover other people's chickens for five eggs a time, and that improved their lives a lot, and the rooster started a new breed of 'randy' red roosters (that is, they were insatiable in covering the hens) in Stroganovka. The first bird himself was pecked to death by the neighbours' roosters a year later – he was very quarrelsome.

Pelagia heard this story out and then started asking about Manuil – what kind of man he was, how he behaved, if he had offended Durka in any way. Remembering why the peasants had driven out the wretched prophet, she couldn't understand, if it was true, why Durka was so concerned for the 'filthy beast'.

The girl didn't say anything bad about the man who had supposedly attacked her – quite the opposite, in fact. When she spoke about him, her voice became dreamy, even affectionate – as if meeting the 'wild Tartar' was the most important event in her pitiful little life.

He was kind, Durka said. It was good to 'talk' with him.

'But how could the two of you "talk"?' Pelagia couldn't resist asking. 'You were tongueless, and so was he; they say he couldn't speak at all.'

To herself she thought: Or was he pretending to the peasants?

'We talked,' Durka repeated stubbornly. 'The way as Manuila spoke, you couldn't understand a single word, but it was clear as day.'

'But what did he tell you about?'

'All sorts,' the girl replied and looked up at the sky and the moon. There was a strange half-smile, not at all childish, playing on her face. 'Still little, I was, a real fool. I wanted to beg him: "Don't go away, live here with me and granny," but all I said was "meh", "meh".'

'When did you learn to talk?'

'It was Emmanuel as cured me of the dumbness. He said, "Girl, you didn't want to talk before, because you had no one to talk to and nothing to talk about. But you'll start talking with me."'

'And he told you all this without words?' Pelagia asked doubtfully.

Durka thought about that. 'I don't remember. He led me to the river and said I should get undressed. He started pouring water on top of my head and stroking my shoulders. It felt so sweet! And he kept saying magic spells. But Vanyatka the miller saw us and ran for the men. They came running and started threshing Emmanuel, and dragging him over the ground by his hair and his legs! I started yelling that loud: "Leave him alone!

86

Leave him!" I yelled in words, only no one heard – they were all yelling so loud as well. And I was so stounded [surprised] that I could yell in words – I fainted and lay like that for a day, and another day. And when I woke up, they'd already thrown him out ... I wanted to run after him, to the Holy Land. That's where Emmanuel's from.'

'From the Holy Land? Why do you think that?'

'Where else could someone like that come from?' Durka asked in surprise. 'And he talked to me about it himself. Only I didn't run off. Because he told me not to. I asked him about it earlier – "Take me," I moaned, "take me." I was afraid he wouldn't understand, nobody but Granny had ever understood me before. But he understood. "It's too soon", he said, "for you to go to the Holy Land. How will Granny manage without you? When the Lord sets you free, then come to me. I'll be waiting."'

It was only then, with hindsight, that Pelagia realised the girl was surely lying or, to put it more gently, fantasising. She had invented her own fairy tale and was comforting herself with it. But then, what else did the poor thing have to take comfort in?

Pelagia stroked Durka's head. 'Why don't you say anything? In the village they think you're dumb and half-witted, but just look how clever you are! *Talk* to the villagers, and they'll start treating you differently.'

'Who can I talk to?' Durka snorted. 'And what about? I only talk with Granny, quiet-like. Every evening. I tells her about Manuil, and she listens. She can't answer, can't speak, just lies there. When I was little, Granny used to talk and talk to me and I was a fool, I could only bleat. Now it's round tother [the other way round]. I talk, Granny bleats. She's poorly, she'll die soon. I'll bury her, then I'll be set free. And I'll go to him, to Emmanuel. To the Holy Land. Only afore [first] I'll grow up into a maid. What does he want with a little girl? I can wait a year or two. Just take a look at what I've got,' Durka said proudly and opened the front of her tattered little dress to show her small breasts that were just barely beginning to swell up: first one, then the other. 'See! Won't I be a maid soon?'

'Yes, soon,' sighed Pelagia.

Both of them fell silent, each wrapped in her own thoughts.

'Listen,' said the nun: 'could you show me that "hollow"? The one where you found Manuil?'

'Why not? I'll show you,' Durka agreed readily. 'When the cocks crow twicely [for the second time], come to us mill again. I'll take you.'

A shameful dream

There was still a long time to go, probably five or six hours, until the cockcrow which, according to the law of nature, ought to herald the dawn, and so she had to make some kind of arrangements for her night's lodging.

Pelagia went back to the communal hut to ask the elder where she could spend the night. The windows in the hut were lit up, and the nun glanced in through one of them before entering.

The elder was not in the room. Sergei Sergeevich was sitting alone at the rough planking table, and the other members of the expedition had stretched out on the benches along the walls.

From this it was clear that the hut had been allocated to the investigator and his team for the night. That was right; where else could they be accommodated? There was no hotel to be found in Stroganovka.

The holy sister stood there without moving for quite a long time, looking at Sergei Sergeevich. Ah, how the investigator's face changed when he thought that no one could see him! Not a trace left of sarcasm or dry humour.

Dolinin's forehead was cut across by wrinkles of intense suffering, there were tragic folds at the corners of his mouth, and his eyes were glowing with a suspicious brightness – could it possibly be from tears?

Sergei Sergeevich suddenly lowered his forehead on to his crossed arms, and his shoulders began shaking.

No words could express how sorry she felt for him. What terrible torment the man was carrying around inside him, and still he didn't bend, he didn't break. And the nun caught herself thinking how much she wanted to press the sufferer's brown-haired head to her breast, stroke his tormented brow and shake the tears from his eyelashes.

Stop it, she told herself, suddenly frightened; is this really pity? And what if it's something else?

If she was completely honest with herself and dropped all

pretence, what had made her agree so easily to make the journey to Stroganovka with Dolinin? Was it only for the sake of the investigation and to defend Mitrofanii's cause?

No, holy Mother, you took a liking to the master detective from Petersburg, the nun rebuked herself. And sinner that you are, you sensed that he liked you too. And so you wanted to be with him. Wasn't that the way it was?

It was, thought Pelagia, hanging her head, it truly was.

She remembered the way her heart was wrung when he spoke those impossible words to her – about how there was no one else like her in the world, and if she hadn't been a nun . . .

Oh, for shame! Oh, this was iniquitous!

And the worst thing of all was that Sergei Sergeevich's terrible story about the sulphuric acid had touched some string in her heart. Nothing was more dangerous than when some string that had long ago seemed broken beyond repair suddenly began sounding subtly in a female heart maintained with meticulous discipline – indeed, one might almost say ruled with a rod of iron.

The nun was so badly frightened that she whispered the prayer for deliverance from temptation. Fright begat determination.

Pelagia walked up on to the porch, into the hallway and knocked on the door of the room. She waited for a little while, to allow Sergei Sergeevich to straighten up and wipe away his tears, then stepped inside.

Dolinin rose to his feet to greet her. He hadn't managed to control his face – he looked at the nun with an expression of amazement, almost terror, as if he had been caught red-handed at the scene of a crime. This only served to convince her yet again of the correctness of her decision.

'I tell you what,' Pelagia declared, 'don't you wait for me. You go on back, today. Why you should mope about here? I can see that you can't even sleep. 'I'll stay in Stroganovka for another day or two. Since, thanks to you, I now find myself in this remote spot, I'll do my job. After all, I am the headmistress of a school. I'll take a look around, have a word with the peasants and the elder. Maybe they'll let me have the girls who are still little, to teach? Why should they grow up in ignorance here?'

She thought: That's right, and I'll definitely have to take Durka, and I can put her granny in the convent hospital.

She was sure that Dolinin would try to change her mind, perhaps even grow angry. However, the investigator looked at her in silence, without saying a single word. Surely he can't have guessed the real reason, Pelagia thought, horrified. He must have guessed – he's an intelligent, keen-witted man. She turned her eyes away, and perhaps even blushed. In any case, her cheeks suddenly felt hot.

Sergei answered dryly, forcing out the words: 'Well then . . . Perhaps that's the best . . .' He began to cough.

'It's all right,' Pelagia told him in a quiet, affectionate voice. 'It's all right . . .' She couldn't allow herself to say any other words, and she shouldn't have spoken these. That is, the words themselves were completely meaningless, there was nothing reprehensible about them; but of course the tone in which they were spoken was impermissible.

Dolinin started when he heard that tone, his eyes glinted in fury, almost hatred. He blurted out: 'All right, goodbye, good-bye.' He turned away.

He shouted at his subordinates: 'What are you all lying around for, damn you! Everybody up!'

He said that – 'damn you' – on purpose, Pelagia realised. To make her go away as quickly as possible.

A strange man. It was hard for someone like that to live in this world. And living with him must be hard too.

She bowed to the investigator's angry back and walked out.

She had decided to spend the night in the communal yard, in the barn. It was less stuffy there than in the hut and she could hope that there were no cockroaches.

She climbed the lean-to ladder to the loft and stirred up the flattened straw. She lay down. Covered herself with a rug. Told herself to go to sleep.

She had no fear of oversleeping: yet another reason for choosing the barn for her night's lodging was that there were chickens clucking in its lower level. And there was also a lively rooster jumping about – to judge from his colouring, a descendant of the one from the cave. This alarm clock certainly wouldn't allow her to oversleep: the first, pre-dawn cockcrow would wake her and give her enough time to get washed and gather her thoughts. And at the second cockcrow she would have to hurry to the mill, to meet Durka. She could hear Dolinin's men hitching up horses and stowing baggage in the yard.

Pelagia sighed at the sound of Sergei Sergeevich's brusque, tense instructions. The harness jingled, the wheels creaked and the expedition set off on its way back. Pelagia sighed for a little longer and fell asleep.

And she had a terrible, sinful dream.

Of course, she had had terrible dreams before. She had even had sinful ones – is a rare nun indeed who never dreams of anything shameful. The Bishop had explained that there was nothing to be ashamed of in these dreams and had even forbidden her to repent of them at confession, because they were mere nonsense and illusion. There was no sin in that – quite the opposite, in fact. If a monk or a nun drove the devil of the flesh away from themselves during their waking hours, then he lay in hiding until the hours of sleep, when a person's will grows weak, and crept up out of the cellar into the soul, like a little mouse in the night. But a dream that was at the same time terrifying and shameful – Pelagia had never had one like that before.

The most astonishing thing was that it wasn't Sergei Sergeevich that she dreamed about at all. Pelagia saw the dead peasant Shelukhin – sitting the way he had been when he was tied to a chair: looking perfectly alive, but actually dead. His eyes were open, they were even gleaming, but that was because of the nitroglycerine. And they were held open, Pelagia remembered, by cotton wool.

She looked more closely at the dead man and suddenly noticed that he didn't really look like Shelukhin after all. Shelukhin's lips had been pale purple and thin, and this man's were full and bright red. And the eyes weren't exactly the same: they were more deep-set, piercing.

It was definitely not Shelukhin, the sleeping woman determined. Like him, but not him. It was Manuil; it couldn't be anyone else. And the moment she guessed the dead man's identity, he suddenly started moving, stopped pretending to be a corpse.

He winked at her, first with one eye, then the other. Then he slowly licked his bright-red lips with an even brighter, moist tongue. There didn't seem to be anything special about that, for what is so strange about a man licking his lips? But Pelagia had never seen anything more terrifying in her life and she began groaning in her sleep and tossing her head about on the hay.

Manuil opened his huge eyes as wide as wide could be: he began beckoning the holy sister with a yellow finger. And whispering: 'Come here now, come.'

She wanted to run as fast as her legs could carry her, but a strange power swayed her forward and drew her towards the seated man.

A firm, rough hand stroked the helpless Pelagia on her cheek and her neck. It was sweet, but it was shameful. 'My little bride, my lovey,' said Manuil, drawing the words out the way they did in Stroganovka. The man's hand began stroking Pelagia's breasts.

'In the name of Christ the Lord . . .' the nun implored him.

The prophet's finger sought out the chain of her cross, snapped it casually and tossed the cross into a corner. And then Manuil chuckled, wagged his beard and mimicked her, mocking her: 'In the name of Christ the Lord . . . Ooh, my little chicken. Co-co-co, co-co-co.' Then he roared out at the top of his voice: 'COCK-A-DOODLE-DOO!'

Pelagia sat bolt upright, gagging on her own shriek.

Down below the rooster was crowing raucously.

Oh, Lord!

Then there was silence

Something began rustling and clicking in the darkness. It was the loud herald fluttering his wings and scrabbling at the rungs of the ladder with his claws as he scrambled up to get acquainted with Pelagia.

'Well, hello, hello,' the nun said to her visitor, who was examining her with his crested head inclined to one side.

'Co-co,' the young rooster said, examining her. He seemed to have taken a liking to Pelagia. He came closer and pecked familiarly at the knee covered in black cloth with his beak.

'And the same to you,' the holy sister rebuked him.

It was hard to make out the details of her feathered guest by the pale moonlight that filtered through the holes in the roof.

But why examine him anyway? He was just a rooster like any other.

'Ah you, Rousty Rooster, sleek and shiny, silky beard,' the nun said, giving his fleshy wattle a gentle tug.

The rooster leapt back, but not very far.

'When are you going to crow for the second time? Soon?'

He didn't answer.

She went down and out into the yard, to the well. She splashed water on her face and combed out her hair, since there was no one there to make her feel ashamed.

The entire sky was covered with stars. When Pelagia glanced up, she froze, motionless.

The rooster was there, right beside her. He hopped up on to the wall of the well and also threw his head back. Perhaps he thought there was golden millet scattered across the sky. He hopped up higher, on to the winch, and stretched out his neck, but still couldn't reach the little grains. He began clucking angrily and crowed again: 'Cock-a-doodle-doo!'

Pelagia was thrown into consternation. What had made him crow this time? His rooster's clock or simply his annoyance? Could this call be counted as the second cockcrow or couldn't it?

But the cocks had started crowing in the other yards too. It was time.

While she was crossing the meadow, the moon hid behind a cloud and it turned completely dark, as it was supposed to do just before dawn.

She could barely make out the grey path in the gloom, and every step she took echoed hollowly. At first the nun even thought there was someone following her, but then she realised it was an echo. Only she hadn't known before that there could be an echo in an open space. Perhaps it was due to the uncommon transparency of the air?

In the middle of the meadow she discovered that the rooster had tagged along with his new acquaintance. He was skipping behind her, fluttering his wings.

'Ah, you're so reckless,' the nun scolded him. 'You feather-brain, abandoning your family and your home for the first skirt that comes along!' She hissed and waved her hands at him: Go away, go on back. But Rousty Rooster wouldn't do as he was told. All right, she decided, let him do as he wants. He can always find the way back.

Durka was waiting by the mill.

'Look, I've come with an admirer,' Pelagia said to her. 'He tagged along. I tried and tried to make him go away . . .'

'He's taken a shine to you. He won't let you off now. Those red fellows cling as tight as tight. Well, are we off to the rock, then?'

'Yes, let's go.'

Of course, it would be better to visit the place by day, Pelagia thought. But during the day someone might notice, and that wouldn't be good. What difference did it make, day or night – it was dark in a cave anyway.

'Karaseen?' the girl asked respectfully, with a nod at the lamp the nun was carrying.

'Yes, it works on kerosene. They're all like that in the town nowadays. And there are gas lamps in the streets. I'll show you some day for certain.'

They crossed the little river on stepping stones: Durka ahead, Pelagia following, with one hand holding up the hem of her habit. The cockerel hopped along behind.

They walked through scrubby bushes for quite a long time, probably for about a verst. And then the cliffs began.

The girl walked quickly and confidently. The nun could barely keep up with her. And once again Pelagia got the feeling she had had in the Forest, as if the night was watching her, like a thief, not looking her in the eye, but staring at her back from behind. She even glanced round and, of course, she spotted some shadows moving behind her, but she didn't allow herself to feel frightened. If she was afraid of the night shadows, how could she go into the cave? That was where it would be really frightening. Perhaps I won't go in after all, Pelagia thought with a shudder. I'll just take a look at it, and that's all.

'But why bother to look?' she asked herself. 'What do I need with this cave in any case?'

She couldn't find an answer to that, because there was no rational answer. And yet she knew, even without understanding the reason, that she *had* to look at the place where Durka had found the prophet Manuil. It was irrational, so Sergei Sergevich would not have done it. But then he was a man; she was made differently.

'There's the Devil's Rock,' the girl said and stopped, pointing one finger at a dark hump that rose up in a sheer wall. 'Shan't we turn back now?'

'Lead me to the cave,' Pelagia ordered and gritted her teeth so that they wouldn't start chattering.

The place really did feel eerie. It was probably terrifying here, even during the day – with those cliff faces crowding together and that absolute silence ringing in your ears. And at night it was far worse.

But Durka didn't seem to be afraid at all. For her, no doubt, memories of Manuila painted this ominous landscape in different colours that were not frightening at all.

'Do you often visit the hollow?' asked Pelagia.

'I haven't ever gone inside again. But sometimes I run to the Devil's Rock.'

'Why don't you go inside?'

The little girl twitched one shoulder: 'I just don't.' She didn't want to explain.

Rousty the Rooster also seemed to feeling just fine. He hopped up on to the big boulder and spread his wings in lively fashion.

So am I the only coward here? Pelagia rebuked herself and asked: 'Well, where is it? Show me?'

The entrance to the cave proved to be in a fissure overgrown with bushes. It pierced the cliff face in a narrow wedge shape.

'There,' said Durka, parting the branches.

Through the pre-dawn twilight Pelagia made out a narrow black opening, about one and a half arshins high – you had to bend over to enter.

'Will you go in?' Durka asked respectfully.

The rooster darted between her legs. He looked at the hole inquisitively, hopped forward and disappeared inside.

'Of course I will. And you?'

'No, I can't.'

'Will you wait here?'

Durka shook her head. 'I've got to run now. Fediushka the shepherd will be driving the flock out soon. Don't you be scared, Aunty. Only don't go too far in. Who knows what the hollow's like . . . When you go back to the village, stick to the path. Well, 'bye now.'

She turned round and dashed back, her white calves glimmering in the darkness.

Pelagia crossed herself and held the lantern out in front of her. She went in.

Durka was running on air, so lightly that it seemed to her she wasn't running at all but flying over the white haze of dawn that was spread out just above the ground. She even threw her hands out to the sides, like the stork bird. To get back in time to drive out the sheep out she'd have to run faster and faster, or that Fediushka would give her a good lashing across her backside.

''S all right, 's all right,' Durka whispered as she dashed along between the rocky walls of the cliffs. It helped you run better, if you kept saying that: 's all right, 's all right.

She'd already figured it out in her head: she'd run as far as the bushes, then she'd be out of breath and she'd have to walk to the river. And there she could fly on again, all the way across the meadow. If only she could get there in time – look, it was almost completely light now.

But she never did get out of breath, because she didn't run very far from the Devil's Stone – only about fifty strides. At a point where the path squeezed right up against the wall of rock, a large black shadow swayed away from the cliff and moved to meet the girl.

'Emmanu—' Durka started to call, but she didn't finish.

Something sliced through the air with a predatory whistling sound.

There was a brief crunch of bone.

Then there was silence.

In the cave

It should be said that, in deciding to enter the black opening, Sister Pelagia had to surmount more than simply the usual female wariness, of which the nun probably had almost none anyway (at least, in her case curiosity always won a decisive victory over timidity, even in situations fraught with greater risk than the present one). No, there was a more serious reason for her trepidation.

The problem was that for some time now, following a certain adventure that had taken place in the non-too-distant past, the nun had had special reason to be wary of caves. And the mere awareness that there were invisible stone walls squeezing in on her on all sides out of the darkness, and a vault of stone pressing down over her head, was enough to set Pelagia's soul trembling in raw, mindless terror.

Reaching one hand above her head and failing to find the ceiling, she straightened up and forced herself to calm down. Now what could possibly be so terrible in this 'hollow'? Some predatory beast?

Unlikely. If a bear or a pack of wolves had made the cave their dwelling place, there would have been a sharp odour in the air.

Bats?

It was too cramped for them in here – they couldn't flap their wings properly.

By and large, she more or less managed to reassure herself and calm her nerves. Lighting the lamp, she shone the light in all directions.

She proved to have been wrong about the cave being cramped: inside the narrow entrance hole the cave expanded both side-ways and upwards, so that the walls were lost to sight, drowned in the darkness. At the very edge of the circle of light she glimpsed a small, low shadow. It was Rousty the Rooster, explor-ing the new territory.

'What did I come in here for anyway?' Pelagia asked herself. 'What need was there for it?' She walked forward a little and saw that in the far corner the walls and the ceiling converged again, but the cave did not end there, it simply seemed to turn upwards.

The holy sister put the lamp on the floor and sat on a pro-jecting ledge of rock. She started wondering why destiny was always driving her into caves of one kind or another. What kind of parable was this at all – these niches under the ground? What did the Lord want them for? What was the significance of their invention? There was a meaning to it, and a special meaning too – that was clear to everybody who had ever, even once in his life, wandered into an isolated cave that was in any way deep.

And after all, there was so much commentary on them in Holy Writ.

The ancient Israelites had lived in caves and buried their dead in them. The prophet Elijah heard a Voice from a cave that asked him: 'Why are you here, Elijah?' And could it really be a coincidence that Christ's resurrection had taken place in a cave?

A natural passage into the bowels of the earth – surely that was an opening from one world to another? From light into darkness, from the visible to the invisible? A cave was like the crater of a volcano that led from the surface into the essential core of the Earth – a planet which, according to science, consisted ninety-nine per cent of blazing fire. We were all flying through the darkness on a ball of fire, with nothing but a thin crust of solid ground over it. Death was above our heads, but also below our feet.

Perhaps as a result of her philosophical ponderings, or perhaps for some other reason, Pelagia thought she saw the darkness around her start to quiver and flow. She began feeling drowsy and she heard a low, vague ringing sound that couldn't possibly have been caused by anything in this place. And then something else happened.

From out of the darkness on the side where the entrance was, she heard a crack, followed by a rumble. At first indistinct, then louder and louder.

Pelagia went dashing towards the sound. She crawled into the narrow passage on all fours, her heart pounding furiously. And her hands encountered a solid barrier of rocky scree.

A landslide!

She tried to clear the stones, but it was hopeless. Pressed down from above, they were locked solid.

Pelagia broke her nails as she tried desperately to shift the heap at least a little, but she got nowhere. On the contrary, she heard the sound of new landslip on the outside. The heap shifted slightly towards the nun as it was subjected to an even greater load.

Calmly now, let's not have any female hysterics, Pelagia told herself, wiping the fine beads of cold sweat off her forehead with her sleeve.

Tomorrow – that is, already today – Durka will see that I haven't come back, she'll come running here and realise what's happened. If she can't clear the stones away herself, she'll bring the peasants. For something like that she'll recover the gift of speech.

A few hours to wait. A day at most. It was bad, of course, but not fatal. The nun made her way back to the spacious open area and forced herself to sit down. She wound down the wick in the lamp to use the kerosene more economically.

She carried on sitting there until suddenly her heart was seared by a horrible thought: You were trying to guess what was drawing you to this cave, weren't you? Perhaps you were drawn here because this is the very place appointed for you to meet your destiny? What if the instinct that drew you here was not the instinct of life, but the instinct of death?

This sudden surmise frightened Pelagia very badly and made her jump to her feet. What a cruel trick of fate it would be if she were to die here! Truly a case of curious Varvara getting her nose pulled off! And worst of all, it was so stupid; there was no need for it, no sense to it!

I have to do something, the nun told herself. Otherwise I shall go insane in here. What do they want with me, these cursed caves? What are they tormenting me for? What have I done to displease them?

She picked up the lamp and set off upwards over the gravel and the small stones. What if she could find another entrance?

The cave narrowed so far that she had to scramble along on her elbows and knees. She crawled a couple of paces, then dragged the lamp from behind her and set it higher up ahead. Then she crawled again. The poor nun tried not to think about the fact that there could quite easily be snakes here. They would just be waking up after their winter hibernation. April, the vipers' venom was at its strongest. Lord, Lord . . .

After a while the passage widened and led out into a new hall, much larger than the lower one. Pelagia explored the empty space. She walked to the left and the right and found at least nine passages – if they weren't simply cracks. Which path should she choose?

It turned out that the rooster had also managed to make his way in there. And he hadn't lost any of his high spirits – he was running backwards and forwards, with his claws clattering gaily.

Then the holy sister remembered that Durka had said a rooster would always find its way out of a maze.

She squatted down in front of the bird and started coaxing him: 'Rousty Rousty Rooster, you show me the way out of here. I'll get a whole sack of millet for you. Eh, Rousty?'

He looked at her with his face turned sideways on, listening to her tender voice. But he didn't actually go anywhere.

Then Pelagia lost patience. She picked him up and started carrying him to each of the passages by turns. She brought him, put him down and watched to see if he would go in or not.

The rooster skipped into the first crack, but immediately jumped back out again. He didn't even stick his beak into the second. But then he darted nimbly into the third and immediately disappeared from view.

Pelagia picked up the lamp and squeezed in after him.

This burrow was even narrower than the one that led from the first level to the second. Pelagia almost got stuck in one place, like a bottleneck. Somehow she managed to force her own way through, but afterwards she couldn't reach the lamp, and it was left behind and below.

She scrambled on in pitch-black darkness, feeling for anything to hold on to. She was soaked through and shuddering – there was cold water running over the rocks. But that still didn't mean that there was a way out higher up: everyone knows that water can seep through any crack and sometimes it even filters through solid rock.

The nun tried to drive out of her mind the terrible thought that now the passage would narrow down to such a tiny crack that it would be impossible to go any further. Then that would be the end, and a terrible one, because it was quite impossible for her to reverse direction. She would be stuck here in this stone shroud, and nobody would ever find her ... Why, oh why had she decided to follow the rooster? She ought to have stayed sitting down below and waited for help! Where had he got to, the perisher? It was fine for him, he could squeeze through anywhere.

Exhausted, Pelagia pressed her forehead against the wet stone and closed her eyes.

And then Rousty announced his presence at the top of his cocksure voice, somewhere higher up, but quite close: 'COCK-

A-DOODLE-DOO!' The time must have come to crow for the third and final time.

The holy sister opened her eyes, threw back her head – and saw a pale, trembling light.

She gasped and started scrambling forwards. The sky, God be praised, the sky. Its glow was unbearably bright, stinging her eyes that were accustomed to the darkness.

Pelagia thrust herself out of the burrow up to her waist and filled her lungs with the blessed scent of freedom. There was Rousty, sitting on the rock beside her, as if nothing special had happened. He was busily pecking something out from under his red wing, paying no attention to the nun.

The light was not as bright as it had seemed to the holy sister from the darkness. In fact, it had only just got light and the sun had not yet appeared above the horizon.

Strange – the nun could have sworn that she had spent several hours incarcerated underground, but the colour of the sky indicated that it had only been half an hour at the most. What a mysterious substance time was, after all. Sometimes it stood still and sometimes it hurtled along at breakneck speed, and no minute, or hour, or day, or year was ever equal to another.

But anyway, she had to figure out where it was that she had emerged.

Then she discovered that she couldn't climb out of the hole completely – there was nowhere for her to go. The crack out of which the holy sister was peering was located in a sheer vertical surface: she couldn't go either up or down. The cockerel had somehow managed to install himself in an indentation in the rock, but a human being is not a bird. And so, her joy proved to have been premature.

Leaning over, Pelagia was alarmed to see that there was not merely a sheer drop, the surface was actually concave. There was absolutely no way she could climb down that.

Jumping was even more impossible. She was about ten sazhens up, and there were sharp rocks below.

How could she get out of here? She could go back into the cave. The very thought of it set her shuddering. And then, what point was there in going back? – the entrance was blocked off.

On looking more closely, the nun realised that she was exactly above the spot where she had entered the cave. She recognised the wedge-shaped hollow and the bushes. And she had an excellent view of the passage itself, *which, moreover, was not blocked off at all, but completely free!*

She couldn't believe her own eyes. How could that be possible? Could someone have managed to clear away the rubble during that interminable half-hour while she had been climbing upwards? But then there would have been rocks scattered all around. Only she couldn't see any.

There was a rumbling sound from down below – quiet at first, gradually growing louder.

Another landslip?

Sticking her head out even further, the nun suddenly saw a man on the slope above the entrance passage. He was acting very strangely. In his hands he had a massive club and he was using it as a lever, prising loose a huge block of stone, from beneath which smaller stones were already scattering downwards. Then the block swayed and went plunging down.

The branches of the bushes cracked as the boulder was followed by a shower of rock, and the passage was completely blocked off.

Pelagia watched as if spellbound, not so much at the landslip itself as at the man who had caused it. Or rather, at the malefactor's head.

She could not see his face from above, because it was concealed by a shaggy cap with a wolf's tail dangling from it. The tail was what held the nun's gaze so fixedly. It was the same tail, definitely the same one! – Struk's tail, the one that had been dangling from a fir-tree branch that evening in the forest thicket!

Pelagia's greatest fear was that she was asleep and dreaming – that she had dozed off in the sealed cave and fallen into a reverie. Now she would wake up and discover that none of this had happened – there was no light, and no fresh air, only a stone cell.

She squeezed her eyes shut so tight that her temples started to ache, and put her hands over her ears. She mustn't see anything or hear anything!

When the strain of it gave her a ringing in her ears, she took her hands away and opened her eyes.

No, it wasn't a dream. The sky, pink patches of dawn light, a wall of stone.

Only the spectre in the wolf-skin cap had disappeared. But

the work of his hands was still there – the entrance to the cave was totally blocked.

Or had all that been a dream?

For a long time after that Pelagia simply prayed, without attempting to fathom what was inaccessible to reason. It was good to be a nun after all: when she didn't know what to do or what to think, she could simply turn round and pray – she had learned lots of different prayers: against the wiles of the Evil One, and against the assaults of the darkness, and against the blinding of the soul.

It took some time – perhaps an hour, or even two – until the sun was shining at full strength, before she calmed down and started pondering how to get out of there. And she thought of something.

It was Rousty Rooster who gave her the idea. He clearly got bored of hanging about on the tiny shelf as if it were some kind of perch. He clucked a little bit and then leapt off the vertical slope. He glided down, desperately fluttering his short, iridescent wings. When he landed, he shook himself and ran off along the path, without so much as a backward glance at his abandoned comrade in misfortune.

Pelagia was roused from her paralysis.

The cloth is strong, she told herself, fingering her habit. If she tore it into strips and tied them together, she would have a rope, and a long one. She could tie the end of it round this stone finger here.

It wouldn't reach all the way down, of course, but it didn't need to. She could get as far as the slope on which Wolf-Tail had been standing; that was only five sazhens, and after that the descent was more or less shallow. Well, and if the rope turned out to be too short, she still had her thread stockings.

It was all right, it was all right, she would manage somehow.

V
Scrambled Brains

The Achilles heel

The district prosecutor Matvei Bentsionovich Berdichevsky had a distinct inclination towards resounding turns of speech – it was a habit he had picked up from addressing members of the jury in court. And even in everyday life he would sometimes start speaking in ordinary language, and then get carried away or become overenthusiastic, and various 'hithertos' and 'verilys' immediately began getting woven into the fabric of his discourse.

'And yet another thing,' he said, shifting his gaze from Mitrofanii to Pelagia. 'Permit me to say that I am, verily, lost for words to express the extent of my admiration at your presence of mind and thoroughness of approach, my dear Sister! After such a terrible shock you did not suffer a nervous breakdown, as any other individual of the weaker sex would have done, not to mention nine out of ten men! You actually carried out an absolutely authentic, highly competent preliminary investigation of fresh evidence! And moreover, entirely alone, without your Mr Dolinin! I am filled with admiration for your heroic valour!'

Embarrassed by such an abundance of exclamation marks, and especially by the admiration, the nun replied as if she were trying to justify her actions: 'How could I not investigate, if the girl didn't come to drive the cows out? I had to find out where she had got to. You haven't told me yet what the spots are.'

Matvei Bentsionovich sighed sadly and replied, flaunting his scientific terminology just ever so slightly: 'The laboratory analysed the bag of soil that you collected on the spot. You were right in what you thought: it really is blood, as confirmed by the Van Deen reaction to a solution of guaiac resin. And a serodiagnostic analysis according to the Ulengut method has demonstrated that the blood is, alas, human.'

'Ah, how terrible,' the nun exclaimed, throwing her arms up in the air. 'That was what I was afraid of! They killed the poor little thing, hid her in some crevice in the rock and covered her with stones! She lost her life because of me. Now what is going to happen to her "granny"?' And she burst into tears – that is, on this occasion she behaved exactly as the aforementioned members of the weaker sex are supposed to.

Mitrofanii frowned – he found women's tears hard to bear, especially if they were not cried out of self-indulgence but for some substantial reason, as now.

'I'll send for the old woman, let them put her in our hospice. But what a villain this Wolf-Tail of yours is! It wasn't enough for him to kill you, a nun, he had to destroy the girl as well. What had the girl done to get in his way?'

'That was so that she wouldn't tell anyone in the village where she took the nun,' the prosecutor explained, crumpling a clean handkerchief in his hand – he wanted to offer it to Pelagia to wipe her eyes, but he didn't dare.

The holy sister made do with her own little handkerchief. She dabbed her eyes and blew her nose, then asked in a nasal voice: 'What about the footprint? Did I copy it well?'

Delighted at the conversation's return to a less emotional channel, Matvei Bentsionovich hastily responded: 'My specialist says that the print of the boot was sketched almost perfectly. Why were you not afraid, all alone at the scene of a suspected murder?'

'I was, really afraid?' Pelagia sobbed, trying to suppress her tears. 'But what else could I have done? I felt so bad when I got back to Stroganovka from the Devil's Rock and found out that Durka had never arrived to help drive out the livestock. I went running to the elder and told him we had to search. He wouldn't give me any men, he said they were all at work, and some little halfwit or other wasn't much of a loss. I went back to the Devil's Rock alone, by the same path. I was afraid, of course, but I thought: Why would the villain still be there? After all, he's certain that he did what he wanted to do and shut me in the cave. I walked all the way to the rock, looking around. But on the way back, I only looked down at my feet. And I found a track on the ground, under the cliff: a line, as if something had been dragged along, a dark spot and the imprint of a boot. The villagers don't wear boots, only bast sandals: I asked afterwards specially. There's only one pair in the whole of Stroganovka, and they belong to the elder. He puts them on for saints' days and when he travels to the district centre. But the sole on them is quite different.'

'Yes, the sole is unusual,' Berdichevsky said with a nod. 'And that, if I may make so bold, is our only clue. The cap with the wolf's tail is not a distinctive feature. The Zytyaks have been making caps like that since time out of mind. You can even buy them in the market here in Zavolzhsk for five roubles. But the boots, now – that's a different matter. An interesting sole, if one might put it like that, with a pattern of small nails. I held a conference in the department, including the best police officers and investigators. Here, if you please.' He took out a little note-book and started reading: '"Blunt toe with three rhomboids formed of four nails, a ten-millimetre welt, double steel tip. Square heel of medium height. Conclusion: not factory-made, the work of a high-class craftsman with his own signature." This is a good thing, because it makes a search possible,' the prosecutor explained. 'The bad thing is that there is no such craftsman in our own province. What else can we extract, so to speak, from the imprint? Applying Parville's formula, which determines that a man's height is 6.876 times the length of his foot, with a correction of four or five millimetres for the foot-wear, we arrive at a height between 1.78 and 1.84 metres for our subject – that is, extremely tall.'

'How much is that in Russian?' His Eminence asked, frowning. He took a dim view of the new-fangled tendency to translate everything from Russian measures into metres. 'All right, God be with the centimetres. But now why don't you tell me, Matvei, what you make of all this?'

Berdichevsky did have a theory, although a rather indefinite one.

'The criminal (following Your Eminence's example, I shall refer to him as "Wolf-Tail") followed Sister Pelagia all the way from Zavolzhsk. For lack of evidence I shall, for the time being, resist the temptation to assume that Wolf-Tail and Glass-Eye are one and the same individual. However, there can be no doubt that the reason for the malefactor's paying such importunate attention to a certain individual so dear to us should be seen in nothing other than a desire to take the life of the presumptive prophet.'

'Matvei,' His Eminence appealed to him. 'Speak more simply, you're not performing in court, you know.'

The public prosecutor was thrown off balance, but only for about half a minute.

'Generally speaking, I am certain that he *is* Glass-Eye,' he said in simple words devoid of all pomposity. 'Somehow he found out that Pelagia had cast suspicion on him and decided to get even. If so, he is psychologically abnormal. You know, I recently read a German research treatise on the subject of obsessive maniacal obsessive resentment. Everything fits. All these individuals live with a constant sense of a global conspiracy directed against them personally; they constantly seek the culprits and sometimes wreak a vicious revenge on them. Who would believe it – pursuing a woman for hundreds of versts, almost all the way to the Urals! Through the Forest, and before that along the River. He must have followed her in a boat, then. But what a monstrous way of killing her he invented! And he had no mercy on a little girl. I'm sorry, but he is quite clearly a maniac.'

'Why didn't he kill me in the Forest?' asked Pelagia. 'Nothing could have been simpler.'

'As I told you: a malicious obsession. He wasn't interested in killing you as simply as possible. Permit me to affirm that these pathological personalities like to act out spectacular performances, such as entombing someone alive in a cave. And what's more, he must have wanted to draw out the pleasure, to savour his power. Surely that is why he growled at you from behind the fir tree? He was toying with you, playing cat-and-mouse.'

The nun nodded in acknowledgement of the prosecutor's sound reasoning. 'But there is something else that worries me. I can't stop thinking about it. Where was I when the landslip happened? Down in the cave, or up at the top? And when I was up at the top, how could I have seen what happened earlier?'

Mitrofanii and Berdichevsky exchanged glances. The two of them had already discussed this strange detail of the nun's story and reached a certain conclusion, which His Eminence now tried to put to Pelagia – naturally, in the most delicate manner possible.

'I believe, my daughter that as a result of shock, reality and appearance became confused in your mind. Might it not be the case that this Wolf-Tail simply arose in your imagination, following the incident in the forest that had given you such a serious fright? Very well, very well,' Mitrofanii added hastily when he saw Pelagia's agitated response to his words. 'It is quite possible that the reason lies not in you, but in external circumstances. You said yourself that the air in the cave was special in some way, that it made you feel slightly dizzy and set your ears ringing. Perhaps there is some natural gas produced in that place, one that induces a delusional state – I have read of such things happening. There are substances and emanations unknown to science, and their effects are imperceptible to the human sense organs. Do you remember what happened on Canaan?'

Pelagia remembered very well. And she shuddered.

'This is how we are going to proceed,' Matvei Bentsionovich declared cheerfully, turning the conversation back from the chimerical to the real. 'Let the criminal believe that he has succeeded in killing the nun and eliminating the only witness. And meanwhile we shall seize him by this Achilles heel.' He tapped the drawing with one finger. 'I have forwarded an enquiry to Moscow, St Petersburg and Kiev, to the forensic-science analytical offices. They have fine card indexes there, on the most various subjects. We could well find our master cobbler before you know it. And through the cobbler, God willing, we'll find the killer too.'

'Don't count too much on God,' said Mitrofanii, quenching his spiritual son's optimism. 'He has plenty of other things to worry about, apart from boot heels.'

The *Tractatus de speluncis*

And then the ordinary daily round of life was restored, and Sister Pelagia had no time for thinking about mysterious caves.

The responsibilities of the headmistress of the diocesan college were troublesome and fraught with agitations of all kinds. To be entirely truthful, a large part of these agitations derived from the headmistress herself.

Having accepted as a work of penance the headship of the school in which she had previously served as a teacher, Pelagia had undertaken a revolutionary change in the syllabus, for which she had come under attack both from above and below.

From above the attacks came from His Eminence Mitrofanii, who did nothing to hinder the innovations but by no means approved of them and passed caustic remarks, as well as promising trouble from the Holy Synod. He even threatened that in such a case he would not bother to defend the rebel, but surrender her to judgement and retribution.

You will defend me, Your Eminence, you will – you will have no choice, Pelagia replied to this in her own mind, although outwardly she demonstrated imperturbable meekness.

The criticism from below caused her far more problems. That is, the holy sisters of the conventual calling, who were accustomed to acquiescence, did not even think of opposing the headmistress's will, but Maria Vikentievna Svekolnika, a teacher employed under contract and a recent graduate of the pedagogical courses in St Petersburg, was ablaze with the fervour of enlightenment and gave Pelagia no end of trouble.

At this point we should perhaps explain the essential nature of the reforms.

The school had a four-year programme, and pupils cannot be taught a great deal in that time. Pelagia had decided to retain only the four subjects without which, in her opinion, it was impossible to get by. Better fewer, but better – that was the headmistress's motto. With an aching heart, she excluded the natural sciences and geography from the curriculum as being unnecessary for children from poor families – in any case, when they finished their studies, they would forget all about the laws of physics and foreign capital cities. She made domestic science the central subject, devoting half of the lessons to it, and she also kept gymnastics, literature and religious studies, which was also singing.

Pelagia explained her choice as follows.

How to run a household was the most important knowledge for future wives and mothers. Gymnastics (including swimming in summer and, during the cold season, exercises in the school hall and bracing dousings with cold water) was required for sound health and a good figure. Literature was essential for the development of exalted feelings and correct speech. And as for teaching the law of God through singing, it was easier for the children to come to know the Almighty through music.

In only a short time the school choir became famous throughout the province of Zavolzhie. On occasion the Governor himself, von Haggenau, wiped away a tear of emotion as he listened to the female pupils (all wearing brown dresses and white headscarves) running through the strains of 'My soul doth glorify the Lord' or 'Dear to my heart' in their angelic voices.

Pelagia tried to demonstrate to the pedagogical graduate that any of the girls who developed an interest in further study could be sent to the municipal college at state expense or, if they proved very capable, even to the grammar school. The provincial budget included a special item for such cases.

Svekolnika would not listen to her arguments and showered the headmistress with various terms of abuse, which sometimes reduced Pelagia to tears: a retrograde cleric, an obscurantist and servant of male despotism who dreamed of locking women into the prison of housekeeping.

Three days passed in dealing with work matters that had accumulated during her absence and battles with the progressive feminist. But even during this busy period it sometimes happened that Pelagia would suddenly forget herself in the very middle of performing some task or other and freeze on the spot, lost in thought. Afterwards, of course, she collected her thoughts and returned to her interrupted business with redoubled zeal.

On her very first free evening (it was the fourth day after her return from Stroganovka), the nun set out for the diocesan centre. She had permission to go there at any time and make use of the Bishop's chambers as if they were her own home. And so she did.

She did not disturb His Eminence. She knew that he usually spent the hours before sleep writing his 'Notes on a Life Lived'. This was an interest that the Bishop had developed only recently, and he devoted himself to his writing with total self-abandon.

Mitrofanii had not conceived the idea of setting forth events from his own past out of idle vanity or egotism. 'Life is passing,' he said; 'how much longer do I have left? I could depart without having shared my accumulated riches. After all, the only genuine treasure a man has, which no one can take away him, is his accumulated experience of life. If you are able to string words together, it is a great sin not to share your thoughts, mistakes, sufferings and discoveries with humankind. For the majority it will probably mean nothing, but someone will read it, and perhaps avoid disaster, or even save their own soul.'

The Bishop would not let anyone read what he had written. He would not even allow his secretary near it, but wrote out the fair copy himself. He kept saying: 'You can read it when I die.' But why would he want to die, we ask, when he had such sound health and clarity of mind?

Pelagia slipped through into the library and murmured a greeting to Father Userdov, who was copying something out of the theological texts for a future sermon. Of all things on Earth, Father Serafim most loved preaching to the flock. He declaimed the most learned sentiments, with numerous quotations, at quite remarkable length. He prepared seriously, taking a long time over it. The only problem was that no one wished to pay attention to his learning. On discovering that Userdov would be taking the day's service, the parishioners considered it the wisest course to take themselves off to a different church and poor Father Serafim had not infrequently found himself delivering his oration to an audience of deaf old women who had only come to church to smell the incense or to get warm.

Mitrofanii could not permit such an affront to the authority of the service of worship, but he did not wish to offend the assiduous preacher, and so in recent times he had only allowed him to give his orations in the diocesan church, in the Bishop's own *metochion*, for the cloistered clergy and the servants, who could not go anywhere else.

Spotting Pelagia walking along the bookshelves, the secretary politely offered his help in searching for books. The nun thanked him but refused his offer. She knew that, once this man attached himself, he would never leave her alone until he had wheedled everything out of her. And this was a delicate matter, none of Userdov's business.

Father Serafim went back to scraping his feather pen over the paper. And then, as if in search of inspiration, he opened a pocket prayer book and stared into it.

Pelagia bit her lip to stop herself laughing out loud. Once, purely by accident, she had seen what kind of prayer book this was. It had a little mirror mounted on the inside of the binding – Userdov had a very high opinion of his own comely features.

After sitting there for a while, the secretary eventually went out, but the holy sister was still walking from shelf to shelf, quite unable to find what she was looking for – either among the Catholic literature or the canonical texts or the hagiography. She even looked in the natural science cabinet but didn't find it there either.

The door opened with a creak and Mitrofanii came in. He nodded absent-mindedly to his spiritual daughter, then went across to a bookshelf, took out some book or other and started rustling through the pages. No doubt he needed a quotation or wanted to check something. It was perfectly clear that just at that moment the Bishop was lost somewhere far away in years gone by.

Pelagia moved closer and saw that His Eminence was leafing through Valuev's *Diaries*.

She cleared her throat.

He didn't look round.

Then she pushed the *Ancient Hebrew–Russian Dictionary* off the table on to the floor. The massive volume weighed a third of a pood, and the noise it made was so loud that Mitrofanii almost jumped out of his shoes.

He turned round, fluttering his eyelids.

'I'm sorry, Your Eminence,' the nun lilted, picking up the ponderous tome. 'I caught it with my sleeve . . . But since you've already been distracted . . . There's a book I can't find. You remember, after that business on Canaan you told me that you had a book on miraculous caves by some Latin author.'

'Still puzzling over your Devil's Rock, are you?' Mitrofanii guessed. 'There is a book about caves. In the medieval-literature section.'

He went over to a large oak bookcase, ran his finger along the spines of the books and pulled out an in-octavo with old calfskin binding. 'Only it's not by a Latin author, but a German one,' the Bishop said, absent-mindedly stroking the faded gold embossing. 'Adalbert the Beloved, one of the junior Rhein mystics. Here, study it, I must be going.' And he went out, without even asking what exactly it was that Pelagia hoped to find in the medieval treatise. Such is the authorial itch.

In fact the holy sister herself was not really sure what she was looking for.

She opened the volume uncertainly and frowned at the Gothic script that was so hard to take in at first glance.

She read the title:

Tractatus de speluncis.*

Below it there was an epigraph: *'Quibus dignis non erat mundus in solitudinibus errantes et montibus et speluncis et in cavernis terrae.'*†

In the prologue and the first chapters, the author painstakingly listed all twenty-six mentions of caves in Holy Writ, accompanying each episode with extensive commentaries and pious thoughts. For instance, in his investigation of the First Book of Kings, Adalbert demonstrated true medieval naivety in a detailed discussion of precisely which call of nature – the greater or the lesser – had led King Saul to enter the cave where David and his supporters were hiding. Citing other authors, and also his own experience, Adalbert convincingly demonstrated that the King must have gone into the cave to address the more substantial of his corporeal needs, since in relieving the less significant call of nature, a man is less distracted and he does not produce *'crattoritum et errantum'*‡ and there could be no doubt that these were precisely what had prevented the victor from noticing David slicing off the bottom of his cloak.

Weary of the effort of making out the medieval Latin, Pelagia was already thinking of setting the meticulous researcher's work aside. She absent-mindedly turned a few more pages, and her gaze fell upon the heading *'Kapitulum XXXVIII de Speluncis Peculiaribus tractans'*.§

She began reading – and then she could not tear herself away.

And there are also caves that are called Special, they are concealed from man for as long as he is alive. These caves connect the fleshly

---

* Latin: *A Treatise on Caves*
† Latin: 'Those of whom the entire world was unworthy have wandered through deserts and mountains, through the caves and the ravines of the earth.'
‡ Latin: 'groans and internal rumblings'.
§ Latin: 'Chapter XXXVIII, which treats of Special Caves.'

world with the non-fleshly world, and every soul passes through them twice: when it enters into the flesh and when it leaves the flesh after death, only the unrighteous souls fall downwards from the cave, into the fires of hell, and the righteous soar upwards into the heavenly spheres. Special Caves, the number of which is one hundred and forty-four are by God's mercy scattered equally throughout the world, one every thousand leagues, so that the journey of the soul to the flesh and back might not be too lengthy, for there is nothing more painful than this transition.

The Special Cave nearest to our parts is located in the Land of Stier, close to Mount Eisengut, concerning which the Father Prior of the Blaugarten Abbey was informed by a worthy individual from the town of Innsbruck, who was either unable or unwilling to name the precise spot.

It sometimes happens, and not so rarely, that the Lord will summons some soul to His Judgement, but the Merciful Mother or a patron saint will intercede for the sinner, and the soul returns to the earth, but it retains a certain vague memory of its movement through the Special Cave. I also have once seen a man whose soul departed from the flesh but then returned. He was a knight who had formerly been in the service of the Landgrave of Hessen and went by the name of Gothard von Oberwald. This Gothard fell from his horse, struck his head against a stone and was accounted dead, but the following day, being already placed in the coffin and his funeral service read, he suddenly opened his eyes and soon recovered completely. He told how his soul, being temporarily parted from his body, had squeezed through a narrow, dark underground place. But when a bright light began to shine at the end of this cave, an unknown power had pulled the distraught soul back to earth. The Father Prior of the Blaugarten Abbey, who was also present at the telling of this story, asked Gothard if anyone had prayed to the Holy Virgin or St Gothard of Hildesheim for him, and it eventuated that all the time when the knight was lying dead, his wife had prayed ceaselessly for his soul, for she loved this Gothard with all her heart.

In appearance Special Caves are indistinguishable from ordinary ones, and anyone who accidentally wanders into them, if he possesses a sensitive soul, will hear a heavenly ringing, but if his soul is insensitive, he will not hear anything and will experience an insuperable desire to leave that place as soon as possible and never return to it again.

When she read the words 'heavenly ringing', Pelagia shuddered and felt a chilly shiver run down her spine. However, the most serious shock was still to come.

Woe unto him who shall find himself in a Special Cave at the hour of dawn if a red rooster shall crow nearby, for both the soul and the body of one who has heard this cockcrow is suspended in the space between worlds, where there is no passage of time [*in intermundis ubi non est aemanacio temporis*] and may disappear for all eternity or else be cast out in another time and even in another Special Cave.

The aforementioned worthy individual from Innsbruck told how a certain dealer in poultry, overtaken by bad weather, decided to spend the night in such a cave, unaware that it was Special. He had with him a cage, in which there was a rooster and some chickens. And this man entered the cave in the evening of the day before the Day of the Resurrection of the Holy Virgin, but he emerged three months earlier on the Day of the Discovery of the Holy Cross and, moreover, from a different cave, located on land held by King James of Scotland, and he made his way home, begging for alms for exactly three months, so that he returned to his native parts at exactly the Day of the Resurrection of the Holy Virgin, and nobody believed him when he said that he had been in the Kingdom of Scotland, although this dealer had the reputation of being an honest man.

And I have also heard tell of a certain hunter from Zealand by the name of Rip who heard a rooster crowing from an underground burrow, realised that a fox must have carried the rooster away and went in to get the fox's skin. He came back out only a very short time later, but when he went back to the village nobody recognised him, because he had been away for twenty years.

And a certain Ligurian merchant, on returning from the land of Cathay, told the noble gentleman Klaus von Weiler, who is well known to me (it was in the town of Lubeck, in the victualling house 'Under the Ship', in the presence of witnesses) that the people of

Cathay had told him, the merchant, about a certain fisherman from the Kingdom of Japon, which lies in the Ocean-Sea close to the land of the Tsar Ioann. This fisherman, while gathering oysters, entered a sea cave at dawn, just as a red turtle cried out, of the kind that announce the arrival of day in the country of Japon instead of cockerels, as a punishment for the local inhabitants not following the Christian faith, and this fisherman fell asleep for a short time, but it transpired that he had slept for all of eighty-eight years, and they would not admit him into his native village, because nobody there remembered him, and he wandered round various places, and those Chinese people had seen him themselves when they sailed to Japon for gold, of which there are immense amounts in that kingdom and it costs no more than silver or even copper.

And concerning the question of why the crowing of a red rooster produces such a remarkable effect on the soul, I have written in *Disputacio ypothetica de rubri galli statu preelectu** and so I shall not write again about that, but shall instead move on to.

Chapter XXXIX, which treats of the cultivation in caves of edible mushrooms

Let it be said that, on reading about the red rooster, Pelagia leapt off her chair and read to the end of the chapter standing up, such was the extent of her excitement. Running on by sheer inertia to read of mushrooms as well, she soon realised that there was no mention of 'Special Caves' here. She leafed through the volume carefully all the way to the end, hoping to come across some further mention of the 'conjectural discourse', but failed to find anything. Then she furiously slammed the book shut and went dashing to His Eminence's study.

Mitrofanii looked round in amazement – never before had his spiritual daughter burst in on him at this hour of sacred solitude, and without even knocking.

'Your Eminence ... the "Discourse on the Red Rooster"?' the nun blurted out.

The Bishop took a moment to come down to earth from his

* Latin: 'A Conjectural Discourse on the Select Nature of the Red Rooster'.

exalted thoughts. 'Eh?' he asked rather inelegantly.

'The treatise on the red rooster, written by that same Adalbert – where is it?' Pelagia asked impatiently.

'On what rooster?' the Bishop asked, overcome by even greater astonishment. 'What is wrong with you, my daughter? Do you have a fever?'

When he understood what the nun was seeking, he explained that apart from the *Treatise on Caves*, no other works by Adalbert the Beloved had survived to our times. The monastery in which the mystic lived and died had been burned by the soldiers of Count Nassau during the religious wars. This composition was the only one to survive, and that was owing to a fortunate coincidence: the manuscript had been at the binder's. This was the first time Mitrofanii had heard that Adalbert had written a work about the rooster.

'In the fifteenth century it was fashionable to ascribe marvellous properties to various animals,' His Eminence went on to say. 'Some of the scholiasts of those times were obsessed by the idea of duality – in other words, that the Lord created everything in pairs: man and woman, black and white, sun and moon, heat and cold. They tried to find a pairing for the human race in the animal kingdom – some kind of beast chosen and marked out by the Lord on a level with man. Some proposed the ants for this role, some the dolphins and some the unicorn. Judging from the title of the work, Adalbert was an apologist for the chosen status of roosters, but why red ones in particular, God alone knows.

'The proposal of ants is understandable enough: an anthill really does resemble human society. The reason for dolphins is clear, too: they are intelligent. The medieval authors had never actually seen a unicorn, so they could imagine anything they liked about them. But what is the point of a rooster? A quarrelsome, stupid bird that does nothing but cover chickens and screech?'

'Ah, but no,' said the Bishop, raising one finger. 'Roosters have been regarded in a special light since ancient times, during the pre-Christian period. And this attitude is particularly common everywhere the species *Gallus domesticus** is to be found. To the Chinese, for instance, it embodies the principle of Yang – that is,

* Latin: 'domestic cock'.

courage, benevolence, dignity and fidelity. And a rooster with red feathers is also a symbol of the Sun. If we turn our gaze to a completely different corner of the planet, to the ancient Celts – for them a red rooster was an embodiment of the gods of the Underground. In Greco-Roman culture a rooster is a harbinger of renewal. And in general, in a majority of mythologies this bird is linked with the gods of the dawn, light, the fire of heaven – in other words, with the inception of new life. The rooster drives out the night and the darkness, fear and blindness that accompany it.'

Improvised lectures of this kind, sometimes given on the most unlikely of pretexts, were a favourite hobby horse of Mitrofanii's, and every time Pelagia listened to them with great interest, but never before had she listened as avidly as she did now.

'Let us take Christianity,' His Eminence continued. 'In our religion the feathered creature that interests you also holds a special status. The rooster is a symbol of light. He greets the rising of the Christ-Sun who puts the powers of darkness to flight. At the festival of Easter, when we remember the Passion of Christ, the rooster signifies the resurrection. Are you aware that the cross, now the generally accepted symbol of Christianity, only appeared relatively recently, in the mid-fifth century? Until that time the Christians used other symbols, and very frequently a rooster, which is an image of the Son of God, who came to awaken mankind. Nor should we forget the prophecy of the wise Ecclesiastes: "And man shall rise at the crowing of the cock, and the daughters of song shall be silent," that is to say, it is a cockerel that shall announce the Judgement Day to men.'

The longer Pelagia listened to Mitrofanii's learned speechifying, the more thoughtful her expression became, so that by the end her gaze seemed to have turned entirely inwards.

When the Bishop finished, the nun did not ask any more questions. She bowed to thank him for his instruction, apologised for distracting His Eminence from his writing and took her leave until the following day.

The lair of the Cyclops

The holy sister was intending to leave the episcopal centre the same way as she had entered – not by the long way through the yard and the main gates, but by the short way, through the garden gate, to which she had a key of her own.

The lights in the windows of the communal block had already been extinguished and not even the lamp beside the front porch was burning, but there was a bright crescent moon shining in the sky and it was a clear night. There was a smell of young foliage in the air, the fountain could be heard gurgling in the avenue of apple trees, and in response to all of this the mood of intense concentration that had held the nun in its tight grip began to ease slightly.

The Bishop's garden was regarded as one of the sights of the town and was maintained in exemplary condition. The snow-white pathways, covered with a special fine-grained sand, were swept several times a day, and so Pelagia had the feeling that she was walking across the Milky Way, not over the ground. She even felt ashamed to leave the trail of her own tracks on this image of beauty and tried to keep to the very edge.

Suddenly she saw footprints ahead of her, right in the very centre of the snow-white strip. Someone had walked this way very recently, after the unvarying late-evening sweeping.

Who could it have been? Pelagia thought absent-mindedly, her thoughts still occupied with caves and red roosters. Not many people were permitted to stroll in the garden, especially at a late hour. Father Userdov? No, the cleric's stride would be far shorter, for it was restricted by a cassock, Pelagia deduced.

She adjusted the spectacles on her nose, still thinking her own thoughts, but at the same time looking at the tracks, which led towards the garden gate.

Suddenly the holy sister gasped and went down on all fours, almost pressing her nose against the surface of the ground. Then she gasped again, more loudly.

Square toes! That outline of the heel! And if you looked closer, you could see three rhomboids!

The nun's heart leapt in her chest. He had been here! Recently! Perhaps even only a moment ago! He had left through the little gate.

She leapt up and went dashing towards the building, but immediately turned back again. Before she could wake up the servants he would be gone! And there would not be any tracks on the street, with its surface of cobblestones.

What if he was still close by and she could follow him?

Gathering up the hem of her habit, Pelagia dashed forward – not actually along the tracks, but alongside, in order not to trample them. She didn't bother to think what this sudden appearance of Wolf-Tail in the episcopal centre might mean.

The footprints turned off the main avenue on to a side branch that seemed to lead, not to the gate, but into a distant, deserted corner of the garden.

The holy sister halted for a moment, trying to understand the meaning of this manoeuvre. And she guessed it: the villain could not have a key, so he would have to climb over the railings.

She started running even faster.

The path was narrower here, hemmed in on both sides by tall bushes casting shadows that made the tracks invisible but, on the other hand, there was nowhere to turn off. Here was the end of the garden already. The little planking shed, where they put the boxes of apples in autumn, and behind it the railings. She had to run up to it, stick her head through between the railings and take a cautious peep to see if there was a dark figure receding into the night. And if there was, she had to climb over on to the other side and follow it.

Even if it turned out to be someone entirely innocent, at least she would be able to find out who had made his boots. And then she . . .

Pelagia had just drawn level with the shed. Her peripheral vision detected a black crack – the door was slightly open – and the thought flashed briefly though her mind that this was an oversight.

But then the door suddenly swung wide open. A long arm reached out of the darkness, a hand seized the holy sister by the collar and snatched her into the little building. The bolt clanged home.

Stunned by the shock of it and blinded by the sudden darkness, Pelagia cried out, but a broad, rough hand immediately squeezed her mouth shut.

'Well hello, my little steamship dame,' a voice said in the darkness.

She realised instantly who it was – not even from the voice, which she had only heard once, but from that repulsive word 'dame'. Glass-Eye (alias Wolf-Tail – Berdichevsky had been right) paused, apparently savouring his captive's distress.

The darkness no longer seemed so impenetrable to her. The shed had deliberately been built flimsily, with cracks in the walls, so that the apples could breathe, and the moonlight came in through the gaps.

The first thing that Pelagia made out was a pair of eyes glittering, but glittering differently, so it was hard to tell which of them was real and which was false.

'I've been running around after you so long, it would be a shame to polish you off straight away,' the appalling man said. 'So you can have another minute to live, OK? Only on one condition: if you so much as squeak you're on your way into a coffin with pretty tassels.'

'We're not allowed,' the nun replied, her voice muffled by the hand.

'What's not allowed?' asked Glass-Eye, taking his hand away.

'A coffin with tassels. Nuns aren't allowed to have them,' she explained, thinking of only one thing: to keep saying anything at all, any nonsense, as long as it postponed the inevitable for a moment or two.

Not in order to escape – what escape could there possibly be here? In order to prepare her soul for the great mystery and recite the words of her final prayer in her own mind.

'You're joking. Good girl!' the killer said approvingly. 'And you have a lively brain. If only it was a bit dimmer, you'd have lived longer. Have you seen this gadget?' He took some object out of his pocket. It bobbled about strangely in his hand, and when Pelagia looked closer, she saw it was a weight on a spring.

'My invention,' Glass-Eye boasted. 'It can strike from a good sazhen away, and It's very accurate.'

He moved his hand ever so slightly, the spring straightened out, something whistled through the air and a clay jug on a shelf, no doubt used by the gardener for his drink, shattered into smithereens. The weight returned to the hand that had thrown it.

'How did you get out of the cave? A really slick dame, no two ways about it. And you sketched the sole of my boot. And now I've caught you with that sole, like a gudgeon on a rod.' He laughed quietly and triumphantly.

The most terrible thing was that the nun could not see his face, and she didn't remember it properly from the first time.

So this is what death is like, Pelagia thought with a shudder: faceless, laughing quietly.

'How ... how did you know that I sketched the boot print?' the nun whispered.

He chuckled again. 'Aren't you the curious one ... You'll find out everything soon enough. Up there.' He pointed one finger up at the ceiling.

'Where?' she asked, puzzled.

His merriment redoubled at that. 'Where, where? In the next world. Where all earthly secrets are revealed.'

'Why do you want to kill me?' the nun asked meekly. 'What have I done to offend you?'

'Not you; your brains.' The frivolous killer tapped her on the forehead. 'So I'm going to smash them out in a moment. It will be interesting to see what that dish looks like – scrambled brains.'

Pelagia glanced involuntarily at the shelf where the shards of the jug lay. Spotting this movement, Glass-Eye was overwhelmed by a fit of giggles – the way the girls in Pelagia's classes used to giggle when one of them got the stupid, ticklish laugh bug and infected the entire class.

The nun fitfully pressed her hands to her chest. Something pricked her palm. A knitting needle! As usual, the holy sister's knitting bag was hanging round her neck. A knitting needle might not seem like much of a weapon, but what if there was no other to be had? And those two steel rods had already saved their mistress in situations no less desperate than the present one.

Pelagia jerked the bag off her neck and grabbed tight hold of it.

'What's that you have there, a prayer book? Oh no, we're not going to pray, that's boring. Goodbye, dame.' He stepped back, and in order to get a good swing – or, perhaps in order to savour his victim's terror – he brandished the weight in a circle through the air.

But Pelagia didn't wait for the second circle: with a sickening squeal, she thrust the two needles straight through the cloth of the bag into the murderer's only eye. At the final moment she suddenly felt frightened: what if she hadn't remembered which eye was the natural one?

However, to judge from the wild howling, her blow had struck home as intended. The howl turned into a groan. The killer grabbed his face in his hands and immediately pulled them away again.

Pelagia staggered back it was a terrible sight, the satin bag dangling and swaying there in front of that human face. She dashed to the door and tugged hard on the bolt, but she couldn't open it – it was rusty and she wasn't strong enough.

The wounded man pulled the bag off his face and cast it aside, and a dark mass trickled down his cheek. He gathered it in his hand and started stuffing it back into the socket.

Pelagia squeezed her eyes shut.

'Bitch!' the blinded man roared. 'Poisonous snake! I'll kill you anyway!' He swung his arm back, and the nun barely managed to squat down in time. The weight flew over her head with a terrifying whistle. And then the throwing began in that narrow space of three by three sazhens.

Glass-Eye swung his arm about, striking to the right and the left. The weight cut through the air, crushed empty wooden boxes on the shelves, crashed into the walls with a crunch, snapped the handle of a garden fork in half.

The nun dashed into one corner, then another, squatting down. Once the killer squatted down too and tried to catch her on the legs, but Pelagia managed to jump up in time. It was all like some monstrous game of tig or cat-and-mouse. And the nun also inappropriately recalled the scene with Odysseus in the cave of Polyphemus. 'The eyeball burst, the eye splashed out with a hiss. The cannibal howled wildly and the cave resounded with his howls.'

This Cyclops wailed and sobbed, he howled incomprehensibly, but Pelagia, short of breath from all her darting and jumping, still tried to make him see reason.

'Calm down! You need a doctor!'

But in so doing she only gave away her position. Each exhortation was followed by a blow more accurate than the one before.

Then the nun squatted down on her haunches and fell silent.

Glass-Eye carried on throwing his weight across the shed for a while, until he realised that his opponent had changed tactics. He also froze and listened.

He was standing only two paces away, and the nun pressed her hand to her left breast, afraid that the beating of her heart would betray her.

'You'll croak anyway, you'll croak,' the blind man hissed. 'I'll finish you without the weight, with my bare hands ...' And he really did put his weapon away in his pocket, stretch out his great paws and start turning round on the spot ...

This was bad. If he got the idea of squatting down, it would all be over. Pelagia jerked the spectacles off her nose and flung them into the corner.

The killer swung round rapaciously and dashed towards the sound.

Then she flew over to the door and threw her full weight on the bolt: thank God, it opened. Leaping out into the garden, she saw there was another bolt on the outside of the door and quickly closed it. And then she went dashing towards the building, shouting at the top of her voice: 'Over here! Over here! Help!'

Behind her, she could hear banging and crashing – it was Glass-Eye struggling with the locked door.

On resistance to evil, the motherland and truth

By the time all the monks had come running up and grasped the meaning of the nun's fitful shouts, then argued over whether they should go into the garden themselves or call the police, at least ten minutes must have gone by. It would have taken even longer if the Bishop himself had not come out to see what all the fuss and bother was about. Grasping the essential points in a few moments, he took hold of Pelagia by the shoulders and asked only one question: 'Are you all right?' When she nodded, he set off into the garden, taking broad strides. He did not run, because unseemly commotion is incompatible with the station of a Bishop, and yet the servants running after him could hardly keep up.

The door of the garden shed was still bolted – Glass-Eye could not have escaped. But there was no sound from inside.

The monks and servants timidly surrounded the rough wooden structure.

'Sir?' Userdov called in a trembling voice. 'Are you there? It would be best if you abandoned your thoughts of violence and surrendered yourself into the hands of justice.'

Mitrofanii took hold of Father Serafimov by the shoulder,

moved him aside and pulled back the bolt with no hesitation.

He stepped inside.

Pelagia closed her mouth tight shut. She absolutely must not call out – God forbid, the Bishop might look round, and to turn away from a wounded, deadly dangerous beast would be madness.

The Bishop stood in the doorway for a few seconds. He shook his head and made the sign of the cross. Then the others rushed into the hut, jostling each other aside. They gasped and they also crossed themselves. Pelagia went up on tiptoe to glance over the shoulder of the brother purser.

There was a rectangle of bluish moonlight falling on to the floor, and she could see Glass-Eye sitting in the corner, slumped back against the wall. His hands were clutching the broken handle of the garden fork, the sharp points of which the suicide had thrust into his own throat, with such great force that the prongs had passed straight through and stuck into the wood.

That night, while the district public prosecutor and the police were carrying out their various duties (the blazing lanterns and torches made the garden as bright as day), Pelagia suffered a belated hysterical reaction which, fortunately, no one apart from His Eminence observed.

'What terrible wickedness I have committed to save my own life!' the holy sister lamented, wringing her hands. 'I forgot who I am! I behaved like an ordinary woman in fear of her life. But I am a nun! I did not follow the law of Christ, which tells us not to resist evil and to turn the other cheek, but the law of Moses! An eye for an eye! I shall never touch any knitting again in my life!'

Mitrofanii decided that this fit of self-castigation would be best calmed by a pretence of severity, and he addressed his spiritual daughter strictly: 'And what if you are a nun! There are different kinds of monks too. There are warrior-monks. Take Oslablya and Peresvet, who fought for their motherland and the truth with weapons in their hands!'

'But are "for the motherland" and "for the truth" really the same thing?' Pelagia objected, with her teeth chattering. 'Every nation has its own motherland, but the truth is the same for all people everywhere. What is so good about your Peresvet? Of course, for the principality of Moscow and for Russians he is a hero, but Christ did not ascend the cross for the principality of Moscow or for one single nation, but for the whole of mankind. The Tartar Chelibei, whom Peresvet slew, also had a living soul. A servant of God must never take up a weapon, even if he is facing certain death. Ah, My Lord, imagine how terribly afraid a man who has already lost one eye must be of losing the only one he has! He must have had nightmares about going completely blind . . . But in my cruelty it seemed a small thing to take away his sight, and I even locked the door from the outside so that he wouldn't get away. Where could he have gone, now that he was blind? I can imagine how the poor man felt at the walls, looking for a way out, and didn't find it . . . If he had, perhaps he would not have damned his immortal soul. Surely I am right?'

Seeing her in such torment, Mitrofanii abandoned severity and took the nun by the hand. 'No you are not right, you are not! Evil must be resisted. I disagree with Count Tolstoy about that and about his interpretation of Chris's teaching. Life is the overcoming of Evil and the struggle with Evil, and not capitulation to villains. You are like David, who defeated Goliath, or St George of Cappadocia, who slew the fiery dragon. And I admire you even more than these heroes, because you are a weak woman, and your knitting needle is a far more courageous weapon than David's sling or George's lance.'

But, instead of taking pride in these flattering comparisons, Pelagia merely waved a hand at His Eminence and sobbed even more bitterly.

So that is the answer

All of this happened during the night of Thursday (which was the day of Ioann the Cave-Dweller) and the next Wednesday – that is, before even a week had passed – Matvei Bentsionovich Berdichevsky presented the Bishop and Sister Pelagia with a full and exhaustive report on the investigation that had been held.

The attacker's identity had proved much easier to establish than the public prosecutor had anticipated. First of all they had found the hotel where the man had been staying. This was not hard, since Zavolzhsk was not a very large town. They had searched his room and found a passport in the name of honorary citizen Mavrikii Iriparkhovich Persikov.

Berdyshevsky had not believed the passport, mindful of the fact that on the steamer the criminal had called himself Ostrolyzhensky, and he had ordered the body to be photographed. Not, of course, in such a highly scientific manner as Sergei Sergeevich Dolinin – he did not comb the dead man's hair or drop nitroglycerine into his eyes (but then the corpse didn't have any eyes anyway).

Together with a verbal portrait, the photographs were sent to all the state security and detective departments in the Empire. And only a few days later a prompt response arrived from the Kiev secret police, and a most unexpected reply it was.

'. . . not Persikov and not Ostrolyzhensky,' Matvei Bentsionovich said with a significant expression as he moved on to the most important part of his report (having begun with a rapturously eloquent panegyric to Sister Pelagia's heroism). 'He was a certain Bronislav Ratsevich, a hereditary noble of the province of Kovensk.' At this point the public prosecutor paused for effect before announcing his most sensational piece of information. 'And, if you please, *a former staff captain of the gendarmes*. He served in the Volynsk gendarmes department, actually in the town of Zhitomir. The report received from Kiev says that Ratsevich was regarded as a courageous and competent officer; during his final period of service he was a member of the flying squad for combating especially dangerous criminals. He lost one eye in an exchange of fire while detaining a gang of dynamiters. He was a decorated officer. But last year he was excluded from the Corps of Gendarmes for violating its code of honour. The regulations forbid gendarmes officers to borrow money, but the staff captain ran up debts and, moreover, to Jewish moneylenders, which his superiors obviously found doubly unacceptable,' said Berdichevsky, unable to resist the jibe as being a Jew by birth himself. 'The business went as far as debtors' prison. That is, to be precise, first Ratsevich was dismissed the service, and then he was put in prison, because an officer of the Corps of Gendarmes cannot be imprisoned. Soon he managed in some way or other to buy his way out and pay off his debts, but there was no way back into the corps for him. Immediately he was released, Ratsevich left Zhitomir for parts unknown. The Kiev

Department of Security has no information on his subsequent actions and place of residence.'

His listeners' shocked response was the best reward the public prosecutor could have hoped for. When he himself had first read the telegram, he had even started running round the office in his excitement, repeating to himself: 'Oh, oh, it can't be true!'

'But . . . But what explanation can there be for this?' His Eminence asked, spreading his hands in perplexity. 'For a gendarmes officer, even a former one . . . I am totally bewildered!'

Unlike the Bishop, Matvei Bentsionovich had had time to recover from his amazement and gather his thoughts, and he had his answer ready.

'I think the situation was as follows. Ratsevich bitterly resented the law that he had served so valiantly for so many years and which had cast him off him so callously – not for some criminal offence but for an ordinary civil misdemeanour. What of it, if he could not pay back his debts on time? Why, you know, that kind of thing is always happening. He had given distinguished service, but he was expelled from the corps he had served and left without any means of support. How was he supposed to earn the money to feed himself?' Berdichevsky smiled cunningly and answered his own question. 'What did Ratsevich know how to do? Track people down, ferret things out and also, so to speak, employ violence – and that was all. Do you know what the "flying squad" is? It is a group of highly qualified officers and agents who posses all the skills of armed combat, fisticuffs and other knowledge required for combating dangerous criminals. And so Mr Ratsevich found himself an occupation as close as possible to his former profession. It is quite a common occurrence in criminal practice for competent policemen to turn into inveterate enemies of society. Perhaps Ratsevich was acting alone. But perhaps not. Permit me also to remind you that he is a Pole. I would not exclude the possibility of the former staff captain being connected with the Warsaw bandits, the elite of the criminal world. Criminals of this class have little in common with other denizens of the social underworld. They live and they commit their villainies, if you will pardon the vulgar expression, with real swank. Many of them come from the Polish gentry. They have education and decent manners.'

'But what was his interest in our Pelagia?' asked Mitrofanii, not entirely convinced by this theory.

Berdichevsky had clearly also prepared his answer to this.

'She threw suspicion on to Ratsevich. I don't know how he managed to get off the steamer after the murder of Shelukhin and the theft of the treasury casket. Most probably by swimming. And it is hardly likely that being forced to swim in icy water was to his liking. He was a spiteful gentleman and, apparently, of a psychopathic temperament. Such types, you know, are not rare among criminals (or among those who catch them). They take any difficulties as a personal insult and they pay back the insult in full. I can only repeat what I have said once already: the killer decided to get even with Sister Pelagia and, moreover, to do it creatively, with sadistic imagination. He bided his time in taking his revenge, waiting for inspiration and a convenient opportunity, such as the one that presented itself at the Devil's Rock. But when he learned that he had failed there, he immediately decided to finish the job quickly, by simply staving her head in, and that's all.'

Pelagia asked the question that was tormenting her: 'But how did he know that he had failed? And especially about the imprint of the boot?'

The public prosecutor frowned. 'If you will permit me to say so, that is hardly squaring the circle. It seems clear enough. When I sent my enquiry to the forensic-analysis departments, I had absolutely no suspicion that the criminal was a former gendarme. In addition to the image of the sole of the boot, it included a description of Mr Ostrolyzhensky – the glass eye and so forth. The enquiry caught the eye of one of Ratsevich's former colleagues. Perhaps they were friends, or perhaps it was a business arrangement – how can we tell? I have heard it said that certain police officials in the provinces of Little Russia and Poland maintain – how shall I put it? – mutually advantageous relations with the Warsaw bandits. But that, I am afraid, is a matter beyond the sphere of my competence, on a scale far too large for Zavolzhsk. Let us be satisfied with the fact that your ill-wisher has been neutralised – thanks to your own bravery and God's providence.'

'Amen,' the Bishop said with feeling. 'All's well that ends well.'

And so they rested content with that.

VI

Intellect and feeling

A beautiful idea

It had taken about five days to gather the necessary information. Some hasty hotheads would have got the job done quicker than that, because the mark's habits and movements were laudably unvaried, but Yakov Mikhailovich was not fond of rushing things, and anyway those types had already done more than enough of their clumsy hustling and bustling. And wasn't it just remarkable that the moment someone bungled something and made a real mess of it, then straightaway it was: Come on, now, Yakov Mikhailovich, help us out here? Clear up all this unsightly litter and make everything neat and tidy. They could at least give him a fresh job to do once in a while, something that hadn't already been mauled by someone else, so that he wouldn't have to shovel up their shit. Who did they take him for – the night-soil man?

Such were the discontented mutterings of the middle-aged man of unremarkable appearance sitting on the terrace of the Café de Paris located on Malaya Borshchovka Street opposite the Bishop's garden, and glancing at the street flooded with sunlight over the top of the *Zavolzhsk Diocesan Gazette*.

He was dressed to match his own appearance, in a style that was decent but somehow dull, so that there was absolutely nothing for the eye to fasten on: a speckled-grey jacket, a collar that was not soiled but not too white, a slightly shabby bowler hat lying on the table. The only even slightly remarkable feature of this extremely modest gentleman was his nasty habit of cracking the joints of his fingers, especially at moments of intense concentration.

Now, for instance, he quickly seized hold of his left hand with his right and began cracking so loudly that the two young ladies at the next table looked round, and one even wrinkled up her nose.

'Pardon me,' said Yakov Mikhailovich, smiling guiltily with his plump lips – he was well aware of his own bad proclivity. 'I shan't disturb you again.'

The aroma and excessive sweetness of the coffee that he was drinking from a fine china cup were somewhat reminiscent of cocoa, but in his travels through the Russian provinces Yakov Mikhailovich had had occasion to drink worse slops. In such cases he usually proceeded as follows: he asked them to bring him a milk jug filled to the top with cream (the cream in the provinces was far finer and richer than in Moscow and St Petersburg), poured as much of it as possible into his cup, and then it was all right – you could drink it up and even enjoy it.

At twenty-nine minutes past seven Yakov Mikhailovich took out his rather inexpensive silver watch and clicked open the lid, but he didn't look at the dial; instead he turned his head to the right, as if in expectation of something or someone. He had to wait no more than a minute – a nun appeared round the corner from the direction of the Kazan Gates – wearing spectacles, with a strand of red hair peeping out from under her headscarf. And now the seated man ran a hand over his own sparse black hair and glanced at his watch (it showed exactly half past), nodded approvingly and jotted something down in a little notebook with a lead pencil – not a word, and not a number, but some kind of squiggle, which made sense to no one but him.

When the nun drew level with the terrace, the dark-haired man concealed his face and his shoulders with his newspaper. And the moment she disappeared into the gate of the episcopal garden, the café's inconspicuous client immediately paid his bill and left, leaving a tip of eight kopecks.

The man from out of town seemed not to have any urgent business. He strolled at a leisurely pace around the lovely town of Zavolzhsk, a most pleasant place, especially on such a fine spring day. Swinging his light travelling bag, Yakov Mikhailovich walked round all the local sights, and at nine o'clock in the evening he dined on cottage cheese and battercakes in the dairy dining hall. Once again he left an eight-kopeck tip, and asked where the privy was. It turned out to be in the yard.

The man who had just eaten supper went off to the latrine and there he disappeared, never to be seen again. Instead of Yakov Mikhailovich, a factory hand emerged from the outhouse – wearing a cap and caftan, with a little greying beard. It was clear straight away that he was a staid individual, a non-drinker and a man who knew his own worth, even though he was not well off. The factory hand had a sack hanging behind his back on a string.

Where the dark-haired man in the worn bowler hat had got to remained a mystery. Perhaps he had drowned in the cesspit? That was how Yakov Mikhailovich joked to himself. From the habit of solitude, which was required by his profession, he had grown used to holding a continuous internal conversation with himself: discussing, arguing and sometimes even joking – why not?

The only points in which the newborn factory hand resembled the gentleman who had sat in the Café de Paris and eaten cottage cheese in the dairy dining hall were his height and his boots, and the latter had been polished and clean before, but now they were grey with dust.

The proletarian set off towards the edge of town with a leisurely stride. By this time it was already dark and the street lamps were lit. Yakov Mikhailovich had noted that the streets here were illuminated in a most excellent fashion, and this was no mere idle observation – the fact was important for his job.

A short while later the man in disguise found himself close to the diocesan college for girls, a rather long, single-storey building that was painted yellow and white. The headmistress's 'cell' was located at one side, with a separate entrance: white curtains on the two windows, a low porch, a door with a little bronze bell.

Yakov Mikkhailovich had been in the apartment two days earlier. A tiny lodging of two rooms, rather cosy, even though it was maintained in a state of disorder.

He stood some distance away from the street lamp, behind a bush, and threw back his head, as if he were admiring the clear crescent moon. In fact, there was nobody watching the dreamer, because there was not a single soul on the quiet street.

Soon there was the sound of a moving carriage.

Yakov Mikhailovich glanced at his watch – twenty-nine minutes to eleven. He entered another incomprehensible squiggle in his notebook.

A small two-seater whirlicote in the English style came driving up. The driver was a middle-aged civil servant with a large nose, wearing a peaked cap. Sitting beside him was the mark – the same nun who had recently walked along Malaya Borshchovka Street.

The man jumped down, raised his peaked cap and bowed. The red-haired nun said something to him, also bowed, and started climbing the steps of the porch. The civil servant watched the holy sister until the door had closed behind her and only then drove away, but not immediately – after perhaps another two minutes. He stood there, twisting the end of his nose, as if he were trying to solve some tricky problem, but Yakov Mikhailovich already knew that this was a habit the civil servant had, like a nervous tic.

When the escort had driven away, the observer came out from behind the bush, opened his little book under the street lamp and looked over his notes.

In five days not a single deviation from routine. He could get down to work.

And so . . .

From 11 p.m. until 6 a.m. – sleep. Half an hour for the morning toilette. Then goes to the nearby church. Comes back home. An interesting fad: from half past seven to eight swims in the River, even thought the water is cold. Then takes breakfast in the school, with the pupils. From nine to twelve – lessons. After that – lunch. From one to five – more lessons. From five to seven' choir rehearsal. Shortly after seven walks to the episcopal residence (route: from Kazan Street turns on to Dvoryanskaya Street, from there on to Malaya Borshchovka Street; at this time the streets are crowded; at twenty past ten leaves the Bishop's apartment with the district public prosecutor, who sees her all the way to her porch.

Those were the terms of the problem, not so very difficult in themselves. But . . .

The snag here was in the rider, the governing condition. They had told him it had to be an accident or sudden death from illness. Not the slightest suspicion of violence. Of course, that was more interesting than a simple ordinary snicker-snack, but also many times more difficult. In short, a real brain-teaser.

'Come on now, come on now,' Yakov Mikhailovich muttered, racking his brains. If those smart alecks hadn't bungled everything so badly, then of course the simplest way of all would have been during the morning swim.

The iron nun (the Lord really had granted her good health), walked to an isolated little cove for her swim, no matter what the weather. She disrobed to her long white chemise, then swam out with rapid overarm strokes to the centre of the River and back again. Just looking at her made you shiver.

The way he ought to have done this was: stun her (ever so slightly, so that afterwards they would find water in her lungs), and slip her into the water. They would have said she got cramp in her leg and drowned. A common story. The water temperature was thirteen degrees – he had checked it with a thermometer. But that wouldn't do. The powers that be were in cautious mood after his predecessor's fine efforts. He had had a totally free hand, but the cross-eyed impressionist had still made a total botch of the job.

They had told him: 'It has to be absolutely perfect' – and what did that mean?

It meant in full public view and no one must suspect a thing.

You just try killing a healthy young woman who swims in water at thirteen degrees in front of numerous witnesses without provoking a single shred of suspicion. After all, every pair of eyes was an additional risk. You could never tell just what natural talent for observation someone might have been born with.

'Oh no, my dear sirs, that's going too far, that's beyond the bounds of the possible! I'm not the Lord God Sabaoth Himself,' Yakov Mikhailovich muttered quietly, but his grousing was not entirely free of affectation: after all, it is flattering when they hand you tricky little problems like this to solve. It shows they respect a man's talent. And what could possibly be more fascinating than trying to find the solution to a problem that actually lies beyond the realm of the possible?

Yakov Mihailovich believed devoutly in the unlimited potential of the human intellect. At least, of his own intellect. He cracked his fingers, smacked his thickish lips, even grunted a little, but he found the solution. And it was such a neat and elegant one – an absolute delight!

No need for any large audience, no need for all those eyes. The important thing here, as in any job, was not quantity, but quality. Let there be only one pair of eyes, but it would be as good as an entire crowd of witnesses (for who knew what they might see, or invent, and testify to under interrogation?). If the nun died right in front of the very man who conducted inquests, there would be no need for any questions and interrogations in any case. How could he possibly not believe his own eyes? He would have to – he would have no choice.

Come on now, come on now!

District Public Prosecutor Berdichevsky brought the nun from the episcopal residence to her official apartment every evening. He drove her all the way home in his carriage and helped her out. He always waited for her to walk up on to the porch and open the door. What could be contrived out of this?

Make the horse bolt somehow? There was a spot on the turn off Dvoryanskaya Street where the cliff edge was quite close. The public prosecutor's horse was docile, but if you used a blowpipe to fire a dart smeared with something that smarted into its side, then it would bolt like a good 'un.

Too risky. In the first place, she might jump out – after all, she was a sportswoman. She'd get off with no more than some worthless fracture. Or they'd both be killed, and that was all he needed.

But it was only a short step from the general idea of a key witness to complete enlightenment. The idea came almost immediately, and it was so brilliant that Yakov Mikhailovich actually squealed in delight. He turned back, driven by inspiration. He didn't simply run up on to the porch, he soared, and stuck his nose right against the door handle, lighting it up with a small electric torch.

That was it! The bounds of the possible had receded under the pressure of human intellect. The public prosecutor would see it all with his own eyes. Yakov Mikhailovich would polish off the little red-headed nun right in front of his big hooked nose, and Mr Berdichevsky would understand nothing, he wouldn't even notice anything.

That was true impressionism for you, that was genuine beauty; none of your setting up idiotic landslides in caves.

At ten o'clock the next evening the specialist in neat and tidy jobs was back in the quiet street at the edge of town, but he was dressed as a rag-and-bone man, not a factory hand.

He installed himself opposite the college building. Then he walked about for a while, calling out dismally: 'Bring out your old junk and bottles! Let's have those old rags and dusters!' –

more out of sheer professionalism than for the sake of the job. As he had already established previously, people didn't walk along this street at this hour; they wouldn't be giving him any old rags or bottles.

He went up on to the porch for no more than a minute, that was all that was needed. The door handle was of the very simplest kind: a wooden bracket attached with nails, God only knew how many years earlier – the heads had turned orange with rust ages ago. Yakov Mikhailovich hammered in another nail, a slim one, angled a little, so that the point protruded ever so slightly from the opposite side – at the precise spot where the fingers grasped the handle. Yakov Mikhailovich smeared the protruding point with some liquid from a little phial, working with extreme care – he even put on gloves. The specialist always took his own special medicine chest with him on his assignments: various glass tubes and phials for every occasion life could offer.

Scratching your hand on a door handle was a paltry, everyday occurrence, who hadn't done it at some time or other? The next morning, an abscess. In the evening, a temperature. Symptoms resembling blood poisoning, then a chilly little shiver, copious sweating and yellowing of the skin. On the second day, intense fever and delirium. That evening or – if you had a strong heart – by the end of the night at the very latest, your soul is at rest with the holy saints. And no suspicion, a perfectly ordinary, everyday incident. The main thing was that the public prosecutor would observe the whole thing in person. With his own ears he would hear her cry out when she pricked herself. Who would ever have thought that a trifle like that could lead to blood-poisoning? Nobody. It was God's Providence.

Yakov Mikhailovich took up his position in the bushes and started waiting. They arrived at twenty minutes to eleven. He had already begun to feel concerned.

Today the public prosecutor did more than merely help his companion down; he gallantly accompanied her all the way to the door.

That was even better – let him have a front-row seat.

The redhead took hold of the handle, pulled it and gave a sharp gasp.

Quod erat demonstrandum.

When he heard that quiet 'Ah!', Yakov Mikhailovich smacked his lips and backed away, and in five short seconds he had completely dissolved into the darkness.

His job was done. As they said, nature would see to the rest.

The public prosecutor in love

State Counsellor Matvei Bentsionovich Berdichevsky, an intelligent and respectable man, thirty-nine years of age, had suffered a misfortune of the kind that he had feared throughout his married life, which had been perfectly happy in addition to being blessed with numerous offspring.

Over the long years Matvei Bentsionovich's love for his wife had passed through several natural phases and finally settled firmly into the channel of habitual affection and a complete harmony of souls that had no need of tender words or handsome gestures. At the age of eighteen, Marya Gavrilovna's temperament had been distinctly passionate and romantic, but giving birth to thirteen children had entirely erased these primary qualities as rather more substantial concerns had arisen to demand her attention. For instance, how to keep the family on her husband's salary, which was, admittedly, very decent – but after all, there were fifteen people!

When she reached the boundary line of thirty, Mrs Berdichevsky had been transformed into a calm, sanguine lady with a firmly defined character and entirely unambiguous opinions concerning which things were important in life and which were mere fribbles unworthy of serious attention.

Matvei Bentsionovich valued these qualities in his wife, and the quality that inspired the greatest admiration in his heart was one ultimately comprehensible to any man: Marya Gavrilovna's self-sacrifice for the sake of those whom she loved unquestioningly, with a love that was entirely natural and completely unaffected.

In Berdichevsky himself the passing years had, by contrast, wrought an increase in his passion, imagination and inclination to dream. Like every healthy man, he enjoyed admiring women who were beautiful or simply attractive (and there are always plenty of those to be found in every time and place). But when he felt a particular liking for one, he took fright: What if I should fall in love? And his imagination immediately started presenting him with such terrible consequences, such heart-rending dramas, that he tried to keep as far away from the dangerous creature as possible. It would be quite intolerable for any worthy man to fall in love with another woman when he had a faithful wife like Masha and thirteen offspring.

Thus far the Lord had spared Matvei Bentsionovich and not tempted him excessively. Or rather, it would be truer to put it this way: the true temptation is not the obvious one. It is quite possible that the lovely charmers whom Berdichevsky shunned so assiduously actually represented no real threat to him for, after all, forewarned is forearmed. As usually happens, calamity waylaid the virtuous spouse where there seemed to be nothing to fear.

Well, how could anyone ever imagine that he should beware of the erotic allure of a black-robed nun?

In the first place, a nun is, as it were, an asexual being.

In the second place, Sister Pelagia had nothing at all in common with the female types from whom Matvei Bentsionovich habitually anticipated encroachments on his heart. Berdichevsky usually experienced a tremulous flutter at the sight of full-fleshed blondes with dimples or, by contrast, of delicately moulded brunettes with a regal gaze and a vulnerable white neck set in a delicate curve. But she was a redhead with freckles, and she wore spectacles.

In the third place, she was an individual he had known for a long time, an old acquaintance, you might say – that is (according to a misconception widespread among men) she was harmless in the romantic sense. In fact, this is the very ground from which dramas spring: as a result of some insignificant trifle, a woman whom one has known for a long time and not previously found even slightly interesting is suddenly enveloped in a tremulous, gauzy haze and acquires a radiant aura of bright radiance. One clutches at one's heart and gasps: O blind man, where have your eyes been looking? And then it is too late to change anything, too late to hide – the sentence of fate has already been pronounced.

This was precisely what had happened to Berdichevsky – the haze, the radiance and the clutching at his heart.

It had begun with his admiration for Pelagia's intelligence, courage and talent. At that stage Matvei Bentsionovich had categorised his feelings for the nun as respectful friendship and not bothered to wonder why he felt so happy in her presence. Surely friends ought to feel happy when they were together?

And then, on a certain especially clear day, after the holy sister's return from Stroganovka, the insignificant trifle had occurred. That moment was etched so firmly in the public prosecutor's memory that he only had to close his eyes and he was back at the scene again.

Pelagia was trimming roses that had been brought to the Bishop from the conservatory, and she had dropped the scissors into the crystal vase full of water. She had pulled up her sleeve in order to lower her hand into the liquid, and Matvei Bentsionovich's heart had suddenly stood still. Never in his life had he seen anything more sensuous than that slim, naked arm emerging from the black sleeve of the habit and plunging into the sparkling water. The State Counsellor had licked his dry lips and gazed at the nun's face as if he were seeing it for the first time: the white skin that seemed to be dusted with golden pollen, those eyes glowing with a gentle light. The features of this face were not regular, it could not be called beautiful, but it was manifestly, indubitably lovely.

On that day Berdichevsky had left the Bishop's chambers early, citing pressure of work. He felt stunned, he was actually swaying on his feet. On arriving home, he looked at his wife with terror in his heart – what if he had stopped loving her? Now he would see his Mashenka, not with the charitable eyes of love, but as she really was: swollen and pernickety, with a hard edge to her voice. But in fact it was worse than that. His love for his wife had not gone away, only she no longer occupied the most important place in his life.

As a meticulously fair-minded individual, Matvei Bentsionovich suffered terrible torment over the sheer depravity and dishonesty involved in this most trivial of conflicts: a forty-year-old husband had grown cold towards his wife, who had lost her youthful charms, and he had fallen in love with another woman. As if his wife were to blame for having withered while bearing him children and providing him with a peaceful, happy life!

For two days after the appalling discovery the public prosecutor stopped going to the Bishop's chambers in the evening, because he might meet Pelagia there.

On the third day he could stand it no longer. He told himself: I shall never, ever leave Masha or betray her, but the heart cannot be coerced. Fortunately, *she* is a nun and so *anything of the sort* is doubly impossible, in fact impossible to the second power. And in this way he appeased his conscience.

And he started visiting His Eminence again.

He watched Pelagia and listened to her. He was bitterly, deliriously happy. He believed so completely in the impossibility of *anything of the sort* that he made it a rule to drive the nun back to the college in his carriage. These journeys became the most important event of Matvei Bentsionovich's day, the secret pleasure to which he looked forward from first thing in the morning.

Ten minutes of riding together on a narrow seat. And sometimes, on the bends, their elbows touched. Pelagia, of course, never noticed this, but every time the public prosecutor felt a sweet surge of pleasure sweep downwards from his solar plexus.

Then there was the crowning touch: offering her his hand when she got down out of the carriage. After all, nuns don't wear gloves. To touch her skin – gently, gently, not prolonging the contact for even a second. What were all the delights of sensual gratification compared with this brief instant?

For most of the journey they didn't speak. Pelagia looked around.

Berdichevsky's entire demeanour indicated that he was concentrating on controlling the horse. But in reality, all the time he was dreaming that they were husband and wife, driving home after visiting friends. Now they would go into the room, she would kiss him absent-mindedly on the cheek and go into the bathroom to prepare for bed . . .

At such moments Matvei's Bentsionovich's dreams were at their most magical, especially when the spring evening turned out as fine as today. In order to prolong the illusion, the prosecutor took an unusual liberty – instead of saying goodnight at the carriage, as usual, he showed her all the way on to the porch. He indulged in an absolute orgy: not only did he squeeze her wrist very gently as he helped out of the carriage, afterwards he even offered her his elbow.

Pelagia showed no surprise at the change in the ritual – she didn't think it of any significance. She leaned on the curved support of his arm and smiled: 'What an evening – it's wonderful.'

Berdichevsky was immediately struck by a bold idea: to promote this escorted walk from the carriage to the porch to the rank of habit. And, in addition, could he not perhaps introduce a farewell handshake? Well, why not? Nuns' hands could not be kissed, but a handshake – that was very restrained, chaste, comradely.

On the porch the public prosecutor doffed his cap – with his left hand, so that his right hand was free, but nonetheless he couldn't bring himself to proffer it, and the idea never entered Pelagia's head.

'Good night,' she said. She took hold of the door handle and suddenly cried out – in a sweet, defenceless voice, like a girl. She pulled her hand away, and Berdichevsky saw a small drop of blood on her middle finger.

'There's a nail sticking out!' the nun said in annoyance. 'It's high time this handle was changed for a brass one.' She began taking out her handkerchief.

'Allow me, allow me!' Matvei Bentsionovich exclaimed, hardly able to believe his good luck. 'You can't use a handkerchief, come now! What if, God forbid, it has lockjaw on it! What if there are microbes? It has to be sucked clean, I know that from . . . a certain article that I read.' Then he completely lost his head – he seized hold of Pelagia's hand and raised the pricked finger to his lips.

She was so astonished that she never even of thought of pulling away. She merely gave the public prosecutor a special kind of look, as if she were seeing him for the first time.

Had she guessed?

But at this stage Berdichevsky no longer cared. The warmth of her hand and the taste of blood had set his head spinning – as if he were some kind of starving vampire. Matvei Bentsionovich sucked in the salty liquid as hard as he could. The only thing he regretted was that this was not a bite from a deadly poisonous snake.

Pelagia came to her senses and jerked her finger away. 'Spit it out!' she ordered him. 'Who knows what sort of filth there was on it.'

He spat delicately into his handkerchief – although, of course, he would have preferred to swallow. He muttered in embarrassment, already regretting his spontaneous impulse: 'I'll pull that detestable nail out right away.'

Oh, disaster! She had guessed, she must have guessed! With her astute mind. It was all over; now she would shun him, avoid his company!

He took the lantern off the shaft of the carriage, took a pair of pincers out of a box under the seat (an essential item for any horse-drawn vehicle – in order to remove a splinter from a hoof if a horse went lame). He walked back up on to the porch, brisk and businesslike. He pulled out the sly nail and displayed it.

'Strange,' said Pelagia. 'The end is rusty, but the cap is still shiny. As if it had only just been hammered in.'

Berdichevsky shone the lantern on it and saw that the point had a dull glint to it. From the blood? Yes, there was blood. But it was glinting higher up than that, from some other, oily substance, lighter in colour.

The public prosecutor caught his breath, but this time the reason was not amorous languor. 'Quick! To the hospital!' he shouted at the top of his voice.

Cr-aa-ck, cr-aa-ck

Professor Zasekin, the senior physician at the Martha and Mary Hospital, and a celebrity famous throughout the whole of Russia, paid no attention to the scratch on the finger. He just looked at it, shrugged his shoulders and didn't even bother to wipe it with iodine. But he paid extremely serious attention to the nail. He took it to the laboratory, spent an hour or so conjuring with it and returned perplexed.

'A curious composition,' he told the public prosecutor and his companion. 'It will take time to determine the complete formula, but it includes both Agaricus muscarus and Strychnos toxifera, and the concentration of Eschericia coli is simply phenomenal. Someone mixed up an absolutely devastating cocktail. If you, my dear fellow, had not sucked that rubbish out immediately after the trauma was sustained, then ...' The doctor shook his head expressively. 'It's remarkable that the wound is absolutely clean. You must have put your heart and soul into it, sucked with real passion. Well done!'

Matvei Bentsionovich blushed, afraid even to glance at Pelagia. But she asked: 'Someone "mixed it up"? Do you mean to say, Doctor, that this mixture was concocted artificially?'

Berdichevsky felt ashamed for being so concerned about trivialities when the matter was so serious.

'Beyond the slightest doubt,' said the professor. 'There's no mixture of that kind to be found anywhere in nature. This is a master's handiwork. And he's not local either – there are no laboratories in Zavolzhsk that could do this.'

The public prosecutor turned cold when he realised the full implications of this statement. And Pelagia's face changed too. At that moment Matvei Bentsionovich loved her so much that the inside of his nose began to itch. If someone were to have said to him just then: This is the individual who attempted to kill the being so dear to your heart – then the State Counsellor would have thrown himself on the fiend, seized him by the throat and ... And at that point Berdichevsky, a man of peace and a *paterfamilias*, was afflicted with a dark mist before his eyes and difficulty in breathing. He had never before suspected himself capable of such fury.

An emergency council was called immediately, in the middle of the night, in the Bishop's chambers.

Matvei Bentsionovich was pale and resolute. Externally he maintained his composure, except that he tugged on his nose more frequently than usual.

'It is obvious now that this is not a solitary maniac, but an entire gang. And that makes the "Warsaw bandits" scenario the most likely. Those people regard it as a matter of honour to get even for one of their own. Once they've got it into their head that Sister Pelagia was responsible for the death of one of their henchmen, they won't rest until they kill her. I'll abandon all my other cases and go to Warsaw if necessary, or Moscow, or even Zhitomir, but I'll find the blackguards. Only there is no way of telling how long the investigation will take. And in the meantime, our dear sister is in mortal danger, and we cannot even speculate from which direction the blow will come next time. You are now our only hope, Your Grace ...'

His Eminence, who had been roused from his bed, was wearing his dressing gown and felt slippers. His fingers trembled as they tugged agitatedly at the cross hanging round his neck.

'We must keep her safe – that's the first thing,' Mitrofanii said in a hoarse voice. 'That's all I'm thinking about. I'll send her as far away as possible, to some quiet hermitage. And let no one know a thing. And I won't even ask you!' he shouted at his spiritual daughter, expecting her to resist.

But the nun didn't say anything. Clearly, the cunning trick with the nail had seriously scared her. Berdichevsky felt so sorry for the poor thing that he started blinking rapidly, and the Bishop frowned and grunted: 'In the Znamensky Convent on the Angara river, the mother superior is a former pupil of mine, I have told you about her. It is an isolated place, and quiet,' said His Eminence, bending down one finger. And then he bent down a second: 'There is also a good hermitage on the Ussuri. You can see strangers coming from ten versts away. The elder there is a friend of mine. I'll take you there myself – all the way to the Angara or the Ussuri, whichever you wish.'

'No!' the public prosecutor and the nun exclaimed in a single voice.

'You can't go,' Berdichevsky explained. 'You are too noticeable. And it's already clear that they are watching us by day and night. It has to be done quietly and secretly.'

Pelagia added: 'It would be best if I go alone.'

'And not in nun's robes, of course – you'd better change,' Berdichevsky suggested, although he was sure the idea would be rejected.

At that Mitrofanii and the nun exchanged glances, but said nothing.

'I swore an oath,' Pelagia said in an uncertain voice, which mystified Berdichevsky (the public prosecutor was unaware of the existence of Mrs Lisitsyna).

'In a case like this I release you from your promise. Temporarily. You'll travel to Siberia as Lisitsyna, and then change your garments. Now tell me, where do you want to go?'

'Instead of Siberia, I'd rather go to Palestine,' the holy sister suddenly announced. 'I have always dreamed of a pilgrimage to the Holy Land.'

The men liked this unexpected idea. 'Yes indeed!' Matvei Bentsionovich exclaimed: 'Abroad is the safest place.'

'And it is educational,' the Bishop declared with a nod. 'I, too, have dreamed of it all my life, but there has never been enough time. And I am a member of the Palestine Society. Go, my daughter. You will find it dreary in the hermitage – I know your restless nature. But there you can travel and gather new impressions. You won't notice the time flying by. I'll write to the father archimandrite at the mission and the mother superior at the Gornensky convent. Travel in Palestine as a pilgrim, live in the convent, while Matvei catches these villains.' And the Bishop sat down that very moment to write the letters of rec-ommendation – on special paper, with the episcopal monogram.

The precautions were thought through in the finest detail.

In the morning Pelagia was taken away in an 'ambulance carriage' – there were many witnesses. When her pupils came running to the hospital, they were told the headmistress was very unwell and orders had been given not to allow anyone in to see her. But that night the nun slipped out through the back door and Berdichevsky drove her more than fifteen versts away from the town, to a small landing stage, where a launch was waiting. The conspirators sailed another five versts away and stopped in the middle of the River.

Half an hour later there hove into view a steamer, aglow with lights, sailing downstream from Zavolzhsk. The lamp on the cutter blinked and the riverboat captain, forewarned by secret telegram, halted his engine – quietly, with no shouting through megaphones and no whistling, in order not to wake the sleeping passengers.

Matvei Benetsionovich helped Pelagia to climb the gang-plank. It was the first time he had seen her, not as a nun but as a lady – in a travelling dress and a hat with a veil. All the time, ever since they left the hospital, he had been tormented by the most outrageous fantasies at the sight of this outfit. He had kept repeating to himself: 'A woman, she is just a woman.' The public prosecutor's soul was all a-tremble with insane hopes.

But Pelagia was preoccupied, her thoughts were soaring somewhere far away.

When they stepped on board the steamer, Berdichevsky's heart was suddenly wrung when he heard a voice saying sadly: Say goodbye. You will never see her again.

'Don't go away . . .' the public prosecutor began, talking con-fused nonsense in his panic. 'I'll be completely . . .' And then he started, struck by an idea that seemed heaven-sent. 'You know, why don't you go to the Angara after all? The Bishop can't go, but I could accompany you. And then I could start on the investigation afterwards. Eh?'

He imagined how the two of them would travel across the whole of Siberia together. He gulped.

'No, I'm going to Palestine,' the traveller muttered, still as preoccupied as ever. 'But I have to be in time. Or they'll kill . . .'

Matvei Bentsionovich didn't really understand the part about 'being in time', but the ending sobered him up. And it made him feel ashamed.

The life of a being dear to him was in danger. And his duty was not to go traipsing across the Siberian expanses with the lady of his heart but to find the villains responsible, and as soon as possible.

'I swear to you that I will find these bandits,' the State Counsellor said in a quiet voice.

'I believe you will,' Pelagia replied affectionately, but once again seemingly with no great interest. 'Only, it seems to me that they aren't bandits, and the stolen money has nothing at all to do with the case . . . But you will work all that out for yourself.'

The captain, who had come to meet his extraordinary passenger in person, hurried them along: 'Madam, we are drifting with the current, and there are shoals to starboard here. We need to start the engine.'

Taking advantage of the fact that Pelagia was not in a habit, but a dress, Berdichevsky kissed her hand – on the strip of skin above the lace glove.

She touched her lips to his forehead and made the sign of the cross over him, then the public prosecutor began walking down the gangplank, looking back every second.

The slim silhouette was first veiled in twilight, and then it merged completely into the darkness.

Pelagia followed the sailor who was carrying her suitcase. The deck was empty, except for some lover of the night air dozing, wrapped in a woollen rug, under the window of the saloon.

When the lady in the hat with the veil walked past, the man in the rug stirred and moved his fingers slightly, producing a dry, unpleasant cracking sound: cra-ack, cra-ack.

PART TWO

Here and There

VII

'Hurry, you're late'

Mysterious and beautiful

Few are granted the good fortune, at their first sight of the Holy Land, to see it as it is in reality – mysterious and beautiful.

Polina Andreevna Lisitsyna was fortunate. The port of Jaffa, Palestine's gateway to the sea, presented itself to her view in the guise, not of a yellowish-grey heap of dust and stones, but of a shiny round Christmas tree decoration – it was like those times in your childhood when you stole up to the doors of the parlour in the middle of the night, to peep in through the crack, and at first you could see nothing, but then suddenly something round shimmered and sparkled in the darkness, and your heart skipped a beat in anticipation of a miracle.

That is exactly how it was with Jaffa.

For all the steamship's puffing and panting and slapping at the water with its wheels, it had failed to reach its destined shore before sunset. Black sky fused with black water and disappointed passengers wandered off dejectedly to pack their things. The only people left on deck were Mrs Lisitsyna and some peasant pilgrims, whose entire baggage consisted of canvas knapsacks, copper kettles and pilgrims' staffs.

But shortly thereafter the doors of darkness opened slightly. First a single solitary light appeared, like a pale star, then another beside it, a third, a fourth, and soon the cliff city came tumbling out on to the sea, a golden apple dappled with paler specks of light.

The peasants went down on their knees and began intoning a prayer. Their foreheads beat so fervently against the deck that Polina Andreevna, who was cherishing the solemnity of the moment, put her hands over her ears. The breeze carried the sweet aroma of oranges from the land.

'Ioppia,' said the traveller, speaking the port's biblical name out loud.

Three thousand years earlier, cedar trees from Phoenicia had been floated to this place to build the temple of Solomon. It was in the midst of these very waves that the Lord had ordered the whale to swallow the obstinate Jonah, and Jonah was in the belly of the whale for three days and three nights.

The steamship slowed down and stopped, its anchor chain clanged and its whistle gave a long-drawn-out blast. The passengers came running out on to the deck, clamouring excitedly in various tongues.

The spell was broken.

In the morning it became clear that the vessel had dropped anchor half a verst from dry land – it could not go any closer because of the shoals. They stood there for half a day without moving, because there was a stiff breeze blowing, but after lunch, as soon as the rough sea calmed down a little, an entire flotilla of boats set out from the shore, oars flailing like grim death. The men sitting in these boats looked terribly like pirates, swarthy-faced, with tattered rags wound round their heads.

The steamer was boarded in the blink of an eye. The pirates scrambled in single file up the gangplank lowered to the surface of the water and scattered in various directions with startling speed. Some grabbed hold of passengers' hands and dragged them to the side, while others ignored the people completely and deftly swung the bundles and suitcases up on to their shoulders.

The navigator Prokofii Sergeevich, whom Lisitsyna had befriended during the voyage, explained that this was how things were done in Jaffa. Two clans of Arab porters held a monopoly on unloading ships: one of them dealt with the people and the other dealt the baggage, a division that was strictly observed.

The women pilgrims, seized round the waist by muscular arms, squealed desperately and some even tried to struggle, pummelling insolent fellows with considerable force, but the porters were accustomed to this and merely grinned.

In less than two minutes the first long boat, crammed full of astounded pilgrims, pushed off from the side and was immediately followed by a skiff loaded with bundles, teapots and staffs. The second boat was filled just as quickly.

Then a hot, sweaty aboriginal came running up to Polina Andreevna and grabbed hold of her waist.

'Thank you, I can . . .'

She never finished the phrase. The intrepid fellow man playfully flung her over his shoulder and went trotting down the gangplank. Lisitsyna could only gasp. Down below her the water swayed and glittered, the porter's hands were rough and at the same time astonishingly gentle, so that she was obliged to suppress an agreeable inner stirring that was distinctly sinful.

A quarter of an hour later the pilgrim from Zavolzhsk set foot on the land of Palestine and began fluttering her arms about in an attempt to keep her balance – in two weeks at sea she had become unaccustomed to solid ground.

She put her hand over her eyes to shield them from the blinding sun. She looked around.

Foul and fetid

What an awful place this was!

Of course, small Russian towns could also be really awful – squalid and dirty with the poverty on every side enough to make you feel sick, but at least there the puddles reflected the sky, there were green trees soaring up over the sagging roofs, and in late May the air was scented with bird-cherry blossom. And it was so quiet! Close your eyes, and there was nothing but the rustling of the leaves, the buzzing of the bees and the chiming of bells from the church near by.

But in Jaffa every single sense organ brought the female pilgrim nothing but distress.

Her eyes – because whichever way they looked they encountered heaps of decaying refuse, piles of fish offal, tattered and dishevelled rags that were anything but picturesque – and besides that the dust made them water and they kept screwing themselves up against the unbearably bright sun.

Her tongue – because the ubiquitous dust instantly began grating between her teeth, and her mouth felt as if it was packed full of emery paper.

Her nose – because the aroma of oranges that Polina Andre-evna had recently found so alluring proved to be an absolute chimera; either she had completely imagined it, or it was quite unable to compete with the vapours of putrefaction and excrement that assaulted her from all sides.

We hardly need mention her ears. Nobody in the port made conversation; they all yelled, and at the top of their voice. The multitudinous choir was led by the asses and camels, and drifting above this overwhelming cacophony was the despairing baritone of the muezzin, who had apparently abandoned all hope of reminding this Babylon of the existence of God.

The sense that caused Polina Andreevna the greatest aggra-vation of all was touch, for from the moment she had passed through the Turkish customs, the nun in lady's clothes was grabbed at by beggars, hotel agents and cab-drivers, and it was quite impossible to tell who was who.

A wretched little Russian town is like a consumptive drunkard: you would like to give him a kopeck and sigh over his lamentable fate; but to Polina Andreevna, Jaffa seemed like a man possessed by demons or a leper, against whom your only defence is to close your eyes tight and run as fast as your legs will carry you.

Gathering her courage, Mrs Lisitsyna told herself strictly: A nun should not run away, even from a leper. In order to distract herself from the terrible filth and the stench, she directed her glance higher, at the yellow walls of the city's buildings, but they also failed to offer her eyes any comfort. The anonymous builders of these unassuming structures had clearly not suffered from any vain aspiration to make their mark on posterity.

Polina-Pelagia picked up her suitcase and squeezed her trav-elling bag under her arm, then made her way through the crush towards a narrow little terraced lane – there, at least, it would be possible to find shade and decide how to proceed.

However, she never left the square.

An unshaven little man, wearing a small waistcoat and trou-sers in combination with a Turkish fez and Arab slippers, jabbed one finger at her triumphantly:

'Ir zend a idishke!* Come quick, I'll take you to an excellent

* Yiddish: 'You are a Jew.'

kosher hotel! You'll feel just like at home with momma!'

'I am Russian.'

'A-ah,' the unshaven man drawled. 'Then you should go to that man over there.'

Polina Andreevna glanced in the direction indicated and cried out in joy at the sight of a respectable-looking gentleman in dark glasses sitting on a folding chair under a large canvas parasol; in one hand he was holding a placard bearing a message in delightfully familiar decorative Slavonic script:

The Imperial Palestinian Society
Travel tickets and advice
for those travelling to the Sepulchre of our Lord

Pelagia dashed towards him as if he were her own brother.

'Tell me, how can I get to Jerusalem?'

'There are various ways,' the representative of the venerable society responded solemnly. 'One can go by railroad for three roubles and fifty kopecks: in only four hours, one is at the gates of the Old City. Today's train has already gone, tomorrow's departs at three in the afternoon. One can go on an eight-seater diligence, for one rouble and seventy-five kopecks. It departs tomorrow at noon, and one arrives in the Holy City that night.'

The pilgrim hesitated. Travel across the Holy Land in a diligence? Or, even worse, on the railway? It wasn't right somehow – as if you were going to Kazan or Samara on some kind of business trip.

Her glance fell on a group of Russian pilgrims gathered at the edge of the square. They knelt down for a while, kissing the dusty roadway, then moved forward, swinging their staffs energetically. But not all of them got to their feet. Two little peasants tied broad birch-bark sandals to their knees and shuffled off, rustling smartly up the incline of the street.

'They're going to scramble all the way to Jerusalem like that,' the society's representative said with a sigh. 'Have you thought which ticket you would like?'

'Probably for the diligence,' Polina Andreevna replied uncertainly, thinking that a journey by steam locomotive would finally destroy her feeling of reverence, which had already been thoroughly undermined by the appearance of the port of Jaffa. At that precise moment someone tugged on her skirt.

Looking round, she saw a rather pleasant-looking man with a swarthy complexion. He was wearing a long Arab shirt and there was a polished watch chain dangling from his broad belt. This native gentleman smiled with a bright flash of white teeth and whispered: 'Why diligence? Diligence not good. I have *hantur*. You know *hantur*? Like carriage, tent on top. You ride like Sultan Abdul-Hamid. Horses – ai-ai, such horses. Arab, you know Arab horses? Where you want, we stop, you look, you pray. I show you everything, tell you everything. Five roubles.'

'How do you know Russian?' Pelagia asked, also whispering for some reason.

'My wife Russian. Clever, beautiful, like all Russians. I also have Russian faith. My name Salakh.'

'Is Salakh really a Christian name?'

'Is most Christian name.' To prove his point the Arab crossed himself with three fingers in the Russian style and mumbled rapidly: 'Ourfathwhoartneaven.'

This was a miraculous sign! To meet an Orthodox Christian only a few minutes after arriving in the Holy Land, and one who was a Russian-speaking Palestinian! How many useful things she could learn from him! And then, riding in your own carriage, with good horses, was not like travelling in a public diligence.

'Let's go!' Polina Andreevna exclaimed, although the kind navigator on the steamer had warned her most strictly that in Palestine it was not usual to accept the price offered, the done thing was to haggle for a long time over everything. But what point was there in bargaining over an extra rouble, when you were on your way to the Most Holy City of Jerusalem?

'We go tomorrow.' Salakh picked up his future passenger's suitcase and gestured with his other hand for her to follow him. 'Today can't go. Too late to get there before night, and night bad, bandits. We go walk now, you spend night at good place, my aunt's house. One rouble, only one rouble. And in morning we fly like bird. Arab horses.'

Pelagia could hardly keep up with her long-legged guide as he led her through a maze of narrow lanes that climbed ever higher.

'So your wife is Russian?'

Salakh nodded. 'Natasha. Her name Marusya. We live Jeru-salem.'

'What?' she asked in surprise. 'Is she Natasha or Marusya?'

'My Natasha called Marusya,' the native gentleman replied mysteriously, at which point the conversation came to a sudden end, because the ascent of the hump-backed little street had left the lady pilgrim quite out of breath.

The 'good place' to which Polina Andreevna's guide had brought her proved to be a wattle-and-daub house, in which the guest was allotted a bare room with absolutely no furniture. Salakh took his leave of her, explaining that there were no men in the house, and therefore he could not spend the night there – he said he would call for her the following morning.

The traveller had to sleep on a slim, scanty mattress and wash in a basin, and the part of a water closet was played by a copper receptacle very similar to Aladdin's lamp.

Spiritual reverence, being a fragile and ephemeral substance, failed to survive these annoying inconveniences – it shrivelled away, leaving behind a mere sprinkling of ash, like an old fire-brand in a dead campfire. The nun tried to read the Bible, in order to rekindle the magical spark, but she was unsuccessful. No doubt her worldly attire was the problem. It was far easier to maintain a thrill of beatific trepidation in a nun's habit.

And when she glanced into the mirror while she was washing, she was really upset. Would you believe it! Freckles had sprung up on the bridge of her nose and her cheeks – a distressing circumstance for any woman, but altogether unseemly for an individual of the spiritual calling. She thought they had been obliterated completely through the use of camomile milk and honey masks!

The desert of all deserts

All night long the unfortunate Mrs Lisitsyna tossed about on her hard bed and early in the morning, following a perfunctory wash, she took up a position beside the gate in anticipation of the imminent arrival of her driver.

An hour went by, then a second, and a third. Still no Salakh.

The sun began to scorch, and Polina Andreevna could positively feel those accursed freckles growing darker and denser.

The appearance of the Orthodox local gentleman no longer seemed like a 'miraculous sign', more like some kind of cunning trick devised by the Evil One to postpone the pilgrim's arrival in the City of God. While the nun wondered whether to carry on waiting or go back to the port, the hour of noon passed, which meant that the Jerusalem diligence had already been missed.

Afraid that she might also miss the three o'clock train, Pelagia at long last set off in the direction of the sea, but she halted at the very first crossroads. Which way should she turn, to the right or the left? And at that precise moment there appeared from round the corner a ramshackle cart with immense wheels and a piece of faded canvas hung over it as protection against the sun. The deceiver Salakh was perched at the front, lazily flicking his whip across the backs of two bony little horses.

'My *hantur*,' he said, proudly indicating his disgraceful vehicle. 'My horses.'

'Arabian?' asked Polina Andreevna, unable to resist the temptation of sarcasm as she resentfully recalled the previous day's dreams of slim-legged thoroughbreds who would carry her off over the mountains and through the valleys to the most important city in all of God's world.

'Naturally, Arab,' the swindler confirmed, tying on her suitcase. 'All horses here Arab. Apart from Jewish ones. Jewish a little better.'

But that was not the sum total of Salakh's villainy.

The cart turned into the centre of Jaffa and stopped in front of the Hotel Europe (apparently there was such an institution here – there had been absolutely no need to spend the night on the floor!). Mrs Lisitsyna had to make room for an American couple, husband and wife, to take their places on the bench. They turned out not to be pilgrims, but tourists, travelling through the Holy Land, equipped with every state-of-the-art convenience that Cook's travel agency could offer. The bountiful baggage of these citizens of the New World was piled on to a dirty, undernourished camel.

'I paid five roubles!' Polina Andreevna hissed at Salakh. 'It's not fair!'

'You think, plenty of space, more fun together,' the native son of Palestine replied blithely, attaching the bridle of his hump-backed trailer to the back of his rattling junk heap. 'Mister, missus, we go Jerusalem!

'Gorgeous!' the 'missus' exclaimed in response to this announcement, and the caravan set off.

To register her protest the nun pretended not to understand English, and she covered her face with her head scarf, but the Americans had no great need of conversation partners. They were full of energy, they were exuberant and delighted by everything, they clicked away with their little cameras, and their lips pronounced the word 'gorgeous' at least twice a minute.

When the cart reached an open space bisected by a main highway that ran off and away over the horizon, the tourists (evidently following advice from Cook's) put on green spectacles, which was a far from stupid thing to do, as Polina Andreevna soon realised. Firstly, the glasses cut out the dazzling brilliance of the sun, and secondly, the colour of the lenses must surely have compensated for the total lack of green tones in the landscape.

On all sides there was nothing but rocks and dust. This was the same valley in which Jesus Navin proclaimed, as he pursued the forces of the five Kings of Canaan: 'Halt, sun, above Gavaon, and the moon above the valley of Aialon!' – and the sun stood in the midst of the sky and hastened not to the west for another day.

The tourists demanded a halt at the dried-up stream where David slew Goliath. The husband picked up a stone and pulled a ferocious face: his wife chuckled as she trained the Kodak camera on him.

Vehicles of both European and Asiatic appearance rolled past them, horsemen rode by and pilgrims walked by on foot, almost all of them Russian and looking strangely out of place in this desert landscape. Polina Andreevna thought dejectedly that Salakh's 'Arabian steeds' moved no faster than these stout peasant walkers did on foot.

Several pilgrims gathered at the stream in hopes of finding water. They raked over the dry gravel, but didn't find a single drop.

Pelagia overheard a scrap of their conversation: 'One of ours, from Vyazma, was blessed last year too. On his way back from

Jerusalem, he was, and the bandits attacked him, stabbed him dead. Granted the mercy of surrendering his soul to God in the Holy Land, he was.'

'There's good fortune for you,' the listeners said enviously.

They moved on.

In the distance hills came into view: the Mountains of Judea. When she spotted the ruins of a fortress (it looked as if it must have been built by the Crusaders), the nun shook her head. Why had people been fighting over this wretched, barren land for so many centuries? And was it really worth so much bloodshed?

No doubt in biblical times this plain was not at all like this; rivers of milk and honey flowed through it, there were green fields and ploughed fields on every side. But now this was a cursed, desolate place. As the prophet Ezekiel said: 'And I shall make the land a desert of deserts, and its proud might shall cease and the mountains of Israel shall be empty, so that that none shall pass by, and they shall know that I am the Lord, when I make the land the desert of deserts for all their abominations which they have committed.'

Pelagia's head was filled with thoughts that were quite clearly heretical and inappropriate for a pilgrim. Why was the Old Testament God so cruel? Why was he concerned with only one thing – whether the Jews worshipped him with sufficient fervour? Was it really so important? And why did he change so miraculously in the New Testament? Or was this already a new God, and not the One who admonished Jacob and Moses?

She crossed herself, driving away the blasphemous ideas. In order to distract herself, she began listening to Salakh's banter.

He rattled on almost without a pause. Since his Russian passenger's response to every attempt to strike up a conversation was an austere silence, the driver chose the American couple as his conversation partners. He could express himself just as well in English as in Russian – that is, with mistakes, but briskly and fluently.

Evidently believing that Pelagia did not understand this language, the sly rogue declared that his wife was an American, 'beautiful and clever, like all American women'. Polina Andreevna snorted, but she restrained herself.

While they were crossing the Valley of Aialon, Salakh continually railed at the Jews for giving the local inhabitants no peace, both in ancient times and now. And he also claimed that the Palestinians had always been here and they were the direct descendants of the biblical Canaanites, who had lived here perfectly happily, until a dastardly, cruel tribe that others did not even regard as human had appeared out of the desert. Their Book ordered them to show no mercy to the Canaanites and to exterminate them completely. And so they had exterminated them in ancient times and were still doing it even now.

Pelagia found all this quite interesting. The newspapers wrote that the indigenous population of Palestine was galled by the influx of Jews, who were settling in the Promised Land in ever greater numbers, and that the wild Arabs were plundering and oppressing the peaceful settlers. It was interesting to hear the opposite point of view.

They had lived for almost two thousand years without them, and lived very well, Salakh complained. And now they had appeared again. So meek and mild, so pitiful. We accepted them in peace. We taught them how to cultivate the land, how to escape from the heat and the cold. And now what? They had multiplied like mice and were bribing the Turks with their European money. Now the Jews had all the best land and our fellahs were labouring for them for a piece of bread. The Jews wouldn't be happy until they drove us out of our motherland, because for them we were not human. That was what it said in their books. They had cruel books, not like our Koran, which called on us to be charitable to infidels.

The Americans listened to these lamentations without paying too much attention, distracted every now and then by the sights ('Look, honey, isn't it gorgeous!'). But at last Pelagia could stand it no more:

'*Our* Koran?' she repeated with venom in her voice. 'Who lied and claimed to be Orthodox?'

'And who lied, claim not understand English?' Salakh parried.

Polina Andreevna fell silent and did not open her mouth again until that evening.

They moved even more slowly across the mountains – mostly because of the camel, who got stuck at the side of the road beside every thistle that had managed to break through the dead soil. They only began moving noticeably faster after the vile animal took an interest in the flowers on Polina Andreevna's hat. It was not very pleasant to feel the hot, damp breath of the cloven-hoofed beast on the nape of her neck, and once a gob of sticky saliva fell inside her collar; but the nun tolerated this harassment, offering up her suffering and only occasionally pushing the thick-lipped face away with her elbow.

They spent the night in the Arab settlement of Bab al-Vad, at the house of Salakh's uncle. That night was even more painful than the previous one. The room allocated to Mrs Lisitsyna had an earth floor, and for a long time she could not bring herself to lie on it for fear of fleas. She was also unable to make use of the 'Aladdin's lamp', because there were two women with blue tattoos on their cheeks stationed at the door, with a young girl who had numerous silver coins plaited into her dirty hair. They squatted there, examining the guest and exchanging comments. The girl soon fell asleep, curled up into a tight ball, but the Arab matrons carried on staring at the red-haired foreign woman until it was almost dawn.

The next day it emerged that the Americans had spent a perfectly wonderful night – on the advice of the ubiquitous Cook's agency, they had hung hammocks in the garden and slept quite gorgeously.

The exhausted Pelagia rattled and bounced along in the *hantur*, occasionally falling into a doze. Constantly jerked back into wakefulness by the sudden jolting, she gazed around incomprehendingly at the bald tops of the hills, then began nodding off again. She gave her hat to the camel so that it would leave her alone and covered her head with a gauze scarf.

Then suddenly, somewhere on the boundary between waking and sleeping, a clear voice declared sadly: 'Hurry, you're late.'

Polina Andreevna's heart was pierced by a strange anxiety. She started. The heavy veil of sleep evaporated without trace, her brain woke up.

'What am I doing, have I completely lost my mind?' Pelagia asked herself. 'I'm nothing but another tourist – the railway wasn't good enough for me. And one day has been completely wasted. What unforgivable, criminal stupidity!' She had to hurry! She must get to Jerusalem soon!

She lifted her head, shook the final remnants of sleep off her eyelashes and saw a city floating in the mist in the distance.

The Heavenly City

There it is, Jerusalem, Pelagia realised, and sat up on the bench. Her hand flew up to her throat, as if she were afraid that her breathing might stop.

The dust and the heat were forgotten, and so was the mysterious voice out of nowhere that had roused the pilgrim from her drowsy stupor.

Salakh explained in two languages that he had deliberately turned off the high road to show them Jerusalem at its most beautiful; the Americans squealed something or other; the horses flicked their ears; the camel crunched the final remnants of the hat, and Pelagia gazed, spellbound, at the city shimmering in the mist, and the lines from 'Revelation' surfaced in her memory of their own accord:

And I, John, did see the holy city of Jerusalem, renewed, descending from God in his heaven, prepared as a bride decked out for her husband. It had twenty gates, and on them twenty Angels. The foundations of the wall of the city were decorated with all manner of precious stones: the first foundation was jasper, the second sapphire, the third chalcydon, the fourth emerald, the fifth sardonyx, the sixth carnelian, the seventh chrysolite, the eighth beryl, the ninth topaz, the tenth crysoprase, the eleventh hyacinth, the twelfth amethyst. And the twelve gates were twelve pearls: each gate made of one pearl. The street of the city was paved with gold like transparent glass.

In the older language the final phrase sounded even more beautiful: 'And streets of the city were of gold most pure, most bright like unto glass.'

There it was, the most important place on earth. And it was right that the road to it was so hard and exhausting. The right to this vision had to be earned, for the light only shines brightly for eyes weary of the darkness.

The nun got down on to the ground, kneeled and recited the joyful psalm: 'Praise the Lord, O my soul, and let all that is within me praise His holy name,' but she concluded the prayer oddly, not in the canonical fashion: 'And teach me, Lord, to do what must be done.'

The *hantur* set off again towards Jerusalem, and the city first disappeared behind the next hill, and then reappeared, this time without any mist and bearing no resemblance whatever to a heavenly city.

The dreary streets followed one after the other, lined with single-storey and two-storey houses. This was not even the East, but some kind of backwater of Europe, and if not for the Arab script on the signs and the fezzes on the heads of the passers-by, it would have been easy to imagine that you were somewhere in Galicia or Roumania.

Polina Andreevna felt quite distraught at the sight of the Jaffa Gate. What on earth was this? Fiacres, the London Credit Bank, a French restaurant and even – horror of horrors – a newspaper kiosk!

The American couple got out in front of the Lloyd Hotel and handed over the camel to a doorman in red livery. Mrs Lisitsyna was now the only passenger in the *hantur*.

'Is the Sepulchre of our Lord there?!', she asked in a tremulous voice, pointing to the wall topped by battlements.

'There, but we not go there. Since you Russian, you need Migrash a-rusim, Russian church centre,' said Salakh, waving his hand vaguely to the left.

The wagon set off along the fortress wall, and a few minutes later the traveller found herself in a small square that seemed to have been transported there directly from Moscow at the wave of some magic wand. Following the torments of the mountains and the deserts, the nun's gaze delighted in the domes of an Orthodox Christian church, unmistakably Russian administrative buildings, and signs with inscriptions in Russian: 'Bakery', 'Hot Water Plant', 'Public Dining Hall', 'Lodging House for Female Pilgrims', 'St Sergius Conventuary'.

'Goodbye, madam,' Salakh said with a bow, suddenly very polite at their parting – no doubt since he was hoping for baksheesh. 'Everyone here ours, Russian. You want go back to Jaffa or like go somewhere else, come Damascus Gate, ask Salakh. Everyone there know me.'

Polina Andreevna didn't give him any baksheesh – he didn't

deserve any – but she bade him a friendly farewell. He was a trickster, of course, but he had got her there.

For the convenience of the pilgrims there was an employee of the pilgrim reception committee sitting here under a parasol in the most conspicuous spot, exactly as in the port of Jaffa. He explained the local customs, answered questions and recommended lodgings to people according to their status and means: for those who were poor, bed and board cost only thirteen kopecks, but it was possible to be accommodated in comfort for four roubles.

'How can I see the father archimandrite?' Polina Andreevna asked. 'I have a letter for him from His Eminence Mitrofanii, the Bishop of Zavolzhsk.'

'His Reverence is away at the moment,' replied the attendant, a benign old man in iron-rimmed spectacles. 'He has gone to Hevron to look for a site for a school. But you take a rest while you wait, madam. We have our own bathhouse, it even has a section for nobility. Good laundresses to wash your linen. And you can confess after the journey. There isn't enough room in the church, so the father archimandrite has blessed the hearing of confessions in tents in the garden, like in the early Christian times.' And indeed, there were four tents crowned with golden crosses standing under the trees at the edge of the square, with a queue leading to each one: one long queue, two moderate queues, and only two people waiting in front of the fourth tent.

'Why are the queues so uneven?' Pelagia enquired curiously.

'Well that, if you please, reflects what people want. They are keenest of all to see Father Iannuarii. But not many are brave enough to go over to the other side, to Father Agapit. He is a harsh and rather intemperate character. I am so sorry, dear madam,' the old man said with a shrug, 'but a confessional is not a hotel, it has no first and second class. All are equal before God. So if you wish to see Father Iannuarii, you will have to wait with the simple folk – that's four hours in the hot sun, at the very least. Some gentlemen, it is true, hire someone to stand there for them, but that, God knows, is a sin.'

'It's all right, I can confess later,' Polina Andreevna replied frivolously. 'When the heat dies down a bit. But meanwhile, please find me lodgings.'

Just then she heard a shout from the confessional that was least popular with the pilgrims (it was the one closest to the square). The canvas walls of the tent swayed and a swarthy-skinned gentleman in spectacles came flying out, almost measuring his full length on the grass. He appeared to have been flung out of the tabernacle of the mystery by the scruff of his neck, as they say.

With an effort, he managed to stay on his feet and stared back at the entrance to the tent, from out of which a hirsute priest, crimson-faced from rage, emerged and howled: 'You get off back to your Moshes! Back to the Rov Ga-Iuda! The Jews can take your confession!'

'There now, you see!' the old attendant for the reception of pilgrims exclaimed in a pained voice. 'He's at it again!'

'But what is the "Rov Ga-Iuda?"' Polina Andreevna asked quickly, gazing at the menacing Father Agapit very attentively.

'The Jewish quarter in the Old City. Inside the wall over there, there are four quarters . . .'

But Pelagia was no longer listening – she had taken several steps towards the garden, as if she were afraid of missing a single word in the escalating squabble.

Having recovered from the initial shock, the swarthy gentleman also began shouting: 'How dare you! I am a baptised Christian! I shall complain about you to the father archimandrite!'

'"Baptised"!' the confessor exclaimed mockingly and spat. 'As the people say: "A Yid's like a devil: he'll never repent!" And another thing they say is: "Baptise a Jew, then push him under the ice!" A Christian, pah! Pah! Begone!' And he made the sign of the cross over the man in spectacles, as furiously as if he were trying to strike him with his bunched fingers, first on the forehead and then in the bottom of his stomach, adding final blows to the right and left collar bones. The rejected supplicant staggered back to avoid these threatening gestures and soon fled from the field of battle, muttering to himself and sobbing.

This scene made a serious impression on the two pilgrims waiting their turn to confess to Father Agapit. They retreated in rapid order, one joining the queue to Father Martirii and the other joining the queue to Father Kornilii.

'Wait!' the old man called to Polina Andreevna. 'I'll tell you how to find the hotel for female pilgrims of noble blood.'

'Thank you. But, you know, I think I'll confess first after all,' Pelagia replied. 'There isn't any queue just now.'

A false brachycephalic

When the female pilgrim pronounced the formula: 'I confess all my sins to the Lord and to you, Father,' the priest suddenly asked: 'Why is your hair so ginger?'

Polina Andreevna was so surprised by the question that she opened her mouth disrespectfully.

Father Agapit knitted his brows: 'You wouldn't happen to be a baptised Jew, would you?'

'No,' said the woman who had come to repent of her sins. 'On my word of honour!'

But the priest was not satisfied with a 'word of honour'. 'Maybe your father was a Cantonist? Do you have any Jewish blood at all, on your father's or your mother's side? You don't get red hair without a touch of the Yid.'

'Oh no, Father, I'm completely Russian. Except for my great-grandfather . . .'

'A Yid, was he?' the confessor asked, screwing up his eyes. 'Aha! I have good eye!'

'No, he came from England, a hundred years ago. But he married a Russian woman and accepted the Orthodox faith. But why are you asking so many questions?'

'Ah-ah, then that's a different matter,' said Father Agapit, reassured. 'It's all right if he came from England. He must have been from Irish stock. That's all right. Red hair comes from two sources: the Celts and the Jews. I questioned you like that so I wouldn't commit a blunder and defile the mystery of the confession. There are lots of Jews and half-Jews nowadays trying to squirm their way into the Orthodox faith. A Yid's lousy enough anyway, but a baptised Yid's twice as bad.'

'Is that why you threw that gentleman out?'

'It's written all over his ugly mug that he's a kike. I tell you, I've got an eye for it. They can burn me at the stake, but I won't stand for any blasphemy!'

Pelagia assumed an expression of total sympathy with such self-sacrificing determination, but out loud she remarked:

'However, our Church does welcome new converts, including those from the Jewish faith . . .'

'Not the Church, not the Church, but the fools in the Church! They'll weep for it some day, but it will be too late. Letting a black sheep into a flock of white ones is either plain stupidity or the prompting of the devil.'

The priest went on to elucidate this not entirely clear allegory. 'There are white sheep, that graze on the slopes of heaven, close to the gaze of the Lord God. And there are black sheep; their pastures are the lowlands of the earth, where the thorns and the tares grow. The white sheep are the Christians, the black ones are the Jews. Let the Yids eat their prickles, just as long as they don't try to join our flock and spoil the whiteness of the fleece. It was said at the Sixth Ecumenical Council: Go not to a Yid for healing, do not wash with him in the bathhouse, do not take him for your friend. And we are God's sheepdogs; the reason we exist is to make sure that God's flock doesn't mingle with the mangy sheep. If a sheep from another flock creeps across to our pasture, we sink our fangs in its legs and give it a good hiding, to teach the rest of them a lesson.'

'And what if it's the other way round?' Pelagia asked with an innocent air. 'If someone wants to move from the white flock to the black one? There are some people who reject Christianity and accept Judaism. For instance, I've heard talk about the sect of the "foundlings" . . .'

'Traitors to Christ!' Father Agapit thundered. 'And that leader of theirs, Manuila, is a devil sent from the depths of hell to kill the Son of Man for a second time! That Manuila ought to be set in the ground with an aspen stake stuck through him!'

Polina Andreevna's voice became even quieter and more velvety. 'Father, I've also heard that this bad man supposedly set out to come to the Holy Land . . .'

'He's here, here! He has come to mock and sneer at the Sepulchre of Our Lord. He was seen at Easter, confusing the pilgrims with his seductive blandishments, and he seduced some! Even the Jews wanted to stone him, even they were nauseated by him! He ran off and hid, the snake. Oh, I wish the brothers would come here!'

'Do you have brothers?' the pilgrim asked naively.

Agapit smiled menacingly. 'Yes, I do. And many of them. Not

blood brothers – soul brothers. Knights of the Orthodox faith, God's defenders. Have you heard of the Oprichniks of Christ?'

Polina Andreevna smiled, as if the priest had said something extremely agreeable. 'Yes, I read about those people in the newspapers. Some said good things about them, and others said bad things. They called them bandits and thugs.'

'Lies from the Yids and Yid-lovers! Ah, if only you knew, my daughter, how cruelly I am oppressed here!' Father Agapit complained. 'It's all fine and well for our lads in Russia, it's our own earth, it warms them from below, and they have the faithful brotherhood at their side. We are strong there. But to be alone in foreign parts is a hard and bitter lot.'

This confession agitated the tender-hearted pilgrim terribly. 'What?' she exclaimed in concern. 'Do you really not have any fellow thinkers here, in the Holy Land? Then who will protect the white sheep from the black? Where are these "Oprichniks" of yours?'

'They're where they ought to be, in Mother Russia. In Moscow, Kiev, Poltava, Zhitomir.'

'In Zhitomir?' Polina Andreevna asked, very interested.

'Yes, the Zhitomir group are faithful knights, militant. They give the Yids no quarter, and they keep an even keener eye on the Yid-lovers. If that Manuila started stirring things up in Zhitomir, or that weasel-face I just flung out of here dared to threaten me, a member of the clergy, their souls would soon be parting company with their bodies!'

The memory of the recent confrontation roused Father Agapit's temper again. 'He'll complain about me to the archimandrite! And won't that tyrant be only too delighted! Our Reverence is possessed by the demon of universal tolerance, I'm like a bone stuck in his throat. They drive me out of here, Sister,' the zealot of pure faith complained bitterly. 'I don't suit them, I'm too intransigent. The next time you come to confess, I won't be here.'

'So you're entirely alone here?' Polina Andreevna murmured in disappointment and then added, apparently to herself: 'Oh, that's no good, no good at all.'

'What's "no good"?' the priest asked in surprise.

At this point the pilgrim wiped all trace of sweetness from her face and gazed fixedly at Father Agapit, feeling as she did so a quite unchristian desire to say something unpleasant to this horrible man – something that would really cut him to the quick. It's all right, I can do that, she thought, giving way to temptation. If I was in my habit, it would be wicked, but in a dress it's permissible.

'You wouldn't happen to have Jewish blood yourself, would you?' Polina Andreevna asked.

'What?'

'You know, Father, at university I attended lectures on anthropology. I can tell you for certain that your mother, or perhaps your grandmother, sinned with a Jew. Take a look in the mirror: your eyes are close-set – an obviously Semitic feature. Your nose is gristly, and your hair has a certain slight curl to it, the ears are typical too and – most importantly of all – the shape of the skull is absolutely brachycephalic . . .'

'Absolutely what?' Father Agapit exclaimed in horror, clutching at his head (which, to be quite precise, was more of the dolichocephalic type).

'No, I don't think so,' said Pelagia, shaking her head. 'I don't want to risk confessing to a Jew. I think I'll go and stand in Father Iannuarii's queue.' And so saying she walked out of the tent, feeling very pleased with herself.

As it happened, there was one other pilgrim waiting outside the tent: a peasant in a large felt cap, with a thick beard that grew almost right up to his eyes.

'You'd better go to the other priests,' Mrs Lisitsyna advised him. 'Father Agapit is not feeling well.'

The peasant didn't reply, in fact he turned away – evidently he didn't want to defile himself by looking at a woman just before confession.

But when the female pilgrim set off, he actually looked round and watched her walk away. And he purred quietly to himself:

'Come on now, come on now . . .'

VIII

The Oprichniks of Christ

Something gets into Berdichevsky

Matvei Bentsionovich was quite unrecognisable, he was such a changed man – or so said all his subordinates, and his acquaintances, and his family.

What had happened to that customary mild manner, that way of becoming embarrassed so easily over the slightest trifle? That habit of looking to one side when he spoke to you? of mumbling and peppering his speech with parasitical phrases, all sorts of 'you knows', 'with your permissions' and 'to tell the truths'? And finally, that laughable habit of grabbing hold of his long nose when he was in the slightest difficulty and twisting it as if it were a screw or a bolt?

Berdichevsky's thick-lipped and rather weak mouth was now permanently set in a tight line; his brown eyes had acquired the gleam of molten steel, and turned partly orange, and his speech had acquired briskness and brevity. In short, this most agreeable and cultured of men had been transformed into the perfect public prosecutor.

The first to experience the transformation undergone by the State Counsellor were his subordinates.

On the morning following Sister Pelagia's evacuation, their boss had arrived at work at first light, stationed himself in the doorway, watch in hand, and severely rebuked every individual who turned up at the office later than the prescribed time, which had hitherto been regarded by everyone, including the district public prosecutor himself, as a rather arbitrary abstraction. Then one by one Matvei Bentsionovich had summoned the employees attached to the investigative section and given each of them an assignment, which in itself seemed perfectly clear but was rather vague as far as the overall goal was concerned. Previously the public prosecutor had been in the habit of gathering everyone together and holding forth at length about the strategy and overall picture of an investigation, but this time no explanations were given, the implication being: Be so good as to do as you are ordered and not to discuss the matter. The officials had left their chief's office with intent, sullen expressions, responded to their colleagues' importunate questions with a dismissive wave of the hand – No time, no time – and gone rushing off to carry out their instructions. The public prosecutor's office, hitherto the most impassive of the province's public departments owing to the low level of criminal activity in Zavolzhie, instantly became like the divisional headquarters of some army at the height of manoeuvres: the officials no longer crept about like flies but scuttled around like cockroaches, the doors no longer closed with a discreet 'click-click', but with a deafening crash, and there was now almost always an impatient queue for the telegraph apparatus.

The next victim of Berdichevsky's newly acquired ferocity was the Governor himself, Anton Antonovich von Haggenau. Following the public prosecutor's sudden transformation, he completely stopped visiting the Nobles' Club, where he had formerly delighted in sitting for an hour or two and analysing games of chess, but he did not dare to neglect the traditional Tuesday game of preference with the baron. He sat there, unusually taciturn, glancing all the time at his watch. However, when he was playing as His Excellency's partner against the head of the chamber of commerce, the Governor committed a blunder by covering the public prosecutor's queen with a king. The old Matvei Bentsionovich would simply have said: 'Never mind, it's my fault for confusing you,' but this unrecognisable individual dashed his cards down on the table and called Anton Antonovich a 'muddle-head'. The Governor fluttered his white Teutonic eyelashes and looked round plaintively at his wife, Ludmila Platonovna.

She had already heard the alarming rumours from the public prosecutor's office, and so now she decided she would waste no more time, but pay a visit to the prosecutor's wife, Marya Gavrilovna, straight away.

She paid the visit and enquired cautiously, over coffee, if

Matvei Bentsionovich was well and whether his character might not be adversely affected by the approach of his fortieth birthday, a frontier that many men find very difficult to cross.

He had changed, the public prosecutor's wife complained. Something seemed to have got into her Motya – he had become irritable, he hardly ate a thing and he ground his teeth in his sleep. Marya Gavrilovna immediately moved on to issues of more immediate concern: her Kiriusha had chronic diarrhoea, and Sonechka was sickening with something. God grant that it wasn't measles.

'When my Antosha reached forty, he went a bit odd as well,' said Ludmilla Platonovna, returning to the subject of husbands. 'He gave up smoking his pipe and started rubbing tincture of garlic into his bald patch. But after a year he settled down and moved on to the next stage in life. And everything will be all right for you too, my darling. You just treat him gently, with understanding.'

After her visitor had left, Marya Gavrilovna thought for another ten minutes or so about the sudden misfortune that her husband had suffered. Eventually she decided to bake his favourite poppy-seed roll and leave the rest to the will of the All-Mighty.

In the entire town of Zavolzhsk, Mitrofanii was the only one who knew the true reason for the public prosecutor's tense and preoccupied state of mind. Bearing in mind the episode of the boot-print that almost cost Pelagia her life, and also the ubiquitous presence of their unknown enemy, they had agreed between them to maintain the strictest possible secrecy.

The disappearance of the headmistress of the diocesan college was explained by medical reasons: the holy sister had supposedly caught a chill in the kidneys from her insane habit of swimming in icy water and been urgently despatched to the Caucasus to take the waters. The progressive ideologue Svekolkina was running riot in the school, tormenting the poor little girls with decimals and equilateral triangles.

Late in the evening Matvei Bentsionovich would call on Mitrofanii and report in detail about all the measures that had been taken, following which they would open the atlas of the world and try to work out where Pelagia was just at the moment – for some reason this gave both of them inexpressible pleasure. For instance, the Bishop would say: 'She must be sailing past Kerch. You can see both shorelines there, the Crimea and the Caucasus. And beyond the bay the waves are different, real sea waves.' Or: 'She's sailing across the Sea of Marmora. The sun's hot there – she's probably broken out in freckles.' And the Bishop and the public prosecutor would smile dreamily, one of them gazing into the corner of the room, and the other looking up at the ceiling.

Then Berdichevsky disappeared from the town, supposedly summoned by the ministry. He was gone for a week.

When he returned he hurried from the quayside straight to the Bishop, without even going home first.

'Well, what a rogue!'

The moment the door of the study closed behind him, he blurted out: 'She was right. But then, she always is ... No, no, I won't start getting ahead of myself. As you recall, we decided to base our search for the bandits on their initial crime, the theft of Manuila's "treasury". That event marked the beginning of the grim trail. The Warsaw bandits were assumed to have picked out their victim in advance and shadowed him in their usual way, waiting for a convenient moment. I was intending to reconstruct the route followed by the "foundlings" and follow it, searching for witnesses.'

'I remember, I remember all that,' said the Bishop, trying to hurry his spiritual son, since he could tell from the narrator's face that he had not come back empty-handed. 'You were hoping to establish who gave the bandits their ... what do you call it? ...'

'Lead,' Berdichevsky prompted. 'Who pointed them towards the sect's "treasure". And from there to reach the bandits themselves. One of the most important rules of detective work is that the shortest path to the criminal is from the victim's own social circle.'

'Yes, yes! Just get on with it. Did you find the person who did the pointing?'

'There wasn't one! And all this has nothing at all to do with the case! Ah, Your Eminence, don't interrupt, let me tell you everything in the right order ...'

The Bishop threw his hands up apologetically, then put one of them to his lips, as if to say: I won't say a word. And the story finally got under way, although His Eminence was unable to maintain a complete silence – that was simply not in his character.

'Shelukhin and his entourage boarded the steamer at Nizhni, where, as I ascertained, they had arrived by train from Moscow,' the public prosecutor reported. 'The conductor remembered the false Manuila, a rather colourful character for first class. He travelled in his compartment alone, and the other ragamuffins, who had places in the standard open carriage, took turns to visit him. The reason for the first-class compartment is clear enough – to make the whole thing more convincing: Look, there really is a prophet on this train! And it is also clear why there was always someone with Shelukhin – because of the casket . . . The "foundlings" have something like a gathering place in Moscow, a basement in Khitrovka, beside the synagogue. We can assume they deliberately stay as close as possible to their fellow believers, but the genuine Jews won't allow these people in fancy costume into the synagogue and they want nothing to do with them. Manuila's flock prays outside in the street. It's an amusing sight: they cover their heads with the edges of their robes and mutter something in broken Hebrew. The idle onlookers poke fun at them, the Jews spit at them. A real fairground show. You should also bear in mind that most of the "foundlings" are extremely unattractive in appearance. Ugly, damaged by drink, with noses eaten away by syphilis . . . It's curious that the Khitrovka ragamuffins leave these holy fools alone – they pity them. I observed the "foundlings" for a while and spoke to a few of them. Do you know what struck me most of all? They ask for alms, but they don't take money – only things that they can eat. They say they don't need kopecks, because money belongs to the tsar, but food comes from God.'

'You say they don't take money? Then where did the "treasury" come from?'

'That's the whole point! Where was it from? You and I assumed that the contents of the stolen casket were alms collected by the "foundlings". That Manuila had changed all those countless kopecks and half-kopecks for banknotes and put them away neatly in a little box. And then I discover, no – he did nothing of the kind! I was even distracted from the "Warsaw" theory, because I was so curious about where the money had come from. I began enquiring cautiously whether the false Jews had heard anything about Manuila's "treasury". I must say that for the most part they are very open, trusting people – exactly the kind who usually fall victim to scoundrels. They said: We know, we've heard about it. Some merchant in the town of Borovsk gave Manuila "a huge amount of money" for projects in the Holy Land. Naturally, I went to Borovsk and had a word with the merchant.'

'But how did you find him?' Mitrofanii gasped, astounded at the depths of persistence and energy that apparently resided within his spiritual son.

'It wasn't difficult at all. Borovsk is a small town. Wealthy, clean, sober – Old Believers live there. Everyone knows everything about each other. They won't forget the appearance of such an impressive character as the prophet Manuila in a hurry. It happened like this. The Borovsk merchant (his name is Pafnutiev) was sitting in his grocery shop and trading, it was a market day. He was approached by a skinny tramp wearing a loose robe with a belt of blue rope, with tousled hair, no hat, and holding a staff. The tramp asked for bread. Pafnutiev is not fond of beggars and started shaming him, calling him a sponger and a cadger. The other man answered him: I'm a beggar, but you're poor, and being poor is a lot worse than being a beggar. "I'm poor?" Pafnutiev exclaimed, offended because he is known as one of the richest men in Borovsk. Manuila said to him: "Of course you are! You've lived to the age of forty-seven and still not realised that a beggar is far more blessed than a moneybags like you." The merchant was astounded – how did this stranger know how old he was? – and the best he could manage was to babble in reply: "How is he more blessed?" "In spirit," the tramp replied.'

Mitrofanii could not resist snorting at that. 'So Manuila doesn't recognise Christ? But it was very smart the way he slipped in that piece from the Gospel about the blessed in spirit.'

'And it wasn't the only piece like that. The prophet also informed Pafnutiev that the gate leading to God is narrow, not everyone can get through it. You just think, he said, who will get through more easily – a beggar or you? And he slapped his own skinny sides. And Pafnutiev weighs at least eight, if not ten poods, just the way a merchant is supposed to look. Well, everyone there started laughing, the lesson was so clear. Pafnutiev didn't take offence, though. In his own words, he "fell into a rather thoughtful state", closed the shop and took the "strange man" home with him, to talk!'

'There's something I don't understand. He was supposed to be dumb, this Manuila. Or at least inarticulate. I was actually thinking what an original prophet he was – managing without words.'

'He is tremendously articulate. He has some kind of speech defect – he lisps or something of the kind – but that doesn't limit the effect he has. Pafnutiev said: "He explains things unintelligibly, but clearly." Allow me to draw your special attention to the "rather thoughtful state" into which Pafnutiev fell and which made him behave in a manner quite untypical of such a man.'

'Hypnotic abilities?' His Eminence guessed.

'And apparently quite exceptional ones. You remember he cured the little girl of her dumbness? He is a most cunning character and very – how shall I put it? – thorough. Do you know how he got round Pafnutiev when they sat down to drink tea? He told the merchant the entire story of his life, with details that not many people know.'

'Perhaps it was no accident that he approached Pafnutiev at the market!'

Matvei Bentsionovich nodded: 'He had gathered his information, prepared in advance. And certainly not, I make so bold as to assure you, for the sake of a crust of bread. Pafnutiev was unable to tell me what they talked about. He mumbled and clicked his fingers, without adducing anything substantial from what Manuila had said.' The public prosecutor paused for effect. 'The "man of God" tried to persuade the merchant to give all his riches to those in need, for only then could he find true freedom and discover the path to God. A rich man's conscience, Manuila told him, is overgrown with fur, otherwise he could not dine on fine white rolls when others do not have so much as a crust of black bread. "If you become poor, your conscience will be laid bare and the gates of heaven will open. But whether these gates are worth your fancy bread – you must make your own mind up about that."'

'Well then, did his arguments persuade the moneybags?' the Bishop asked with a smile.

Berdichevsky raised one finger as if to say: Listen and you will find out.

'In part. "I was terribly frightened," Pafnutiev told me. 'The Devil got into me, and wouldn't let me give away all my wealth." He had a bundle of "unclean" money in an icon case, behind the icon. As far as I understand it, this is a habit the Borovsk merchants have – if they make a sinful profit by selling rotten goods or cheating someone, they put the dishonest earnings behind an icon, to "purify" them. So that was the money that Pafnutiev gave this opponent of riches – all that he had there. At first Manuila hesitated, he didn't want to take it, said he had no use for it. But in the end, naturally, he took it gladly. He said it would come in useful for the naked and hungry in Palestine. The land there was poor, not like in Russia.'

Matvei Bentsionovich could not resist laughing – the cunning rogue apparently inspired his admiration.

'And now what?' Mitrofanii enquired. 'Does Pafnutiev regret giving away his money? Does he understand that he was duped?'

'Believe it or not, but he doesn't. At the end of our conversation he turned sulky and hung his head. "Ah," he said, "I feel so ashamed. It wasn't Manuila, it was God I tried to buy off with that rag full of banknotes. I should have given away everything I had, and then I would have saved my soul." Ah well, never mind Pafnutiev and his woes. That's not the most important thing here.'

'Then what is?'

'Guess how much money the merchant contributed.'

'How should I know? It must have been quite a lot.'

'One and a half thousand roubles. That's how much there was in the rag.'

Mitrofanii was disappointed. 'Is that all . . .?'

'That's the whole point!' Matvei Bentsionovich exclaimed. 'Why would the Warsaw gangs be interested in going after small change like that, and even committing murder for it? And we can't even be sure that Manuila handed over the entire sum to his "little brother". He probably kept the lion's share for himself. What was it that I said at the beginning? Pelagia was right. It has nothing to do with the casket. It's all to do with Manuila himself. So the robbery theory is eliminated. The people we are looking for are definitely not bandits.'

'But then who are they?'

'But then who are they?' asked Mitrofanii, knitting his brows. 'Who hates Pelagia so badly that they want to bury her alive or poison her?'

'As far as the poisoner is concerned, we know absolutely nothing. But we do know quite a lot about the first attacker. So we shall start with him,' the public prosecutor declared with an assurance which indicated that he had already drawn up a plan of further action. 'What, in your opinion, is the most remarkable thing in Ratsevich's story?'

'The fact that he was a gendarme. And that he was dismissed from the service.'

'I think it is something else: the fact that he managed to pay off his debts. Ratsevich had no funds of his own to do that, otherwise he would never have let the whole business get as far as prison and expulsion from the gendarmes corps. *Ergo*, the money to buy himself out of debtor's prison was given to him by someone else.'

'But who?' His Eminence exclaimed.

'There are two possible explanations, which in some ways are diametrical opposites, mirror images. I find the first extremely unpleasant on a personal level.' Berdichevsky frowned painfully. 'It is possible that the debt was not paid off, but forgiven – by the creditors themselves. And as we know, the staff captain's creditors were Jewish moneylenders.'

'Moneylenders forgive a debt? Why, that's unheard of. Why would they?'

'That's the question. What did Ratsevich do or undertake to do in exchange for his freedom? What would Jews need with a specialist in detective work and violence? Alas, the answer is obvious. The Jews hate the prophet Manuila, they think he insults them and disgraces their faith. You should have seen how frantically they drive the unfortunate "foundlings" away from the synagogue.' Matvei Bentsionovich clearly found it hard to say such things about his own compatriots, but in the interests of the investigation he had to be impartial.

'Ah, Your Eminence, our Jewry, until recently the most placid of all the social communities, has recently been stirred to a state of frenzy. Within its general body the most varied forces and movements have sprung to life, each striving to be more furious and fanatical than the others. The mass of the Jewish people has begun to move, it is prepared to rush to Palestine, or Argentina, or even, God forbid, Uganda (as you know, the English have proposed the establishment of a new Israel there). And the Jews of the Russian Empire have become even more agitated than the rest, because they are oppressed and disenfranchised. The youngest and best educated among them, earnestly seeking to make Russia their genuine homeland, have encountered the hatred and mistrust of the authorities. It is hard, in fact, almost impossible, for a Jew to become a Russian – there is always someone waiting to bring up the saying that a baptised Jew is "a thief forgiven". Or have you heard the joke: When you baptise a Yid, stick his head under the water and hold it there for five minutes? Many who have failed in their efforts to assimilate have become disillusioned with Russia and wish to build their own state in the Holy Land, a kind of earthly paradise. But the building of heaven on earth is a cruel business, it can't be done without blood being spilled. But even I, if I had not had the good fortune to meet you, would most probably have found myself in the camp of the so-called Zionists. They, at least, are people with a sense of their own dignity and purpose, nothing like the old-style Jews in their caftans. But then even the old-style Jews are no longer what they once were. They seem somehow to have sensed that the curse which has hung over Jewry for two thousand years is coming to an end, that the restoration of the Temple in Jerusalem is already nigh. This merely renders the animosity between the various groups and factions all the more bitter – the Lithuanian Jews and the Little Russian Jews, the traditionalists and the reformers. All sorts of Judaeophobic rabble have begun to stir, spreading rumours about ritual killings, secret Sanhedrins and the blood of Christian infants. Of course, there are no ritual killings, and there could not possibly be – what would Jews want with goys and their non-kosher blood? But it's a different matter where their own kind is concerned. We could see bloodshed at any moment. Especially over matters in Palestine. There is something worth dividing up in the Holy Land now. Never before have donations flowed there in such abundance. I beg your pardon for this lecture, Your Eminence, I have only given it in order to paint the full picture. And even more importantly – to justify my decision.'

'Are you going to go to Zhitomir?' the Bishop asked with a shrewd glance.

'Yes. I want to take a look at the staff captain's creditors.'

Mitrofanii thought for a little while and nodded in approval. 'Well, that makes sense. But didn't you say there were two possible explanations?'

The State Counsellor brightened up at that. He evidently liked the second explanation much more than the first.

'We know that the pale of settlement, which includes the Volynsk province, provides the stage for every kind of anti-Semitic organisation, including the most extreme of all, the so-called Oprichniks of Christ. These Jew-haters are not content with pogroms, they will even resort to political assassinations. The Oprichniks must hate the prophet Manuila even more than they hate those who were born Jews – after all, in their terms he is a traitor to the faith and the nation, for he lures Russians away from Orthodoxy into Yiddishness. So I wondered whether it was the Oprichniks who had bought Ratsevich out of jail. What if they had decided to make use of a man whose life the Jews had destroyed?'

'Well now, that's very possible,' Mitrofanii admitted.

'But then it turns out that I have to go to Zhitomir in any case. Whether we proceed on the first explanation or the second one, that is where I must look for the trail!'

'It is dangerous, though,' said the Bishop, alarmed. 'If your reasoning is correct, then these are desperate people – both the first group and the second. If they discover why you have come visiting, they will kill you too.'

'How can they find out?' Matvei Bentsionovich asked with a cunning smile. 'They're not expecting me and they don't know me. And it's not me we should be thinking about, Your Eminence, but *her*.'

The Bishop exclaimed plaintively. 'Ah, how I envy you, Matiusha! You are going to *do* something. And I can't even help in any way. Except by praying.'

'"Except"?' the public prosecutor echoed, shaking his head in mock reproach. 'Such belittling of the power of prayer, and from the lips of a prince of the Church!'

Matvei Bentsionovich stood to be blessed. He was about to kiss the Bishop's hand, but instead he found himself embraced round the shoulders and pressed so tightly against the prelate's broad chest that he could scarcely breathe.

Evidently Berdichevsky really had undergone some fundamental change, less external than internal in nature.

As he prepared to go to Zhitomir, he did not feel in the least concerned about the dangers, whereas the former Matvei Bentsionovich, with his overactive imagination, had frequently quailed in the face of trials of courage that were quite insignificant or sometimes even laughable, such as making a speech at the club or a trivial visit to the dentist. Not fear, but feverish impatience and an inexplicable feeling that *time was wasting* – those were the feelings by which the public prosecutor of Zavolzhsk was possessed as he said goodbye to the members of his family.

He mechanically repeated the sign of the cross over all thirteen children (the five youngest were asleep, since the hour was already late) and kissed his wife perfunctorily.

But then the stern Marya Gavrilovna suddenly did something very odd. She flung her plump arms round Berdichevsky's neck and said in a quiet little voice: 'Matiushka, take care now. You know without you my life means nothing.'

Matvei Bentsionovich was taken aback. In the first place, he had no idea that his wife had any suspicions of that kind. And in the second place, Marya Gavrilovna had always been very sparing when it came to pouring out her soul, in fact, you might say she had never had any time for it.

The public prosecutor blushed and turned awkwardly, then half-walked, half-ran out into the street, where the official carriage was waiting.

A *iddishe kop*, or the 'White-Haired Angel'

The closer he came to Zhitomir, the stronger the strange feeling became. As if Matvei Bentsionovich had got stuck on rails from which it was impossible to turn off or to turn back until you reached the final destination, which it was not for you to choose and the name of which you did not even know.

In addition, here and there along this route that Matvei Bentsionovich was taking for the first time in his life and on which he found himself by pure chance, there were signposts that seemed intended especially for him. As if Providence did not entirely trust the State Counsellor's intellectual abilities and felt it necessary to send him signals: That's right, this is your path, have no doubt.

To begin with, the train on which Berdichevsky travelled from Nizhni Novgorod brought him to the town of Berdichev, where he had to change for the narrow-gauge line to Zhitomir.

And when Matvei Bentsionovich arrived in the capital of the province of Volynsk, it turned out that both of the institutions in which he was interested – the prison committee and the police department – were located on Great Berdichevsky Street.

By this time the public prosecutor was completely in the grip of the mystical feeling that he was not going anywhere, but *being sent*, and so he kept his ears pricked and his eyes wide open to make quite sure that he would not, God forbid, miss some important sign.

And what do you think happened?

At the railway station he happened by chance to overhear a conversation between two Jewish businessmen. They were complaining about how hard it had become to live in the town and what a disaster it was when the chief of police was a Jew-baiter. Until that moment Berdichevsky had been intending to direct his steps in the first instance to the prison committee, for which purpose he had come equipped with a letter from the chancellery of the Governor of Zavolzhsk, but now he made a correction to his initial plan: the Jew-baiting police chief was where he had to begin.

He took a room in the finest hotel, the Bristol, where there was a Mixe-Geneste telephone gleaming on the counter, with a directory of all the numbers in the town, only one page long, proudly displayed alongside it.

A porter with plump lips and a dripping nose carried the new arrival's suitcase up to the counter, where the pompous receptionist sat in state, a gold chain trailed across his belly.

'Just arrived on the train, Naum Solomonovich,' the porter with a cold announced, speaking though his nose. 'I was there in a flash, just like that. Come and stay with us at the Bristol, I told him.'

'Well done, Kolya,' the receptionist praised him. His keen glance took in Matvei Bentsionovich's good-quality coat and rested for a moment on his face. Then he smiled sweetly.

But Berdichevsky was looking at the telephone. The State Counsellor perceived even this attribute of progress as a sign from on high. There it was, the police chief's number: 'No. 3-05, Court Counsellor Gvozdnikov, Sem. Lik.' 'Sem.' was Semyon, but what exactly 'Lik.' stood for was not clear.

Nonetheless, he twirled the handle and asked the young woman to connect him. He was acting on inspiration, not logic.

He stated his name, position and rank and agreed a time to meet, and then put the phone down feeling very pleased with himself – the Zhitomir investigation seemed to be getting off to a lively start.

But then Berdichevsky suffered an unexpected blow. The receptionist, who had already opened the guest book and even dipped the pen in the inkwell, said respectfully: 'Welcome, Your Excellency. What an honour for our establishment. How good to see that a Jew is a man of importance.'

The doorman who was loitering close by (looking precisely as a doorman is supposed to – dressed in livery and with a full beard, but also wearing long side-locks) added:

'Af alle yiden gesucht!'*

'What makes you think that I am a Jew?' Berdichevsky asked, stupefied.

The receptionist merely smiled. 'Glory be to God, this isn't the first year I've spent looking at people.'

'Ah, General, of course, anyone could anyone tell just by

* Yiddish: 'May all Jews do as well.'

looking at you – *a iddishe kop!** the doorman added.

Matvei Bentsionovich cursed his own lack of caution. That very day every Jew in Zhitomir would know about the intriguing new arrival, and naturally things would be exaggerated. He had already become a 'general' and 'Your Excellency', and before evening came he would probably be transformed into a minister.

'Porter!' the public prosecutor called to the man with the runny nose. 'Take my suitcase and call a cab!'

'Ai-ai-ai, have you forgotten something?' the receptionist enquired, flustered.

'Yes, I'm going back to the station,' Berdichevsky snapped, already on his way out. And he heard the receptionist remark loudly in Yiddish to the doorman with the side-locks: 'These baptised Jews are even worse than the Goys.'

The doorman replied in Hebrew, quoting the terrible words of the prophet Isaiah, which Matvei Benetsionovich had often heard in his childhood from his own father: 'Death unto all apostates and sinners, and those who have abandoned the Lord shall be annihilated.'

His mood was completely spoiled.

On the central thoroughfare, Kiev Street, the alarmed public prosecutor called into a *Salon de beaute* and bought the patent American hair dye White-Haired Angel.

He found another hotel – the Versailles (which was not at all like Versailles) and walked into the lobby with his hat down over his eyes and his coat collar turned up.

Once in his room he stood at the sink and began transforming himself into a white-haired angel and he did not forget about his eyebrows. Ah, he ought to have thought of it sooner! This place was the pale of settlement, not God's own city of Zavolzhsk, where they didn't know how to tell a person's nationality from his face so smartly.

The result surpassed all expectations. Matvei Bentsionovich had been a little concerned about his flagrantly non-Slavonic nose, but his new-found blondness even dealt with that; what had been a massive Jewish hook was now a haughty bowsprit,

* Yiddish: 'A Jewish head.'

with an aquiline, even thoroughbred profile to it.

Surveying his transformed features in the mirror, the State Counsellor discerned in them all the signs of aristocratic degeneracy, including even the mournful hollows below the cheekbones and the crooked chin. But then, what was so surprising about that? Every Jew, even the most feeble specimen, had a family tree so long that the Romanovs and the Hapsburgs could well envy it.

To complete his battle paint before he set off on the warpath, Berdichevsky changed into his formal short caftan, with the bright stars of a fifth-rank nobleman gleaming on its shoulder tabs (the Jew-baiter was only a court counsellor – that is, a nobleman of the seventh rank).

He peered at himself from the right and the left and felt perfectly satisfied.

As one nobleman to another

'But permit me to enquire, Mr Berdichevsky, what interest do you, a public prosecutor from a distant province, have in information concerning the Zhitomir branch of the Oprichniks of Christ?' Semyon Likurgovich Gvozdikov asked in a quiet voice. The police chief was a flabby gentleman with puffy cheeks and an unhealthy yellow tinge to the circles under his eyes

Matvei Bentsionovich disliked absolutely everything about this retort: the fact that it had been uttered following a lengthy silence, that it was an answer phrased as a question, and – worst of all – the intonation with which the police chief had pronounced that dubious surname.

'What was that you called me?' the visitor asked with a frown. 'Ber-di-chev-sky? Do I look like some Jewish shopkeeper from Berdichev? *Berg-Dichevsky*,' he rapped out, raising one eyebrow as if he were setting an invisible monocle in his eye socket. 'When my great-grandfather married my great-grandmother, the sole surviving heir of the Dichevskys, it was decided to combine the two family crests, so that the ancient line should not die out.'

Horror glinted in the court counsellor's eyes and his plump little face flushed bright red. Gvozdikov's torment at his own blunder was so great that he even sat to attention in his chair.

'My God, in the name of ... A thousand apologies ... I misheard you on the telephone. You know, the connection is terrible!'

In order to accentuate the effect, one more blow was required. And therefore Matvei Bentsionovich dismissed the laughable misunderstanding with a casual wave of his hand, lowered his voice confidentially and leaned forward: 'Tell me, Gvozdikov – is that a noble name?'

The police master turned an even deeper crimson. 'No, I actually come from the merchant class. As yet I have only earned a personal title ...'

The public prosecutor pretended to hesitate, as if he were wondering whether he ought to continue this conversation with such a lowly born individual. He sighed and chose the magnanimous course: 'Never mind, God willing, your service will earn you a hereditary title. The edifice of the Russian state is founded on us nobles. The sovereign himself' – he pointed to a portrait, of a size which compensated for its quality of execution – 'is ultimately only the leading member of the nobility. It was our forebears who elected Mikhail Romanov tsar. We bear responsibility. Do you agree?'

'Yes,' said Gvozdikov, listening most attentively. 'But, Your Excellency, I don't quite ...'

'Let me explain. I see before me an honest, decent man and a patriot. So why prevaricate? After all, I have made enquiries about you. With competent people,' said Matvei Bentsionovich, lowering his voice suggestively. 'And therefore I can move straight on to the purpose of my visit. By virtue of your professional activity, you are undoubtedly acquainted with the various social movements and organisations that exist in Zhitomir.'

'If you mean the nihilists, then that's really a matter for the gendarmes ...'

'I don't mean the nihilists,' said Berdichevsky, interrupting the police master once again. 'Quite the contrary. I am interested in an organisation that is loyal to the throne, to the sovereign. The same organisation that I mentioned at the beginning of the conversation. The point is that the Yids have spawned and multiplied in the province of Zavolzhie as well. They have begun taking great liberties. They have taken over the provincial bank and launched a filthy newspaper; they are putting the true Zavolzhians under pressure in the field of commerce. And so we, the local patriots, have decided to learn from your experience. I have heard many good things about the Zhitomir Oprichniks. If you can help me to contact them, God knows, it will be a good deed on your part.'

Semyon Likurgovich was clearly flattered, but he chose to err on the side of caution. 'Mr State Counsellor, I myself am not a member of the Oprichniks. My official position does not permit it. Especially since, as you know yourself, their methods are not always in accordance with the requirements of the law ...'

'I have not come to you in my official capacity. Not as a public prosecutor to a chief of police, but as one nobleman to another,' Matvei Bentsionovich declared reproachfully.

'I understand,' the police master hastened to reassure him. 'And I say this purely in order to avoid any misunderstanding. I am not a member of the Oprichniks and I do not approve of every action they take, especially those that cause harm to property or danger to life and limb. Sometimes you have to use a little fatherly discipline with them, there's no other way. These are passionate people, and some are reckless, but their hearts are pure. Only sometimes you need to rein them in a little, so they that they won't make a mess of things.'

'How right you are!' the visitor exclaimed. 'I am exceedingly glad that I came to you. You see, that is why I wish to establish a brigade of Oprichniks in Zavolzhsk, before it happens spontaneously. I would like, so to speak, to be there at the beginning and direct things tactfully.'

'That's right, that's right. I direct things tactfully too. And there are things you could learn from our fine young fellows.' Gvozdikov paused solemnly, as befits a respectable man who is weighing up all the pros and cons before making an important decision. 'Very well, Mr Berg-Dichevsky. As one nobleman to another. I will put you touch with the people you want to see and also explain your purpose in coming here. I shan't be able to attend the meeting myself – for which I humbly beg your pardon.'

Matvei Bentsionovich raised an open palm: I understand, I understand.

'... And I would advise you not to advertise your own title. And one other thing ...' Gvozdikov paused delicately. 'I shall introduce you to the captain as Mr Dichevsky, without the "Berg". I beg your pardon but, you know, our Russian lads are none too fond of Germans either.'

'Oh, come now, what kind of German am I?' Berdichevsky exclaimed sincerely.

The fatherland in danger

Matvei Bentsionovich prepared thoroughly for his dangerous undertaking, although he felt ill at ease and even mocked himself ironically, muttering: 'See what a fine pantomime warrior you make. Little boys' game, that's what all this is, little boys' games ...'

The first thing he did was to buy a Lefaucheux revolver in a gun shop – a six-shooter, with a folding trigger, for thirty-nine roubles. The salesman commented on the folding trigger: 'A rational adaptation, especially if you're going to carry the gun in your pocket. It won't catch on anything and go off by accident.' Included in the price, as a present from the firm, Berdichevksy also received a little single-shot waistcoat-pocket pistol that fitted completely into the palm of his hand. 'An invaluable little item if you're attacked by a robber at night,' the salesman explained. 'This tiny tot has incredible firepower for its calibre.'

The 'tiny tot' had an ordinary trigger, not a folding one, and that made the public prosecutor feel nervous. He imagined the pistol, with its barrel pointing downwards, suddenly going off – bang! That little bullet of incredible firepower would rip through his chest and his side.

Well to hell with it. He put the little toy in his trouser pocket.

No, that was not good, either.

Eventually he got an idea: he tugged up his trouser leg and stuck the gun in the top of his sock. The hard metal was a little uncomfortable against his ankle, but that was all right, he could put up with it.

The note that Gvozdikov had sent to the hotel was both brief and odd: 'At midnight on the embankment under the lamp.'

He had to assume it was the small Kamenka river that was meant, since Zhitomir's main waterway, the Teterev, had rocky cliffs along its banks and therefore no embankment as such. And even the Kamenka was not exactly clad in granite – Berdichevsky failed to discover any parapets there, or any of the other usual signs of an embankment. But the mysterious phrase 'under the lamp' was easily explained: there was only one lamp burning on the river bank; the others were all dark, and seemed to have no glass in them.

The public prosecutor let his cabby go and stood in the narrow circle of light. He raised his collar – there was a damp draught from the river. He started to wait. All around it was pitch-dark – that is, he could not make out anything at all.

Naturally, Matvei Bentsionovich immediately started imagining that someone was watching him out of the darkness. At first the thought made him squirm and then he told himself: 'Well, of course they're watching. And it's a very good thing that they are.

The State Counsellor quickly overcame his nervousness. He whispered a single word to himself under his breath – 'Pelagia' – and immediately his fear was replaced by excitement: the victim was instantly transformed into the hunter.

He began turning his head impatiently and even stamped his foot angrily. Where on earth have you got to, Devil take you?

The darkness seemed to have been waiting for this magical sign. It stirred and rustled, and a dark silhouette that seemed quite gigantic to Berdichevsky drifted into the weak kerosene illumination. The figure raised its hand and beckoned.

With his nerve failing him once again, the State Counsellor was just about to take a step towards this stranger when the figure turned its back on him and set off, every now and then looking round and making mysterious invocatory gestures.

The tramping footsteps of Berdichevsky's guide echoed hollowly over the cobblestones of the street. The giant's gait was erect, his back unbending.

The Commandant's statue, Matvei Bentsionovich thought with a start as he struggled to keep up

From the embankment they turned to a narrow little street with no paved surface – nothing but earth, still wet after a recent shower of rain. On one side there was a blank fence and on the other a stone wall, with either warehouses or workshops behind it. There was no lighting at all.

Berdichevsky stumbled over a pothole and swore – for some reason in a whisper.

The wall led to gates with a lamp burning above them. The public prosecutor read the signboard: 'Savchuk's Intestine Cleaning Plant'.

He read it and shuddered. Signs were all very well, but this was sheer mockery, not to say bad taste, on the part of Providence. The point being that the State Counsellor was, after all, in a state of serious funk, and various rather unpleasant processes were already developing in his insides.

Berdichevsky did not follow the Commandant's statue in through the narrow wicket gate, but instead asked in a trembling voice: 'What is this place? Why here?'

He was not really hoping for an answer, but the giant (the great hulk of a man really was almost a sazhen tall) turned back and replied in a voice that was surprisingly delicate and polite: 'This, sir, is an establishment where they clean intestines.'

'In what sense?'

'The ordinary sense, sir. For the manufacture of salami.'

'Aha,' said Matvei Bentsionovich, slightly reassured. 'But why do we need to go in there?'

The Commandant giggled, which finally made it perfectly clear that it was not any kind of menacing intent that had made him remain silent, but the shyness of a provincial faced with a visitor from other parts.

'You can see for yourself what the town's like, sir: more Yids than Russians. That makes this the perfect place. Salami's made with pork. So not a single one of the workers is Jewish – nothing but Russian and Ukrainians, sir.'

The secret meeting of the Oprichniks of Christ militia was taking place in the plant's office premises. These premises were a rather grubby room that was quite large, but with a low ceiling, from which several kerosene lamps had been hung.

There were two rows of chairs facing a table covered with the Russian tricolour. On the walls, icons alternated with portraits of heroes of the fatherland: Alexander Nevsky, Dmitry Donskoi, Suvorov, Skobelev. The places of honour in this gallery were occupied by images of Ivan the Terrible and His Majesty the Emperor.

The chairman was a middle-aged man wearing a jacket and a lace tie, although he had long hair, cut in the Russian pudding-basin style.

Standing in front of the table was a skinny individual in a Russian-style shirt – evidently the speaker. There was an audience of about ten.

Everybody turned to look at the men who had just come in, but in his agitation Berdichevsky failed to get a good look at the faces. Most of those present seemed to have beards and their hair was also cut in the Russian manner.

'Ah, here is our dear guest,' said the chairman. 'Welcome, welcome. I am the captain.'

The Oprichniks got to their feet and someone spoke in a deep bass voice: 'Good health to you, Your Excellency.'

Matvei Bentsionovich was so nervous that he almost corrected the man and told him that he was no 'Excellency', but he stopped himself just in time. He nodded briskly, military-style, and a lock of angel-coloured hair slid down over his forehead.

The captain (that appeared to be the title used for the position of leader of the Oprichniks) got up from behind his table and came towards the public prosecutor.

And once again Berdichevsky almost committed a faux pas – he reached out to shake hands. It turned out, however, that what he ought to have done was not extend his hand, but throw out his arms in a wide embrace. That was what the chairman did: with the words: 'Glory to Rus!' he pressed the guest against his chest and kissed him three times on the lips.

The others also wished to greet the important man, and so he was obliged to kiss every one of them – eleven in all – and every time the sacramental phrase glorifying the fatherland was pronounced.

The smells that Mr Berg-Dichevsky breathed in as he was kissed did not vary greatly: cheap tobacco, raw onions, the fumes of *spiritus vini* processed by the stomach. Only the very last of the kissers, the very same Virgil who had conducted Matvei Bentsionovich to the gathering, had a fragrant aroma of eau de cologne and moustache fixative. And he didn't kiss with a loud smacking noise like the others, but extended his lips delicately.

A hairdresser, the public prosecutor realised, examining the curled locks at the man's temples and the beard combed into two halves.

'Please come this way,' said the captain, inviting his guest to the place of honour.

Everyone fixed their gaze on 'His Excellency', evidently anticipating a speech or a greeting, for which the State Counsellor was quite unprepared. However, he found a way out – he asked them to continue, for he had come 'not to speak, but to listen; not to teach, but to learn'. They liked that. They applauded the modest 'general', shouted 'Grand!' and the interrupted talk was continued.

The speaker, whom Berdichevsky christened the Sexton for his manner of speaking and slightly bleating intonation, was informing the members of the militia about the results of an investigation he had conducted into the Jews' dominant position in the press of the province.

The picture that was drawn was a monstrous one. The Sexton could not even mention the *Zhitomir News* without trembling in indignation: nothing but *perelmuters* and *kaganoviches*, insolent mockery of everything that was dear to the Russian heart. However, even in the *Volynsk Provincial Gazette* everything was by no means well. With the editor's connivance, they often printed articles written by Yids who hid behind Russian names. A list of these wolves in sheep's clothing was given: Ivan Svetlov was really Itzhak Sarkin, Alexander Ivanov was really Moishe Levenson, Afanasii Beryozkin was really Laiba Rabinovich, and so on and so forth. But the speaker kept his most sensational revelation for last. It turned out that the Sanhedrin's tentacles even extended into the *Volynsk Diocesan Gazette*: the wife of the archpriest Kapustin, had been born Fishman, in a family of baptised Jews.

A murmur of indignation swept round the room. Matvei Bentsionovich also shook his head regretfully.

The captain leaned over and whispered to him: 'We are gathering material for a loyal subjects' note to the sovereign. You should see the figures on financial capital public education. Enough to set your skin creeping.'

The public prosecutor frowned severely: terrible, terrible.

The speaker concluded and took his seat.

Everybody started gazing expectantly at the visitor once again, making it quite clear that he could not avoid having to speak.

He recalled the wise saying that seemed apposite: When you don't know what to say, speak the truth.

'What can I say?' asked Matvei Bentsionovich, rising to his feet. 'I am shocked and dismayed.'

The response to that was a general sigh.

'Of course, things are bad in our province, but not to the same extent. This is terrible, gentlemen. Verily, wailing and gnashing of teeth. However, my dear friends, let me tell you this. Investigations and notes to the sovereign are all well and good, but they are not enough. I must confess, this is not what I was expecting from the Oprichniks of Zhitomir. I had been told that you were men of action, that you are not in the habit of sitting about doing nothing. The very sight of the present condition of Rus is enough to make your heart bleed,' said Berdichevsky, gradually warming to his theme. 'We are surrounded on all sides by mere talkers, heroes in words alone! Gentlemen and patriots, this way we shall simply let them take our fatherland! We shall talk it away! But in the meantime the Yid is wasting no time in idle talk; he has everything calculated for years ahead!'

As they listened to the orator's words of bitter experience, the seated men exchanged glances and squeaked their chairs.

Finally the captain could stand it no more. After waiting for the short pause that Berdichevsky required in order to refill his lungs with air, the leader of the Oprichniks exclaimed: 'We are not idle talkers or scribblers! Yes, we have not abandoned all hope of getting through to our thick-eared authorities by legal means, but let me assure you, we do not limit ourselves to mere notes.' It was clear that the chairman could barely hold back, he was so eager to exonerate himself. 'I tell you what, sir, please come into my office and we can talk face to face. And in the meantime, brothers, please help yourself to what God has provided.'

It was only now that Matvei Bentsionovich noticed the table in the corner of the room, set with a samovar, loaves of bread and an impressive range of salamis – no doubt the produce of the intestine-cleaning plant.

The members of the militia moved across in lively fashion to help themselves, but the pubic prosecutor was invited into the 'office' – a cramped little cubby hole, divided off from the larger room by a glass door.

Missing!

Now at last there was a handshake. It should be said that, once he was parted from his fine young fellows, the captain's behaviour changed somewhat, as if he wished to show that he and his guest belonged to the same circle.

'Savchuk,' he said, introducing himself. 'I own the plant. Mr Dichevsky, I noticed the way you were looking at my janissaries. They are a little rough, of course, and their intellectual prowess is far from brilliant.'

Matvei Bentsionovich was flustered (he thought that he had concealed his feelings quite remarkably well) and gestured in protest.

'It's all right,' the factory-owner assured him. 'I quite understand. However, I do ask you to bear in mind that they are not ideologues, but sergeants, in charge of platoons. To use the biblical phrase – "men of force". I jokingly refer to them as my apostles – there are exactly twelve of them. There should be another one here, but he has been delayed for some reason. My sergeants may not be too nimble-witted, but if there is action to be taken, they won't bungle it. Please don't get the wrong idea; we have members of the intelligentsia too. Lawyers, doctors, grammar school teachers – they suffer most of all from the Yiddish onslaught. If you wish, I will introduce you to them later, in more appropriate surroundings. Ilya Stepanovich Glazkov, the deputy mayor of the town – a brilliant mind, a true thinker.'

'You know,' Berdichevsky butted in, 'there are already plenty of thinkers about. What we are short of is men of action. To act fearlessly, with no concern for legal considerations – that is what it would be good to learn. And not just swinging a crowbar and smashing the Yids' shops – that's very simple business. Tell me, do you have any people with experience of real work – in the police or security forces? But no longer in service, so that they are not bound by the letter of the law.'

'How do you mean?' Savchuk asked with a puzzled frown.

Matvei Bentsionovich took the bull by the horns. 'I decided to come to see you in Zhitomir after a heart-to-heart talk with a certain highly interesting man who recently spent some time in Zavolzhsk. Former gendarmes staff captain Bronislaw Veniaminovich Ratsevich . . .' And he paused, waiting with a sinking heart to see what the response would be.

The response was not long in coming. The captain's face contorted in an expression of disgust.

'Ratsevich? And what lies did he tell you, that Yid-lover?'

'W-Why is he a Yid-lover?' the public prosecutor asked, amazed. 'I understood it was quite the opposite: the Jews, that is, the Yids ruined his life . . . They destroyed his career and clapped him in debtors' prison!'

'They clapped him in, and then they dragged him out again,' Savchuk hissed.

'So it was the Jews who bought him out?' the State Counsellor babbled in confusion. His heart had now sunk as low as possible.

'And who else? They say the slimy little Pole had debts of fifteen thousand. Who else but the Yids could have found that kind of money? It was a thank-you to him from the Sanhedrinites, and we know what for. Two years ago in the Lipovetsk district our knights executed a sheriff, a well-known Yid-lover. The gendarme investigation was led by Ratsevich. He sniffed everything out, dug everything up and sent two Russian men off to hard labour. For this abomination he even received a formal letter of gratitude from the "Goel-Israel". They're the ones who let that Judas out of the debtor's prison – You're free now, off you go, destroy the Orthodox people. It was their Goel-Israel, it couldn't have been anyone else.'

' "Goel-Israel"?'

'Yes, we have an ulcer by that name, pure Yiddish pus. Rabbi Sherafevich's *hatzer*. A *hatzer*, pardon me for the expression, is like a bishop's conventuary, only for Yids. They have a synagogue in there, and an *eshibot*, the Yiddish seminary. Shefarevich is member of the secret Sanhedrin, we know that for certain. He raises his wolf cubs in hatred for Christ and everything Russian. He doesn't let anyone near his little devils. What he's particularly afraid of is Russian women turning young Yids away from the Jewish faith. That's the way it is with them – anyone who gets involved with a goy woman is lost to Jewry, he has stained his name himself for ever.' The captain spat. 'Stained their names, have they? There was a case here only recently. They found a peasant girl in the river. We carried out our own investigation. Discovered that the slut had been going with a little Yid from Shefarevich's *hatzer*. The Yids found out about it. The rabbi summoned him and started telling her: Get rid of the goy girl. But this little Yid was a stubborn one, he wouldn't have it. I love her, he said, and that's all there is to it. So they sent him off to Lithuania, and almost the very next day the girl was found in the Teterev. A clear case of murder. And it's clear enough who killed her, too. But our Yid-lovers were afraid of creating a rumpus. She drowned herself, they said, out of unhappy love. Then we decided to implement our own justice for ourselves, but we were too late – Shefarevich had cleared off to Palestine with his brood. That's the sort of thing that goes on around here!'

Berdichevsky listened sceptically to the story of the Russian girl's murder. And then he suddenly started having doubts. There were just as many madmen among the Jews as in any other race. Or perhaps even more. You could never tell – what if some Jewish Sanhedrin or other really had been established in Zhitomir? He could only hope that Pelagia would not cross paths with the furious rabbi in Jerusalem. Thank God, there was nothing to bring them together.

The sound of voices in the next room became louder, and one that stood out above all the others seemed vaguely familiar to Berdichevsky. The State Counsellor involuntarily started listening.

The nasal voice was telling a story: '. . . all smooth and pompous, with a great big conk on him. "I'm a public prosecutor," he says. "A real big-wig, such-and-such counsellor."'

'A Yid – a public prosecutor?' the other interrupted him. 'You're raving, Kolka!'

'Ah, there's my twelfth disciple,' said Savchuk, peering at the clamouring Oprichniks through the glass door. 'He's turned up at last. The sergeant of the Kiev section, he works as a porter in the Bristol Hotel. Hey, Kolya, come in here, I'll introduce you to a good man.'

Berdichevsky rose to his feet, feeling a chill in his bones. His sweaty hand slipped into his pocket – to the handle of the revolver. His finger started feeling for the folding trigger, but it was stuck – it simply would not unfold.

The thick-lipped porter from the Bristol came into the room.

He bowed. With a loud declaration – 'Glory to Rus!' – he flung his arms wide, looked at Berdichevsky's face and froze.

IX

Shmulik – Ruler of the Universe

A desirable bridegroom

If only little Shmulik Mamzer had known that he would never again see the sun rise over the bright city of Erushalaim, may it stand for all eternity, then he would probably have regarded the lamp of morning with greater affection; but as it was, he merely squinted at the round pink patch that had appeared from behind the Mount of Olives and muttered: 'May you burst, curse you.' It seemed like only just five minutes ago that he had laid his head on the volume of the Talmud wrapped in cloth, which served as his pillow for the night, and now all of a sudden it was time to get up again.

Rubbing the side of his body that had turned numb from sleeping on the floor, Shmulik stretched. The other pupils who had spent the night in the *eshibot* were clearing away their beds – all the same as Mamzer's: a meagre piece of matting, a book or rags instead of a pillow, and in summer, thank God, no blanket was required. The faces of the *eshibot* boys were crumpled and sleepy – quite different from the way they would look once they were washed.

In all his fifteen years of life, Shmulik had only slept in a real bed three times: twice when he was ill and another time on the eve of his bar mitzvah, but otherwise always on the floor or sharing with three or four others and that, let me tell you, is even worse than the floor, and so it doesn't count. That was the way it had been in Zhitomir in the *heder*, and then in the *eshibot*, and now here, in the bright city of Erushalaim, may it stand for all eternity.

But what can you expect if someone has no father or mother, not even a lousy distant cousin twice removed? Shmulik had not made his appearance in the world in a maternity home, the way all normal children do, but on the doorstep of a synagogue, wrapped in a scrap of a bed sheet. At first people had doubted if he really was a Jew at all – some shameless *shiksa* might have planted him there, calculating that the child would be better fed with the Jews. Respected people had gathered together and tried to lay down the law on whether the little orphan ought to be given to a Russian orphanage, but Rabbi Shepetovker, may the earth be a feather mattress to him, had said: 'Better bring up a Russian as a Yid than doom a Jewish child by putting him in a goy orphanage,' and Shhmulik had been circumcised and the abandoned child had been joined to God's chosen people. (He was horrified to think what might have happened otherwise.) They had joined him all right, but they hadn't been generous enough to hand a state official three roubles to give the child a beautiful family name such as Sinaisky or Iordansky; they hadn't even given the official a rouble so that he would write simply something like Haikin or Rivkin. And the official had been furious. The other clerks used to mock the nameless too – they would write them down as Soloveichik (Nightingale!) or Persik (Peachy!), or if the child had a large nose, Nosik (Nosy!), but unfortunately this cursed goy knew a little Yiddish and he had decided to poison Shmulik's entire life by giving him the worst possible name. '*Mamzer*' means born out of wedlock, illegitimate, a bastard. With a name like that you could never marry or become a respected rabbi. When did you last meet a girl who would like to be 'Madam Baistriuk'? And 'Rabbi Bastard' – what do you make of that?

Well then, you ask, did the rascally state official achieve his goal – did he ruin Shmulik's life completely?

It would seem not.

Ever since the boy's earliest years the shameful surname had inspired him with a great, almost impossible dream: to go away to the Holy Land, where surnames were not even needed, because there every Jew was visible to the Lord, and he would not confuse which of them was which.

Shmulik had always studied, for as long as he could remember. Jewish boys like to study, but there was no more fervent swot in the whole of Zhitomir, which, by the way, is home to twenty-five thousand Jews, many of them boys zealously seeking learning.

By the age of thirteen Shmulik had learned the Pentateuch – by heart. And not merely by heart, but by 'pinpoint'. A man who knows the Holy Writings in this way can take a needle, stick it into any letter and immediately tell you what words the point has pierced on the following pages.

On coming of age, Shmulik had taken up the commentaries on the Torah and learned off word for word all 613 laws corresponding to the 613 parts of the soul: the 248 in its upper region and 365 in its lower. He had also mastered to perfection the articles of the *eidut*, in which mention is made of historical events, and the easily understood laws of the *mishpatim*, and even the commandments of the *hukim*, which were beyond human comprehension.

Once mature in erudition, he had plunged into the labyrinths of the Talmud. But now he no longer blindly learned things off by heart, because there, concealed in the wily twistings and turnings of the book Zogar, there were indescribable treasures. It is known that a highly learned man endowed with the gift of penetrating the hidden meaning of letters can discover in that book the keys to great mysteries and wonders, he can even become the ruler of the Universe. In the combinations of letters used in the Names of the Lord, in the holy number 26, the numerical equivalent of the four letter '*iud-hei-vav-hei*', there lies concealed the key to the hidden knowledge that has tantalised many generations of Talmudists. Some of the *eshibot* boys tried repeating one prayer or another twenty-six times, like parrots; others struck their heads against the Wailing Wall twenty-six times, or walked twenty-six times round Mount Meron, where the great Shimon bar Iohai, author of the Zogar, was buried; but Shmulik could sense that this was all stupid nonsense: mindless repetition would not get you anywhere. His heart told that it was all immensely more complicated and at the same time far simpler. One day at sunset (he knew for certain that it would happen at sunset), the truth itself would be revealed to him in all its beautiful simplicity, and he would be able to pronounce the unpronounceable, hear the inaudible and see the invisible. God would appoint him to manage His world order, because in His all-embracing wisdom He would know that Shmulik Mamzer could be trusted, he would cause no harm to the human world.

You may be quite certain that, once having become the ruler of the Universe, Shmulik would have arranged everything in it in the most excellent fashion possible. Nobody would ever again have made war because, after all, it is always possible to reach agreement with each other. Nobody would ever again have tormented anybody else: if people were happy together, let them live side by side, and if they were unhappy – well then, they could separate, there was plenty of space in the world. And all the goys would have begun to observe the teachings of the Torah – at first only the compulsory ones, known as *hova*, and then also the desirable ones, the *rishut*. Soon absolutely everyone would have become Jews, and then Shmulik would have been hailed as the very greatest of men, even greater than the prophets Moses and Elijah. To call things by their proper names, he would have become the Messiah who is to save the world and reconcile it with the Lord.

As it happens, Shmulik had made a great discovery using his own mind, but he had not, God forbid, shared his surmise with Rabbi Shefarevich: *The Messiah would not come from the sky; the Messiah would be the one who decoded the name of the Lord and was not afraid to pronounce it aloud, who would accept responsibility for everything that happens on the earth.* And then would come the morning after which the sun would no longer glance out from behind the mountains, because there would be no reason for it to dry up the earth, since man had fulfilled his assigned task, and dust would return unto dust, and the spirit would return unto the Lord. And all thanks to Shmuel of Zhitomir, who was once known as Mamzer.

Among the pupils of the great rabbi Shefarevich – round-shouldered and shortsighted, with constantly runny noses – he was not the only one ablaze with divine ambition that was beyond all compare with the goys' pitiful dreams of a career and wealth. But Shmulik's flame blazed brighter than all the rest, because he was an *ilui*. Madam Perlova, who had lived all her life in Kiev and knew no Hebrew at all, used to say it in Russian: 'a boy of genius'. And after all, that didn't sound too bad either. And once she had also called him 'the Mozart of the Talmud'; but when he discovered that Mozart was a musician, Shmulik had taken offence. How was it possible to compare the noble art of the Kabala with scraping on a violin! But on the other hand, what could you expect from a woman who could not even recite the very simplest prayer in the Jewish language?

The *ilui* from the great Rabbi Shefarevich's *eshibot* – that was the reputation that Shmulik had earned for himself in Jerusalem, and he had hardly been living here for any time at all, only a few days really.

Of course, none of this would have happened if not for the rabbi, the fame of whose learning and godliness had even reached as far as here, so that the *rishon le-tsion* himself, the chief rabbi of all, who had a medal from the Sultan hanging round his neck and a *ksive* with seals from the Turkish pasha, had asked the wise man from Zhitomir to move to the Holy City, together with his pupils. Just how often had an Ashkenazi rabbi been accorded such a great honour?

The Jews argued a lot over whether Rabbi Shefarevich should be regarded as one of the *gaons* – the great teachers of the faith – or one of the *lamed-vovniks* – that is, those thirty-six righteous men who must always be present in the world, because it is only for their sake that the Lord does not destroy our sinful Earth. If there should ever be even one *lamed-vovnik* less in the world – that would be the end. Thirty-five righteous men would not be enough to ensure His tolerance.

The year before, Rabbi Shefarevich had fallen ill with the mumps (and everyone knows what a dangerous illness that is for a man who is no longer young) and Shmulik had been terribly frightened: God forbid that his teacher might die, and there might be some kind of hitch with the new *lamed-vovnik* – what then? But the rabbi had been all right, he hadn't died, only become even fiercer.

The great Shefarevich was a special man. It is well known that God's spark is placed in every soul from its birth, but what he had was not a spark, not even a candle – it was a torch, a blazing campfire – standing beside it made you feel hot. And it could be dangerous, if you weren't careful you could get burned. Because of this the rabbi had many enemies in Zhitomir, and even in Jerusalem. Although it was only a month since they had moved here, some people were already beginning to look askance: they said he was too wrathful.

Well now, that was true. Shmulik's teacher was strict. If he glanced into the classroom and saw that someone had not washed yet, and was just sitting there batting his eyelids, then there would be *az och'n vei*, that is cries of 'oi' and 'vei', or to put it in biblical terms, a wailing and gnashing of teeth.

So Shmulik screwed his eyes up against the sun as he put on his lower *tales*, smoothed down his long hair as best he could and recited the prayer on awakening from sleep: 'I thank Thee, living and substantial King, for Thy mercy in returning my soul to me.'

He poured water over his hands (three times for each one, as prescribed) and recited the prayer of ablution. Then he paid a visit to the privy and thanked the King of the Universe for his wisdom in creating man and providing his body with all the necessary openings and internal hollows.

After another three prayers – for the blessing of the soul, for the partaking of breakfast (may our enemies breakfast like this: a mug of hot water and half a flat bread cake) and for study – Shmulik and the other *eshibot* pupils sat down at the table and immersed themselves in the Gemara.

The others behaved noisily, not to say rowdily: some read out loud, some nodded their heads and swayed backwards and forwards, some even waved their hands about, but Shmulik did not see or hear anything around him. There is no occupation in the world more absorbing than copying out combinations of letters in a notebook and figuring out calculations. Time no longer seems to exist, it reverently stands still: any moment now Shmulik would touch the Mystery, and the world would no longer be as it had been. And this could happen at absolutely any time, at any instant!

The sound that returned the future saviour of mankind to base reality was a rumbling in the stomach of his neighbour, the *balabes* Mendlik. *Balabes*, or *balbes*, was the name given to young *primaks* who lived and ate with their wives' families until they attained the age of maturity. Mendlik was only fourteen years old, so he still had plenty of maturing to do.

Earlier Shmulik's neighbour on the right had been Mikhl-Byk, whose name it was now forbidden to pronounce – but, after all, you can't place a prohibition on thought. Shmulik often thought about the unfortunate Byk, Where was he now? How was he?

Someone could be just living his life, even someone as stupid and coarse as Mikhl, but still a Jew, a living soul, and then from out of nowhere destiny suddenly appeared, in the form of a barefooted *focusmacher*, and suddenly the Jew was no more. What a terrible fate.

There was more gurgling from Mendlik's belly, and Shmulik's stomach responded in sympathy. The sun was already past the high point of noon. It was time for lunch.

Immediately upon arrival in Erushalaim, may it stand for all eternity, each *eshibot* pupil had been given a list of the local families in which he would be fed on Monday, Tuesday, Wednesday and all the other days of the week. It was a matter of the luck of the draw. One day was not like another. If the family was poor or miserly, you were left hungry. If it was hospitable and compassionate, you could stuff yourself until you could eat no more.

Today it was Shmulik's turn to go to Madam Perlova. That was both good and bad. Good, because the widow would feed him better than at Passover: with meat, and fish, and even cream buns (praise be to the Lord for creating such a wonder). And it was bad, because she would sit beside him, look at him with her wet cow's eyes and stroke his shoulder, or even his cheek. This made Shmulik feel ashamed; it even made his éclair stick in his throat.

Like the other rich widows, Madam Perlova had come to Erushalaim, may it stand for all eternity, in order to die close to the cemetery on the Mount of Olives. She had already bought a plot of land for the grave, in the very finest spot. But she had health enough for another fifty years, so she needed to attend to the question of how to live them. It is well known that as a reward for feeding her husband and running his household, in the next world a woman is granted exactly half of the blessings that he has earned. In this respect she could hardly place any great hopes in the deceased Mr Perlov – he had been a broker on the stock exchange. Yes, he had earned what was needed to support his wife in this life, but as for the afterlife – alas ... So the widow's interest was quite understandable: Shmulik Mamzer was bound to become a great scholar, at the very least.

He wondered himself whether he ought to marry. The fluff was already beginning to sprout on his chin. Why bother to wait until he grew a moustache? Without that vile surname, which had been left behind in Zhitomir, and would soon be completely forgotten, Shmulik had been transformed into a most desirable bridegroom. It was true that he didn't have a penny to his name, but when had the Jews ever paid any attention to wealth? Learning and a good name were more valuable than money. They would be glad to welcome an *ilui* into an old Erushalaim family. Sephardics never married Ashkenazi girls, because they were spoilt and wilful, but they welcomed Ashkenazi bridegrooms, who made fine, caring husbands.

Only why did he need a Sephardic family, when he had Madam Perlova? She was a kind woman who kept a good house and she had capital, which meant that Shmulik would not be distracted from the main business of his life by the concerns of earning his daily bread. Of course, she was really very fat, and you couldn't exactly call her very beautiful, but wise men said that bodily beauty meant nothing, and wise men would not lie.

And Rabbi Shefarevich also told them: Marry. Next week he had promised to take them to see Rabbi Menachem-Aizik, who explained to bridegrooms the correct way to lie with a woman in order not to transgress a single provision of the Law – after all, three parties were involved in the mingling of the flesh: the husband, the wife and He Whose Name is Blessed.

As he walked along the street on the way to Madam Perlova's house, Shmulik took a decision. I'll go and listen to Rabbi Menachem-Aizik. What I don't understand I'll remember by heart and then, so be it, I'll marry the widow and make her happy. I've had enough of sleeping on the floor.

In the Armenian quarter he speeded up to a trot. The bad boys who lived here threw asses' droppings at Jews. Never mind, in Zhitomir the *kundeses* from the Workers' Settlement could even fling a stone.

What would you rather be hit with in the back, a sharp cobblestone or an ass's turd, which will stick for a while, but then fall off?

Of course.

From every point of view, during the spring just past Shmulik had certainly advanced a long way up the stairway of life – you could even say he had leapt from the very bottom to the very top, right over God only knew how many steps: the Zhitomir *mamzer* had become a desirable bridegroom, and he had done it in the glorious city of Erushalaim, may it stand for all eternity.

The red-headed *shiksa*

After lunch, which had been particularly good today, Shmulik
lounged in comfort for just a little while on the soft cushions in
the courtyard. He recited from the Torah for Madam Perlova.
She didn't understand a single word, but she listened reverently
and didn't dare pester him with her stroking. The widow had a
shady tree growing in her courtyard, a very rare thing in the Old
City. He could have gone on sitting there for ages, but he had to
hurry back to the *eshibot*. During the afternoon Rabbi Shefarevich himself taught the pupils, and you'd better not be late for
him. He wouldn't care if you were an *ilui* – he'd lash you across
the fingers with his pointer, and that hurt. The teacher made no
allowances for the flesh – neither the flesh of others, nor his
own, because the body belongs to the *asia*, the lowest sphere of
phenomena, and it is not deserving of indulgence.

Even in the heat of Erushalaim the rabbi dressed as befitted
an Ashkenazi sage: in a long-skirted black frock coat with a
velvet collar and a fox-fur *shtraimel*, with his grey side-locks,
stuck together with sweat, dangling below it. And this was in
May – what was going to happen in summer? They said it could
be so hot in the Promised Land that an egg laid on the sand
would be hard-boiled in two minutes. Would the rabbi's holiness
withstand such a trial?

It will, Shmulik thought as he glanced at the teacher striding
round the classroom.

Rabbi Shefarevich stopped beside cross-eyed Leibka and
prodded the back of the boy's head with one finger. 'Why haven't
you copied out the chapter from the *Mishna* as you were told?'

'I had a bellyache,' Leibka replied miserably.

'He had a bellyache,' the teacher informed the other *eshibot*
boys, as if they hadn't heard for themselves. 'Let us discuss this.'

This last phrase indicated that a learned discussion had
begun – now the spring of wisdom would burst forth from the
rabbi's lips. And so it did.

'It is written: all illnesses are visited on man as punishment
for sins. Agreed?'

Leibka shrugged – this beginning promised him no good at all.

Rabbi Shefarovich pretended to be surprised. 'Is it not so?
He whose thoughts are of the vain and the dishonest suffers a

headache. The lover of sweet things who nibbles too much sugar suffers a toothache. The libertine consorts with indecent women and his *ud* rots. Do you agree with this?'

Leibke was obliged to nod.

'Well, that's good. Since you had a bellyache, your belly must have sinned: eaten something that it shouldn't have. It is responsible for your illness. Agreed? And who does this belly belong to? You. So you yourself are to blame. Agreed?'

If I were Leibke I would reply with a quotation from *Iuda Gabirol's Scattering of Pearls*, Shmulik thought: 'The fool blames others; the intelligent man blames himself; the wise man blames no one.' In recent times Shmulik had developed the habit of arguing with the teacher. This was a highly praiseworthy habit for a student of the Talmud, but not without its dangers where Rabbi Shefarevich was concerned, and so the *ilui* conducted his polemic with himself, inside his own head.

Leibke was not able to adduce quotations in his own defence, and so he received a blow from the pointer.

The teacher was out of sorts again today, as he had been recently. Shimon also received the pointer across his fingers for reciting the lesson hesitantly and incompletely.

'Have you said all that you know?' the rabbi asked with a frown.

'Yes, I have said all that I know,' Shimon replied in due form, as required.

But that didn't save him.

'The fool says what he knows. The wise man knows what he says!' the teacher barked.

In his head, Shmulik immediately parried with another aphorism: Foolishness shouts, wisdom speaks in a whisper. An excellent reply. It would be grand to debate with the Rabbi – no matter what the subject was. Who could tell which of them would win? There was this thing – a 'telephone', it was called. The very thing for a dispute with Rabbi Shefarevich: say whatever you liked, the pointer couldn't reach you.

Shimon had not replied so badly that he deserved to be beaten with such energy. The poor boy howled out loud and the tears poured down his cheeks. None of the *eshibot* pupils apart from Mikhl-Byk, with that thick skin of his, could ever have borne a lashing like that without crying out.

Again he had remembered that forbidden name, for the second time that day.

Rabbi Shefarevich was apparently thinking about the same thing, because the theme he chose for the day's discussion was apostasy.

'Modern Europe represents a terrible danger for Jewry,' the great man said. 'Earlier, when we were robbed, murdered and locked in the ghetto, things were easier – oppression merely united us. But now the governments of the so-called advanced countries have abandoned their anti-Semitism and the Jews there have been faced with the temptation of becoming the same as everyone else, of being no different from the goys. For after all, being a Jew is not merely an accident of birth, it is also a conscious choice. If you do not wish to be a Jew – that is up to you. Have yourself baptised or simply stop demonstrating your Jewishness, and immediately all roads will be open to you. In the countries of Peil and Lite, which are now part of the Russian Empire, the situation is still tolerable, because there the Jews who have ceased to be Jews are allowed no true freedom and persecuted for their origins. But in Western Europe things are really bad. In the country of Taits the greatest harm has been done to the Jewry by Bismarck, and thousands of Jews have turned away from the faith of their fathers. The situation is also appalling in the country of Tserfat, which proclaimed the equality of the Jews a hundred years ago. Thanks be to God, the stupid goys decided to put the baptised Jew Dreyfus on trial there, and that gave many apostates pause for thought. The enemies of the Jews belong to two types. The first wish to annihilate us, and we should not be afraid of their kind, because, for the Lord will always protect His chosen people. The second type is a hundred times more dangerous, because they do not attack our bodies, but our souls. They lure us with gentle words and kindness, they want us to reject our own special character, to stop being Jews. And many, very many give way and become *meshumeds*. A *meshumed*, having accepted Christ, is a thousand times worse than the most vicious goy. In order to curry favour with his new masters, he maligns us and our faith. And when he appears among us, he sows doubt and temptation in the hearts of the cowardly by putting on airs with his rich clothes and the fine position he has won.'

Rabbi Shefarevich grew more and more incensed. His eyes

flashed with the fire of holy wrath, the forefinger of his right hand was repeatedly raised towards the ceiling.

'These traitors should be eliminated, as a sheep infected with murrain is eliminated before it can destroy the entire flock! The Lord said: "If any of the house of Israel should detach himself from Me, I shall turn My face against that man and crush him in portent and parable, and eliminate him from My people, and you shall know that I am the Lord."'

Shmulik objected to this as follows: 'The Lord did not say "eliminate", full stop, but "eliminate from My people" – that is expel them out of Jewry, and let them carry on living as they like, without Me.'

But, naturally, this was said 'over the telephone', so that the rabbi did not hear the argument and continued with his thundering, this time against the *apikoireses*.

'We Jews are the only keepers of the fire of God, which would long ago have gone out without our people. We do not change, we have remained the same, since the times of Abraham and Moses. But what do the Zionist-*apikoireses* want? They want the Jews to become an ordinary nation and an ordinary state. But ordinary nations do not live long, they appear and disappear. Where are the Mohabites, the Philistines, the Assyrians, the Babylonians, the Romans who tormented us? They are all long gone, they were squeezed out by new nations: the English, the Germans, the Turks, the Russians. Two or three centuries will go by and the torches of these nations, which now blaze so brightly, will be extinguished and new, brighter ones will be ignited in their place. But our candle will go on burning with the same quiet, unquenchable flame which is already thousands of years old! Is there any other nation on earth whose candle has been burning for so long?'

And at this Shmulik could hold back no longer. 'What about the Chinese, Rabbi?' he said out loud. 'They have maintained their customs for as long as we have. Perhaps even longer. For as long as four thousand years.' He had read about the Chinese in an encyclopedia, at Madam Perlova's house.

The sally hit home, the rabbi's beard trembled. Well now, what would he say to that, what quotation would he adduce?

Shmulik was not granted any quotation, he was granted the pointer – not across his fingers, but across his neck and the back of his head. He went flying out of the classroom, howling, under a hail of blows and insults. It was hard to dispute with Rabbi Shefarevich.

Now he had to wait until the teacher cooled off, then go back and beg his pardon – but only after an hour or two.

Shmulik stuck his hands in his pockets and started strolling up and down the street, but he didn't stick his nose into the Armenian quarter.

Near the Dung Gate someone called to him in Russian: 'Boy! Boy!'

A *shiksa* in a dark silk dress came over to Shmulik, her ginger hair covered with a transparent scarf. She had a travelling bag in her hand. The woman's freckled face seemed vaguely familiar to him.

'Your name's Shmulik, isn't it?' the redhead said with a happy smile. 'I was the one who spoke to you on the steamer? Remember? I was dressed as a nun then?'

Right, now he remembered. He had seen this *shiksa* before when they were sailing down the river from Moscow – Jewish parents had brought their children there from various towns in order to hand them over to study in Rabbi Shefarevich's *eshibot*. Only the *shiksa* hadn't been so beautiful in a nun's habit. With those golden speckles on her face and that glowing halo of hair she looked much prettier.

'Hello,' Shmulik said politely. 'How are you?'

'Well, thank you. What a good thing that I met you!' said the redhead, still delighted.

And what exactly was so good about it?

Here was a pupil of the venerable Rabbi Shefarevich, standing in the middle of the street and chatting with a *shiksa*. God forbid that anyone should go telling tales to the teacher – Shmulik had enough problems without that. That Lithuanian Jew over there in the black hat and robe had stopped and he was squinting at them. Shmulik would have liked to remind him of the wise saying: Better to talk with a woman and think of God than the other way round. But to be quite honest, Shmulik was not thinking about God at all at that moment, but about how much more pleasant it would be to marry Madam Perlova if only she had white skin like that.

'I really need to have a word with you,' said the *shiksa*.

But the Lithuanian was still staring. This was sure to end badly – he was bound to tell the rabbi.

'I'm in a hurry,' Shmulik muttered. 'I don't have any time.' And he tried to walk on.

But the beautiful *shiksa* suddenly swayed and leaned on his shoulder, moaning. 'Oh, I feel so dizzy . . . Boy, take me into the shade . . . Give me some water . . .' She squeezed her eyes shut and reached one hand up to her temple. It was the hot sun that had given her a headache, she wasn't used to it.

One of the most important of God's commandments, surpassing all the prohibitions in importance, said: Be charitable. I'll take her into the shade, give her a drink and then run off straight away, Shmulik decided.

He took the stricken woman by the arm and waved his hand in front of her face, like a fan – that was so that the Lithuanian would see there was no flirting going on here, just someone feeling unwell because of the heat.

It was shady in the narrow alley, not hot. Shmulik sat the Russian woman on a stone step, ran to the well and brought some water in his yarmulka.

The *shiksa* took a sip and immediately felt better. She said: 'I'm looking for a certain man.'

At this point Shmulik ought to have gone on his way. He had shown charity, and that was enough. But he suddenly felt curious about who she was looking for. The narrow little lane was not the street. There was nobody much strolling about here, no one to stare at an *eshibot* pupil talking to a *shiksa*.

'What man?'

'He's called Manuila. The prophet of the "foundlings" sect. Do you know him?' Shmulik shuddered. How strange! The *shiksha* was talking about the barefooted *focusmacher*!

Some glimmer in his eyes must have given him away, because the redhead asked quickly: 'He was here, wasn't he? You saw him, didn't you?'

Shmulik took his time before he answered.

It had happened on the first Sabbath after Passover, an entire two weeks ago now, but it seemed like just today.

Rabbi Shefarevich had taken the boys from the *eshibot* to the Wailing Wall.

They had stood in a row and started to pray. Shmulik had closed his eyes in order to picture the Temple in all its imperishable magnificence – the way it had been before and the way it would be when the hour struck.

Suddenly the next boy along had nudged him with his elbow and pointed off to one side.

There was a tramp standing there, dressed in a dirty robe, belted round with a blue rag. He was holding a knotty stick in his hand, and on his feet he had peasant sandals of birch bark, stained with dried clay. His shaggy head was uncovered and he had a sack hanging behind his back on a string – in the land of Peil those were called *sidor*.

The ragamuffin was watching the Jews with curiosity as they swayed and lamented. He absent-mindedly pulled up the hem of his robe and scratched his sinewy calf, overgrown with hair – he had no trousers under his ragged robe. 'What are you doing, people, and why are you crying?' he had asked in Hebrew, pronouncing the words outlandishly.

So despite the birch-bark sandals, he was a Jew after all, only a very strange one. How could a Jew not know what they were crying about at the Wailing Wall? He must be a madman.

The Law ordered him to treat the mad with pity, and Shmulik had replied to the tramp politely though of course, not in Hebrew (the sacred language was not intended for idle talk), but in Yiddish: 'We are weeping for the destruction of the Temple.'

Rabbi Shefarevich gave the ignorant man a fleeting glance, but didn't say anything to him, because it was beneath his dignity as a *gaon* or, perhaps, even a *lamed-vovnik* to make conversation with just any riff-raff.

'I don't understand your language very well,' the barefooted man had said in his laughable Hebrew, which was like the clucking of a bird. 'You say you are weeping for the temple? For the temple that stood here before?' And he pointed at the Temple Mound.

Shmulik nodded, already regretting that he had got involved in the conversation.

The tramp had been amazed. What point was there in crying about it, he had asked? Stones were just stones. It would be better if they wept for the 'Messiha' to come. Shmulik didn't understand straight away exactly who the 'Messiha' was, but when realised it was a mispronunciation of the word 'Messiah', he felt frightened. Especially since the rabbi had stopped whispering his prayer and turned round. Berl, who knew everything, had trotted over to him and whispered: – 'Rabbi, that's the Russian prophet Manuila, the same one who ... I told you, he has already been seen in the city.'

The teacher's forehead had gathered into menacing folds and he had spoken loudly in Russian: 'I am Aron Shefarevich, a member of the Rabbinical Council of the City of Erushalaim. And who are you to go making idle conversation in the language of prayer, which you do not even know properly? Where have you come from and what is your name?'

The tramp had said that his name was Emmanuel, and he had come from the Mount of Har-Zeitim, where he had spent the night in one of the caves. He was not very good at speaking Russian either – they say people like that have porridge in their mouths. And what caves were these on the Mount of Olives? Surely not the burial chambers? Well now the rabbi would let him have it for sacrilege.

But the teacher did not ask any questions about the cave, instead he asked contemptuously: 'Is that why you are so dirty on the Sabbath?'

'I was digging in the earth, and I got as filthy as a pig,' Emmanuel had laughed light-heartedly. 'That's a funny expression, isn't it?'

'Digging in the earth? On the Sabbath? And after that you call yourself a Jew?'

Quite a crowd had gathered round. They all wanted to hear the great Talmudist and master of verbal duels make short work of this miserable excuse for a prophet.

The man who called himself Emmanuel had waved his hand casually. 'Eh,' he had said, 'the Sabbath is for man, not man for the Sabbath.'

'Jews do not say that – that is what the Christians' god, Jesus, says,' Rabbi Shefarevich had noted in an aside, especially for his pupils. 'No, Emmanuel; you are no Jew.'

The tramp had squatted down on his haunches, set his staff across his knees and looked up merrily at the teacher. And the gist of his answer had been this: I know no god called Jesus, and I am a Jew – you can take my word on that. But you, angry man, are not a Jew. A Jew is not someone who is born of a Jewish woman, wears side-locks and does not eat pork, but someone who wishes to cleanse his soul. Anyone can become a Jew, if he concludes a covenant with the Lord, and there is absolutely no need to go inventing stupid prohibitions and cutting small pieces of flesh off little boys. God will trust a person without that. And at that point Emmanuel had burst into laughter and concluded his sacrilegious speech in an absolutely shameful fashion. 'Judge for yourself,' he had said, 'O member of the Rabbinical Council, what would God, to whom all the treasures of the heavens and the earth belong, want with a treasure like that – a little piece of your *pipiske*?'

The comical word had come so unexpectedly that some of the *eshibot* pupils had started giggling, and Shmulik had squeezed his eyes shut to drive away the picture that his overactive imagination had instantly drawn: the Lord God inspecting Rabbi Shefarevich's gift and wondering what to do with this little trifle – keep it somewhere safe or throw it away.

The giggling broke off and an ominous silence fell. Nobody had ever paid the venerable rabbi such a terrible insult anywhere, let alone in a public square full of Jews. And this was not just anywhere, but right beside the Wailing Wall!

Was it any wonder that the teacher had lost his temper? 'Jews!' he had shouted, brandishing his fists. 'Stone the son of Belial!'

The only one to throw a stone had been Mikhl-Byk, the most hopeless of all the pupils, whom the rabbi kept in the *eshibot* for all sorts of heavy work. Mikhl was twice as broad as the other *eshibot* boys and four times as strong. Everyone was afraid of his malicious cruelty. Shmulik had once seen Byk grab a street dog by the tail and smash its head against a wall. And the dog had not bitten him or even barked at him – it was simply lying in the middle of the road, the way dogs like to do.

The stone struck the squatting man in the chest. He staggered and rose rapidly from his squatting position, clutching at the spot where he had been hit with one hand.

Mikhl had picked up another stone, and then Emmanuel had looked his attacker in the eye and spoken strange words, very, very quickly. 'Boy,' he exclaimed plaintively, 'that hurts me. *As much as it hurt your father when they killed him.*'

And Byk had dropped the stone and turned pale. Shmulik

would never have believed that Byk's flat, copper-coloured face could ever be so white.

But it was only natural! How could a perfect stranger have known that the Oprichniks of Christ had beaten Mikhl's father to death during a pogrom in Poltava?

Then Rabbi Shefarevich had come to his senses and waved his hand for all the others to drop their stones too.

'So you claim that you are a Jew?' he had asked.

'Of course I am,' the amazing tramp had muttered, pulling down the collar of his robe. On his bony chest there was a visible dent, rapidly flooding with blue and crimson.

The teacher had declared ominously: 'That's excellent. *Genekh, gei-no mit mir!*'* And he had walked off at a rapid pace towards the Mahkamah Palace, which stood beside the Wailing Wall.

Genekh, a pupil from the local population who knew Arabic and Turkish, had dashed after him.

Shmulik had immediately realised where the rabbi was going in such a hurry and why. The municipal court and the *zaptiya* (Turkish police) were both located in the Mahkamah. By law all Jews were subject to the Rabbinical Council, and if a member of the council gave the order for one of the Jews to be put in prison, it had to be carried out.

Apparently Emmanuel was not aware of this, and so he had not been even slightly alarmed. And none of the Jews warned him.

Byk had asked hoarsely: 'How do you know about my father?'

The tramp had replied: 'I read it.'

'Where did you read it? In a newspaper? But it was seven years ago!'

'Not in a newspaper,' Emmanuel had said, 'in a book.'

'In what book?'

'In this one,' the tattered tramp had replied with a serious expression, pointing at Mikhl's forehead. I can read faces, he had said, the same way that other people read books. It's very simple, you just have to know the letters. The face alphabet doesn't have thirty-seven letters, like the Russian alphabet, or even twenty-

* Yiddish: 'Genekh, come with me!'

two, like in the Jewish alphabet; it only has sixteen. A face is even more interesting to read than a book – it will tell you more and it will never deceive you.

And then Byk had suddenly recited the prayer that was meant to be said if you saw some wondrous marvel, or if you were lucky enough to meet a truly distinguished individual: *'Baruch ata Adonai Elocheinu melech cha-olam she-kacha lo be-olamo'* – 'Blessed be Thou, Lord our God, the Lord of the Universe, in whose world such things exist.'

Mikhl reciting a prayer, of his own free will, with no compulsion? Incredible!

After his prayer, Mikhl had said: 'You have to leave, Rabbi. The police will come running now, they will beat you and put you in prison.'

Emmanuel had looked round in alarm at the large building into which Rabbi Shefarevich had disappeared. 'Ah,' he had said, 'I'm going now. Going away altogether.' And he had informed the people nearby in a confidential voice that that there was nothing for him to do in Erushalaim just yet. He had taken a look at the Pharisees, now he was going to take a look at the Sadducees. He said he had been told the Sadducees had settled in the Isreel Valley, where the city of Megiddo once used to be. Then he had lifted up the skirts of his robe and hurried away.

Mikhl had overtaken him and caught hold of his shoulder. 'Rabbi, I'll go with you! The road to Megiddo is long, there are bandits everywhere, you will be killed on your own! I am strong, I will protect you. And you will teach me the sixteen letters!' And he had looked at Emmanuel as if his entire life depended on the reply.

But Emmanuel had shaken his head.

'Why?' Byk had shouted.

'Because you,' the *focusmacher* had said, 'will not master these letters. It is not what you need. And to go with me is not what you need, either. Nothing will happen to me, God will protect me against misfortune. He will protect me, but not those who are with me. That is why I go everywhere alone now. And if you wish to become a Jew, you will do it without me.' And he had gone skipping off in the direction of the Dung Gate.

He had barely disappeared round the corner and less than

half a minute had passed, before Rabbi Shefarevich appeared, with two Turkish gendarmes.

'Where is he, Jews?' the great man had shouted.

'Over there, over there!' the Jews had cried, pointing.

Genekh had translated into Turkish for the gendarmes: 'Over there, over there,' and the Turks had gone running after the disturber of public order.

But a few minutes later they had come back, gasping and limping. One's head was split open, the other was spitting out blood and teeth.

The Jews had been unable to believe their eyes. Could the skinny tramp really have given two hulking brutes like this a thrashing?

The policemen had talked gibberish. Apparently they had almost overtaken the tramp when he just managed to slip away from them into an alley. The men in uniform had dashed after him – and suddenly something terrible had happened in the dark passage. Some diabolical force had seized one of them by the collar and swung him hard against the wall, knocking him out. Before the second man could even look around, the same thing had happened to him. The badly frightened policeman had kept repeating: 'Shaitan, Shaitan!' and Rabbi Shefarevich had hissed through clenched teeth: 'Ga-Satan!' and spat.

The *focusmacher* had turned out to be pretty smart, but to look at him you would never have thought it.

That very evening, Mikhl-Byk had gone away. And how could he not go away, after what had happened at the Wailing Wall?

When he left he had said: 'I'll go and wander round the world a bit. I'll take a look at Africa, see what it's like. And America too.'

He had sewn a blue ribbon on to his white shirt and left. Eliminated himself from his own people . . .

That was what had happened on the first Sabbath after Passover. But Shmulik didn't tell the *shiksa* about Mikhl-Byk, or about the barefoot conjurer who stole Jewish souls. All he said was: 'The man you are asking about was here and he went away.'

'When?' the Russian woman asked anxiously.

'Two weeks ago.'

'And do you know where he went?'

Shmulik hesitated, wondering if he should say or not. But what was the problem? Why shouldn't he say? 'He mentioned the Isreel Valley and the ancient city of Megiddo, and something about Sadducees.'

'Megiddo?' the *shiksa* echoed, and her eyes opened wide in fright. 'Oh, Lord! But where is it and how can I get there?' She took a little book out of her travelling bag. There was a folded map inside it.

Shmulik wanted to tell the stupid woman that the journey to the Isreel Valley was long and difficult, that Emmanuel wouldn't get there anyway, because nobody went to those parts on his own – they were crawling with bandits. And a European woman would be absolutely crazy to think of going to such a desolate place.

He wanted to tell her, but he didn't have time, because he happened by chance to look round, and everything inside him turned cold. That cursed Lithuanian, the one who had been staring in the street, had proved stubborn: he had trailed them and there he was – peeping round the corner. It was terrible to think what lies he would tell Rabbi Shefarevich. The only hope was that he might not have recognised which *eshibot* this lover of idle tattle with *shiksas* came from.

Shmulik darted headlong into the nearest side street, slipped into a broad doorway and hid. He heard a pair of lady's heels go clacking past – that was the *shiksa* walking by. A minute later they were followed by soft, muffled footsteps.

Glory be to Thee, Lord. The danger has passed

Life in an Arab harem, seen from the inside

Megiddo? Sadducees?

Polina Andreevna walked quickly along the tiny street that was like a deep trench, the ringing echo of her footsteps bouncing off the walls that were separated by a gap of no more than a sazhen.

It was the Zionists that he had called Sadducees. In actual fact, they were similar. The Sadducees had also defended freedom of will and claimed that man's fate was in his own hands. The plump girl on the steamer the *Sturgeon* had mentioned the Isreel

Valley and the City of Happiness that would be built close to ancient Megiddo.

Ah, how terrible! Ah, how awful! And two whole weeks had already gone by!

Her decision was taken in a moment, without the slightest hesitation. It was simply remarkable that she had guessed that she ought to bring a travelling bag with all the essentials – underwear, a folding parasol, various ladies' accessories – just in case. She didn't have to go back to the hotel.

In addition to the map of the Holy Land, the pilgrim's guide-book also had a street map of Jerusalem. There was the Jewish quarter, below the Old City. She had to keep moving straight forward all the time – through the Christian section, then the Moslem section – and she would come out at the Damascus Gate.

Only the alley simply did not wish to be straight – it kept swerving, first in one direction, then the other, so that very soon Mrs Lisitsyna had completely lost her grasp of the four points of the compass. She could not see the sun, because the first floors of the houses, which were fronted with wooden grilles so that they resembled chicken hutches, stuck out towards each other and almost met.

The nun stopped, wondering what to do. There was no one for her to ask the way from. Perhaps someone would look out of a window?

She raised her head – and just in time. A pair of woman's hands were thrust out of an open grille. The hands were holding a basin, out of which a stream of soapy water came pouring downwards, glinting like a strip of silver. At the very last moment Polina Andreevna leaped aside into a narrow gap and also jumped up in the air, so that she would not be caught by the water splashing up from the surface of the street.

Since she was already lost in any case, it made no sense to go back, so she walked on along the side alley in front of her. Only now she kept looking up fearfully every now and then. To judge from the traces she spotted on the ground, the waste poured out of windows included other items less innocuous than soapy water. She had to get out on to a normal street as soon as possible!

The alleyway led her to a monastery, and from then on things were simpler. Following the wall, Pelagia reached a small square, where she asked the first passer-by, a man dressed in a European suit, how to get to the Damascus Gate. And finding Salakh's house was really not difficult at all.

The nun stopped in front of an Arab street coffee-house, said, 'Salakh', and gestured as if she were holding reins. They understood exactly what she meant and replied in the same language: straight ahead, then right, and you'll see the gate (a semicircle drawn in the air, and 'knock-knock' with a hand).

In response to the knock, the gate was opened by the master of the house himself, who had parted from Polina Andreevna only some three hours earlier.

'I expect you are surprised,' his visitor said, panting for breath. 'But I have a job for you.'

When he saw his recent passenger, Salakh opened his brown, slightly protruding eyes wide in surprise; but when he heard about the job, he began waving his arms about. 'No can do job! No can do! You come visit as guest – welcome. We drink coffee, eat baklava. Then talk job.'

Pelagia wanted to say that the job was too urgent to postpone, but she recalled how sensitive Eastern etiquette was and gave way. In the final analysis, what difference would a few minutes make, and in any case, she didn't know any other drivers in Jerusalem.

From the outside Salakh's house did not look very impressive, with flaking walls and rubbish and offal dumped beside the gate, so Polina Andreevna was fully prepared for a depressing scene of poverty and neglect. However, the visitor was in for a surprise.

The house was in the form of an enclosed rectangular space with an open yard in the middle. The inner walls of the structure gleamed brilliant white and in the centre of the yard, under a canopy, there was an extremely comfortable raised dais, covered with a carpet.

Pelagia was reminded of a comment she had read in a book by a certain traveller: the Asiatic dwelling, as opposed to the European, was not concerned with external appearance, but with internal comfort. That was precisely why Orientals were so phlegmatic and uncurious – the world that they inhabited was contained within the walls of their own home. Europeans, on the other hand, did not feel comfortable under their own roofs, and so they wandered all over the world, exploring and conquering distant lands.

But the Asiatic way is more correct, Polina Andreevna suddenly thought, leaning back in delight on the soft cushions. If life is the search for yourself, then why go traipsing off to the ends of the earth? Stay home, drink coffee with honey cakes and contemplate your inner world.

A fat woman with a rather conspicuous moustache set a bowl of candied fruit on the carpet and poured the coffee.

Salakh exchanged a few phrases with her in Arabic, then introduced her: 'Fatima. Wife.'

Fatima did not come up on to the dais. She squatted down on her haunches beside it, holding the coffee pot in her hands, and every time the guest put her cup down, even for a moment, she topped it up again.

Having spent five minutes on the requirements of etiquette (beautiful house, wonderful coffee, charming wife), Pelagia announced the purpose of her visit: she wanted to go to Megiddo. How much would it cost?

'Not a thing,' her host replied, shaking his head.

'How do you mean?'

'I not mad. I not go any money.'

'Twenty-five roubles,' said Polina Andreevna.

'No.'

'Fifty.'

'Not even thousand!' Salakh exclaimed, fluttering his hands angrily. 'I not go!'

'But why not?'

He began bending down his fingers, counting off reasons.

'Swamp fever. One. Bedouin bandits. Two. Circassian bandits. Three. I not go no matter how much.'

It was not said in order to raise the price, but definitively – the nun realised that straight away. So she had simply wasted her time.

Disappointed, Pelagia put down her cup. 'But you boasted: I'll take you wherever you want.'

'Wherever you want, but not there,' Salakh retorted.

Seeing that the guest was no longer touching her coffee, Fatima asked her husband about something and he answered – no doubt explaining what was the matter.

'So it was yet another lie,' Polina Andreevna declared bitterly. 'Like the lie to me about a Russian wife and the lie to the Americans about an American one.'

'Who lied? I lied? Salakh never lied!' the Palestinian exclaimed indignantly. He clapped his hands and shouted: 'Marusya! Annabel!'

A woman peeped out of the door leading into the interior of the house. She was dressed in oriental style, but her pink cheeks and snub nose left no doubt at all as to her nationality. The woman's hair was tied back with an Arab scarf, not knotted at the chin, as the local woman did it, but at the back of her neck, peasant-fashion. Shaking her hands, which were covered in flour, the Slav woman gazed at Salakh enquiringly.

'Come here!' he ordered her and shouted even louder: 'Annabel!'

When there was no response, he got to his feet and disappeared into the house.

He could be heard inside, appealing in English: 'Honey! Darling! Come out!'

'Are you really Russian?' Polina Andreevna asked.

The round-faced woman nodded, coming closer.

'You're Natasha, aren't you? Your husband told me.'

'Nah, I'm Marusya,' the nun's fellow-countrywoman drawled in a thick voice. 'Natasha's what the men round here call all our women. That's their custom.'

'Are there really many Russian women here?'

'Plenty of them,' Marusya told her, taking a candied fruit from a tray and popping it into her full-lipped mouth. 'The pilgrims with any brains – as don't want to go back to Russia. What's so good there, anyway? Slave away like a horse. Your man drinks. In winter you get froze half to death. But this place is paradise. Warm and free, all sorts of fruits and berries. For them lucky enough to find a husband, it's heaven. Your Arab doesn't guzzle vodka, he's affectionate, and then you don't have to handle him on your own. With three or four women around, it's a lot easier. Right, Fatimushka?' She rattled away in Arabic, translating what she had just said.

Fatima nodded. She poured coffee for herself and Marusya and they both sat down on the edge of the dais.

The appeals in English could still be heard from inside the house.

Marusya shook her head. 'Anka's not going to come out. She writes that book of hers round about now.'

'What's that?' Pelagia asked, blinking. 'What book?'

'About woman's life. That's what she got married for. Said "I'll live with an Arab husband for a year or so, then I'll write a book like there's never been before." And the title of the book is "Life-in-arabian-harem-seen-from-inside",' said Marusya, pronouncing the English phrase without stumbling once. 'That's in American, but in our language it's "A Tale of Arab Men". She says everyone in America will buy a book like that, she'll earn a million. Anka's an educated women, terribly clever. Almost like Fatimka. "Afterwards", she says, "I'll go to China and marry a Chinaman. I'll write another book, 'A Tale of Chinese Men'. Women have a right to know how our sister lives in different places."'

Intrigued, Polina Andreevna exclaimed: 'But how can she go? She's married!'

'Very simple. Round here, nothing could be easier than that. Salasha just has to say: "You are no longer my wife" three times, and that's it – go wherever you like.'

'But what if he won't say it?'

'He will – what choice has he got? He'll say it thirty-three times, never mind three. A woman can always drive a man crazy if she wants. And with three women it's even easier . . .'

Marusya translated for Fatima, who nodded again.

The nun found sitting there with the other two, drinking strong, flavoursome coffee and talking about women's concerns so unusual and absorbing that for a while she even forgot about her postponed business.

'But how do you all get along with just one man?'

'Really well. It was hard for Fatima with him on her own: keep the house and keep an eye on the children. And then she invited me to be a wife – we met at the bazaar. She could see I was a strong, working woman, and honest.'

'And Salakh agreed?'

Marusya laughed and relayed the question to her female comrade, who also tittered. She replied (and Marusya translated into Russian): 'Who asked him?'

Polina Andreevna found all this terribly interesting. 'And what does our American do?'

'Anka? Teaches the children and stands in for us in bed, especially during the hot season. She's young and skinny – doesn't feel the heat. And it's good for her book too. When she finishes writing it and goes away, we'll get someone to take her place, another pretty young one. We've already made our minds up, it has to be one of the local Jewish girls. They're full of go.'

'But does Islam allow men to marry Jewish women?'

Marusya was amazed. 'What, did you think I'd swapped my faith for theirs? Oh no, I'll die in the same faith I was born in. Salasha didn't try to force me. Islam's a good faith – it's kind. For them Christian and Jewish women are "people of the Book" – of the Bible that is. There's no shame in marrying them. It's the cursed pagans you can't marry, and who's ever seen any of them round here?'

At this point Fatima said something for the first time without waiting for a translation from Marusya.

'She asks, why do you want to get to Megiddo so bad?'

'There's a man I really need to find, but Salakh doesn't want to go. Not even for fifty roubles.'

The fat woman with the moustache looked closely at the guest, as if she were trying to weigh her up.

'Do you love him very much?'

The unexpected question left Pelagia confused and unsure how to explain. The easiest thing was to tell a lie. 'Yes . . .' she said, and blushed furiously. It was shameful for a nun to tell an untruth. But Fatima interpreted the blush in her own way.

'She says: If you turned red, it means your love really is strong.'

The wives spoke to each in Arabic for a while. Then the senior wife patted Polina Andreevna on the cheek and said something brief.

'He'll go,' Marusya translated. 'And you give the fifty roubles to Fatimka here.'

A hitch

The lengthy journey over sea waves, mountains and valleys had put Yakov Mikhailovich in philosophical mood. In his profession you didn't often get the chance to travel so peacefully and unhurriedly across the face of Mother Earth. The section across water had been especially gratifying. There had been no point in trailing the mark – where could she go to, once she was on the ship? On the contrary, he had had to keep away from her, not get under her feet too much. During the voyage Yakov Mikhailovich had even filled out a bit from the rich food and healthy naps on the deck.

However, the newly acquired layer of fat had soon melted away – just you try covering seventy versts on your own two feet.

Once on shore, Yakov Mikhailovich had felt it imperative to transform his appearance – on the steamship he had been an unremarkable gentleman in a panama hat and a two-piece linen suit, and now he became an even less remarkable peasant pilgrim. There were any number of those dragging themselves along the road to the most blessed city of Jerusalem. The mark was travelling in a horse-drawn vehicle, but a really lousy one, so there had been no need for him to trot along like a little goat.

In Jerusalem Yakov Mikhailovich had thought it more appropriate to transform himself into a Jew. This species was present here in an unprecedented variety of forms and, what was more, they all shunned each other, and each of them spoke their own language. On several occasions the false Lithuanian had been approached by other individuals in loose coats and hats, who had started talking to him about something or other, but Yakov Mikhailovich had only moaned and grunted in reply – after all, Jews could be deaf-mutes too. The Lithuanians had clucked their tongues compassionately and left the poor fellow in peace.

Everything had been going absolutely fine, until the hitch happened.

Yakov Mikhailovich was following the mark along a narrow alleyway. He was keeping his distance, not sticking too close, but not letting her out of his sight either, not relying just on the clacking of her heels. And suddenly a supernatural event, a real piece of magic – there was nothing else you could call it.

He looked round for just a split second, to see if anyone was following him. Suddenly there was a splash of liquid further up ahead. When he looked back, there was water pouring from a window on the first floor of a house, and the nun seemed to have vanished into thin air. He rubbed his eyes to make sure he wasn't dreaming. She was there just a moment ago, but now – abracadabra, and there was nothing but a soapy puddle on the surface of the alley. Could his little snow-maiden really have melted? Or had she noticed she was being followed and taken off as fast as her legs would carry her?

He rushed forward, but after a hundred steps he reached a dead end. And it was only on the way back that he discovered a narrow little opening on the right that Ginger must have slipped into. But it was too late – he wouldn't catch her now.

He dashed around the alleyways for a little while, getting soaked in sweat. Anyone without his strength of character would certainly have fallen into despair, but Yakov Mikhailovich, as we have already said, believed fervently in the power of the human intellect. There are no insoluble problems, only incompetent problem-solvers.

He stopped in a patch of shade and used his head. Come on, now, come on now. What does the intellect have to say in a situation like this?

Go to the Russian conventuary, to the women's hotel? Wait for the frisky lady there?

But why was she carrying a travelling bag? And if she wasn't intending to go back to the hotel, what then?

He used his brain a bit more, then nodded to himself and said: 'Clever lad.'

And he turned back, towards the Jewish quarter.

The round-shouldered little Yid was still at the same spot where Ginger had called to him. He was standing, slumped back against the wall, sniffing. Then he squatted down, picked up his stick and started drawing some kind of squiggles on the ground. He was so absorbed that he didn't even notice Yakov Mikhailovich walk up to him.

The 'Lithuanian' waited for the street to empty and touched the kid on the shoulder. The black eyes that gazed at Yakov Mikhailovich reflected the pink glow of the sunset, but he could see fear in them too. The little rascal started gabbling away in the Jewish patter and shaking his head – as if he was making excuses for something.

'You come along with me, my little friend,' Yakov Mikhailovich told him, gently squeezing one skinny shoulder and jerking the little Jew to his feet.

'I didn't do anything,' the little squirt babbled in Russian. 'All I did was give her some water . . .'

'Come on, come on,' the 'Lithuanian' repeated peaceably, leading the boy along. 'This way, into this little gap. We're going to have a cosy little chat, and no one's going to interrupt us. What did she ask you about, that ginger-headed one?'

The little Yid looked into Yakov Mikhailovich's calm eyes, and he must have seen something special in them, for he gulped convulsively and his lips started trembling.

It was good that the boy was so quick on the uptake. To make quite sure no time was wasted, the man poked him with his finger under the collarbone, where the nerve point is, at the same time stopping the lad's mouth with his other hand, so there wouldn't be any unnecessary shouting.

There was no shout, nothing but silence. The boy's pupils dilated – that was from the pain. In his line of work, Yakov Mikhailovich had repeatedly observed this remarkable phenomenon, and only recently he had read in a certain scientific journal that it was a physiological reaction caused by intense stimulation of the visual nerve.

'So, what was she asking you about?' Yakov Mikhailovich repeated, after waiting for the pupils to contract a little bit.

He took his hand away from the mouth, but not very far, just a couple of vershoks. And he held the finger that he had jabbed into the painful spot where it could be seen, as a reminder.

'About the Russian prophet,' the little Jew said quickly. 'About Emmanuel . . . He's here now.'

The man smiled and gave him a pat of approval on the forehead – the boy squeezed his eyes shut in terror.

'I believe you're telling me the truth. And where did she go to, do you know?'

Yakov Mikhailovich's own heart skipped a beat. If he didn't know, what then?

'I don't know, mister . . .' the little Jew said, which upset Yakov

Mikhailovich, but when the boy saw how dark this terrible man's face had turned, he added hastily: 'She said something about the Isreel Valley, asked how she could get there. And about Megiddo too.'

The 'mister' breathed a sigh of relief. 'And there was nothing else said?'

'N-no, n-nothing . . .'

It looked like he really had milked the boy dry. Yakov Mikhailovich started pondering.

'Word of honour, mister, I've told you everything . . .'

'Quiet, my little friend, don't interrupt. I'm just wondering if I can let you live,' the man muttered, scratching his temple.

Then the little Jew just blurted it out – so solemnly, it was clear he really meant it. 'You can't kill me, you mustn't. I've still got to save mankind!'

That decided it. If he was one of those saviours of mankind, then he was bound to blab, Yakov Mikhailovich realised. We know all about them and their Jewish telegraph.

He smiled reassuringly at the lad, stroked the lumpy back of his head with one hand, took hold of the narrow chin with the other and jerked it powerfully to one side. There was a faint squeal in the little scallywag's narrow, bird-like chest, and when Yakov Mikhailovich took his hands away, he slid silently down the wall. The head swollen with learning slumped on to one shoulder, and the saviour of mankind joined his people.

X

The Spider's Lair

'Well done, Berdichevsky'

Matvei Bentsionovich looked the sergeant of the Kiev section straight in the eye, stared at the wet lips puckered up ready to kiss him and hissed contemptuously through his teeth, borrowing a useful term from the captain: 'The kiss of Judas. Well, recognised me, have you, Yid-lover?'

Savchuk gaped in amazement, while Kolya pulled his lips back in and the lower one dropped together with his jaw.

The important thing now was to continue the onslaught, pile on the pressure. 'Fine apostles you have!' exclaimed Berdichevsky, rounding on the factory owner. 'I saw this specimen in the Bristol! A nest of Yids – the place is piled high with them. And him crawling around in front of them on his hands and knees. They treat him with disdain, and he says "sir" to all of them. When I see Russians trampling their own pride underfoot, it makes me see red!'

The captain hastily interceded for Kolya: 'He does that on purpose! It's what we instructed him to do! All the important people stay at the Bristol. Nikolai is our eyes and ears.'

'He bows down to the floor at their feet for a lousy ten-kopeck piece,' the public prosecutor cried, refusing to hear a word. 'Perhaps he's the Yids' eyes and ears here?'

Matvei Bentsionovich's wrath was magnificent. The saliva sprayed from his mouth, and his arms flailed about so furiously that the porter backed away, ran into a chair and fell flat on the floor.

The others ran to help the fallen man up.

'I assure you, Mr Dichevsky, you are mistaken, he is our man!' said the captain, trying to coax Berdichevsky round. 'Tried and tested many times over! He has even taken part in secret operations.'

Eventually the State Counsellor allowed himself to be calmed down, but not straight away, oh no.

And then came the counter-attack from the insulted Kolya. He began shouting in a voice trembling with resentment and jabbing his finger at Matvei Bentsionovich: 'His hair wasn't like that – black it was!'

The public prosecutor retorted contemptuously: 'You fool! Have you never heard of hair dye?'

'You really are a fool, Kolya,' said the hairdresser, rushing to Berdichevsky's aid. 'Come round to my place, and I'll turn you into a kike in two ticks.'

'But why did you colour your hair to look like a Jew?' Savchuk asked with a frown.

In reply, Berdichevsky gestured with his eyes, as if to say: Let's step aside for a moment. He whispered in the captain's ear: 'Tomorrow I'm going to dye my hair again. I have a plan. I'm going to pretend to be a Jew. I'll infiltrate their inner circle, get a feel for what they're like and the best way to handle them. I hope you can give me the information I need. Who's the leading Sanhedrinite now that Shefarevich has gone?'

'You must be insane!' said the factory owner, throwing his arms up in the air. 'How could you possibly pass for a Jew, with your appearance? They'll spot an outsider straight away. Then it'll be just like it was with that girl – head down in deep water . . .'

'You can only die once, and beneath that slab of stone – you know yourself . . .' Berdichevsky said with modest courage and without the slightest trace of posturing. 'Come on, Savchuk, tell me everything you know.'

Infernal Zizi

First thing on Friday morning the State Counsellor went to Great Berdichevsky Street to see the head of the provincial prison committee, and there he made a few enquiries.

After lunch he carried out raid number two – but not on the Goel-Israel *eshibot* (of which, as it happens, nothing remained except the building). A more interesting target had come to light.

The weather was excellent, almost summer-like, and Matvei Bentsionovich decided to go for a stroll, especially since he felt the need to gather his thoughts.

How different Zhitomir was from the public prosecutor's beloved Zavolzhsk! Heaven and hell, Berdichevsky repeated to himself as he looked around. This place was undoubtedly hell, despite the sticky young leaves, the fresh breeze and the blue sky. In fact, the magnificence of the natural setting only rendered the abhorrent wretchedness of the town all the more offensive to the eye. How strikingly different the world of man was from that of God!

God had granted the people of Zhitomir the aforementioned high sky, and the singing of the birds, and the marvellous view of the Teterev river from Castle Hill.

As their contribution, people had added to God's gift these grey streets with crooked houses, this pavement fouled with ordure and gobs of spittle, and their own malevolent faces.

Everywhere in Zavolzhsk there was a sense of sound quality and unpretentious solidity, but the dominant theme here was grinding poverty and a certain fragility, as if the little houses were on the point of crumbling into dust, sending their inhabitants scattering in all directions, like scalded cockroaches. And he could also sense a peculiar tension in the atmosphere, as if the entire town were about to be tossed up into the air at any moment and transformed into a site of carnage. What kind of glances, what kind of faces were these? Berdichevsky wondered, shaking his head and feeling homesick for the people of Zavolzhsk.

The population of Zhitomir was quite remarkably diverse. In addition to Jews, Russians and Ukrainians, you could also meet Poles, and Germans, and Czechs, and schismatics, and each of these groups dressed in its own way and stuck to its own manners; they regarded outsiders with disdain and had no desire at all to mingle with them.

Perhaps this heterogeneity was the problem? No, Matvei Bentsionovich told himself. There were all sorts of people in Zavolzhsk too – Tartars, and Bashkirs, and Zityaks and Votyaks and Mordvinians, and those Poles yet again. Some were Orthodox Christians, some were Old Believers, some were Moslems, some were Catholics and some were even pagans. But it was all right, they got along together, they weren't at each others' throats all the time.

Berdichevsky suddenly had a disgustingly anti-Semitic thought, the very thing for a baptised Jew to think: Perhaps the Jews were to blame for everything after all? It was an individualistic religion, every Jew existed face to face with God, all on his own, you might say. If there were a lot of them, or if they were the majority, as in Zhitomir, the concentration of energy was too intense, it set the atmosphere sparking. But no: the number of Jews in St Petersburg was tiny, because they weren't allowed to live there, but the feeling of a dormant volcano was even stronger in the capital than in Zhitomir.

His memories of St Petersburg gave him his answer. The problem was not the Jews, and it was certainly not the variety of races and multitude of faiths. The problem was the authorities.

In Zavolzhsk, now, the authorities were even-handed, and everybody there lived in peace, neighbours didn't bear grudges against each other or look down each others' trousers to see who was circumcised and who wasn't. And anyone who tried it would soon get a cuffing from the earthly authorities in the person of the Governor and the spiritual authorities in the person of the Bishop.

But in Zhitomir, discord between the city's residents was encouraged, as demonstrated by that police chief, Likurgovich. It was the same in St Petersburg and therefore throughout the great Empire as a whole.

Nationalities and religions were sorted and graded from up above – some were better, some were worse, and some were no good at all. And that created a great tall stairway that Russia could easily come tumbling down and break its legs, or even its neck.

Standing on the very top step were the Orthodox Great Russians, then came the Orthodox Slavs of non-Russian blood, then the Lutheran Germans, then the Georgians, the Armenians, the Moslems, the Catholics, the Old Believers and the Jews. The only ones considered worse than the Jews were the prohibited sects, such as the Dukhobors or the Khlysts. And each subject knew which step his place was on, and every one of them was dissatisfied. And that included the apparently privileged Great Russians, because nine out of ten of them were hungry and illiterate and they lived worse lives than others on lower steps.

This allegory had a whiff of socialism about it, and socialism was a thing of which Matvei Bentsionovich disapproved, regarding the theory of coercive equality as a harmful Teutonic temptation that preyed on immature minds. And so the public prosecutor abandoned his philosophising and returned to reality. And it was high time – the Castle Hill had already been left far behind, and he was already entering Podgurka, the area that the provincial prison inspector had called 'an appalling Jewish weed patch'.

The inspector seemed to have been right, Berdichevsky thought as he strode along the dirty streets of the Jewish quarters. How did the Oprichniks ever manage to arrange pogroms with all this poverty? Everything here was smashed and broken already.

People stared curiously at the clean gentleman in the bowler hat. Many of them greeted him in Yiddish, one or two tried to engage him in conversation, but Matvei Bentsionovich politely declined: *Unshuldigen zi mir*, dear fellow, I'm in a hurry.

The State Counsellor had tried to reverse his hair colour from angelic to brunet, for which purpose he had visited the familiar *salon de beauté* and purchased the dye Infernal Zip, which promised hair that was 'the colour of a raven's wing with a remarkable anthracite shimmer'.

But he had not succeeded in restoring the natural colour of his hair (evidently the angel and Zizi had been chemically incompatible) and the thinning growth on the public prosecutor's head had acquired a reddish-brown tone. But then, some Jews had natural colouring exactly like that, and so Matvei Bentsionovich accepted it. In fact, he was rather delighted by his newly acquired gingerness, which seemed somehow to bring him closer to Pelagia (may the Lord preserve her from all trouble and misfortune).

Outside the synagogue there was a jostling queue of incredibly ragged and tattered beggars. The air was filled with a raucous hubbub, only not in the Russian style, with crude obscenities and women's squeals, but a plaintive lament, complete with wailing and the lifting up of hands – in short, an absolutely genuine Jewish *chipesh*. Ah yes, it was Friday evening. They were giving out the *chalyav* – crocks of milk and *challah* bread – the indigent Jews, so that they would have something with which to celebrate the Sabbath.

Only a stone's throw from the synagogue, thought the State Counsellor, recalling the inspector's instructions. All he had to do was turn on to Little Vilenskaya Street.

There it was – the single-storey grey house with a crooked attic storey (the one the inspector had called the 'spider's lair').

The signboard was in Russian, Polish and Yiddish: 'Efraim Golosovker's Pawnshop and Loan Office'.

A piece of advice worth twenty-five thousand

Berdichevsky jangled the little bell and went into the front office, which at first glance produced a strong impression of squalor and neglect. However, if one looked a little more closely, the dusty, cracked window panes turned out to be protected by extremely solid steel rods, there was a triple English lock fitted to the door, and the safe had the matt glint of Krupps' steel.

So we like to look a bit poorer than we really are, the public prosecutor thought to himself as he surveyed the owner of the establishment.

Mr Golosovker was wearing a grubby yarmulka, the bridge of his spectacles was held together with a piece of string and his elbows were adorned with worn bookkeeper's sleeve-protectors. He glanced briefly at the visitor and made a show of being terribly busy, clicking the beads on his abacus.

There was one other person in the office – a rather dapper young man with a perfect parting in his gleaming blond hair. He was standing in a corner by the counter, copying something out into a tattered accounts book.

'Shabat shalom,' Matvei Bentsionovich said, on the occasion of the approaching Sabbath.

The young man murmured: 'Hello.' His gaze was extremely gentle, positively silky in fact.

The moneylender himself merely nodded. He looked at the visitor again, for a bit longer, and held his hand out with the palm upwards. 'Show me.'

'Show you what?' Berdichevsky asked, astonished.

'Show me what you've brought.'

'Where did you get the idea that I've brought something?'

Golosovker rolled up his eyes, sighed and explained patiently, as if he were talking to a retarded child: 'People come to me either-or. Either to take out a loan or to pawn something. You're not a *tsudreiter*, you don't think I'd give a loan to someone I don't know, do you? No, you're not a *tsudreiter*. If a Jew's a *tsudreiter* or, to put it more politely, an idiot, he doesn't wear a bowler hat worth twelve roubles and an English tweed jacket worth forty or maybe forty-five. That means you've brought something. Well what is it you've got? A gold watch? A ring with a precious stone?' He slid his spectacles down to the tip of his nose, shifted a magnifying glass down from his forehead on to one eye and clicked his fingers,

'Come on, come on. Of course, I'm not a *tsadik* or a rabbi, but on Friday evening I go to the synagogue, and then I sing *"Shalom aleichem, mal'achei ga-shalom"* and sit down to festive supper. Kesha, what are you fiddling about with there?' he asked, turning to the young blond man. 'Honest to God, I'd do better to hire some atheist Jew to sit in the shop on Friday evening and Saturday.'

'Almost done, almost done, Efraim Leibovich,' Kesha said meekly and started scribbling in the book at twice the speed. 'I can't seem to find Madam Slutsker's turquoise beads in the inventory. Is she not coming back to redeem them? Tomorrow's the last day.'

'She'll come, of course, even though it's the Sabbath, and she'll cry, but she hasn't got any money, and that means the beads can't be given back to her. I'm locking them in the safe.'

Matvei Bentsionovich took advantage of the pause to examine the 'spider' and try to work out how to talk with someone like this. The best thing to do was probably to assume the same tone as he used.

'I haven't brought you anything, Mr Golosovker,' the State Counsellor said, and his voice naturally started weaving that sing-song intonation that he thought had been banished for ever by the long years of study and state service. 'On the contrary, you have something that I want to take.'

The moneylender took his hand down from his face and screwed up his eyes. 'And am I going to give something to a man

I don't know, even if he is wearing a bowler hat? Do you think I'm a *shlimazl*?'

Berdichevsky smiled demurely. 'No, Monsieur Golosovker, you are not a *shlimazl*. The great Ibn-Ezra said: "If a *shlimazl* takes it into his head to become a gravedigger, people will stop dying, and if a *shlimazl* starts selling lamps, the sun will stop rising." As far as I am aware, everything is in perfect order with your business.'

'As far as you are aware?' Golosovker echoed. 'And may I enquire *exactly how far* you are aware? Begging your pardon, but who might you be, and where are you from?'

'Mordechai Berdichevsky,' the public prosecutor said with a bow, using the name that he had borne before he was baptised. 'From Zavolzhsk. And I really do know quite a lot of things about you.' Seeing the other man's face stiffen at these words, Matvei Bentsionovich hastily added. 'Don't worry, Monsieur Golosovker. What I want from you is something that any Jew will gladly give – advice.'

'And you've come all the way from Zavolzhsk to Zhitomir to ask Efraim Golosovker for advice?' the moneylender asked, screwing up his eyes suspiciously.

'You will laugh at me, but that is so.'

Efraim Golosovker did not laugh, but he manage a smile that seemed rather alarmed and flattered at the same time

Berdichevsky cast a sideways glance at the young man, who was doing everything possible to appear so busy with his work that he could not possibly see or hear anything that was going on.

'Speak, Monsieur Berdichevsky. Keshe's a good boy, *a idishe chartz**, even if he is a *katsap*. He knows that what is said within these walls has to stay within these walls.'

The owner of the Jewish heart seemed not to have heard this flattering testimonial – he was intently rustling through the pages in the book, trying to find something.

But even so, the public prosecutor lowered his voice: 'I have a loan and credit company in Zavolzhsk – something like your own. Well, perhaps just a little bigger.' He demonstrated with

* Yiddish: 'a Jewish heart'.

his thumb and forefinger that the difference was only a tiny one.

'And how did you manage that? The province of Zavolzhie is outside the pale of settlement. Did you get baptised?'

'No, how could I possibly do that?' Berdichevsky asked, raising both hands in a gesture of reproach. 'As they say, you can't make a yarmulka out of a pig's tail. But, I can tell you, there was still *makes* to pay. I had to register as a merchant of the first guild – *tsimes mit kompot*. The certificate alone cost 565 roubles, and then they require you to trade wholesale, and what kind of wholesale is there in our business? If you don't want to trade, pay the chief of police, *a loch im in kop*,'* said Matvei Bentsionovich, taking on his soul the sin of slandering the perfectly honest police chief of Zavolzhsk. He was surprised at himself – how freely the words and phrases from his childhood rose up out of his memory.

'Eh, you haven't seen what our police are like yet,' Golosovker said with a dismal smile. 'I've never met worse *urls*, even in Belaya Tserkov.'

The public prosecutor blinked in puzzlement, then he remembered that an *url* was the same as a goy.

But it was time to get down to business. And Berdichevsky began cautiously: 'A certain man has come to me. He wants to set up his own business and he's asking for a loan of twenty-five thousand.'

Efraim Leibovich rolled his eyes up as a sign of respect for such a large sum.

'I wouldn't have given it to him, because he is a new man in Zavolzhsk and he has no real estate there, but there is one special circumstance to the case. This man is a goy, a nobleman, but he brought a guarantee from a Jew, and not just from some *laidak* or other, but from your town's highly respected Rabbi Shefarevich.'

Golosovker raised his eyebrows, and Berdichevsky immediately stopped speaking to see if there would be any comments. But no comments followed.

'Mr Shefarevich is such an important man that he and his Goel-Israel are even known in Zavolzhsk. A guarantee from the rabbi cannot be so easily dismissed. And the interest rate is advantageous too. But I am a thorough man. I decided to come

---

* Yiddish: 'a hole in the head to him'.

and check. And what do I discover when I get here? It seems that the rabbi has moved to *Erushalaim, eliger itot*.'* As he pronounced the name of the Holy City, Matvei Bentsionovich reverently raised his hands in the air. 'And it also turns out that my would-be client spent some time in the debtors' prison here.'

'Ah, I knew it,' the moneylender remarked with satisfaction. 'A villain.'

'Wait, it's not all quite that simple. He only spent a short time in prison. Everything was paid off for him, right down to the last kopeck. And someone whispered to me that it might have been the Rabbi Shefarevich himself, or his deputies, who paid the debt. Does that mean I can rely on the guarantee? And I have come to you, Monsieur Golosovker, because you know my client well. He is a certain Bronislav Ratsevich, who once owed you money. It was you who clapped him in jail, was it not?'

'It was,' said the owner of the loan office, smiling like a man recalling an old victory. 'What does a clever businessman do with his money? He divides it into three parts: he puts the biggest part into deals that are reliable but don't earn a lot of profit. He puts the next part into undertakings with medium risk – and with medium earnings. And he spends a small part on projects that are highly dubious, where he can simply lose his money, but if he is lucky the earnings can be very high. In our *gesheft* the high-risk capital investment is buying up irredeemable IOUs. For ten, or sometimes even five per cent.' (Berdichevsky nodded, although this moneylending wisdom was new to him.) 'Most of the time you lose, but sometimes you can be lucky. I bought up Ratsevich's debt for a thousand roubles. People had no hope of ever getting their money back because of the kind of man he was: he served in the gendarmes department. But I wasn't afraid. And I got everything in full, all fifteen thousand. That's high-risk investment for you.' Golosvker raised one finger to emphasise the point.

After first expressing his admiration for the other man's generosity with advice, Matvei Bentsionovich enquired cautiously: 'But who paid off the IOUs? The venerable Rabbi Shefarevich?'

---

* Yiddish: 'Jerusalem, the Holy City'.

Efraim Leibovich grimaced disdainfully. 'Would Shefarevich buy a gendarme out of jail? *A chits in parovoz?*'*

'Is there steam in a locomotive?' Berdichevsky repeated, puzzled. 'What does that expression mean?'

The moneylender laughed. 'With your surname you ought to know that. It comes from Berdichev, from the time when the railway line was built. What I mean is: Shefarevich needs this gendarme like a locomotive needs extra steam.'

'But they might have some special, private dealings that we don't know about . . .'

'No, no and no again,' Golosovker snapped. 'People can have dealings of any kind at all, of course, but there's nowhere Shefarevich could lay his hands on fifteen thousand. Who should know that, if not me? Shefarevich and fifteen thousand? Don't make me laugh. You can only believe *umzin*† like that if you live in Zavolzhsk. Send Ratsevich packing, he's a swindler. He won't give you back your money, and he forged the guarantee – he must know that Shefarevich has gone away and won't be coming back. There's a piece of advice worth twenty-five thousand for you!'

The moneylender spread his arms in an expansive, generous gesture.

The triumph of emancipation

'Wait, wait,' exclaimed Matvei Bentsionovich, alarmed at the collapse of his second and final theory. 'You say the Goel-Israel had no money to buy Ratsevich out of jail. That is hard to believe. A highly respected man like Shefarevich has no need of capital. All he has to do is give the order, and the rich Jews will contribute as much as is necessary. Someone who is completely trustworthy told me that the venerable rabbi is like the prophet Ezekiel. People say there hasn't been such a formidably belligerent Jew since the times of Judas Maccabeus, that Rabbi

* Yiddish: 'Is there steam in a locomotive?'
† Yiddish: 'nonsense'.

Shefarevich is the new incarnation of the might and wrath of Israel.'

'Spit in the face of whoever told you that. Shefarevich is an ordinary pompous blabbermouth; the thin soil of the diaspora breeds plenty of his kind. They wag their beards and their eyes flash and they bluster and thunder, but they're just like grass-snakes: their hiss is loud, but their bite is nothing to worry about.' Golosovker heaved a sigh. 'The Maccabeans have been reborn all right, but they don't wear side-locks and they don't observe the Sabbath – you can take my word on that.'

'You mean the Zionists?'

'Some of them.' The moneylender glanced round at the young man and began speaking in a whisper. 'Do you know what I spent those fifteen thousand on, and then another five thousand on top of that?' He spread his hands plaintively. 'You'll never believe it. On draining the swamps in some valley in Palestine. How do you like that? Where is Efraim Golosovker and where are those swamps?'

'It's a noble deed,' Berdichevsky said absent-mindedly, think-ing of something else.

'You'd be noble too, if you were asked so persuasively, *az och-n-vei* . . .'

The State Counsellor was intrigued by the emphasis given to these words.

'You were coerced? Extortion?'

'No,' Efraim Leibovich said with a bitter laugh. 'This gentle-man didn't actually extort the money. He simply came to see me in my hotel. Such a polite young man, with a tie and a calling card. He spoke to me in a pleasant voice: "Golosovker, you're a rich man, and you've grown rich mostly by sucking the blood of poor Jews. The time has come to share with your people. I would be most grateful if you would kindly contribute twenty thousand roubles to the Megiddo-Khadash commune fund within the next three days. And if you don't make the contribution, we'll meet again." And you know, he said it in such a quiet voice, nothing like the way that Rabbi Shefarevich talks. I thought: There's a snake that doesn't hiss, but if he bites – *neshine gedacht*.* And

---

* Yiddish: 'God forbid'.

I really didn't want to meet that young man again.'

'When was this? Where? And who is this man?'

'You ask me when? Four months ago. You ask me where? In the city of Odessa, *zol dos farhapt vern.** I went there on business.'

Matvei Bentsionovich reminded him of the third question: 'I also asked you who this bandit is.'

'You used the word, not me,' the moneylender said, glancing round at the door, although Odessa was a good five hundred versts away. 'Many Jews regard him as a hero. If you ask me, I'll tell you that heroes and bandits are baked from the same flour, but that's not important. The polite young man who came to visit me was called Magellan. I made enquiries, spoke to respectable people. And what they told me about this Magellan made me think it was best to let those swamps – or rather, let them not – be any longer. Twenty thousand is very big money, but what good is it to a dead man?'

'Oh really?' laughed Berdichevsky, amused by the story. Who would have thought that a Zhitomir Gobseck could be so impressionable?

'I won't tell you everything those respectable people told me about the Jew called Magellan, because it would take a long time, and it would be sure to give you nightmares, and who needs nightmares on the Sabbath? What I will tell you is what I saw with my own eyes, and then you can say "oh really?" and laugh, all right?' Golosovker shuddered at the hideous memory. 'You think I'm *mishuginer*, to go throwing away twenty thousand on some lousy swamps, even if I was seriously frightened? Two days is two days, I thought. In two days the Lord God divided the light from the darkness and the water from the dry land – since we happen to be talking about swamps. I read in an Odessa newspaper that the next day the Megiddo-Khadash was holding a meeting, and I decided to see what kind of people they were. If they were really frightening, I was going to take off to Zhitomir the same day, let Monsieur Magellan try to catch the wind in the meadow. And if they weren't very frightening, I was going to finish my business in Odessa first, and then take off.

'So I went to see. Well, it was a typical meeting – one Jew

* Yiddish: 'may it rot'.

240

shouting a lot of loud words and others listening. Then another Jew came out and started shouting too. Then a third one. They shouted for a long time at the tops of their voices, but they didn't listen too well, because Jews like to do the talking themselves, they don't like listening to anyone else. And then Magellan came out. He spoke quietly and not for long, but they listened to him the way they listen to the cantor Zeevson in our synagogue, when he comes from Kiev with his choir of eighteen singers. And when he finished speaking and said: "If you're with us – sign the Charter" (they had a charter, something like an oath of loyalty or allegiance), a long queue of young men and women formed. They all wanted to drain swamps and fight Arab bandits. And I thought to myself: Never mind my business in Odessa, I'm leaving for Zhitomir today. Then suddenly Fira Dorman pushed her way through the crowd and started giving a speech herself. You know who Fira Dorman is, of course?'

'Isn't she the American socialist and suffragette? I read about her in the newspapers.'

'I don't know what a suffragette is, but if it's someone who claims a woman is just as good as a man, then Fira's the one they mean. She was taken to America as a little girl, picked up all sorts of stupid ideas there and came back to stir up confusion in poor Jewish heads that are already topsy-turvy ...

'So anyway, Fira comes out with her cropped hair and papirosa, wearing some kind of riding breeches, and she starts yelling in this hard voice – just like a sergeant major on the parade ground: "Don't you believe this *shmuk*, girls! He's lying to you about equal rights and the new brotherhood. And I ask you, what kind of word is that – 'brotherhood'? If we're talking equality, then why not 'sisterhood'? And why is the leader of the commune a man? Because this glib speechifier wants to lead you into a new slavery! People like him came to us in America too, to set up communes! I can tell you how it all ended! The poor girls did the same work as the men, but they also did their laundry, and fed them, and bore their children and then, when they grew old prematurely and lost their looks, their 'brothers' of yesterday brought in new wives, young ones, and they didn't tell them anything about equal rights!"

'Firka shouted a bit more about the same sort of thing, and then she grabbed hold of their Charter with the signatures and tore it into little pieces. There was uproar. And she stood face to face with Magellan, with her hands on her hips, and said: "Well, exploiter, cat got your tongue?" And he answered, even quieter than usual: "I'm for equality of the sexes. I think woman are people, just like men. And now I'll prove it." And she said to him: "Words, just more words!" Magellan said: "No, deeds. If any man dared to tear up our sacred text, I'd break his lousy arms, and I'm going to do the same to you". Before anyone realised what was going on he grabbed hold of her sleeve and yanked so hard that she sat down on the ground. And then the nice young man broke Fira's arm across his knee. Then he grabbed her other arm and did the same to that. Well, I tell you, that was some sight! A crack and a crunch! Fira's mouth hanging wide open, her eyes right up on her forehead, and her arms dangling down from the elbows like ropes: one sleeve was pulled up and you could see the blood pouring out and the bone sticking through the skin!'

'Mm, yes indeed, a fine fellow,' said Berdichevsky, wincing at the naturalism of the description. 'Then what – did they arrest him? According to the Penal Code, that's "aggravated bodily harm", up to five years of prison or three years of hard labour.'

After he said it he felt embarrassed – it sounded altogether too much like a public prosecutor speaking. But Golosovker was too agitated by his terrible memories, and the legal reference went straight over his head.

'Are you kidding? Fira didn't complain to the police. The next day she went to this Magellan, put her plastered arms round his neck and kissed him – for acknowledging the equal rights of women. Only I didn't see that for myself, because I was already halfway back to Zhitomir.'

'You did take off, then?'

'I was in a hurry, to get the money together,' Efraim Leibovich replied sadly.

'That's a fascinating story, of course, but it has nothing to do with my problem,' Berdichevsky said slowly. 'If the rabbi didn't buy Ratsevich out of jail, then who did?'

The moneylender shrugged. 'The money was transferred to my account from the Kiev branch of the Russian Bank for Trade, Industry and Commerce.'

'And you don't know who paid it?' Matvei Bentsionovich asked in a trembling voice.

'No, I don't. Of course, I tried to find out, but the Russian Trade and Industry is a goy bank, I don't know anyone there. Ah!' said Efraim Leibovich with a philosophical shrug of his shoulders. 'What business is it of mine? Kesha, have you finished that at last?'

A secret sign

The public prosecutor emerged on to Malaya Vilenskaya Street in a state of total frustration. His trip to Zhitomir had proved to be an absolute fiasco, nothing but a waste of precious time.

Both of his plausible theories had come to nothing. There was still a tiny little clue in the bank in Kiev, but that was poor consolation to him. As a legal specialist, Berdichevsky knew all about the confidentiality of banking, an institution that he respected. Of course, he could send an official enquiry from the public prosecutor's office, but paperwork like that would take weeks, and it still might produce nothing. If whoever sent the money wanted to remain incognito, there were plenty of ways for them to do it.

Matvei Bentsionovich stopped, perplexed as to what he should do and where he should go now. Was this really the end of the investigation? Then what about Pelagia? Suddenly he heard a gentle tenor voice speak behind his back: 'Mr ... What is your name ... Mr Berdichevsky!'

Looking round, the State Counsellor saw the good-looking young clerk Kesha.

'How can you leave the shop like that?' the public prosecutor asked in surprise. 'Has Mr Golosovker already gone?'

'He's locking the safe, in person,' the blond-haired young man said with a subtle smile. 'At times like that I'm expected to be outside.'

'What can I do for you? Did you want to tell me something?'

Kesha inclined his head to one side ambiguously and asked hesitantly: 'Tell me, you don't really own a loans and credit company, do you?'

'Where did you get that idea?' asked Berdichevsky, looking at the office boy with growing interest.

'What you're really interested in is Ratsevich, I guessed. And I think I know why.'

'Why?'

Then the young man did something very odd: he took hold of Matvei Bentsionovich's left hand and tickled the palm with his little finger.

The public prosecutor shuddered at the unexpectedness of it and was about to protest at such outrageous familiarity, but he restrained himself. The outlandish tickling was like some kind of secret sign.

'Aha, I knew it,' Kesha said with a nod. 'Now it's clear why you want to know who bought Ratsevich out. I have a very definite hunch on the subject that interests you. Only I'm not a Jew, so I don't give free advice.'

'How much?' Berdichevsky asked in a voice hoarse with excitement.

XI

The City Of Happiness

The luck of the Jews – 1

They didn't make any speeches over the grave. Or weep over it. The communards had an understanding that they would not do that. And before the deathbed delirium set in, Rokhele herself had told them: 'Don't cry'.

Malaria turned out to be quite different from what Malke had thought. That morning Rokhele had got up as usual and milked the cows. Then they had sat down together to sort the seeds and sung 'Awaken not the memories' in two-part harmony, and suddenly Rokhele had said 'Everything's gone dark; never mind, it will pass in a moment.' But half an hour later she was already burning up with the fever.

Malke had led her back to their house, the *han*, but Rokhele had kept saying: 'I can manage, I can manage; you go, or the boys will come back from the field, and our dinner won't be ready.'

Magellan had come running, felt her forehead and gone galloping to Zihron-Yaakov for Dr Sherman. But by nightfall, when the doctor arrived, Rokhele had already passed away. Apparently there was a galloping form of malaria too.

They buried the best and most beautiful of the group in the dark, by torchlight. Malke washed the body that had not grown stiff yet – it was a pure, clear white, without a single mole anywhere – and dressed up the departed in the silk dress and the town shoes that Rokhele had never worn.

The members of the commune dug a hole near the edge of the little river, under the eucalyptus tree that they had planted only a week earlier. The tree was still very small, but some day it would grow tall and mighty.

A group of Arabs from the nearby village stood a little way off, watching to see how the Jews buried their dead.

The Arabs didn't see anything particularly interesting.

Magellan walked out to the front and said: 'This is the first death, there will be others. We must not weaken.' Then they sprinkled earth on the body, which was wrapped in a sheet, and went back to the *han*.

There was no wake at all, because drink was prohibited and anyway, as Magellan said, there was *no point*.

Malke controlled herself for as long as she could, but when she felt she could hold out no longer, she grabbed a bucket and went outside – as if she were going for water. She ran out through the wall of the *han* and once out there, of course, she burst into tears.

As she was walking back, she heard someone else sighing and sobbing in the bushes. Who could it be? Probably Senya Levin – he had always looked at Rokhele in a special kind of way. Although it could have been anyone at all of the remaining twenty-five. Even Magellan himself.

Malke slipped past the bushes as quietly as a mouse.

The New Megiddo commune had just celebrated a month since the day of its birth.

In that short time they had not managed to do very much.

First they had repaired and painted the abandoned *han* that they had acquired together with the land. The *han* was a fortress-house, a faceless rectangular block with only a single gate. The living quarters were set along the first inner wall, the cowshed along the second, the storehouse for tools and equipment along the third, and the barn along the fourth.

Misha the agronomist had shown them the best place to sow the wheat, the best places to plant the orange trees and the maize, the best place to lay out a pasture. The land they had bought along the banks of the Kisson river was good, rich.

Magellan had done well, anticipated everything. He had even bought eucalyptus saplings to suck the excess moisture out of the swampy ground. And he had managed to collect so much money for the commune! He was a real magician. There had been enough to buy a large plot of land, and all the equipment and stores they needed, two carts, four horses, two cows and a prefabricated mechanical mill.

According to the Charter, the property was held in common and indivisible. All the members of the commune were equal, and they shared in everything equally. At the very first meeting they had decided there would be no flirting and love affairs – not out of sanctimonious hypocrisy, but because there were only two girls to twenty-five young men, and the very last thing they needed was quarrelling and dramas of the heart. And then, a family meant children, and it was still too soon to start having children in the City of Happiness. So they had deferred love until later, when they would be settled in more comfortably and more women would come from Russia. They had curtained off a corner for Malke and Rokhele, and that was their only element of segregation. They dressed in the same way as the men, they did not ask for any special indulgences and did not receive any.

It had proved harder to implement the other resolution: to speak to each other only in Hebrew. The only commune member who knew the ancient Jewish language well was Izya, a former *eshibot* student. He gave the others lessons every evening, and everybody tried hard, but during the day they still spoke to each other in Russian. How could you say 'matches' or 'rifle' in Hebrew? Uzya had invented some new words, such as 'fire splinters' and 'thunder-stick', but whatever they might be, they certainly weren't the ancient language of the Jews.

What other decisions had been taken?

Not to accept any help from Baron Rothschild, as other settlers had done. In the first place, Rothschild was a capitalist and an exploiter, and in the second place, they had to get used to relying on their own efforts in everything.

No hired labourers – they would work the land only with their own hands. They hadn't founded a commune to live like parasites on the labour of the indigenous proletarians, had they? (This had immediately spoiled relations between the communards and the local Arab village – the fellahs had been hoping that the Jews would give them work.)

But the most risky decision had been to do without 'protection', since the Circassians, the Bedouins and the settled Arabs had long ago grown accustomed to this source of income and even fought among themselves for the right to play guardian to each Jewish settlement.

New Megiddo had been visited by ambassadors from the Bedouin camp, and the Circassian *aul* and the local sheikh, but Magellan had turned them all away, saying: 'We have weapons, we will defend ourselves.' And that meant they had to live as if they were in a fortress under siege.

The Arabs mostly just stole things, but the Bedouins and Circassians had proved to be genuine bandits.

One night there had been shouting out in the darkness and shots had been fired at the walls. The way the bullets slammed into the clay had been very frightening. But Magellan had given out the rifles and told them to fire a volley. And it had worked – the shouting had stopped.

In the morning, though, they discovered that the three draught horses that were grazing outside the gate had disappeared. The Bedouin camp had disappeared too. The nomads had just folded up their tents and left. Magellan had wanted to pursue them on the only remaining horse, and they had barely managed to dissuade him.

The Bedouins had gone, but the Arabs and Circassians were still there, just waiting for their chance.

Dr Sherman, who lived in the Rothshchild settlement of Zikhron-Yaakov had told Magellan: 'Do not be like the biblical king Josiah, young man. He refused to submit to Pharaoh and was killed, and in this way he destroyed the entire Kingdom of Judea. And you know, the fateful battle took place in the very same Valley of Megiddo where you and I are now standing.'

But Magellan had told him: 'This is the place our kingdom was destroyed, this is the place from which it will be reborn.' It was a good answer, a beautiful answer.

But today, after they had buried Rokhele in the silty soil, the doctor had started remonstrating with Magellan again, and this time the young man had no answer for him, because there was nothing he could say.

Dr Sherman had said: 'You can shoot at bandits – sometimes it works. But you can't shoot at malaria. How could you buy land in this pernicious place without consulting the old-timers like us? And then this is only the beginning: the worst disaster will come in summer, at the peak of the fever season. As well as the lowland pasture, you ought to have bought a plot on a hill. Surely you can see that the locals only ever settle on high ground? The wind disperses the swamp vapours up there. But then, the Arabs would never have sold you a plot on a hill. The cunning rogues will wait until the malaria season begins and most of you die, and then buy the land back for a song. Or just take it back . . . It's the Jews' own fault, we have spoilt them. They used to live by their own labour – meagrely but honestly. But we've driven them crazy with our European money. Why should they cultivate their own land if they can earn more by cultivating ours? Why should they bother to exert themselves, if there are fools like you around?'

Magellan's face had gradually turned darker and darker. He glanced sideways at the other members of the commune, who were listening to the prophecies of doom. And he roared: 'Get out of here, you old raven! I'm sick of your miserable squawking!'

The doctor took offence and left. Malke felt sorry for him, but Magellan had done the right thing. They had sworn an oath to lay down their lives in this land, but never abandon their goal.

And Rokhele has already laid down her life, Malke thought with a shudder as she remembered the repulsive champing of the rotten ground under the blades of their spades. But she hardened her heart and told herself: Never mind, others will come. They're already on the way. And even if they bury me in that filthy swamp too, it will be better than if I had stayed at home and lived to the age of fifty, or even a hundred. What sort of pointless life would that have been? A female vegetable with a husband, children, a daily routine . . .

And then, Magellan was so handsome!

'Hey! Hey! Over here, quickly!' the lookout Sasha Briun shouted from the roof of the *han*. 'Look!' Earlier, when they'd had a dog, they hadn't bothered to set a lookout. Magellan said they ought to get a new dog, but where could they find another one like Polkan?

Everyone went dashing up on to the roof, to the lookout tower, and started peering into the twilight.

There were dark shadows bustling about over by the river – at the spot where they had buried Rokhele only an hour ago.

'They're digging up the grave!' Sasha shouted. 'I didn't realise at first what they were up to over there, but then I took a closer look . . . Honestly, they're digging it up!'

They started dithering and dashing about, not knowing what to do. But then Magellan appeared and shouted: 'Follow me!' And they each grabbed something – an axe, or a Berdan rifle – and ran towards the eucalyptus tree.

Rokhele was lying there, half-covered by a sprinkling of wet dirt – absolutely naked. They hadn't even left her undershirt on her, they'd taken every last thread.

Squealing in fury, Magellan pulled his revolver out of its holster and loped off, taking huge bounds along the path that led to the Arab village two versts away.

Malke was the first to go dashing after him, panting for breath and smearing the tears across her face, but she kept up, even with her short legs. The others ran behind.

When they had covered half the distance, someone at the back shouted: 'Magellan! Look! Fire!'

Looking round, they saw the *han* silhouetted against a background of flickering red flame.

They rushed back. It was harder to run now, because they were worn out.

They saved the house – thankfully there was water in the barrel. Only the lean-to shed for equipment was burned down. But the sacks with their collection of seeds had disappeared and both cows and the horse were gone too. The safe with their reserve funds of three thousand roubles had been torn out of the wall. And the brand-new American harrow, which was worth its weight in gold in Palestine, had disappeared as well.

There were hoof-prints left behind on the ground.

'Shoed,' said Magellan as he shone the torch on them. 'So it's the Circassians, not the Bedouins. They must have been lying in wait until night came. And then, what a stroke of luck – we all went rushing off without even locking the gate . . .'

'That's what they call "the luck of the Jews",' Coliseum said with a sigh. 'What are we going to do now, with no seeds, no harrow, no money?'

Someone (Malke didn't recognise the voice, it was trembling so badly), sobbed: 'We ought to go to Zikhron-Yaakov. We'll die here . . .'

Some snivelled and wailed, some shook their fists in the air in helpless fury, and some just stood there, hanging their heads.

Malke, for instance, was crying. Not because she was afraid, but because she felt sorry for poor Rokhele and for the cows, especially Pestrukha, who used to give two full pails of milk . . .

But Magellan didn't swear or wave his arms about. When he was finished with the hoof-prints, he went to see if the marauders had got as far as the cellar where the weapons were kept. And when he came back, he said calmly: 'They didn't find the guns. So not everything is lost. If they want war, we'll fight.'

'Fight who? – Daniel-bek?' Shlomo the apothecary asked.

The luck of the Jews – 2

The Circassians were known to have appeared in Palestine twenty or twenty-five years earlier on the initiative of the Sultan, who had rewarded his faithful *bashi-bazouks* for their bravery in the war against the Russian and Serbian infidels with good land. Before they became Turkish warriors, these men from the Caucasus had fought under the green banner of the great Shamil and they had left their native mountains after refusing to become subjects of the Tsar. His Osman Majesty had decided to follow the example of his northern neighbour and acquire his own Cossacks, who would prop up the Sultan's power in his decaying realm. Abdul-Hamid had been expecting that, after he gave his soldiers land and exempted them from the payment of tribute, they would feed themselves. They would keep an eye on the restless Arab population, plough and cultivate the land, breed sheep. But yesterday's *bashi-bazouks* had not turned into Cossacks, they had already lived for too long – almost a hundred years – by nothing but war and pillage, and completely lost the habit of any kind of peaceful occupation.

The Circassians' mode of service officially consisted in maintaining order on the roads. However, they had interpreted this mission in their own way, and soon every passing traveller had to pay them a toll. And when the trade caravans started avoiding the Circassian *auls* and the road taxes starting drying up, these intrepid warriors had found themselves new sources of income:

they hired themselves out to the caravans as guards, or hunted down criminals with a state price on their heads and sometimes they themselves even plundered villages or kidnapped rich travellers for ransom.

The police didn't get involved with the Circassians, because every Circassian was a born warrior who had been riding horses since he was a baby, could shoot straight and never missed and slashed with a sword like the very devil.

The *aul* that was located close to the New Megiddo commune had a reputation as the most belligerent of all. While the Circassians in the other settlements had gradually been drawn into a slightly more settled way of life and begun to abandon their pillaging ways, Daniel-bek's clan still regarded any form of work as a disgrace for a *dzhigit*, or horseman, and they earned their living exclusively by means of the rifle and the dagger.

The real reason for this was the *bek* himself. He had spent his entire life on a horse and was fond of saying that he would die in the saddle. But Daniel-bek wasn't ready to die just yet. At the age of seventy-something, he was still strong, still restless: he had recently taken a new thirteen-year-old wife, and they said she was already pregnant.

As many as fifty horsemen rode to Daniel-bek's banner (a six-pointed star with a half-moon and a horse's tail). The arrangement of their village was exactly the same as in their native Caucasus: they had set a stone watchtower at the top of a steep hill and surrounded it with low huts, or *saklyas*. A sentry stood on the tower day and night, keeping a sharp lookout in all directions. The Circassians did not keep dogs, because the high-mountain variety they had brought with them had not survived the Palestinian climate, and the immigrants despised the local breed.

Magellan saw this circumstance as the weak spot in the Circassian defences.

When the communards realised that their leader was not joking and he really did want to declare war on Daniel-bek, a sudden silence filled the inner yard of the *han*. Even Malke, who was always ready to support Magellan in anything, felt frightened and wondered if he hadn't gone too far this time and alienated the others.

But Magellan behaved as if such a possibility had never even entered his head.

'Look here,' he began briskly, heaping up a mound of earth and sticking a twig into it. 'This is the hill, and this is the tower. The stones are the *saklyas*.'

'And what's that?' someone asked, pointing to a wavy line.

'The river. The slope here is very steep, almost a cliff. And in the south-west, over here, the slope is shallow and the road . . .'

It was a fine idea of his, this model. Everybody crowded round and studied Magellan's handiwork, instead of snivelling and arguing.

'The goal is clear,' he said, wiping his hands on his trousers: 'to teach the Circassians once and for all to leave us alone. And, of course, to get back what was stolen.'

'Magellan, they won't give it back willingly. They'll shoot at us,' Coliseum said gloomily.

'And we'll shoot at them. Didn't I teach you how?'

'If we kill even one of them, it will start a blood feud. They told us about that . . . And there'll be no end to it . . .'

Magellan sliced through the air with his hand: 'We'll try to manage without any deaths. But if we can't, we'll have to eliminate all the male Circassians. Every last one. Otherwise, Coliseum's right – we'll never be free of them.'

'Absolutely all of them?' Malke asked. 'Even the little boys?'

There was the sound of nervous laughter.

Sasha Briun said: 'I don't really think I can shoot a grown man, let alone a child. Drop it, Magellan; this is real life, not some novel by Fenimore Cooper.'

'That's just the point, Sashulya: this isn't a novel, but real life. Either it defeats you and puts you down on your knees or you defeat it.' Magellan shook his head, so that a strand of chestnut hair fell down across his forehead, and Malke couldn't help admiring him – he looked so fine just at that moment. 'The Arabs call the Jews *uliad-el-mot*, "sons of death", because we are afraid of everything. It's time to show the Arabs, and the Circassians, and the Bedouins that new Jews have arrived, and they aren't afraid of anything. Or, rather, the old Jews have come back – the ones to whom all this land belonged two and three thousand years ago. If you can't shoot at people – then learn how. So, who's with me?'

Malke immediately raised her hand and shouted: 'I am!'

After a girl had put her hand up, it was embarrassing to play the coward. One by one the other members of the commune raised their hands.

'I never doubted it,' Magellan said with a shrug. 'So this is what we're going to do. Shlomo and Coliseum stay here to guard the *han*. Malke, you stay with them; you're in charge. Make sure the Arabs don't raid the place and steal all that's left. The rest of you, follow me!'

Ah, how cunning! Trying to soft-soap her by leaving two crocks to look after the house and putting her in charge. Oh no, she wasn't having that! 'Oh no, I'm not having that!' Malke declared. 'Shlomo and Coliseum can lock themselves in and not open up for anyone. But I'm going with you. Do we have equality or not?'

They did – she insisted on it.

The twenty-four communards advanced in single file along the empty road through the wide valley. There was no moon or stars to be seen, the sky was veiled by clouds. Magellan led his army at a brisk pace, almost a run – no doubt deliberately, so that they would put all their energy into the movement and there would be no time to think and hesitate.

Only six of them had Winchesters, the others had Bedan rifles or hunting guns. Malke had ended up with a shotgun for hunting ducks. As she hurried along, barely able to keep up with Magellan, she kept repeating to herself: First you lift the two little metal bits, then you press the trigger with your index finger: first the metal bits, then the trigger . . .

The plan (or, as Magellan called it, military-fashion, 'the disposition of forces') was as follows: scramble up the hill from the cliff side, because the view from the tower was not so good in that direction. Hide in the bushes and wait for the dawn. As soon as there was enough light to aim a gun, Magellan would shoot the sentry, and then they had to run as fast as they could to get into the tower, occupy it and keep the entire *aul* in their sights. Fire at anybody who poked their nose out of a *saklya* – from up there the entire village would be in plain view. 'We'll force them to capitulate,' Magellan declared cheerfully. 'We'll get back what was stolen and make them pay a fine too. There'll only be one dead body, and that will be my problem. I'm not afraid of the Devil himself, never mind some blood feud.'

Malke looked at him and suddenly thought that if he only loved her, there was nothing she wouldn't sacrifice for such happiness. But, of course, she drove the absurd thought out of her mind immediately, because it was uncomradely and anyway, how could he love her, with these short legs that made her look like a little goose?

A comedy in five acts could have been written about how they climbed the steep slope. Or a tragedy.

Yankel the violinist went tumbling down into the river. He climbed out soaking wet, hiccupping and with his teeth chattering violently.

Meir Shalevich tore his trousers on a thorn bush, and the white rent on his backside stood out clearly in the darkness.

That clumsy oaf Briun reached up and caught hold of a snake instead of a branch. Luckily it didn't bite him, but darted away, startled out of its sleep. And it was a lucky thing too, that Sasha had asthma. He tried to yell, but he just choked. Otherwise the entire 'disposition' would have been ruined.

But somehow or other they managed to clamber up, and then lay down on the very edge, gulping in the air. Soon their sweat dried and the communards started feeling chilly, but there was still a long way to go until dawn.

This was the hardest part. Now, while they lay there without moving, they started getting all sorts of bad thoughts into their heads. If not for the cliff behind them, someone could well have broken down and taken to their heels.

Magellan could sense that. He didn't lie still, he kept moving along the line all the time – whispering a couple of words to one of them, giving another an encouraging slap on the shoulder. But he squeezed Malke's elbow and whispered: 'That's my girl! You're a great kid.'

And suddenly she wasn't even a little bit frightened. 'My girl!' 'Great kid!'

Lyova Sats, the youngest member of the commune at just barely seventeen, was lying on Malke's right. He kept squirming about and sighing to himself, and as soon as the darkness grew just a little brighter, he began scribbling something on a piece of paper.

He crept across to Malke with his lips twitching. 'I'm going to be killed,' he whispered. 'I can sense it. Take this letter, send it to my mother in Moscow.'

'Don't go imagining things!' she hissed.

'I'm not imagining things. Men who are killed in battle can always sense it beforehand, I read that in a book.'

Malke took the letter and began listening carefully to her own feelings, to see if she had a premonition of death or not. And straight away she felt that she did. She was going to die today. It was an absolute certainty. She ought to write to her family and friends too. The entire street would read it and weep . . .

She borrowed a sheet of paper and a pencil from Lyova and she had already written the beginning: 'Dear Mama and Papa! You know, I don't regret . . .' – when suddenly the word came rustling along the line:

'It's time! It's time!'

Magellan hunched down and ran towards the fence behind which they could see the first *saklya*. The others hesitated. Malke grabbed her gun and was the first to go trotting after their commander.

They advanced in arrowhead formation, like storks in flight: Magellan in the centre; Malke hanging back a little on his right, Lyova on his left, and the others stretching out in both directions.

Magellan set his rifle on the wicker fence, carefully unwrapped the rag from the optical sight and set the sight in its groove.

The crude stonework of the tower soared up above the low, flat roofs. Three levels, with a narrow embrasure on each one, and an open platform at the top. The sentry's head and shoulders could be seen between the teeth of the battlements.

Is it really possible to hit anything at this distance? Malke wondered. It must be a hundred paces, at least.

Magellan set his cheek to the gun-butt and closed one eye.

She squeezed the shot gun between her knees and put her hands over her ears. What a terrible bang there would be now! And then they would have to make a dash for the tower, before the Circassians woke up.

But Magellan didn't fire. He prodded Malke on the shoulder, and when she took her hands away from her ears, he whispered: 'He's asleep! My God, he's sleeping like a log. I can see it through the sight!' And he added angrily. 'They don't think we're real men at all. It doesn't even enter their heads that we might take revenge. Right then, forward! Let's try to manage everything without any bloodshed. Pass it down the line: take your shoes off.'

Everyone took their shoes off and ran after Magellan, jerking their knees up in that funny way you do when you're running on tiptoe. No arrowhead formation now, they were moving in a tight bunch.

Malke bit her lip to stop herself gasping out loud when she sharp stones stuck into the soles of her feet. She had her boots in one hand and the gun in the other. The front of her shorts was soaking wet with dew.

The yards of the *aul* were quiet, with only a rooster crowing somewhere. There was the square, actually a square only in name – just a broad triangle of empty space between the tower, the small wattle-and-daub mosque and a two-storey stone house (which must belong to the *bek* himself).

Standing by the porch was an Arab cart, a *hantur*, with no horse.

Malke suddenly froze on the spot. There was a man sitting beside the cart, attached to it by a chain round his neck. He wasn't asleep, he was watching the Jews with his eyes starting out of his head in terror.

It was certainly no sight for the faint-hearted. In the dim light of the new day the communards looked like a collection of weird scarecrows.

At the front – Magellan in his Mexican sombrero, with two cartridge belts criss-crossed over his chest. Mendel was wearing a colonial pith helmet, and Briun had a felt bowler hat, while various others were wearing Arab kerchiefs or fezzes. Malke was wearing her mother's farewell present: a straw hat with porcelain cherries.

Magellan threatened the slave with his Winchester, and the man pulled his head down into his shoulders and put one hand over his mouth to show that he was not going to shout. But they still didn't manage to reach the tower without making a sound.

Lame Dodik Pevsner stumbled over a rock and dropped his Bedan rifle, and the drowsy silence was shattered by the sound of a shot.

Magellan swore loudly and obscenely, then bounded across to the tower and disappeared inside. The others dashed after him, holding their weapons at the ready. The only ones who hung back were Malke and Lyova – they felt sorry for the poor man who was kept on a chain like a dog.

'Your mother! Your mother!' the slave repeated after Magellan. He had black eyes set in a lively, intelligent-looking face. 'You Russian! I Russian too! Save and preserve me!'

And he crossed himself rapidly in the Orthodox manner.

'You don't look Russian to me,' Lyova remarked as he tried to break the chain with the butt of his gun.

'I have Russian faith! Arab, but Russian.'

'And we're Jews,' Malke told him.

Lyova threw caution to the winds – what point was there now? He set the barrel of the gun against the chain and fired. The chain parted.

'Hurry!' Malke cried, grabbing the Russian Arab by the hand.

After hearing that they were Jews, the man slumped down and tried to creep away under the wagon, but Lyova grabbed him from the other side and the three of them ran to the tower together.

Two members of the commune were waiting inside and they immediately barred the door with a thick beam of wood. Then they all dashed up the stairs.

The warriors of the detachment were crowded together on the third level and the upper platform.

Magellan had done well, managed to get to the sentry before he had any idea of what was going on. The lookout, a mere boy, was squatting in the corner, holding his head where it had been clubbed with a rifle butt but, thank God, he was still alive.

Malke gestured for him to take his hands away – the wound needed to be bandaged – but the young Circassian snarled at her like a wolf.

'Two men with Winchesters at the loopholes on the second level, two on the third,' Magellan commanded. 'Everyone else stand between the battlements and point your guns out. Let the

Circassians see that there are a lot of us and we're armed. Nobody shoot without being ordered.'

Malke stuck her head into a gap. The view of the *aul* and its immediate surroundings was simply wonderful. The streets were empty. In places she could see women dashing about in the yards, but she couldn't spot a single man.

'Where are the *dzhigits*?' Magellan asked, bemused. 'I don't understand what's going on here . . .'

Then the Arab they had released said: 'All men gallop in night. Get on horse and gallop. Not back yet.'

'Why, of course!' said Magellan, slapping himself on the forehead. 'I ought to have guessed! From our place they went to El-Lejun to sell their loot. It never even entered their heads that we might attack them ! Now that's the real luck of the Jews – do you understand that, you little mother's boys?' Then he turned to the freed prisoner. 'Who are you? How do you know Russian?'

'I Arab, but my bride Jewish,' the man said, bowing. 'I marry here. Perhaps I become Jew too. Good faith, I like.'

'Why were you chained?'

'I driving Russian lady, from Jerusalem. Rich lady, only little crazy. Circass attack, bring us here. Want ransom. Going write Russian consul, tell him send ten thousand franks. And for me want thousand franks, but I said I very poor man. Then put chain on me . . . Took my *hantur*. Took two Arab horses. When *bek* come, tell him give everything back: *hantur* and horse, and must give lady back too.'

Magellan was not looking at the Arab, but down into the valley. He screwed his eyes up and spoke quietly through his teeth: 'There he is, your *bek*. You can tell him everything yourself.'

Malke also looked down and saw a long string of horsemen moving up the incline of the road at a trot. There was a loud crash right beside her ear – Magellan had fired into the air. He fired again.

The women in the *aul* started wailing more loudly.

Why wars happen

The shots and the shouting did not wake Pelagia, because she was not asleep. She had spent the whole night walking backwards and forwards in the cramped little room with bare walls, without lying down even for a moment on the cushions on the floor.

Sometimes she prayed, and sometimes she abused herself roundly, using all the words that it was appropriate for a nun to use, but neither prayer nor abuse brought her any relief.

How stupid! To ruin everything because of her own sheer carelessness! She should have hired bodyguards at the Russian mission. They had Orthodox Montenegrins there, especially for accompanying pilgrims setting out to Lake Tiberius, Bethlehem and other trouble spots. They looked absolutely terrifying, with their bushy moustaches, silver-embroidered jackets, crooked swords and pistols in their belts. The Montenegrins' reputation was so fearsome that no bandit would even come near them.

Mitrofanii was right, a thousand times right: his spiritual daughter could be very adroit, but her approach completely lacked thoroughness. She acted first and only thought afterwards. And it was all because she had been afraid of losing another day, or even another hour. She had been spurred on by an irrational, inexplicable feeling that *time was wasting*, and that there was almost none left. She had felt she could actually see the final grains trickling from the glass cone of the future into the glass funnel of the past.

And she had followed the Russian habit of trusting her luck. For the first two days luck had lured her on, then on the third day it had abandoned her.

At first they had travelled for a long time through mountains. On the steep climbs they had to climb out and walk behind the *hantur* – the horses were not strong enough to pull the load. On the third day they had reached the broad, green Isreel Valley, almost ten versts long. The Har-Megiddo mountain, which was close to where she ought to search for the commune, was just to their west.

Har-Megiddo: Armageddon. This boggy field would be the site of the final battle on Earth, when the forces of the Devil would fight against the angels, Polina Andreevna thought, but she did not feel the appropriate thrill of awe. And even when she saw in the distance the geometrically regular form of Mount Tabor, the site of the Transfiguration of the Lord, she was not really moved: although she muttered a prayer, it was mechanical, it had no soul. Her thoughts were too far away from the divine.

There were only a few versts left to go to the dwelling of the 'Sadducees', and the nun still had not decided how she ought to behave with their iron-eyed leader Magellan.

Stupid, stupid Manuila. What was it that was drawing him here, like a moth to a candle flame? On the steamer Magellan had threatened to take the prophet by the legs and smash his head against a chain locker. Perhaps that was what he had done, and Glass-Eye had nothing do with the case?

It would certainly be like Magellan – the Byronic type, the superman. For a man of that kind a principle or a grand pose was more important than his own life, not to mention the lives of others. He had told his boys and girls that Manuila was an agent of the Okhranka. But why would he do that? Perhaps what he had in mind was killing the supposed police spy in order to bind the members of the commune together with blood? After all, didn't another superman, Nechaev, do the same with the student Ivanov . . .

But regardless of whether Magellan had been involved in the murder of the peasant Shelukhin or not, when the genuine Manuila turned up at the commune the Zionists were sure to imagine that the ubiquitous Okhranka had tracked them down even in Palestine. What if they did away with the importunate prophet? The police would never find out, and anyway, what police was there here in this Turkish backwater?

Salakh distracted the traveller from her alarming thoughts with his chatter.

'The Jews were wrong to decide to live here,' he sighed, wafting away the mosquitoes. 'In summer they'll all die of malaria. What do they want land for? The Jews are an urban people. They should have stayed in the city. They've gone completely insane, it's Allah's punishment. I even pity them.'

As became clear later, what made him pity the Jews most was that they could only marry female Jews, and they were the most unbearable women in the whole world. Devious and deceitful, sticking their hooked noses into everything. 'Sleep with Jewish woman is like stick your manhood into a scorpion's burrow,' said Salakh, making Pelagia wince at the crude force of his metaphor.

Her driver dwelt on the theme of the guile of Jewish women for a long time. Naturally, he mentioned the villainous Judith, who murdered Holofernes in his sleep, but he was most incensed of all by Jahel, who had desecrated the sacred law of hospitality. The general Sisara (whom Salakh called 'the ancestor of the Arabs') asked for sanctuary in Jahel's tent after he was routed in battle. And what did this perfidious woman do? According to the Book of Judges, she said to him: Come in to me, my lord; come in, fear not. He went into her tent and, being covered by her with a cloak, said to her: Give me, I beseech thee, a little water, for I am very thirsty. She opened a bottle of milk and gave him to drink, and covered him. And Sisara said to her: Stand before the door of the tent, and when any shall come and enquire of thee, saying: Is there any man here? thou shalt say: There is none. So Jahel, Haber's wife, took a nail of the tent, and taking also a hammer; and going in softly and with silence, she put the nail upon the temples of his head and, striking it with the hammer, drove it through his brain fast into the ground: and so passing from deep sleep to death, he fainted away and died.

Listening to Salakh retelling this biblical story and adorning it with heart-rending details, Pelagia felt sorry for the man – not Sisara, who had lived God knows how long ago and in the end received no more than his just deserts, but the narrator. The simple soul did not know that his fate had been decided and his own next wife would be Jewish.

'The man was very tired, he was really weak. So he lay down, and straight away – cr-r-runch.' Salakh snored to illustrate the point and rested his cheek on his folded hands.

Then suddenly he started and pulled on the reins. Two horsemen slowly rode out of the bushes on to the road ahead.

When she saw the rifles sticking up over their shoulders, Polina Andreevna cried out: 'Are they bandits?'

'I don't know,' Salakh replied and dropped the reins

'What are you doing? Turn back!'

'We can't. They'll see we're afraid and come after us. We have to drive straight on and ask them something. That's the best thing.'

'What should we ask?'

'The way. How to get to El-Lejun. I'll say you're on your way to see the chief of police. You're his mother-in-law.'

'Why his mother-in-law?' Polina Andreevna asked, surprised and a little offended.

'You can't take a ransom for a mother-in-law.'

'Because that's the custom, is it?'

'Because nobody pays a ransom for a mother-in-law,' Salakh explained abruptly, preparing for his conversation with the armed men.

He started jabbering to them from a distance, bowing and pointing vaguely in the direction of the hills.

The horsemen examined the cart and its passengers without speaking. Their appearance was very strange for Palestine: both in Circassian jackets, one wearing a hood on his head and the other a Cossack hat. Just like our Kuban cossacks, Polina Andreevna thought, and her spirits rose slightly.

'They not understand Arabic,' said Salakh, turning towards her. He was pale and frightened. 'They Circass. Very bad Circass. Now I speak Turkish to them . . .'

One of the horsemen rode up and leaned down towards Pelagia, and she caught a smell of garlic and mutton fat.

'Muskubi?' he asked. 'Ruska?'

'Yes, I am Russian.'

The Circassians held a guttural conversation. There was no way to tell whether they were arguing or quarrelling.

'What are they talking about?' Pelagia asked nervously.

Salakh merely gulped.

The same bandit leaned down again and grabbed hold of the hem of Polina Andreevna's dress. She squealed, but the villain did not try to tear her clothes, he merely rubbed the silk with his fingers, demonstrating something to his comrade. Then he picked up the parasol from the seat and showed his comrade the ivory handle.

'What is he saying?' the nun exclaimed in fright.

'He say, you rich and important. Russians will give much money for you.'

Salakh joined in the discussion. He started babbling in a pitiful voice and waving his hands about. Polina Andreevna did not like the look of those gesticulations: first the Palestinian flapped one hand towards his female passenger as if he were disowning her, then he jabbed himself in the chest and pointed back the way they had come. He seemed to be saying that they should just take her and let him go. The scoundrel! Jahel would be too good for him!

But the Circassians did not take his advice. They replied curtly and rode on down the road.

Salakh hesitated.

But then one of the bandits looked back and threatened him with his whip, and Salakh drove on.

'I told her, I told her,' he wailed. 'Must not go to Megiddo, bad place. No, take me. What happen now? What happen now?'

Soon it got dark and Polina Andreevna could not really see what the road to the Circassian *aul* was like: some hills, followed by a hollow, and then a steep climb.

All she saw of the village was some low, flat roofs and dimly lit windows. The *hantur* halted on a small triangular open space and two mute women in white headscarves led the nun into a small house set at the back of a yard. The hut turned out to be special, with tightly shuttered windows and a lock on the outside of the door. No doubt it was kept for 'rich and important' prisoners, Pelagia thought.

Her guess was soon confirmed when the master of the house, who also looked like the master of the entire village, arrived – an old man with a long beard, wearing an astrakhan Cossack hat with a turban wound round it. For some reason he was fully armed – surely he didn't walk around at home wearing a sword, a dagger and a revolver in a holster?

The chief Circassian said that his name was Daniel and the 'princess' would be given a bread cake and goat's milk for her supper. He spoke surprisingly clear and correct Russian, with only the very slightest accent.

Polina Andreevna was very frightened to hear that she was a 'princess' 'I am not a princess!' she exclaimed. 'You are mistaken!'

The old man was upset. 'Musa said you are a princess. A silk dress, a white face. Who are you then? What is your name?'

'I'm a pilgrim. Pelagia . . . that is, Polina Lisitsyna.'

Daniel-bek bowed respectfully, but stopped short of scraping his foot on the ground and kissing her hand. 'Who is your husband?'

'I have no husband.' She almost added, 'I am a nun,' but how could she prove that?

'That is bad,' said the *bek*, with a click of his tongue. 'Already an old maid, and no husband. That is because you are so skinny. But you should get married anyway. Your father should find you a husband.'

'I have no father.'

'Then let your brother find one.'

'I have no brother either.'

Her host rolled his eyes up to the ceiling – his patience was almost exhausted.

'No husband, no father, no brother. Then who is going to pay your ransom – your uncle?'

This sounded so strange that for a moment Pelagia was taken aback and did not realise that he really did mean her uncle. Was there actually anyone in the world who would be willing to pay a ransom for her? Apart from His Eminence Mitrofanii, that is. But he was far away.

'I have no uncle either,' she replied despondently, almost sobbing, she was feeling so sorry for herself. 'Perhaps you can simply let me go, without any ransom? Taking hostages is a sin in our religion and in yours.'

Daniel-bek was amazed. 'Why is it a sin? When I was a boy my *papa*' – he pronounced this word in the French fashion, with the stress on the second syllable – 'was an important *nahib* with Shamil. The Russians took Shamil's son, Djemal-ad-din and me as hostages. Djemal-ad-din went into the Corps of Pages, and I went into the Cadet Corps. I learned Russian there, as well as many other things. But my *papa* was brave. He took a Russian princess and her son hostage and exchanged them for me. But Shamil's son was a prisoner of Tsar Nicholas for a long time. So you see, the Russians take hostages. And so do I. How else am I to live? I have to feed my wives and children, don't I?' He sighed heavily. 'If you do not have a husband, or father, or even a brother, it is not good to take a big ransom. Let the Russian consul send ten thousand franks, and you can go wherever you want. You will write the consul a letter tomorrow: "Ai-ai-ai, send ten thousand franks quickly, or the evil bashi-bazouk will cut off my finger, then my ear, then my nose."'

'Will you really do that?' Pelagia asked, cowering away from him.

'No, only the finger. The smallest one.' He held up the little finger of his left hand. 'There are lots of fingers, you won't miss one. In two weeks, if the consul doesn't send the money, I'll send him your little finger. Hey, hey, why have you turned white? Are you afraid of cutting off a finger? Buy one from one of our people; they won't take much for a little finger.'

'What do you mean – buy?' the unfortunate captive babbled.

'Has the consul kissed your fingers?' the *bek* asked.

'N-no . . .'

'Good. He will not recognise it. A women or a boy will cut off their own finger, and the consul will not realise – he will think it is yours. If it is a woman, give her your dress, and she will be happy. If it is a boy, buy him a good saddle or a silver dagger.'

'But what if the consul won't give the money anyway? We're not even acquainted.'

The old man spread his hands in a broad gesture. 'If he does not take pity on you after the finger, I will marry you off. To Kurban – his wife has died. Or to Eldar – his wife is in a bad way: she is sick and he needs another one. Calm down, woman; what do you have to be afraid of?'

But Polina Andreevna did not calm down. In the first place, it was absolutely impossible for her to get married. And in the second place, getting stuck for a long time in this bandits' lair did not enter into her plans at all. Time was passing, precious time!

'You will write the letter tomorrow,' Daniel-bek said in farewell. 'I have no time now. We are going to rob the *uliad-el-mot*.'

'To rob whom?'

But he walked out without answering her.

A few minutes later she heard the stamping of a large number of hooves, and then all was quiet. Pelagia was left alone to languish in her despair until dawn; but when the pale light began percolating through the crack in the shutters, there was the loud crack of a shot somewhere in the village and women began shouting on all sides.

What had happened out there?

Polina Andreevna pressed her ear to the door, but it was hard to make sense of anything. There were several more shots, and the sound seemed to be coming from somewhere above her. The women carried on shouting for a while and stopped. Then there was total silence, broken occasionally by isolated shots.

An hour and a half later she heard steps in the yard. The bolt clanged.

She had expected to see Daniel-bek, but the person in the doorway was Salakh, with one of the women from the previous day beside him. 'Come on,' the Palestinian said with a nervous sniff. 'I exchanged you.'

'For what?'

'The Jews let the *bek* go into his house, for that the *bek* lets you go.'

Pelagia was totally bemused, but the Palestinian took hold of her hand and pulled her along.

The situation in the *aul* was what the chess-player Berdichevsky would have called stalemate.

The communards were ensconced in the stone tower. From there they had a clear view and a clear line of fire at the yards and the streets and all the approaches to the village, so the women and children had all hidden in the *saklyas*, while the *dzhigits* had taken cover round the hill. They had made several attempts to creep closer, but then Magellan started firing with his optical sight, placing the bullets close, just as a warning.

When it became clear that the Circassians could not enter the village and the Jews could not leave it, Salakh emerged from the tower as a truce envoy. He had been instructed to deliver an ultimatum. The Circassians must return everything they had stolen and pay a fine, and then the Jews would leave.

Daniel-bek said that he would not talk with a man who had a metal collar round his neck, he would only talk with the Jews' *bek*, and for that he had to go into his own house, because it was not seemly for honourable men to conduct negotiations in the bushes, like a pair of jackals.

'I realised straightaway that he wanted to see if his wives and children are alive or not,' Salakh told the nun proudly, 'And I said, very well, *bek*, but for that let the Russian princess go.'

'Oh, why "princess"?' Polina Andreevna groaned. 'If the Circassians win, we won't get away with ten thousand franks now.'

They were sitting in Daniel-bek's house, waiting for the owner to arrive.

Then he appeared, riding slowly up the street, holding both

hands in full view. The old bandit's face was absolutely rigid; his white beard fluttered slightly in the wind.

At the porch he jumped down lightly, like a young man, and handed the reins to a woman. He asked her something in a low voice; she replied, and the *bek*'s face became a little less stony. He must have been told that no one has been hurt, thought Pelagia.

She and Salakh walked out of the door to go across to the tower, but Daniel-bek suddenly grabbed hold of Polina Andreevna's arm and dragged her back into the house.

'Hey, hey,' Salakh cried. 'That's not what we agreed!'

The old man bared his teeth. 'The princess will stay with me! Daniel is no fool; he has lived in this world for a long time. Now the Jews will come running out and kill me. That is what I would do! Go to them and say: The princess will die with me! Let Magellan-bek come here alone, we will talk.'

He sat Pelagia down beside him at the table and took a firm grip of her arm. Squinting sideways, the nun could see that his other hand was on the handle of his dagger.

'If the Jew comes in and starts shooting at me, I will cut your throat,' said Daniel-bek. 'It is not your fault, it is not my fault. It is just fate.'

'Why me and not him?' she said, asking the logical but entirely un-Christian question.

'I am already old, but he is young and agile. I will not be fast enough to kill him,' the *bek* replied sadly.

The dialogue broke off at that point, because Magellan came in.

Pelagia recognised him immediately, although the leader of the commune had changed. He was tanned, his moustache had grown longer and was curled up at the ends, and the Jewish warrior's head was crowned with a huge comic-opera sombrero.

The new arrival did not even glance at the woman, he was not interested in her. He set one hand on his open gun holster and declared: 'Right then, you old bandit. First, you're going to give us everything back. Second, you're going to take back from the Arabs what they stole during the night. And third, you're going to pay a fine – twenty sheep. Then we'll leave.'

'Give you our sheep?' Daniel-bek said through his teeth. 'No, Jew. You will give me all your guns, and then we will let you go.

What do Jews need guns for? You will pay us five hundred franks every moon, and nobody will bother you any more. I heard about the clothes stolen from the dead Jewish woman. I will tell Sheikh Yusuf; he will give them back. Think, Jew: my *dzhigits* will not stand up to be shot by your bullets. There is no water in the tower. Tomorrow or the next day you will come creeping out, and then we will kill you.'

Magellan said nothing for a moment, twitching the muscles in his jaws. His light-coloured eyes narrowed.

'Circassian, your *saklyas* are made of clay and camel dung. A bullet will go straight through them. I will order my men to fire in salvoes, and soon the houses will be nothing but piles of rubbish. Red with blood.'

The *bek* also paused before he answered.

'You are not like the *uliad-el-mot*. Perhaps you are not real Jews? Or are the ones who came here before you not real Jews?'

'We are absolutely genuine Jews. And there will be more and more just like us.'

'Then we ought to kill you. Even if our women and children will die,' Daniel-bek said in a flat voice. The knuckles of the fingers gripping the hilt of the dagger had turned white. 'Otherwise you will seize all this land and leave no Arabs or Circassians here.'

'You are the *bek*. You must decide.'

The two men stared at each other with intense, stony expressions. Pelagia saw the dagger slip silently out of its· sheath. Magellan's hand gradually crept into his holster.

'What do you think you're doing!' the nun exclaimed indignantly, slapping her hand down on the table.

The two enemies had forgotten that she was there. They started and turned their gaze on her.

'Whenever you men have the slightest problem, you start talking about killing! And as usual, the first to die will be the women and children! Only a fool breaks down a door with his head because he hasn't got the wits to turn the key! Intelligent people find a different use for their heads! Later they'll say you were two fools who couldn't come to an agreement, and because of that the Jews and Circassians started killing each other all over Palestine! Give him back what you stole,' she said, turning to Daniel-bek. 'And you, Mr Magellan, forget about your fine. What do you want sheep for? You don't even know how to shear them!'

There was no obvious change in the room after these words – the *bek* was still holding his dagger and Magellan was still clutching his revolver, but the tension had eased imperceptibly. The men looked each other in the eye again, this time with less menace and more enquiry.

'I've seen you before somewhere,' Magellan said, without looking at Pelagia. 'I can't remember where, but I've definitely seen you . . .' From his tone of voice it was quite clear that he was not really very interested just at the moment. Which was not surprising.

The *bek*, as the more mature individual who possessed the wisdom of experience, was the first to take a half-step towards reconciliation.

He put both his hands on the table and said: 'The princess speaks the truth. One *dzhigit* can always reach an understanding with another.'

Magellan also took his hand away from the holster and folded his arms. 'Very well, we'll forget about the fine. But what about the sheikh?'

'Yusuf is no *dzhigit*, he is a dog. I have wanted to teach him a lesson for a long time. Moslems do not rob graves and undress the dead. Sit down, let us be friends.'

The Circassian gestured in invitation and Magellan sat down, putting his sombrero on a bench. 'We'll go straightaway, together,' he demanded. 'Rokhele cannot lie there naked in a grave that has been dug up.'

The *bek* nodded. 'Straightaway. We will surround the Arab village completely.'

'No,' the Jew interrupted. 'We will leave one way out.'

Daniel-bek's eye glittered youthfully. 'Yes, yes! We will leave a passage to the ford! Let them run that way!'

They both leaned over the table and began drawing on it with their fingers, speaking at the same time and interrupting each other. An anti-Arab league began taking shape before Polina Andreevna's very eyes.

She did not really understand what was going on, but she did not like it at all. This business about a grave that had been dug up, stolen clothes . . .

'Wait,' the nun exclaimed. 'Listen to me! I don't know who Sheikh Yusuf is, but if he's a sheikh, I suppose he must be quite rich?'

'He has five hundred sheep,' Daniel-bek replied, glancing round. 'His fellahs are paupers, but Yusuf himself is rich.'

'If he is rich, why would he steal a dead woman's dress? That was the work of cheap scoundrels, and the Sheikh himself will probably punish them when he finds out about it. You must not surround the village and leave a passage to the ford! Or later people will say: Three fools were unable to come to an agreement, and—'

'Woman,' the *bek* roared, 'that is the second time you have called me a fool!'

'She's right,' Magellan put in. 'There are more Arabs in these parts than Jews and Circassians taken together. It would start a war. We ought to invite the Sheikh to negotiations. That would be more intelligent.'

'You are not only, brave, Magellan-bek, but wise too,' said the Circassian, pressing his hand to his heart. And the men bowed ceremonially to each other, once again completely ignoring the woman.

Girls' talk

The joint mission to Yusuf-bek was led by the Circassians riding at the front with the Jews following on foot. In order to impress their allies, the communards formed up into a column, set their guns on their left shoulders and tried to march in step.

Shrouded in dust, the united forces set off down the road. The Circassian women watched them go. They did not shout or wave their hands – evidently that was not the custom.

The *bek* had told Polina Andreevna that she was free to go anywhere she liked, but there was only one place she wanted to go. She had waited for her chance to have a word with Magellan alone. She complained that after what had happened she was afraid of travelling without protection and asked permission to spend the night in the commune.

He magnanimously gave his consent and asked once again:

'But where was it that I saw you before? It must have been in Russia, but where?'

Pelagia thought it best to say nothing, and he had no time just then to go delving into his memory.

She waited in the *aul* until noon for the goods stolen from the commune to be delivered from the small Arab town of El-Lejun. The trophies were received by the young woman called Malke, with whom the nun had exchanged a few words on the river steamer.

Woman being the way they are, Malke recognised Pelagia immediately, even with her secular clothes and freckles. And she was as pleased to see her as if they were old friends. The nun's appearance in the Isreel Valley did not rouse the fat girl's suspicion at all.

She immediately started talking to Polina Andreevna in a familiar manner and told her a lot of details about herself, and the commune and everything else that came to mind. And of course, she asked questions too, but for the most part she answered them herself.

For instance, she asked: 'How did you come to be here? Ah, yes, you were on the steamer with us. Going to Palestine, right? On pilgrimage? And you took your nun's habit off so you wouldn't feel so hot? Of course, in this kind of heat a silk dress is far better. I expect you're not a nun, still a novice, right?'

All Pelagia had to do was nod.

When they set out for New Megiddo, the sun had already moved into the western half of the sky. Malke harnessed the horse that had been recovered to a Circassian cart and hitched the two cows on at the back. They put the harrow and the safe – battered, but not opened – in the bottom of the cart and set the sacks of seeds on top of them. Then the two women sat down beside each other and set off.

Salakh trundled along behind on his *hantur*, singing shrill, whining songs at the top of his voice. He was happy to have got his horse and cart back without having to pay any ransom.

Polina Andreevna admired the way her new-found friend handled their heavily loaded cart. Malke sat with her legs crossed under her, Turkish-style (her tanned knees were as brown as two crispy-roasted piglets), set her gun across them and cracked the whip, without stopping talking for a single moment.

It was light conversation – girls' talk.

'Polina, I just can't understand why you want to be a nun. I could understand if you were some kind of ugly freak, but you're really beautiful, honestly you are. I suppose it's all because of an unhappy love, right? Well even so, even if it is, it's still not worth it. Why lock yourself away in a convent, in a tiny little world, when the big world is so interesting? I could have carried on living in my Borisovo until I got old and never have discovered who I really am. I used to think I was a coward, but you've no idea just how brave I turned out to be! Perhaps you think Magellan didn't take me to the Arab village because I'm a woman? Nothing of the sort! There won't be any shooting there, or else I would definitely have gone with them. What he said to me was: Malyutka, you're the most sensible helper I have, the only one I can ask to do this. (He does that sometimes – calls me Malish or Malyutka, instead of Malke). Get it all back safe and sound, he said, and make sure those two blockheads Coliseum and Shlomo don't water my horse straight away, but walk it a bit first. And lay out the seeds to dry – they've got damp from the night dew.'

Pelagia felt a little guilty about exploiting this nice girl's openness, but at the first opportunity (when Malke started telling her about how isolated the commune was) she asked casually: 'Do you ever see any strangers?'

'Rarely. The Rothschild Jews think we're insane atheists. Relations with the Arabs are bad. And as for the Circassians – you've seen for yourself.'

'Well, what about wandering pilgrims? And I've been told Palestine is absolutely full of itinerant preachers,' the nun said, rather clumsily turning the conversation in the required direction.

Malke broke into loud laughter. 'There was one prophet. He was funny. And from Russia, as it happens. You remember Manuila, who was killed on the steamer? Or, as it turned out, it wasn't him who was killed, but someone else – I'll tell you all about that later. As soon as he got to the Holy Land, this Manuila started calling himself Emmanuel, to make himself sound grander.' She laughed again.

If she was laughing, it meant that nothing bad had happened to him. Pelagia's heart suddenly felt less heavy.

'Is it a long time since he was here?'

The girl began counting, bending down her short fingers. 'Seven, no eight days ago. Ah yes, that was the night Polkan was killed.' Her merry laughter was suddenly replaced by a sob, then she sniffed and smiled again. 'He died for *Erets Israel* too, Polkan did.'

'For who?'

'For the Jewish state. Polkan was a dog who attached himself to us in Jaffa. He was terribly clever and brave, like a regimental dog. He was wonderful at keeping watch at night – we didn't need any sentries. We could just tie him to the outside of the gate and no one would come anywhere near. He was long-haired, black and yellow, a little bit lame in one leg, and on his side—'

'And what about this prophet?' Polina Andreevna interrupted. She was not interested in a portrait of the deceased Polkan. 'Where did he come from?'

'He knocked at the gate in the evening. We'd already finished work and we were sitting there, singing songs. We opened up and saw this bearded peasant, wearing birch-bark sandals, with a stick. He was just standing there, fondling Polkan's ear, and the dog was wagging his tail. He didn't even bark once – I couldn't believe it. I suppose the prophet must have converted him to his own faith,' Malke laughed. '"Good evening, good people," he said, "you sing well. Are you Russian then?" And we asked him: "Who are you? One of Manuila's foundlings?" (He was wearing a loose robe with a blue belt, the same as they all wear.) He said, "I am Emmanuel himself. I'm walking about, looking. I've been in Judea, and Samaria, and now I've come to Galilee. Will you let me in for the night?" Well why wouldn't we? We let him in. I asked him: "What's going on – you were killed on the steamer; have you risen from the dead, then?" And he answered, "It wasn't me they killed, but one of my *shelukhin*."'

Polina Andreevna started. 'What was that?'

'In ancient Aramaic *shelukhin* means "apostles". When there are many, it's *shelukhin*; when there's only one, it's *sheluakh*. Magellan told us that; he knows everything about Jewish history.'

Sheluyak, thought Pelagia, suddenly remembering. The peas-

274

ants at Stroganovka had said that was what Manuila called his friend.

'And what did Emmanuel tell you about the killing?

'He said his *sheluakh* wanted to protect him, and that was why he died. But there is no need to protect him, because the Lord does that. And he started telling us about a miracle that had happened to him that morning. The way he tells his lies, you just can't help listening. With his wide blue eyes, like some innocent angel!' Malke laughed as she remembered. '"When they threw me out of Zikhron-Yaakov," he said . . . The Jews who live in Zikhron-Yakov are prosperous, they get money from Baron Rothschild. They don't plough the land themselves, they hire the Arab fellahs . . . Anyway, the rich Jews threw Emmanuel out, they wouldn't listen to him. He set off on foot along a valley in the mountains, and he was attacked by bandits.' The girl began lisping like a child, evidently imitating Manuila. '"A vewy angwy man, waving a sword. I haven't learned to speak Bedouin yet, I couldn't expwain to him that I didn't have anything. When he saw that for himself, he got even angwier and wanted to cut off my head with his sword. Chop it wight off. And he would have done, because his nervous system was completely unbalanced . . ."' Malke dissolved into laughter.

'He actually said that – "his nervous system was unbalanced"?' Pelagia asked in astonishment.

'Yes, the way he speaks is absolutely wonderful – I can't really imitate it properly. Well, after that it was all like a fairy tale. The moment the bandit raised his sword to kill him, suddenly, taram-taram! – there was a peal of heavenly thunder. And the villain dropped down dead, with blood pouring out of his head. "And there was no one anywhere awound there – just the mountain this side, the mountain that side, and the path. Not a soul! I thanked the Lord, buwied the dead bandit and went on." We laughed so much, we almost split our sides. But Emmanuel didn't mind at all, he laughed with us.'

'And what about Magellan?' the nun asked. She almost asked if he had shown any hostility towards the prophet, but she stopped herself.

'Well, at first Magellan was very strict with him. He put him through a kind of interrogation. Why did you come here? On the steamer your people were hanging around us, now you've come in person! What do you want from us? And so on. But Emmanuel told him: It's not surprising that you met my *shelu-khin* on the boat. Many of them follow me to the Holy Land, although I told them a man's Holy Land is where he was born. What do they want with Palestine? I'm a different case, there's something I have to do here. But they don't listen to me, he said. That is, they listen, but they don't hear. And there's nothing surprising about us meeting here like this. Palestine is a small place. If someone decides to walk round it ... Oh no,' Malke said with a smile, 'what he said was "twavel wound it". If someone decides to travel round it, then he'll get to everywhere, and very quickly too. And then Emmanuel started telling lies about his miracle and Magellan lost interest in him. He gave up and went to bed.'

'Then it wasn't him,' Pelagia said out loud in her absent-mindedness.

'Eh?'

'Oh no, it's nothing. What else did the prophet tell you?'

'Well, it was then that all the fuss and bother started,' said Malke, turning serious. 'Polkan started barking. We thought there must be a jackal. Then we heard the barking moving away – he must have broken his rope. We went running after him, shouting Polkan! Polkan! But he was lying there dead. About a hundred steps from the *han*. He'd been stabbed with a sword. It wasn't jackals at all, it was the Arabs or those Circassians. The Bedouins had already gone away by then ... We woke Magellan. He said we had to go after them! But how could we catch up with them? Which way should we run, to the Arabs or the Circassians? Everyone was arguing and making a racket. Some shouted: There are too many of them, and not enough of us. They'll kill us all, like Polkan! This is a bad place, we have to go away! Magellan told them that if you can't stand up for yourself, any place in the world will be bad. And it went on and on ...' The girl gestured dismissively, and then suddenly threw her hands up in the air. 'Ah, yes, Emmanuel had just said something really odd. How could I forget! Nobody was taking any notice of him, they were all yelling and shouting, and he suddenly said: "You will defeat the Arabs and the Circassians. You are few, but you are strong. Only," he said, "your victowy will be your defeat." How can a victory be a defeat, we asked him? But we couldn't understand his answer. He said that a victory over another person is always a defeat. A genuine victory is when you overcome yourself. Well, our people wouldn't listen to him after that – they started arguing again. But it turns out that he was right, about victory!'

'Then what happened?'

'Nothing. In the morning he drank some milk and went on his way.'

'And he didn't say where he was going?'

'Yes he did, he's very talkative. Rokhele was pouring his milk and he said: "First I'll go to Capernaum" – then somewhere else – "and then I'll have to go to the Valley of Siddim and take a look at the Avarim Mountains – they say they've built a new Sodom there, I'd like to see it."'

'Sodom!' Polina Andreevna exclaimed. 'Where are these Avarim Mountains?'

'Beyond the Dead Sea.'

'Sodom! Sodom!' the nun repeated in an agitated voice. That was where the family of pederasts on the river steamer had been going! But what had Glass-Eye got to do with them? It wasn't clear. But there must be something to it!

Eight whole days had gone by, but if Emmanuel was planning to visit Capernaum first, she might have enough time. He was a strong walker, though . . .

'What's that you're muttering about, Polya?'

Polina Andreevna took out her guidebook, removed the map and unfolded it. 'Show me where the Valley of Siddim is. How can I get there?'

'Why do you want to go there?' the girl asked in surprise, but she took the red pencil and marked a line on the map. 'This way, to the River Jordan. Then down as far as the Dead Sea and south along the shoreline, all the way. You see this little circle, the village of Bet-Kebir? Sodom is somewhere beyond that. But honestly, Polya, why do you want to got there? Straight from the convent to Sodom!' Malke burst into laughter. 'Rus, whither do you hasten? She answers not!'

Pelagia carefully folded the map and put it back in the book.

'Are you really going to go there?' Malke asked, her eyes wide in horror and curiosity. 'You really are very daring! I can just imagine what goes on there! Write me a letter afterwards, will you? Only with lots of detail!' She nudged Pelagia with her elbow and started giggling.

The nudge knocked the guidebook into the bottom of the cart. The nun picked up the precious volume and put it away safely in her pocket.

Meanwhile the cart came out on to the top of a hill from which there was a broad view across the valley and the surrounding mountains.

'You can see our *han* there, in the distance,' said Malke, half-standing to point. 'Now we'll go down here and along the little river. We'll be there in about forty minutes. You can have a rest and get washed.'

'No thank you,' said Polina Andreevna, jumping down on to the ground. 'It's time I was going. Tell me, which way should I go to reach the Jordan?'

Malke sighed – she obviously felt sorry to say goodbye. 'Go along that little track. It's bumpy and overgrown with grass, but it will lead you straight to a fork in the road. To get to the Jordan, go right. But what about the bandits? You told me you were afraid without any protection.'

'Never mind,' Pelagia answered absent-mindedly. 'God is merciful.'

God does exist!

There was only one road from Jerusalem to the Isreel Valley, so Yakov Mikhailovich had managed to catch up with the mark on the very first day. He fell in behind and strode along, breathing the mountain air.

The sun in the Holy Land was so fierce that he was burnt as black as an Arab. And that was very convenient, because he had dressed himself up as an Arab for his travels. It was the most comfortable mode of dress for the climate here: the long shirt of thin material allowed the wind to blow through, and the scarf (it was called a *kufia*) protected the back of your head against the burning rays of the sun.

Whenever Yakov Mikhailovich met someone on the road and they spoke to him in Arabic, he respectfully touched the palm of his hand to his forehead, then to his chest and walked on. You could make what you liked of that: perhaps the man did not wish to talk to you, or perhaps he had taken a vow not to engage in idle chatter with anyone.

He had a stroke of bad luck on the third day, when Ginger turned left on to a road that ran between the valley and the mountains. Yakov Mikhailovich saw the Circassians capture the *hantur*, but he did not interfere. They were serious people, with carbines, and all he had was a six-shooter, a pop-gun. It was good for the city, where there were corners and walls everywhere, but out in the open it was a pretty useless object. And anyway, he couldn't afford to give himself away.

That evening he installed himself near the Circassians' hill and observed the Jews' entire operation. My, my, he thought, they're really fighting seriously now. What if they turn that audacious in old Mother Russia?

As the old saying has it: 'Less haste, more speed,' and Yakov Mikhailovich did not try to hurry things. He waited until the Circassians and the Jews had reached their agreement and gone away, and a little while later everything was arranged in the most convenient way possible when the nun left the *aul* in the company of a plump little Jewess and her faithful Arab. The proper order of things was restored.

The surrounding area was level and smooth, and he had to drop further back – you can see a man a long way off in open country. But then, thank God, he could see well too. They wouldn't get away.

When the carts started climbing up a hill, Yakov Mikhailovich allowed himself a little indulgence. He could see that after the hill the road ran down into a hollow, and he thought: The clever man doesn't climb a hill; the clever man goes round it.

Why get himself soaking in sweat when he could walk round the hill on the low ground? Sometimes your own two feet were handier than a set of wheels. And that way he would save enough time to give his feet a quick rinse in the stream. Then he could hide in the willow thicket and wait for the mark to drive by. So that was what he did. He had a quick wash, and drank some fresh water and even had a bite to eat.

Just as soon as he had brushed off the crumbs, he heard creaking and rumbling. They were coming.

Come on now, come on now. He poked his head out of the bushes and froze in confusion.

Instead of two carts there was only one. You're not such a clever man after all, are you, Yakov Mikhailovich? – you're an idiot! Now you'll have to run back up the hill!

He hunched down to let the cart pass. It drove on a little further and turned towards the stream – the Jewish girl obviously wanted to cool off too.

Yakov Mikhailovich trotted up the incline of the road, with the sweat streaming across his face and pouring down his back. In five minutes he had run all the way to the top.

Things were getting worse by the minute!

There was a crossroads up there: one road led to the right, the other to the left. And if you looked closely, there was a little overgrown track too. The coarse grass on it was dead and hard, he couldn't see if a cart had passed that way recently or not. What should he do? Which way should he run?

He appealed to his intellect and, as always, it came up with the answer.

Yakov Mikhkailovich went dashing back to the stream. It was easier running downhill.

The little Jewess had already washed her horse and was leading it back to the cart by the reins. She heard the tramping of feet and swung round, pulling the shotgun off her shoulder.

'Disaster, girl! Disaster!' Yakov Mikhailovich yelled in Russian from a distance.

Her jaw dropped: what was this – an Arab shouting in Russian? She completely forgot about her gun.

'Who are you?' she shouted. 'What disaster?'

He stopped in front of her, caught his breath and wiped the sweat off his forehead. 'I've lost her, that's the disaster.'

'Who have you lost? Who are you?'

'Let me have that. Or else, you never know . . .' He took hold of the barrel of the shotgun.

The girl did not want to let the weapon go, but Yakov Mikhailovich gave her a gentle tap under the ribs with his fist, and the little Jewess doubled over and started flapping her lips like a fish hoisted out of the water. He tossed the gun into the bushes and slapped the fat girl across the back of the head – she plumped down on to her backside.

She said: 'Bastard!' And she gave him a searing look from those dark, fearless eyes.

Ai-ai-ai, I'm going to have a bit of bother here, the man of experience realised. He didn't waste any time on idle conversation. First he had to reduce this 'little cow' to a state of reason, eliminate her stubbornness. 'Little cow' was a special term that Yakov Mikhailovich used. A 'little cow' had to be milked for various kinds of useful information and then, depending on the circumstances, either let back out into the meadow or slaughtered for beefsteak.

Of course, the stubborn little Jewess would go for beefsteak, that was clear, but first let her give some milk.

He beat her with his feet for a while – without swinging too hard, because it was hot. He kicked her on the ankle bones, then twice on the kidneys, and when she curled up in pain, on the coccyx. When she unfolded again, he kicked her female parts. It didn't matter how loudly she yelled, there was no one around to hear her in any case.

He decided that was enough for now. He sat on the girl's breasts and squeezed her throat in his fingers to make her think the end had already come.

But when she turned blue and her eyes started popping out of her head, Yakov Mikhailovich let go of her and allowed her to breathe, get a taste of life. And only then did he start talking to her.

'Where did she go? Which road did she take?'

'Bastard,' said the 'little cow'. 'Magellan will put you in the ground . . .'

He had to squeeze her throat again.

Yakov Mikhailovich was disappointed – he was always upset by stupid stubbornness, that very worst of human sins. One way or another, she was going to tell him everything anyway; she was only putting herself and a busy man through unnecessary anguish.

He glanced around. Picked up a branch lying nearby and broke off a piece. 'You stupid fool, now I'm going to poke your eye out with this stick,' said Yakov Mikhailovich, showing her the jagged end. 'And then the other one. If that's not enough, I'll shove this thing all the way up through your back entrance. Understand me, girl, I'm not an animal – I just have a very important job to do. Talk, my little sweetheart, talk. Which way did the redhead go?'

He released the pressure on her throat a little again. But the ungrateful bitch spat at him. The gob of spit didn't reach Yakov Mikhailovich – it fell back on to her own chin. But it wouldn't have bothered him if it had.

Well, what could he do with her?

'Who is she to you – your sister, your friend?' he complained. 'All right then, it's your own fault.' He adjusted his sitting position, pinned the little Jewess's arms down with his knees and pressed her neck against the ground with his elbow. Then he took hold of the stick close to the pointed end and held it right up to the little fool's nose.

'Well?'

From the way her eyes glinted, he could tell she wasn't going to say anything.

He thrust the stick into her eyeball and the blood bubbled out and ran across her round cheek. A sob broke out of the 'little cow's' throat and she bared her white, even teeth.

And then the little Jewess did something quite outlandish. Yakov Mikhailovich was prepared for her to press her head back against the ground, but she suddenly jerked it up towards the stick, with a strength that he couldn't possibly have expected from such a plump little thing.

The stick sank into her eye as far as his fist. Yakov Mikhailovich jerked it back out, of course, but too late – the girl's head thudded lifelessly against the ground. Where one eye should have been there was a crimson pit that looked disgusting, and there was something grey dripping off the end of the stick – it had pierced all the way through to her brain.

What a bitch! For a moment Yakov Mikhailovich simply could not believe his own bad luck.

Ah, disaster! This was a real disaster! Lord God, why do you punish me so? Help me, show me the way! What should I do now to find Ginger? Yakov was suffering, but he didn't just sit there and do nothing. You never knew who might happen along the road! He shoved the dead Jewess under the water, beside the bank, and washed the blood off his hands at the same time.

He walked across to the cart and started wondering what to do with it. Perhaps he could ride it himself? It would be easier than walking. First he could try one road – drive until he met someone and ask if a woman in a *hantur* had passed that way. If he had no luck, he could come back and try the same thing on the other road. If that was no good either – then he could go along that overgrown track.

He realised that it was a lousy plan. You could travel for an hour, or even two around here, without meeting anyone. And then, how would he explain what he wanted? And what if there more forks in the road?

He dropped the sacks of grain in the stream, followed by the harrow and the safe. He hesitated for a moment over the money box, though. Ah, if only he had a stick of dynamite and he could take a look inside. But there was no way these ragamuffins could have really big money, and there was no point in carrying the excess weight with him. He simply lashed the cows across their backsides with the whip.

Just as he was about to get in and go to try his luck, he noticed a folded sheet of paper in the bottom of her cart. He unfolded it, and it was a small map of Palestine, like the ones they put in guide books. Ginger had a book like that – he'd seen it. Had she dropped this?

There was a route marked on the map in red pencil.

'Bet-Kebir' Yakov Mikhailovich read. That was the point at which the red line stopped.

He crossed himself with broad sweeps of his hand.

God does exist, he definitely does.

XII

Castle Schwartzwinkel

Theory number three

'A hundred,' the handsome young man whispered, looking around.

'A hundred roubles?' Matvei Bentsionovich asked indignantly, but mostly for form's sake, because just at that moment he was willing to pay any amount of money, even a sum like that – a quarter of his monthly salary. Of course, life was cheaper in Zavolzhsk than in many other places, not to mention the two capital cities, but when you have fifteen people in the family, you can't help getting into the habit of economising. The main problem is that I can't take a receipt, Berdichevsky thought in passing, and that means I can't put it through as official expenses.

'Come on, come on,' said Kesha, holding out a slim, well-manicured hand; 'if my advice turns out to be no good, you'll get it back.'

That was fair. The public prosecutor took out his wallet with the picture of Catherine the Great and paid up. The young man with the blond hair was in no hurry to hide his fee – he held the banknote lightly between his finger and thumb, as if demonstrating his willingness to return it at a moment's notice.

'So, who was it that bought Ratsevich out of jail?' Matvei Bentsionovich asked hoarsely.

'I believe it was the man who loved him.'

A romantic story? The public prosecutor started. This was an entirely new twist, and he could not tell in which direction it would lead.

'You mean to say, "the woman who loved him"?'

'No, I don't,' Kesha said with a smile.

Matvei Bentsionovich took hold of his nose. 'I don't quite . . .'

'Do you think Ratsevich was thrown out of the gendarmes for his debts? Stuff and nonsense. If they threw everyone out for little trifles like that, there'd hardly be anyone left. And the top brass wouldn't have allowed an experienced officer to be put in a debtor's prison. No, that was just an excuse.'

'And what was the real reason?'

'Nobody knows that – except for the local gendarme bosses and *our people.*'

'Our people?'

The clerk took hold of Berdichevsky's left hand again and repeated the strange manipulation – tickling the palm with his finger. Seeing the look of absolute amazement on the other man's face, Kesha snorted: 'What, do you find that hard to believe? Well just imagine, there are people in the gendarmes who like men too.'

Matvei Bentsionovich's mouth fell open in astonishment.

'I can see I've earned my hundred roubles,' the young man observed with satisfaction and put the banknote away in his wallet.

The public prosecutor was still struggling to recover his wits. Was it really possible?

And then he was struck by a sudden realisation. Yes, yes! Pelagia had told him that there was a group of pederasts on the river steamer, settlers travelling to the rebuilt city of Sodom . . . But that sent the investigation off in a completely different direction!

The State Counsellor took a firm grip on the young man's elbow.

'You still haven't told me who paid the money to get him out.'

'I don't know for certain, but I'm sure it must have been Charnokutsky; it couldn't have been anyone else.'

'Who is this Charnokutsky?'

'You've never heard of the counts Charnokutsky?' Kesha asked incredulously.

'Yes, I have. A noble Polish family.'

'Noble! Never mind noble! The Charnokutskys are the richest family in the whole of Volynia. The Chernokutsky district is just

285

twenty versts away from here, and the district town, Chyorny Kut, belongs completely to the count.'

'The whole town? Do such things happen?' Matvei Bentsionovich asked in amazement. 'This isn't the Middle Ages.'

'It certainly is in Volynia. The city of Rovno belongs to Prince Liubomirsky, Staro-Konstantinov belongs to Princess Abamelek, Dubno belongs to the Princess Bariatinskaya. And the Charnokutskys have been in Volynia for seven hundred years. Look, do you see that rock?' Kesha asked, pointing to a picturesque cliff overhanging the river in the distance: 'One of the sights of Zhitomir. It's called Chatsky's Head.'

The cliff really did bear a certain resemblance to a proudly bowed head.

'What has it to do with Chatsky?'

'Absolutely nothing. The cliff used to be called Charnokutsky's Head. In the sixteenth century the *gaidamaks* here beheaded the present count's ancestor. But after eighteen sixty-three, the order came down to change the cliff's name. And the reason was that several of the Charnokutskys were involved in the Polish rebellion, and one of them even paid for it with his head. So to avoid any ambiguity, they changed it to Chatsky.'

'So the count is one of the rebels of eighteen sixty-three?'

'No way! His Excellency has quite different interests. Pretty much the same as you and I do.' The clerk laughed. 'It's a pity he can't stand Jews, or I would definitely introduce you to him.'

'But I'm not a Jew at all,' Berdichevsky declared. 'I pretended to be, in order to win Golosovker's trust.'

'You pretended very well,' Kesha remarked, examining the public prosecutor's face sceptically.

'No, it's true! My hair is dyed. I'm actually blond. If you'll take me to the Count, I'll wash the dye out. And my name is not Mordechai Berdichevsky, it's Matvei Berg-Dichevsky. You guessed right when you said I wasn't a moneylender. I'm ... I'm a district marshal of the nobility,' Matvei Bentsionovich lied, unable to think of anything more aristocratic. 'From the province of Zavolzhie.'

It was impossible to tell if the young man believed him or not. But he thought for a moment and said: 'Two hundred roubles.'

'You're out of your mind!' the State Counsellor gasped, trying to work out if he had that much money with him.

'You can pay when we come back. If I'm wrong and the Count didn't buy him out, you don't have to pay at all,' the sharp-witted youth quipped.

Matvei Bentsionovich readily agreed to these terms. If this was the right trail, and his trip proved fruitful, he could probably include the expenditure in the bill for the investigation.

'Where are you staying?' Kesha asked.

'At the Versailles.'

'I close the office at seven. Only don't be mean – hire a carriage with spring suspension, or we'll get battered black and blue. I can have a word with Semyon Pochtarenko, he has a good carriage. It's a long drive . . .'

Travelling meditations on the sad future of mankind

Once again the State Counsellor turned to the White-Haired Angel for help, but his blond hair colour was not restored completely. The actual result was a kind of golden-reddish colour. Never mind, it would be good enough for the evening light, Berdichevsky consoled himself.

Kesha arrived on time, in a most respectable-looking phaeton that cost the public prosecutor eight roubles. The clerk was quite unrecognisable. He had decked himself out in the very latest fashion, put on perfume, and his neatly parted hair gleamed like a mirror. Who would ever believe that this dandy earned an extra penny by taking care of a Jewish shop on the Sabbath?

'Where are we going?' Matvei Bentsionovich asked after making himself comfortable on the soft seat.

'To the Count's castle at Schwartzwinkel.'

'The Black Corner?' the public prosecutor asked, translating the name.

'Yes indeed. "Chorny Kut" in the Volynian dialect, and in Great Russian it's "Chorny Zakut", or something of the kind. It was built by His Excellency's grandfather, in the Gothic style. He was very fond of novels about knights and chivalry.'

Berdichevsky had managed to ask the hotel receptionist about the Count, but the absolutely incredible stories he had been told in reply had only served to inflame his curiosity. He had to check which of these fantastic tales were true and which were not.

'This magnate would appear to be an unusual man, then?' Matvei Bentsionovich asked casually.

Kesha chortled. 'You and I couldn't exactly be called ordinary, could we? But, of course, there's no way we could be compared with His Excellency. He is absolutely one of a kind.'

Hungry for more details, the public prosecutor put on a thoughtful expression and remarked: 'The scions of ancient families have the predilection for sodomy in their blood. It must come from being so spoilt. Or perhaps it's the result of degeneracy.'

'Oh, the Count hasn't always been interested in boys. In his young days he was a real enthusiast for the female sex; it was like a madness or, as he puts it, an obsession. That's a medical term – something like a bee in your bonnet.'

'I know.'

'After all, he's a doctor by education. He was so interested in women that after the Corps of Pages he didn't go into the Guards, or even into the diplomatic service; instead he went to the medical faculty to study gynaecology. But not in order to earn money, of course. He says: "I wanted to know everything about women: how they're made, what they have inside them, what little key turns them on. I learned every little detail."' Kesha chuckled again. 'Yes, obviously he must have had too much of it. When he graduated from university, he opened a women's hospital, but he soon gave it up. Now he can't even look at a woman; they make him shudder.'

Matvei Bentsionovich's information was rather different. The receptionist had told him: 'Before the Count went crazy, he ran a hospital and treated female ailments for free. First he killed one woman during an operation, then another, and then another. The business got as far as the court. Any ordinary doctor would definitely have been convicted, but he was a Charnokutsky. But they closed the hospital down anyway.'

'Then His Excellency went travelling,' said Kesha, continuing his story. 'He spent a long time travelling round the world. He went absolutely everywhere – to Amazonia, and the Dutch East Indies, and Papua. He has an incredible collection – you'll see for yourself . . .'

Berdichevsky had heard about the collection as well. Supposedly it included severed heads in glass jars. 'They say he brought them back from savage countries, but who really knows?' the receptionist had said.

'Eventually the Count even got tired of travelling round the world. And now he's living in Schwartzwinkel and hasn't left the place for years. He's arranged his home in a quite original manner – you'll see for yourself. You should consider yourself lucky. Not many people are allowed into the castle. *Exclusivité* – that's a French word. It means—'

'I know what it means,' Berdichevsky interrupted. 'You carry on with your story. The things I've heard about this count of yours . . .'

Kesha seemed offended at not being allowed to show off his erudition. He mumbled: 'You could never have got in there without me. And all this gossip is just from envy and ignorance.' He fell silent after that.

So the public prosecutor did not discover if it was true that the castle was surrounded by a thick forest that it was strictly forbidden to enter. And, to make sure that no one did go in, that that forest was full of wolf-pits, snares and man-traps. The State Counsellor had been told that several lads and lasses who had been tempted in by the mushrooms and berries growing there had disappeared without trace. The police had searched the forest and the castle. They had seen the snares and the pits but had found no clues. 'In the moat under the walls,' the receptionist had whispered, 'there's an immense swamp snake, five sazhens long. It can swallow a man in a single gulp.' Well, after that Berdichevsky hadn't bothered to listen to any more, because it was all such obvious make-believe. But now he regretted not having heard the man out.

The carriage rolled on over hill and dale. It gradually got dark and stars appeared in the sky – pale at first, but growing brighter every minute.

What am I doing here? Matvei Bentsionovich suddenly thought with a shudder, surveying this Gogolesque landscape. *What will I say to the Count? What lies in wait for me there? Especially if the homosexual theory turns out to be right and this rich man really is linked with the murderers?*

The excitement of the hunt was to blame; it had made a

rational man, a respectable paterfamilias, throw all caution to the winds.

Perhaps I ought to turn back, the public prosecutor wondered. After all, if I disappear, no one will ever know what happened to me.

But then he remembered Pelagia – the way she had walked up the gangplank and on to the deck, with her head lowered and the light from the lamp falling across her defenceless shoulders. The State Counsellor stuck out his chin and knitted his brows menacingly. We'll soon see who should be afraid, Berdichevsky or this Volynian magnate.

'You have a very handsome profile,' said Kesha, breaking the silence. 'Like on a Roman coin.' And he rubbed his knee against the other man's leg. Matvei Bentsionovich glanced severely at the dissolute youth and pulled away.

'It's all Ratsevich's fault, is it?' the young man sighed. 'You love him that much? Oh well, I respect men who are faithful to one love.'

'Yes, I am faithful to one love,' the public prosecutor declared, and turned away.

Just what is homosexuality, and why do people need it? Matvei Bentsionovich wondered. And the remarkable thing is that the higher the level of civilisation, the greater the number of people who indulge in this vice condemned by society and all religions. But is it a vice? Perhaps it is a natural development resulting from mankind's ever greater distance from the natural state as it moves from the primeval campfire to the bright glow of electricity? No matter what big city you go to – Petersburg, Moscow or Warsaw – they are everywhere, and every year there are more of them, and they are more and more open in their behaviour. This is no accident, this is a sign, and it is not a matter of declining morals or debauchery. There are certain important processes affecting the human being, and we do not yet understand their meaning. Culture brings sophistication, sophistication leads to unnaturalness. Men no longer have to be strong – that is becoming a relic of the past. Women can no longer understand why they ought to allow men precedence, if men are no longer the strong sex. In another hundred years or so society (or at least its cultured section) will consist entirely of effeminate men like Kesha and masculine women like Fira

Dorman. That will make a fine muddle of all the instincts and desires of the flesh! Matvei Bentsionovich's thought wandered further and further, into the far distant future. Humankind would die out because in the end the difference between the two sexes would disappear altogether and people would cease to reproduce. Unless, of course, science were to invent a new means of reproducing human individuals, something like budding plants. Take a rib, for instance, as the Lord God did with Adam, and grow a new human being. All very passionless and proper. No wild frenzies, no fiery intermingling of the male and female energies.

How fortunate that I shall not see that heaven on earth, the State Counsellor thought with a shudder.

'There it is – Schwartzwinkel,' said Kesha, pointing upwards.

A unique collection

When he stuck his head out of the carriage, Matvei Bentsion-ovich saw a large dark cone in the distance, with lights flickering on its summit.

'What are those, fires?' he asked in amazement.

'Torches on the towers. I told you, it's a medieval castle.'

The road that ran off from the rough, bumpy high road in the direction of the incomprehensible cone was narrow, but paved with smooth stone. It was a large hill, covered with forest, Berd-ichevsky realised. And right on the top there was a castle. Now he could make out the battlements on the walls, illuminated by the dancing tongues of flame. A minute later the phaeton drove into the forest and the castle disappeared. It was completely dark.

'It's a good thing there's a lantern on the shaft,' the public prosecutor remarked as he felt the phaeton heel over to one side. 'You can't see a thing.' For a moment he imagined they were about to go rolling over down a steep slope, tumble into a thicket and fall into some wolf-pit studded with sharp stakes . . .

'It's all right, Semyon knows the road.'

The forest road spiralled round the hill, gradually climbing higher. On both sides the trees pressed right up against it, like a stockade fence, and it was hard to believe that close by, only a hundred paces away, there was light and live people. And as ill luck would have it, Kesha said nothing.

'We seem to be driving for a long time,' said Matvei Bentsiono-vich, feeling anxious. 'Will it still be long?'

The question was asked with no particular purpose in mind, simply in order to hear the sound of a human voice; but the young man who had been so talkative before did not answer now.

The carriage straightened up and started rolling along a hori-zontal surface. After one final bend, the road led them out on to a large square paved with cobblestones. A massive tower loomed up straight ahead, with gates flanked by two flaming torches. In front of the gates there was a drawbridge, and below the drawbridge, a moat – the same one that the hotel receptionist had claimed was home to a swamp monster.

'Br-rr-rr, a Gothic novel,' the State Counsellor said with a chilly shudder.

From somewhere above them a loud, coarse voice called out: 'Whossere?'

Kesha opened the door on his side and stuck his head out. 'Foma? It's me, Innokentii! Open up. And switch on the lights, I can't see a damn thing.'

Two lamps, the very latest word in electrical illumination, lit up the square. Time ceased its vacillation, returning from the middle of the second millennium to its end. Berdichevsky noted with delight the pillars and the wires, the post box on the gates. Medieval horrors and swamp snakes be damned!

A narrow little door opened and a heftily built man came out, dressed completely in black leather. The shirt with a low neck that showed his hairy, muscular chest was made of leather, and so were the high boots, and the tight-fitting trousers with a leather pouch at the crotch, like in sixteenth-century paintings. A codpiece, thought Berdichevsky, recalling the name of this absurd item of the medieval wardrobe. Only this was no cod-piece: it was an entire, huge cod.

Kesha jumped down lightly to the ground and stretched like a cat.

'Whossat?' Foma asked, pointing to Matvei Bentsionovich.

'With me. A guest. I'll tell His Excellency. Let Semyon go,' the young man said, addressing the public prosecutor. 'The

Count will give us his carriage for the drive back.'

When Berdichevsky paid the driver, the man seemed confused, as if there was something he was hesitant to say, and at the last moment he decided not to. He merely grunted, pulled his cap down over his eyes and drove on his way.

The State Counsellor watched the carriage leave with a wistful gaze. Matvei Bentsionovich did not like the look of Castle Schwartzwinkel, despite the electric light and the post box.

They went inside.

Berdichevsky did not get a very clear impression of the courtyard and the buildings, because it is hard to make out architectural details in the dark. The setting seemed to be bizarre and fantastic: little towers, gryphons on waterspouts, stone chimeras silhouetted against the starry sky. In the main building there was electric light behind the curtains: dim on the ground floor and bright on the first.

The visitors were met in the doorway by another servant, whom Kesha called Filip. He was dressed in exactly the same fashion as Foma, which indicated that this was the livery of the Count's servants. Once again the dimensions of the codpiece were impressive. Do they stuff them with cotton wool or something? the public prosecutor wondered, stealing a sly glance. And only then did the naive man realise that these fine bucks were probably used by His Excellency for more than just running the household.

With his black leather creaking, Filip led the guests up a marble stairway decorated with sculptures of knights. When they reached a spacious, tastefully furnished room on the first floor, he bowed and went out, leaving Matvei Bentsionovich and Kesha alone.

The young man nodded towards a tall door that led into the inner chambers. 'I'll tell the Count about you. You wait here in the reception room for a while.'

The public prosecutor had the impression that Kesha was nervous. The clerk straightened his tie in the mirror, then took out a little porcelain tube and deftly touched up the colour of his lips. The sudden surprise of it set Berdichevsky's eyes blinking.

No sooner had the young man with blond hair disappeared into the next room than the State Counsellor leapt up out of his chair and tiptoed across to the door. He pressed his ear against it and listened.

He could hear Kesha's rapid tenor patter, but he couldn't make out the words.

An unnaturally taut, springy voice that sounded as if it had been inflated with a pump said: 'Oh, really?'

More unintelligible gabble.

'What's that you say? Berg-Dichevsky?'

Kesha replied: gabble-gabble-gabble.

'Very well, let's have a look at him.'

Matvei Bentsionovich swung round and in three swift, silent bounds he was back at his armchair and fell into it, casually crossing one leg over the other.

Then suddenly he noticed Filip standing in the doorway that led to the stairs. The servant was watching the guest with a stony expression on his face and his strong arms, naked up to the elbows, crossed on his chest.

Curses! Not only had he not heard anything useful, he had disgraced himself in front of a servant! The public prosecutor felt his face flooding with colour, but there was no time to ponder his error. The door of the drawing room opened, and the master of the house came out.

Berdichevsky saw an elegant gentleman with very white skin and very black hair. From a distance the moustache with curled-up ends looked like a line drawn in charcoal, dividing the face into two halves. Ah, the infernal Zizi has been at work here, the State Counsellor thought, drawing on his own recently acquired expertise in the dying of hair.

Charnokutsky was wearing a Chinese silk cap with a tassel and a black dressing gown with silver dragons, beneath which could be seen a white shirt with a lace collar. The magnate's absolutely motionless face appeared to be ageless: there was not a single wrinkle on it. Only the faded colour of the blue eyes made it possible to surmise that their owner was closer to the sunset of his life than to its dawn. However, the gaze of His Excellency's eyes was not sated and bored with life but as sharp and inquisitive as a little boy's. An old child – that was the definition that occurred to Matvei Bentsionovich.

'Welcome, Mr Berg-Dichevsky,' the host said in that rubbery voice with which the public prosecutor was already familiar.

'Please forgive my informal dress. I was not expecting visitors at this late hour. People rarely come here without some advance arrangement. But I know that *Innocent*' – the word was pronounced in the French manner, with the stress on the final syllable – 'would not bring anyone . . . *inappropriate*.'

It took Matvei Bentsionovich a moment to realise that the count was referring to Kesha: 'Kesha' – 'Innokentii' – '*Innocent*'.

Charnokutsky flared his nostrils slightly, as if he were repressing a yawn. Suddenly it was clear why his voice sounded so unnatural: the Count hardly moved his lips at all and employed no facial expressions – that must be in order to avoid wrinkles. Flaring the nostrils was undoubtedly his substitute for a smile.

When asked if he was related to the deceased Field Marshal Count Berg, the State Counsellor replied cautiously that he was, but only very, very distantly.

'Better not tell the other Poles about that,' His Excellency said with another twitch of the nostrils. 'It's all the same to me; I'm an absolute cosmopolitan.'

As a result of this reply Matvei Bentsionovich, firstly, recalled who Field Marshal Berg was – the oppressor of the Poles during the reigns of Nikolai Pavlovich and Alexander the Second – and, secondly, realised that his host had taken the cautious tone of his reply the wrong way. And thank God for that.

'What is it, Filip?' the Count asked, gazing at his servant.

Filip bowed, walked up to the Count and whispered in his ear.

He's told on me, the brute.

Charnokutsky's eyebrows lifted very slightly, and a spark of merriment glinted in the eyes turned towards the public prosecutor.

'So you are a marshal of the nobility? From the province of Zavolzhie?'

'What do you find so funny about that?' asked Matvei Bentsionovich, and knitted his brows darkly, having decided that the best form of defence was attack. 'Do you imagine Zavolzhie is such a hopeless backwater that it has no nobility?

The Count whispered something to Filip and patted him affectionately on his taut thigh, and then the scurvy lackey finally cleared off.

'No, no – what I found amusing was something quite different,' said the master of the house, examining his guest openly, in fact absolutely frankly. 'It is amusing that Bronek Ratsevich's friend of the heart should be a marshal of the nobility. That joker will always land on his feet. Tell me, how did you come to meet him?'

Berdichevsky had prepared an explanation to meet this eventuality on his way there. 'You know Bronek,' he said with a congenial smile, 'Always up to mischief. He got himself into a silly spot of bother in our province. He tried to give a certain nun a fright, for a joke, but he tried a little too hard and found himself in court. As a stranger who had no acquaintances in the town, he appealed to the marshal for help in choosing a lawyer ... Naturally, I helped – as one nobleman to another ...' Matvei Bentsionovich paused eloquently, as if to say: You can guess how events developed after that for yourselves.

The smile that was like a yawn appeared once again on the Count's face. 'Yes he always did have a certain penchant for servants of the Church. Do you remember that nun, Kesha – the one who wandered into the castle, looking for charitable contributions? Remember how Bronek dealt with her, eh?' The trembling of the nostrils was joined by a suppressed sobbing – this was obviously not simply laughter, but an entire paroxysm of mirth.

Kesha smiled too, only his smile seemed somehow crooked, even frightened. But the State Counsellor tensed inside at the mention of the nun. He seemed to be getting warm!

'But why are we standing here? Please come through into the drawing room. I'll show you my collection, which is absolutely unique after its own fashion.' Charnokutsky gestured to invite them in, and they all moved to the next room.

The walls of the drawing room were lined and draped with red velvet in a wide variety of tones, from light crimson to dark vermilion, which produced a strange not to say malevolent impression. The electric lighting emphasised the shimmering transitions of this bloody palette, creating a glowing effect somewhere between a distant conflagration and a blazing sunset.

The first thing to catch Berdichevsky's eye in this incredible drawing room was an Egyptian sarcophagus that contained an incredibly well-preserved female mummy.

'Twentieth dynasty, one of the daughters of Ramses the

Fourth. I bought it from grave-robbers in Alexandria for three thousand pounds sterling. She could be alive! Just take a look.' The Count raised the muslin, and Matvei Bentsionovich saw a slim body, absolutely naked.

'You see, this is the mark of the embalmer's knife.' A slim finger with a polished nail followed a line stretching across the yellow, wrinkled stomach until it reached the *mons pubis*, when it was fastidiously withdrawn.

Turning his eyes away, the State Counsellor almost screamed out loud: there was a little negro girl gazing out at him from a glass cupboard, her eyes glinting as if she were alive.

'What's that?'

'She's stuffed. I brought her from Senegambia. For the sake of the tattoos. A genuine work of art!' The Count switched on a lamp below a shelf and Matvei Bentsionovich saw purple designs in the form of intertwined snakes on the dark-brown skin.

'There is a tribe there in which the women are decorated with delightful tattoos. One little girl had just died. Well, I bought the body from the chief – for a Winchester rifle and a box of ammunition. Apparently the natives there thought I was a consumer of dead human flesh.' The Count's nostrils twitched again. 'But in fact one of my servants at the time was an outstanding taxidermist. Impressive work, isn't it?'

'Yes,' Berdichevsky replied with a gulp.

They moved on to the next exhibit.

This proved to be less frightening: an ordinary human skull, and hanging above it a portrait of a powdered lady with a plunging décolleté and a capriciously pouting lower lip.

'And what's this?' Matvei Bentsionovich asked with a feeling of relief.

'Do you not recognise Marie Antoinette? This is her head,' said the Count, stroking the skull's gleaming crown lovingly.

'How did you hold of get it?' Berdichevsky gasped.

'I acquired it from a certain Irish lord who happened to be in straitened circumstances at the time. One of his ancestors was in Paris during the Revolution and was quick-witted enough to bribe the executioner.'

The State Counsellor shifted his gaze from the portrait to the skull and back again, trying to discover at least some similarity between the human face in life and after death. He failed. The face existed in its own right, and so did the skull. What a swine that Parisian executioner was, Matvei Bentsionovich thought.

Next there was a glass cube containing a doll's head with curly hair – as small and wrinkled as a newborn baby's.

'That is from the island of New Guinea,' the Count explained. 'A smoked head. Not really a great rarity – there are plenty like it in European collections – but this one is remarkable because I was, so to speak, personally acquainted with this lady.'

'How's that?'

'She had committed an offence, broken some taboo or other, and for that she had to be killed. I was a witness to the killing and also the subsequent smoking process – in fact it was shorter than usual, because according to the rules the process ought to take several months, but I could not afford to wait for so long. I was warned quite honestly that my souvenir might spoil after a few years. But so far all is well; it is surviving.'

'And you did nothing to try to save this unfortunate woman?'

'Who am I to interfere with the administration of justice, even aboriginal justice?'

They walked up to a large display case in which little bags of various sizes with leather drawstrings were displayed on the shelves.

'What's this?' asked Matvei Bentsionovich, failing to find anything interesting in the exhibits. 'They look like tobacco pouches.'

'They are pouches. Made by the Indians of the American Wild West. Do you not notice anything special? Take a closer look.' The magnate opened the door, took out one of the pouches and handed it to his guest, who turned the object in his hands, marvelling at how thin and soft the leather was. There was nothing else remarkable about it – no pattern, no embossed work. Except that at the centre there was something like a little button. He looked at it closely, and then tossed the pouch back on to the shelf in horror.

'Yes, yes,' His Excellency clucked. 'It is a nipple. The warriors of certain Indian tribes have the delightful custom of bringing back men's scalps and women's breasts from a raid. But there are even more startling trophies.' He took something that looked like a bunch of dried mushrooms off a shelf: a series of dark rings, some of them with little hairs, threaded on a string.

This is from the jungles of Brazil. I visited a certain forest people who were at war with those brutish, bloodthirsty female warriors the Amazons, whom, thank goodness, they later exterminated completely. I bought this garland from their most valiant hero, who had personally killed eleven Amazons. See, there are exactly eleven rings here.'

'But what are the rings?' the slow-witted Berdichevsky asked, then suddenly felt sick as he realised the answer.

A gong boomed quietly somewhere in the depths of the house.

'The hors d'œuvres are ready,' the Count declared, breaking off the terrifying excursion. 'Shall we?'

After what he had just seen, the public prosecutor was not really in the mood for hors d'oeuvres, but he replied hastily, 'Thank you, with pleasure.'

Anywhere at all to get out of this room.

The wolf driven into the pit

In the hall next door, the dining room (a perfectly normal one, thank God, with no smoked heads or dried genitals), Matvei Bentsionovich drained two glasses of wine one after the other before he could rid himself of the repulsive trembling in his fingers. He ate a grape. His stomach convulsed, but it was all right – it withstood the test.

Kesha bolted down stuffed quails as if nothing unusual had happened. The Count himself did not touch the food; he merely took a sip of cognac and immediately lit up a cigar.

'Well then, so there is *society* in Zavolzhsk?' he asked, pronouncing the word in a way that made it quite clear exactly what kind of society was intended.

'Not very numerous, but there is,' Berdichevsky replied, preparing to lie.

Charnokutsky asked several more questions with lively interest, some of which the Zavolzhian did not understand at all. What could 'Do you have a spring chick farm?' mean? or 'Do you organise a carousel?' The devil only knew what sort of carousel was meant. Some kind of filthy pederasts' perversion.

In order to avoid being exposed, the public prosecutor decided to seize the initiative. 'I was very impressed by your collection,' he said, changing the subject. 'Tell me, why do you only collect ... er er ... the remains of the fair half of the human race?'

'Woman is not the fair half of the human race, she is not even a half at all,' the Count snapped. 'She is a cheap caricature of a human being. I tell you this as a medical man. An ugly, absurd creature! Mammary glands like jellyfish, cushions of fat in the pelvis, an absurd skeletal structure, a squeaky voice ...' Charnokutsky shuddered in disgust.

A-ha, thought Matvei Bentsionovich, you might be a medical man, but there's a hospital ward just crying out for you. The kind that is locked from the outside.

'I beg your pardon, but it is not possible to manage entirely without women,' he protested mildly. 'If only from the point of view of continuing the human race ...'

The Count was not floored by his argument. 'A special strain should be bred from the most fertile of them, the way they do with cows and farrowing sows. Kept in a barn. And fertilised, of course, by using a syringe – in no other way.' A tremor of revulsion ran across the misogynist's face.

Is he mocking me? thought Berdichevsky, suddenly doubtful. Is he playing the fool? Never mind, damn this psychopath's idiotic theories. It's time to get down to business.

'How marvellous it would be to live in an exclusively male society, associating only with others like oneself,' the State Counsellor mused. 'Have you heard that some American millionaire is restoring the biblical Sodom?'

'Yes. An amusing fruit of American didacticism. From the point of view of philanthropy, of course, those millions should have been spent on bread for the poor, but you won't amaze the world that way. And what good would it do? The poor will eat the free bread and then demand more tomorrow; you can never have enough. But this is a lesson to humanity. Mr Sairus is a respectable family man and he can't stand "perverts", but he wants to show his contemporaries an example of tolerance and compassion for pariahs. Oh, the Americans will teach everyone to be moral, given enough time.'

'No doubt the Sodom project has plenty of enemies?' asked

Matvei Bentsionovich, venturing on to his main subject. 'Amongst the prudes and religious fanatics. So many sects have appeared just recently, calling for Old Testament-style intolerance.' From there he was intending to go on to Manuila – to feel out His Excellency's attitude to the prophet whom one-eyed Bronek had tried to kill.

However, the conversation was interrupted. Filip entered the dining room with a crunch of gleaming leather, bowed and handed his master a long paper ribbon.

So there was a telegraph in this medieval castle? Somehow the public prosecutor did not find this discovery to his liking.

After running his eyes over the rather long message, Charnokutsky suddenly said to Kesha: 'Innocent, you foolish little boy, I'll have to give you a good whipping. Who is this you have brought?'

The handsome boy with blond hair choked on a segment of orange and Berdichevsky's heart skipped a beat. He exclaimed in a trembling voice: 'What do you mean by that, Count?'

'What an insolent breed you Yids are,' the magnate said, shaking his head, and then spoke no more to Matvei Berdichevsky, only to Kesha. 'Listen to what Mickey writes':

The provincial marshal of the nobility in Zavolzhsk is Count Rostovsky. The district marshals are Prince Bekbulatov, Baron Stakelberg, Selyaninov, Kotko-Kotkovsky, Lazutin, Prince Vachnadze, Barkhatov and Count Beznosov, and there are also three districts that do not have a marshal because of the small numbers of nobles there. The individual about whom you enquire does indeed reside in Zavolzhsk, but the name has been confused and the position is incorrect. He is not Matvei Berg-Dichevsky, but Matvei Berdichevsky, the district public prosecutor. A State Counsellor, forty years of age, a baptised Jew.'

The colour of Kesha's cheeks suddenly changed from pink to green. He collapsed on to his knees and sobbed: 'I didn't know a thing about it, I swear!'

The Count pushed the boy's forehead with the toe of his shoe, and Kesha collapsed back on to the carpet, snivelling.

'Who sent you this nonsense?' asked Matvei Bentsionovich, who had not yet adjusted to the catastrophic change in the situation. After all, until this moment everything had been going so smoothly!

The Count blew out a stream of cigar smoke. He looked the public prosecutor up and down with an expression of curious loathing, as if he were some peculiar insect or a squashed frog. But even so, he condescended to reply: 'Mickey, one of ours. An important figure. Any day now he'll be a minister, and so he should be – he's a brilliant worker. The kind of man you can send a telegram to at midnight and be sure of finding him at work.'

This called for an urgent change of tactics – Matvei Bentsionovich had to abandon blunt denial and lay all his cards on the table, as they say.

'Well since you now know that I am a public prosecutor, you should understand that I didn't come here to play foolish games,' Berdichevsky declared sternly, actually feeling a certain relief that he no longer needed to continue acting out this comedy. 'Answer me immediately: was it you who paid off Ratsevich's debt?'

And then something quite unthinkable happened: someone seized the State Counsellor's elbows from behind and twisted his arms painfully.

'Leave him, Filip,' the Count said with a frown. 'No need. Let the little Jew crow for a while.'

'There's something heavy in his pocket,' the lackey explained. 'Here.' Easily clutching both of his prisoner's wrists in one huge mitt, he took the Lefauchier out of the public prosecutor's pocket and handed it to the Count.

His master took hold of the revolver with his finger and a thumb, gave it a single quick glance and tossed it aside with the words: 'Cheap garbage!'

Berdichevsky wriggled helplessly in a grip of steel. 'Let me go, you villain! I'm a State Counsellor! I'll send you to Siberia for this!'

'Let him go,' said Charnokutsky. 'The poisoned fang has been drawn, and Yids are not known for their skill in fisticuffs. Do you know, Mr Jewish Counsellor, why I dislike your breed so much? Not because you crucified Christ. He got what he deserved, the Yid. But because you are like women, caricatures of human beings. You only pretend to be men.'

'I am a representative of the authorities!' Matvei Bentsionovich shouted, clutching a numb wrist. 'Don't you dare treat me like—'

'No,' the Count interrupted with sudden ferocity. 'You are a rat, who has entered my home like a thief. If you weren't a Yid, I would simply have you thrown out of the gate. But for making me, Charnokutsky, flatter and amuse you for the best part of an hour and feed you thirty-year-old cognac, you will pay with your life. And no one will ever find out. You are not the first, and you will not be the last.'

'You are involved in a criminal case!' Berdichevsky exclaimed, trying to talk some sense into the madman. 'I may have come here clandestinely, but I am conducting an important investigation! You are the main suspect! If I don't go back, the police will be here tomorrow!'

'He's lying about the investigation,' squeaked Kesha, still not daring to get up off the carpet. 'He found out about you from me; he didn't even know your name before that.'

'What about the coachman?' the public prosecutor reminded him. 'He brought me here and went back to the town! If I disappear, the coachman will tell the whole story.'

'Who brought you, Innocent?' Charnokutsky asked.

'Semyon. You don't think I'd use an outsider, do you?'

The Count crushed his cigar into an ashtray. Speaking to Matvei Bentsionovich in a respectful tone again, clearly to mock him, he declared merrily: 'Our Volynian peasants, who have twelve languages mingled together in their dialect, say "Drive a wolf into a *kut,* and then the creature is kaput." Do not be downhearted, Mr Berdichevsky, do not let that crooked nose of yours droop. There is a long night ahead, there are many interesting things in store for you. Now we will go down into the basement and I will show you the secret part of my collection, the most interesting part. I did not buy the exhibits down there, I made them myself. I cannot add you to the collection – as you saw, I only have women. Although, perhaps, some small piece, by way of an exception?'

An intensive interrogation

Gazing at his prisoner's expression of horror, the Count burst into a fit of his stiff, cackling laughter. 'No, not the part that you thought of. That would be a blasphemy against the male body. Innocent, my friend, what do you think of the exhibit "A Jewish heart". In a jar of spirit alcohol, eh?'

Charnokutsky walked up the table, took a peach out of a bowl and stroked its velvety cheek lovingly. 'No!' he exclaimed, continuing with his jest. 'I have a better idea than that! A pound of Jewish flesh!' And he declaimed in English, with an immaculate Eton accent: '"An equal pound of your fair flesh, to be cut off and taken in what part of your body pleaseth me". I will even let you make the choice, which is more than Shylock did for poor Antonio. Where would you prefer?'

Matvei Bentsionovich could not speak English as beautifully, and so he replied in Russian. 'I don't want your charity; let it be as it is in your Judaeophobic play – "as close as possible to the heart."' He unbuttoned his jacket and slapped his left side, where the 'present from the firm' – that single-shot trinket with a barrel slightly thicker than a straw – lay in his waistcoat pocket. Well, they say that a drowning will clutch at a straw.

And that is exactly what the public prosecutor did – he grabbed the pistol, and so furiously that he broke the nail on his thumb against the hammer.

'What's that – an enema tube?' asked the Count, not frightened in the least. 'It seems a little on the small side.'

At that very moment Berdichevsky underwent a remarkable metamorphosis: suddenly he was completely free of fear and fell into a monstrous rage, of a kind he had never experienced before. And there was a reason for this.

We have already mentioned the change that had taken place in the character of this peaceful and even rather timid man as a result of his unexpectedly falling in love, but in this particular case the spark that detonated the explosion was a far less romantic circumstance. Matvei Bentsionovich had always been obsessively concerned with his nails. A microscopic hangnail or – God forbid – a small crack, could completely unbalance him, and the sound of a nail scraped across glass set him shuddering convulsively. The essential hygienic procedure that the civilised part of humanity performs on its nails once every four days was a torment for Berdichevsky, especially its final phase, which involves working with a file. But now a whole piece had broken off his nail and was dangling from it in a most repulsive fashion!

This minor unpleasantness, a mere trifle in the context of the situation as a whole, was the last straw: the whole world darkened in front of the State Counsellor's eyes and fear gave way to frenzy.

'It's a waistcoat pistol!' Matvei Bentsionovich growled, his face flushing bright red. 'An indispensable item when you are attacked by a robber in the night! It possesses incredible fire power for its calibre!'

The Count frowned ever so slightly. 'Filip, take that abominable thing away from him.'

How the public prosecutor would have liked to fire at the dastardly aristocrat, to demonstrate to him the remarkable qualities of the pistol he had insulted, but Matvei Bentsionovich recalled the warning he had been given by the salesman in the gun shop: 'Of course, at a distance of more than two sazhens the firepower weakens a bit, and at five sazhens there's no point at all in wasting the bullet.'

The distance to the magnate was not as much as five sazhens but, alas, it was not as little as two sazhens either. Therefore Bedichevsky leapt abruptly to one side and trained the barrel on the ox-like Filip. Wasting no time on stupid warnings ('Stop, or I'll fire!' and so on) he simply raised the hammer and immediately released it again.

The pop was not very loud – quieter than a champagne cork. His hand hardly felt any recoil at all. The smoke that poured out of the tiny gun barrel was like cotton wool, although not really the kind you might stick up your nostril. However, the result was quite remarkable: the huge thug doubled over and clutched at his stomach with both hands.

'Your Excell —' Filip gasped. 'He got me in the belly! It hurts – I can't stand it!'

For several moments the dining room was transformed into something like a pantomime or *pas de quatre*. The Count's face was a picture of extreme astonishment that threatened the appearance of two or three wrinkles at the very least; His Excellency's arms rose smoothly out to both sides. Kesha froze on the floor in the pose of a dying, or perhaps already dead, swan. The wounded servant swayed back on his heels, completely doubled over. And even Berdichevsky who, in his heart of hearts had not really believed in the effectiveness of his weapon, froze rigid for an instant.

But the State Counsellor was the first to recover his wits. Tossing the useless little pistol aside, he made a dash for the Lefauchier lying on the floor, grabbed it and began jerking his finger in search of a trigger. Ah, yes, it had a folding trigger!'

He raised the hammer, transferred the revolver to his left hand and stuck his broken nail into his mouth – to feel it with his tongue.

The Lefauchier might be 'cheap garbage', as the Count had put it, but even so it had six bullets, not one. And it was effective at a distance of more than two sazhens.

'Oh, it hurts!' Filip howled at the top of his voice. 'He shot right through my insides! Mummy, it burns! I'm dying!' He stopped swaying, tumbled to the floor and pulled up his legs.

'Quiet!' Berdichevsky yelled at him in a repulsive, shrill voice. The public prosecutor was white with fury. 'Lie quietly, or I'll shoot you again!'

The big brute immediately fell silent and didn't make another sound: he just bit his lips and wiped away the tears that looked so odd on his coarse, bearded face.

Berdichevsky licked at his nail as he gave Kesha an order: 'You fifthy sfine, get under ve table, and don't wet me heawa sound out ovyou!'

The young man immediately repositioned himself as indicated, performing the manoeuvre on all fours. Now Matvei Bentsionovich could turn his attention to the main target.

The target had not yet recovered from his stupefaction – he was still standing on the same spot, holding a bitten peach in one hand.

'And you and I, Your Exfewency, are going to have a wittle talk,' Matvei Bentsionovich said, still not removing the finger from his mouth and smiling as he had never smiled in his life before.

The State Counsellor did not understand what was happening to him, but it was exhilarating. All his life Berdichevsky had thought of himself as a coward. He had occasionally managed to perform brave actions (sometimes a public prosecutor has to), but every time he had needed to strain his inner resources to the utmost, and it had left him with a weakened heart and fluttering nerves. But this time Matvei Bentsionovich experienced no strain at all – as he waved the revolver about, he felt simply magnificent.

In his childhood, when he was a cobbler's son and the only little Yid in the entire artisans' settlement, there had been times when he sniffed with his bloody nose and imagined how he would run away from the city, join the army and come back as an officer, with epaulettes and a sword. Then he would get even with Vaska Prachkin and that rotten Chukha. They would crawl on their knees and beg him: 'Mordka, dear Mordka, don't kill us.' He would wave his sword and say: 'Don't call me Mordka; I'm Lieutenant Mordechai Berdichevsky!' And then he would forgive them anyway.

Now it had all almost come true, except that in the years that had passed Matvei Bentsionovich had evidently grown more hard-hearted – he did not feel like forgiving Count Charnokutsky, he wanted to kill the repulsive reptile there and then, and preferably not outright but in a way that would make him squirm.

This desire must have been only too easy to read in the frenzied public prosecutor's eyes, because His Excellency suddenly dropped his peach and clutched at the edge of the table, as if he were finding it hard to stay on his feet.

'If you shoot me, you'll never get out of the castle alive,' the magnate said hastily.

Berdichevsky glanced at his wet finger and winced: 'I don't intend to go anywhere, with the night coming on. First of all I'll finish you off, because I find your very existence an insult to the Universe. Then, if your Filip doesn't want another bullet, he'll go with me to the telegraph room and tap out a message to the chief of police. How about it, Filya – will you tap out that telegram?'

The servant nodded; he was afraid to answer out loud.

'There you are. I'll barricade myself in there and wait for the police to arrive.'

'For the murder of Count Charnokutsky they'll give you hard labour!'

'After the police find your secret collection in the basement? They'll give me a medal, not hard labour! Right, then!'

Matvei Bentsionovich aimed at the centre of His Excellency's figure, then changed his mind and trained the barrel on his forehead.

Charnokutsky's face, already white, turned absolutely chalky. One side of his blue-black moustache had drooped in some incomprehensible manner, while the other was still swaggeringly erect.

'What . . . what do you want?' the master of the castle babbled.

'Now I'm going to put you through an intensive interrogation,' Berdichevsky informed him. 'Oh, my feelings about you are very intense! It's going to be very difficult to stop myself putting a bullet though your rotten head.'

The Count kept glancing from the State Counsellor's contorted face to the barrel of the gun twitching in his unsteady hand.

He said hastily: 'I will answer all your questions. Only keep a grip on yourself. Is that trigger stiff enough? Have some Moselle, it calms the nerves.'

That seemed like quite a good idea to Matvei Bentsionovich. He moved closer to the table. Without taking his eyes off the Count, he groped and found a bottle (Moselle or not Moselle – it made no difference), raised it to his lips and drank greedily.

It was the first time in his life that Berdichevsky had drunk wine straight from the bottle. It turned out to taste much better than from a glass. The State Counsellor really was having a night full of remarkable discoveries.

He put the bottle down and wiped his wet lips – not with his handkerchief, but on his sleeve. That was good!

'What is your connection with Staff Captain Ratsevich?'

'He is my lover,' the Count replied without a moment's hesitation. 'That is, he was my lover . . . I have not seen him for six months and I have had no news – until you appeared.'

'Why should I believe that? So it was you who paid his debt for him!'

'Not at all. Why would I? If I were to pay fifteen thousand for every one of my lovers, the entire Charnokutsky fortune would not be enough.'

'It wasn't you?' The public prosecutor's bravado instantly deserted him. 'If not you . . . then who?'

Theory number three, that had emerged so brilliantly from

the debris of its two predecessors, had collapsed. His time had been wasted! Yet another damp squib!

'You look terrible,' the owner of the castle said nervously. 'Drink some more wine. On my word of honour, I do not know who bought Ratsevich out of jail. Bronek didn't tell me.'

When the public prosecutor realised the implications of the last phrase, he asked: 'So you and he saw each other after he was released?'

'Only once. He acted mysteriously and said things I couldn't understand. He was very pompous. He said: "They threw Ratsevich out like an old shoe. Never mind, gentlemen, just give me time." I had the feeling, that by "gentlemen" he meant his superiors.'

'What else? Come on, remember, damn you!'

The shout made Charnokutsky cringe, pulling his head down into his shoulders and blinking rapidly. 'All right, all right. His explanations were very vague. Supposedly some very important individual had visited him in prison. That was what he said: "An important individual, very important." And after that the money was paid for him. That is all that I know ...'

Not like Pelagia

Berdichevsky heard a noise behind him.

He swung round and saw that the servant he had shot had taken advantage of the fact that they had forgotten about him to get to his feet and was running on bent legs in the direction of the drawing room.

'Stop!' the public prosecutor yelled, running after him. 'I'll kill you!'

Filip fell flat on his face and put his hands over his head.

'I'm bleeding to death! I can't bear it! I'm dying!'

And then there was the sound of running feet again – but from the other direction.

This time Matvei Bentsionovich was too slow. He only caught a glimpse of the figure in a black dressing gown with a silver dragon glinting on its back as it slipped out through a door. A bolt shot home and the most important prisoner was gone.

'Lie there, you brute!' the State Counsellor barked and went dashing after the Count.

He tugged at the door, but it was no good. Then he ran over to the table and dragged Kesha out from under it.

'What's behind that door?'

'The study.'

'Can the servants be summoned from there?'

'Yes. There's an electric bell. And an internal telephone . . .'

Berdichevsky could already hear the bell trilling piercingly and the hysterical voice of the magnate shouting something into the telephone, or perhaps simply out of the window.

'Are there many servants in the building?'

'About ten . . . No, more.'

And I only have six bullets, Matvei Bentsionovich thought, but calmly, without panicking.

He ran to a window, looked out and saw the inner courtyard. There were shadows running from the far end. He dashed to the other side of the room and saw the black forest water glinting down below. He swung the window frame open and stuck his head out.

Yes, there was the moat. The window was a bit high. But then he had no choice.

He had already scrambled halfway up on to the windowsill when he remembered something and jumped back down again.

First he ran to the door of the drawing room and locked it. Then he grabbed Kesha by the lapels of his jacket. 'All right, young man, give back the money; your hypothesis was not confirmed.'

The blond-haired clerk held out his entire wallet with a trembling hand. Matvei Bentsionovich took out his hundred-rouble note.

There was a tramping of feet and the door shook as someone charged it with heavy shoulders.

Casting a final glance round the room, Berdichevsky snatched the unfinished bottle off the table and only then went back to the window.

They were pounding regularly on the door with something heavy. A gilded flourish came flying off one panel.

Moving quickly, so that there would be no time to get frightened, the public prosecutor stepped into empty space. 'Eeeheeh!' – the desperate cry was torn from his throat, but a second later the State Counsellor had to close his mouth, because he was completely submerged in smelly, black water.

His feet hit the soft bottom; he pushed off and surfaced.

Spitting out the slimy scum, Berdichevsky began jumping towards the bank. It was impossible to swim, because in one hand he was holding the bottle, and in the other, the Lefauchier. He had to bound along like a grasshopper: pushing off with his feet, taking a gulp of air and sinking back under the surface again. The water was not very deep, though, and his hands remained above the surface.

After five or six bounds he reached a shallow spot. His knuckles encountered something slippery, round and yielding, and he yelled for all he was worth, remembering the swamp monster. But he didn't drop the bottle or the revolver.

But thank God, it wasn't a snake; it was one of the old water-softened logs with which the walls of the moat were lined. Berdichevsky managed to find a foothold, climb out of the water and creep to the bushes. Then he looked round at the castle for the first time.

He saw two heads in the brightly lit window (which wasn't nearly as high as it had seemed from above), and then they were joined by a third.

'Catch him!' he heard the Count's voice say. 'I'll give a thousand roubles reward!'

The public prosecutor did not have the strength to run through the dark forest – the flight from the window and the bounding through the water had seriously reduced his enthusiasm for physical exercise. He needed to cool the servants' ardour, make them realise that life was worth more than a thousand roubles.

Matvei Bentsionovich emptied the water out of the revolver's barrel and fired twice at the wall. The heads immediately disappeared from the rectangle of light.

'Turn the lamps off,' someone wailed. 'He can see us! He'll kill us!'

The light went out in the drawing room, and then on the entire first floor.

That's the way.

Soaking wet and filthy, the public prosecutor forced his way through the bushes and walked down on to the stone surface of the road. He took a swig from the bottle and set off at a trot, in order to get warm.

Running downhill was easy and pleasant. Take about fifty paces, and then a swig. Another fifty paces – another swig.

The State Counsellor was in a simply wonderful mood.

He finally reached Zhitomir at dawn, in a peasant cart.

He got washed and changed in his hotel room. He bought a bottle of port from under the receptionist's counter, thereby criminally aiding and abetting a violator of the law concerning the regulations governing the trade in alcoholic beverages.

He downed half of it straight away – in his new manner, straight from the bottle. But it did not make him drunk; on the contrary, it helped him to gather his thoughts.

The day was dawning outside the window. The public prosecutor sat on the bed in his braces, swigging from a bottle of port and working out the sequence of his further actions.

There was no point in seeking police action against the Count. During the night Charnokutsky would have hidden, or even destroyed, the secret part of his collection (Berdichevsky wondered what kind of foul items it contained). That degenerate would have to be dealt with in a more thorough manner, working via Kiev and the Governor General's chancellery. It would be a long business, and where it would end was clear in advance: not with hard labour but in a comfortable psychiatric clinic.

All right, that could wait. There were far more urgent things to be done.

What time did the government offices open here on a Saturday?

At precisely nine o'clock Berdichevsky was in the prison-committee office, where his acquaintance the inspector provided him with a note for the warden of the provincial lock-up.

At the prison he did not enter into long discussions, but simply asked straight away: 'Do you keep a register of visits to prisoners?'

'Yes sir, Your Honour. We're very strict on that. When anyone comes, even the provincial governor himself, we make a note of it,' the duty warder replied.

This is where I ought to have started, Matvei Bentsionovich reproached himself, instead of scrambling about in filthy drains. I'm a lousy detective. Not like Pelagia.

He opened the register at 19 November the previous year (that was the day Ratsevich had been released) and ran his finger along the lines, moving up from the bottom.

On 18 November no one had visited the prisoner in 'noble' cell number eleven, although twenty-six people had come to the prison.

On 17 November there had been thirty-two visits, but again no one had come to see Ratsevich.

On 16 November . . . Yes, there it was!

In the 'Visited' column there was an entry in neat clerk's handwriting: 'No. 11, the bankrupt debtor Ratsevich.' And in the facing column, 'Visitor's signature: first name, surname, title', there were several indecipherable squiggles.

The public prosecutor carried the register across to the window, where there was more light. He started deciphering the carelessly written letters.

When the letters finally formed themselves into a name, Berdichevsky dropped the register on the windowsill and started blinking rapidly.

XIII

Sea of the dead

And there shall be a Newer Testament

The journey to Bet-Kebir was exhausting and monotonous.

The River Jordan was a cruel disappointment to the female pilgrim because it was so anaemic and unpicturesque. Polina Andreevna even felt a little offended at Providence for having decided in its wisdom to locate the greatest events in the history of mankind beside this pitiful stream instead, for instance, of the magnificent banks of her own native River, where the sky and the earth did not squint through the dust and the heat but looked at each other with their eyes wide open.

When the Jordan flowed into the Dead Sea, also known as the Asphalt Sea, the landscape became even more dreary.

To the right were the bald humps of the Judaea desert's hills, and to the left the smooth surface of the water, wreathed in mist, extended into the distance. At first it seemed to Pelagia that the water was covered with a shell of silvery ice, which was quite absurd in this kind of heat. The nun went down to the shoreline and reached her hand out towards the water. Even at close quarters the illusion of a covering of ice was absolute. However, instead of encountering a cold, hard crust, her fingers sank into warm, completely transparent liquid, with an unbroken layer of white salt lying below it. Polina Andreevna licked her wet hand and tasted tears.

The unbearable glare made her eyes hurt. It was not only the sea that glittered but also the jagged cliffs, the desert, the road. And the silence was like none that Pelagia had ever encountered anywhere before. No rustling of sand, no splashing of water, and when Salakh stopped the horses to give them a rest, the silence of the world around them became quite intolerable. Dead silence at the Dead Sea, Pelagia said to herself, entirely without intending any pun.

As they approached the southern extremity of the salty lake, their surroundings became even more lifeless and unnatural. Sharp bluffs broke up through the ground, looking like gigantic splinters, or the bared teeth of the Earth. The mountains approached almost to the very water's edge, as if they wanted to shove the cart into the acrid, salty water.

Polina Andreevna began feeling afraid – not because of the menace of the landscape, but at the thought of the monstrous deed that had been committed here many centuries earlier.

This had been a blossoming land, which 'was watered all the way to Sigor with water, like the garden of the Lord, like the land of Egypt'. But an enraged God had rained fire and brimstone down from the sky on Sodom and Gomorrah, and this immense funnel filled with bitter tears had been formed. Lying on the bottom, covered with a thick layer of salt, were thousands of dead evil-doers, and possibly a few righteous men. For before the terrible punishment took place, God had bargained with Abraham:

And Abraham drew near, and said, Wilt thou also destroy the righteous with the wicked? Peradventure there be fifty righteous within the city: wilt thou also destroy and not spare the place for the fifty righteous that are therein? That be far from thee to do after this manner, to slay the righteous with the wicked: and that the righteous should be as the wicked, that be far from thee: Shall not the Judge of all the earth do right? And the LORD said, If I find in Sodom fifty righteous within the city, then I will spare all the place for their sakes. And Abraham answered and said, Behold now, I have taken upon me to speak unto the LORD, which am but dust and ashes: Peradventure there shall lack five of the fifty righteous: wilt thou destroy all the city for lack of five? And he said, If I find there forty and five, I will not destroy it. And he spake unto him yet again, and said, Peradventure there shall be forty found there. And he said, I will not do it for forty's sake. And he said unto him, Oh let not the LORD be angry, and I will speak: Peradventure there shall thirty be found there. And he said, I will not do it, if I find thirty there. And he said, Behold now, I have taken upon me to speak unto the

LORD: Peradventure there shall be twenty found there. And he said, I will not destroy it for twenty's sake. And he said, Oh let not the LORD be angry, and I will speak yet but this once: Peradventure ten shall be found there. And he said, I will not destroy it for ten's sake. And the LORD went his way, as soon as he had left communing with Abraham: and Abraham returned unto his place.

With all her heart, Pelagia was on the side of Abraham, who had trembled with fear as he struggled with the Almighty to save the land of Sodom, but the divine prerogative had overridden the human. So while a single child's tear would prevent Dostoyevsky rejoicing in the salvation of the world, the Almighty had not thought nine righteous men enough, and he had even grown angry and gone away, stopped talking! In those distant times God must have been young, and his youth made him uncompromising and cruel. He had not learned the tolerance and compassion manifested in the New Testament.

God changes, Pelagia realised with sudden insight. Like mankind. As the centuries pass he grows more mature, gentler and wiser. And if that is so, then we can hope that in time a Newer Testament and covenant will be granted to us to replace the New Testament that we have. The burden of the Old Testament was that a Jew must treat other Jews kindly. The burden of the New Testament was that all people should love each other. And the Newer Testament will probably extend love to the animals. Does a horse or a dog not have a soul? Of course they do!

How wonderful it would be if the Newer Testament gave people the hope of happiness in this life, and not only after death, in the Kingdom of Heaven

And again . . . But at this point Pelagia pulled herself up short. What Newer Testament? These matters were beyond her reach! And were not these very thoughts, about the obsolescence of the former Testament, not a satanic delusion, induced by the dead desert?

They made camp at a small oasis, where several trees grew beside a stream. It was the travellers' third overnight halt since they left the Isreel Valley.

And in the morning, when the *hantur* had only just moved

away from their campsite, a miracle happened. Salakh, who had last driven through these parts two years earlier, was even more astounded than Pelagia.

A smooth highway, as straight as an arrow, crept out of the desert of Judaea, swallowed up the wretched road along the lake and turned to the south. Salakh's emaciated horses took heart and started clopping their hooves over the asphalt in a rapid rhythm. All the rattling and shaking disappeared completely, and the *hantur* began moving twice as fast.

Polina Andreevna was amazed and delighted.

The world was suddenly no longer abandoned and deserted. Every so often they encountered identical white wagons coming towards them, pulled by sturdy shaggy-legged Percheron horses. The eloquent emblem on their tarpaulin covers was a picture of the Acropolis and the letters: 'S&G Ltd' Pelagia racked her brains, trying to think what it could mean, and she guessed: 'Sodom and Gomorrah Limited' – that was what it was. She even shuddered at such an unfortunate name.

Shortly after midday they reached the Arab settlement of Bet-Kebir. During her travels, Pelagia had seen more than enough of the local villages, as alike each other as two drops of water: windowless little wattle-and-daub houses barely taller than the height of a man; walls and roofs always plastered with cakes of dried camel dung, which was used as fuel; narrow, dirty streets; a crowd of naked children that always came rushing out to any passers-by, shouting 'Baksheesh! Baksheesh!' and a stench that made you want to squeeze your nose shut.

And suddenly here there were new little white houses with verandas, paved streets, freshly planted bushes! No beggars, ragamuffins or lepers. And to Pelagia, exhausted by her journey, the inn into which Salakh turned to ask directions for the road ahead seemed like a genuine palace.

She got washed in a genuine shower, drank strong tea, brushed her hair, changed her underclothes. Meanwhile Salakh was conducting important negotiations with the owner. He had to drink seven or eight cups of coffee before finding out everything Pelagia wanted to know.

It turned that the newly built city of Usdum (that was how Sodom was pronounced in Arabic) was not far from Bet-Kebir – only fifteen versts away; but women were forbidden to enter it.

The *Luti* were good people; they paid generously for work and goods, but they had their own rules.

'Who are the *"Luti"*?' Polina Andreevna asked.

'The *Luti* are the people of Lut. The same Lut who left Usdum, and the city was consumed by fire.'

Ah, the people of Lot, Pelagia realised – that is, the pederasts.

Salakh explained that the workers from Bet-Kebir entered Usdum with a special pass, and women could not go any further than a guard post that was five versts from the town. There was only one road, squeezed between the lake and the long mountain of Jebel-Usdum. There were Turkish soldiers at the guard post, their officer was called Said-bei. The Turks guarded the road very well, they didn't even sleep at night, which was quite amazing for Turkish soldiers. And they didn't take bak-sheesh, which was twice as amazing. And all because the *Luti* paid them very well. Previously Said-bei and his soldiers had sheltered in tents in the middle of the desert. They used to catch smugglers and had a very, very hard life, but now the *Luti* had asked the respected *yuzbashi* to move his post to the road and the Turks had started living very, very well. This information was not reassuring. Pelagia began feeling nervous.

'But is it not possible to get round the guard post through the desert, from the other side of the mountain?'

Salakh went to drink more coffee with the owner.

'No, impossible,' he said when he came back. 'In day soldiers will see from mountain, they have tower there. And at night can't travel through desert: pits, rocks, break leg, break neck.'

'Tell the owner I will give twenty francs to anyone who gets me past the guard post.'

Her faithful helper set out for more negotiations. Four cups of coffee later he came back with a mysteriously satisfied air.

'Possible. Jebel-Usdum mountain has holes. In spring stream flows, finds hole. Water flow for thousands of years, make cave. Owner knows how to get through mountain, but twenty francs not enough. Cave is frightening, djinns of fire live there.'

Salakh interpreted her grimace in his own way. He thought for a moment and scratched the back of his head. 'Yes, fifty francs very much. Give me twenty-five, I take you without cave.'

'But how?'

'My business,' the Palestinian replied with a cunning air.

And so now they were riding along beside the low mountain crest that was probably the only one of its kind: a mountain located below sea level. Up ahead they could see a large canvas tent and a boom across the road – the Turkish guard post.

Polina Andreevna glanced round. Trailing along behind them was a large wagon with the emblem 'S&G Ltd' on its side, loaded with crumbly black soil.

'Where are you going to hide me?' the nun asked the mysteriously silent Salakh for the hundredth time.

'Nowhere. Turn this way.' He took a small lacquered box out of his travelling bag.

'What's that?'

'Present, bought for Maryusya. Paid three francs, you give back.'

Pelagia saw white make-up, lipstick, powder and something else that was sticky and black, all in little cells.

'Don't turn head,' said Salakh, holding her chin with one hand.

He dipped in a finger and rapidly daubed something across Polnia Andreevna's cheeks. He smoothed it out. He ran the little brush over her eyebrows and eyelashes. Then he coloured her lips with lipstick.

'What's all this for?' the bemused nun babbled.

She took out a little mirror and was horrified. The face looking out at her was gaudily daubed with colour. Bright beetroot cheeks, immense eyebrows like wings, outlined eyes, a vulgarly luscious mouth. 'You're out of your mind! Turn back!' Pelagia shouted, but the *hantur* was already approaching the boom.

'Keep quiet and smile. All the time smile and do this.' Salakh moved his eyebrows up and down and rolled his eyes back up and back. 'Smile wide, very wide, show all your teeth.'

It was too late to rebel. Pelagia spread her lips as wide as she possibly could.

Two soldiers in faded blue uniforms came up to them, with an officer who had a sword – none other than Said-bei himself. He jabbed one finger angrily at Pelagia and swore. And he didn't even glance at the wagon carrying soil; it calmly drove straight through as the boom swayed upwards.

Polina made out the word *kadye* – she thought that meant 'woman' in Turkish. Well, now the officer would turn them back, of course, and that would be the end of her journey.

Salakh was not alarmed by the invective; he said something and laughed. Said-bei gave Pelagia a curious look and asked a question. There was a clear note of doubt in his voice.

Suddenly the Palestinian grabbed the hem of his passenger's skirt and pulled it up. In her fear Pelagia smiled so broadly that her ears started wiggling.

The soldiers chortled, and the officer also burst into laughter. He waved his hand – all right, go on through.

'What . . . what did you tell him?' Pelagia asked timidly when the post had been left behind them.

'That you boy dressed up as woman. The *Luti* bought you in Yaffo. The *yuzbashi* not believe me at first. I say: "You not believe – look between his legs," and try lift up your skirt. Said-bei won't look between boy's legs, or soldiers think their *yuzbashi* is *Luti* too.'

'But what if he had looked after all?' asked Pelagia, pale-faced.

Salakh shrugged his shoulders philosophically. 'Then that bad. But he not look, we get through guard, you owe me twenty-five francs more.'

Since the day of their departure from Jerusalem, Polina And-reevna's debt to her driver, guide and benefactor had increased to an astronomical size. The money paid to Fatima had only been the beginning. To this sum Salakh had added a charge for the terror he had suffered during the Circassian adventure, then the cost of the journey to the Dead Sea, and then separately for the journey from Bet-Kebir to Usdum. And there had been other, smaller sums exacted along the way. Pelagia herself no longer knew what the total was, and she was beginning to fear that she would never pay off this extortioner.

Suddenly she realised that he was looking at her with a rather strange, even agitated expression. 'What's wrong?' she asked in surprise.

'You clever and brave,' Salakh said with feeling. 'First I thought how ugly you are. But that's because your hair is red and you thin. But can get used to red hair, and you not be thin if you stay sit home, sleep a lot, eat well. And if put on powder and lipstick, you almost beautiful. You know what? . . .' His voice trembled and his eyes gleamed damply. 'Come to me as fourth wife. Then you cannot pay debt.'

He's proposing to me, Pelagia realised and, to her own surprise, she felt flattered. 'Thank you,' she replied. 'It is nice to hear you say that. But I cannot become your wife. In the first place, I have a Bridegroom. And in the second place, what would Fatima say?'

The second argument seemed to produce a stronger effect than the first. And in addition, during the process of explaining Polina Andreevna took out a flask of water and started washing the make-up off her face, and no doubt her beauty was dimmed as a result.

Salakh sighed and cracked the whip, and the *hantur* rolled on.

The mountain came to a sudden end in an outcrop with a sheer, almost vertical face, and the town appeared from round the corner without any warning. It lay in a small hollow, surrounded on three sides by hills, and it was inexpressibly beautiful, as if it had been transported here from ancient Hellas.

Polina Andreevna could not believe her eyes as she looked at the pediments decorated with statues, the elegant colonnades, the marble fountains, the red-tiled roofs. Encircled by blossoming gardens, the town seemed to be swaying in the hot, streamy air.

A mirage! A mirage in the desert, the delighted traveller thought. They drove up to a green alley, where there were heaps of rich black soil. The wagon they had seen recently was already standing there, but had not been unloaded yet. The driver had disappeared, probably gone to seek instructions. There were several Arabs digging holes for trees, watering flower beds, cutting the grass.

'This is a genuine Elysium,' Pelagia whispered, breathing in the scent of the flowers.

She jumped down on to the ground and stood behind some rose bushes to avoid attracting attention. She simply could not get enough of this magical vision.

Then, when the initial ecstasy passed, she asked, 'But how shall I get into the town?'

Salakh shrugged. 'I don't know. I only promised to get you past the guard.'

Irodiada's dance

She glided across the marble floor, trying to grasp the fading melody. Pram-pam-pam, pram-pam-pam, twirl twice, spinning out the gauze peignoir in a weightless cloud, bob down into a curtsey and then go soaring up, flying, with her arms like swan's wings.

She used to dance to a gramophone, but now she didn't need mechanical music any more. Divine melodies that Paganini himself could not have rendered were born within her. They were short-lived, not destined for repetition, and that made them especially beautiful. But today there was something hindering the music, killing it, preventing its magical power from developing.

Para-para-ram-pa-pam, para-para-ram-pa-pam. No that wasn't right!

In this blessed oasis, securely sheltered from the crude outside world, Irodiada had discovered two sources of daily delight, two new talents that she had not even suspected in herself previously.

The first was dancing – not for her family, not for guests and definitely not for an audience, but exclusively for herself. To transform herself into harmony and graceful movement. To feel her body, formerly so rebellious, rusty and creaky, become lighter than a feather, more resilient than a snake. Who would ever have believed that after the age of forty, when it would seem there was nothing more to be expected from one's own flesh apart from betrayals and disappointments, she would only just begin to realise what a perfect organism her body was?

It was absolutely quiet in the house. Lyovushka and Salomeia were cuddling in the bedroom; they would get up as evening drew on, when the heat abated. Antinosha was swimming in the pool – a whole team of bargemen couldn't drag him out of the water.

Every day after lunch, left to her own devices, Irodiada danced in front of the mirror, in total silence. An electric fan drove waves of scented air through the atrium. The dancer performed *pas* of indescribable elegance, the drops of sweat trickling down her face drying instantly.

Half an hour of absolute happiness, then take a delightful cold shower, drink a glass of resinous wine with snow, throw on a silk robe – and off to a rendezvous with her second delight, the gardens.

But today she simply couldn't immerse herself completely in the movement: in addition to the music with which her head ought to be filled, there was another vague, alarming thought wagging its mouse-like tail.

It will die, its light will fade, Irodiada suddenly heard a lisping voice say, and she stopped.

Ah, so that was it.

Yesterday's conversation.

The absurd man in a robe of sackcloth with a belt of blue string had been brought into the town by Zbishek and Rafek, two mischievous scamps from Warsaw. They had been racing chariots along the edge of the sea and picked up the tramp on the highway, because his appearance had made them laugh. When they discovered that the traveller had just arrived from Russia, they had come to show him to their Russian friends.

She had been alone in the house. Lyovushka was in session at the Aeropagus; the children had gone to the beach.

The ragamuffin had amused his hostess by claiming to be Manuila, the leader of the 'foundlings'. The poor fellow didn't know that she happened to know that the genuine Manuila was dead – he had been killed, so to speak, almost in front of her very eyes.

Irodiada had not been in any hurry to expose him; she was waiting for an effective moment. When the Warsaw jokers took the tramp to look at the town, she went with them.

The false Manuila had turned his head this way and that, constantly gasping in amazement and showering them with questions. Zbishek and Rafek had mostly laughed and played the fool, so the role of guide had been played by Irodiada.

'But don't you acknowledge women at all, then?' the pretender had asked, perplexed.

'We acknowledge them and respect them,' she had replied. 'On the West Square we have a monument to Lot's wife – they found a column of salt on the seashore and commissioned a sculptor to carve a statute out of it. Of course, there many who objected to a naked female figure, but the majority took a tolerant attitude. We have nothing against women; it's just that we are better off without them, and they are better off without us.'

'Well then, is there a town of women somewhere?' the 'prophet' had asked.

'Not yet,' Irodiada had explained, 'but there soon will be. Our benefactor, George Sairus, was intending to buy some land on the island of Lesbos for maidenly lovers of female beauty, but the Greek government would not allow it. Then he got the idea of rebuilding Gomorrah – the work there has already begun. We shall be friends with our neighbours, just as men and dolphins are friends. But the dolphin's element is the sea, and man's element is the dry land, and why should man and dolphin copulate together?'

The amusing rogue had admired the beauty of the buildings and the technical advances that were so very numerous in Sodom: the electric tram running from the Acropolis to the beach, the cinematograph, the ice rink with artificial ice and many, many others.

But what had had interested the false Manuila most of all was the relationships between Sodomites: did they have families, or did each one live separately?

Irodiada, anticipating the moment of exposure, had politely replied that there were very few families with children, such as her own. Some people lived in couples, but most simply revelled in the freedom and security.

Then Rafek and Zbishek had tried to get her to go to the Labyrinth, a special place where young people got up to all sorts of salacious devilment in the dark. She didn't go, she was already past the age when mere ravishment of the flesh is amusing – she valued feelings far more now. To her surprise, the tramp had not wished to go to the Labyrinth either; he had said there was nothing new in these amusements – the Romans had them, and so did the Greeks and the Babylonians.

So it happened that Irodiada was left alone with him.

'Well, man of God, will the Lord rain down fire and brimstone on us for these transgressions?' she asked mockingly, nodding in the direction of the Labyrinth, from which they could hear the sound of laughter and wild howls.

'Hardly, not for that,' the prophet said with a shrug. 'They're not coercing each other, after all. Let them do it if brings them joy. Joy is sacred, it's grief that is evil.'

'Well said, prophet!' Irodiada replied merrily. 'Perhaps you are one of us too?'

What was that answer he gave?

No, he had said, I'm not one of you. I feel sorry for you. The path of a man who loves a man is full of sorrow and it leads to despair, because it is barren. He had used other words, spoken less smoothly, but the meaning was exactly the same, and Irodiada had shuddered in surprise.

Out of inertia, she had tried to joke: 'Barren – because we cannot have children?'

And he said seriously: For that reason too. But not only. Man is the black half of the soul, and woman is the white half. Do you know how a new soul comes to be? By a little of the fire of God being struck. And it is struck when the two halves of the soul, white and black, thrust against each other, trying to understand if they are one whole or not. You poor people will never find your other halves because black and black cannot combine together. Your half-soul will die; its light will fade. It is a grievous lot – eternal loneliness. No matter how much you thrust against each other, there will never be any spark. That is where the problem lies: not in bodily fornication, but in spiritual error.

Irodiada quite forgot that she had been planning to laugh and expose the self-styled prophet. What difference did it actually make who he really was? The tramp had spoken about what she felt herself, only she hadn't been able to express it clearly.

She had objected. Naturally, it wasn't just a matter of the body. When the trance induced by prohibition had passed and there was no more need to hide from society, she had discovered that she did not really have such a great need for passionate intercourse with her beloved. The most important things were tenderness and security such as you could never experience with a woman, because women were different. But here there was no need to pretend: you were understood with a single word, even without any words at all – that was what was important. We are together, we are the same. No conflicts of opposites, no strife. A blissful peace.

Irodiada poured all this out to a stranger, speaking with fervent passion, so deeply had his words stung her.

He listened and listened, then shook his head sadly and said: 'But there still won't be any spark. And if there is no spark, God is not there.'

Yesterday Irodiada had refused to agree – she had insisted on her own point of view; but today, when the false Manuila was no longer there beside her, those brief words he had spoken – 'eternal loneliness' and 'spiritual error' – had suddenly surfaced in her memory and driven away the music.

Lyovushka was spending more and more time with Salomeia nowadays. No, this wasn't jealousy, it was what the wandering prophet had spoken about: the fear of loneliness. And Antinous was hardly ever at home now, either – he had new enthusiasms, new friends. Perhaps they were more than just friends . . .

After all, it was only a month since they had arrived in this male heaven. They said families didn't last long in Sodom. And then what would be left?

Quite a lot, Irodiada thought, taking heart. There will still be dancing and gardens.

And on the subject of gardens . . .

It was time to visit the peonies and medlars. And take a quick look at the roses too – to make sure that Djemal hadn't overdone the watering.

Irodiada drove away her sad thoughts. She put on a feather-light robe and tied back her hair with a blue ribbon.

The sun was still scorching with all its might, but already a light breeze was blowing from the Avarim Mountains, bringing a promise of evening coolness. She walked along a shady little street to the Western Gates, nodding amiably to people she met and exchanging kisses with some. All her thoughts were focused on the garden now.

Before sunset she had to hoe the flower bed so that the seedlings could breathe. Tomorrow they were going to bring earthworms from Haifa. Then she could do some serious work on the peach alley. In a year or two there would be gardens in Sodom the like of which this ill-fated region had not seen since the time of Lot.

This was what a life should be dedicated to! Not teaching grammar-school boys Latin, but cultivating gardens and flower beds. Russia was heaven for plants. There was as much water as you could want, and the soil was alive, not like here.

But then in Russia you couldn't find anything like the black soil that the wagons delivered here. Specially treated, it cost a lot of money. But thank God, Mr Sairus had plenty of that.

Once outside the town wall, Irodiada began walking with a brisker, more energetic stride. Forgetting about the heat, she made her rounds of the trees, bushes and flower beds. She scolded the head gardener a bit – she had guessed right: he had watered the rose bushes evenly, but on the eastern side, where the cool breeze blew at night, they needed less water. Djemal listened attentively – he knew that the old *Luti* had a special gift from Allah for understanding the life of plants, and he regarded this talent with respect.

At university, in addition to all sorts of other unnecessary learning, Irodiada had studied ancient Greek, and so she found Arabic remarkably easy to pick up. After only a week of working together, she and Djemal understood each other excellently.

'What's this?' Irodiada asked, pointing in annoyance at the wagon loaded with black earth. 'Where's the driver? Why hasn't he unloaded it?'

'There's a woman over there,' said Djemal, pointing to the rose bush at the end of the row. 'I don't know how she got through. Sadyk has gone to tell the sentry.' He bowed and went to water more flower beds.

Irodiada looked round. There really was someone hiding behind the bush. And when she went closer, she could see it really was a woman. You could tell from a distance that she was a natural, not just dressed up. Not so much even from the figure, but from the inclination of the head and the way the arm was held out slightly to one side.

Irodiada had to tell her to leave while she still could. The head of security was a former British colonel, not to be trifled with. He would hand the trespasser over to the Turkish guard and fine Said-bei for negligence, and Said-bei would take his anger out on the curious fool – these Asiatics did not practise gentlemanly chivalry.

Yakov Mikhailovich eavesdrops

He never thought, never even guessed that everything would turn out so neatly with the wagon. He was lucky –

he'd just been in the right place at the right time.

At first, though, he had cursed himself for being too clever by half – when he was buried alive, so to speak, in the damp earth. And while they were trundling along the highway, he had cursed the entire world. It was hot, the worms crawled in under his clothes. One stubborn brute even crept into his nostril. It was a miracle that he hadn't had a sneezing fit.

Yakov Mikhailovich breathed through a reed that he had pushed up through the black soil. Then he had set himself up to see. He had a clay jug with a long neck, for drinking water. After he had gradually drained its contents (consuming plenty of mother earth in the process) he had thought of a good use for the vessel. He broke its neck off at the base with his fingers, and he had a tube. He pushed it through the surface, and he acquired the ability to see. The jug was earth-coloured, so the broken neck was invisible from the outside even at two paces. To be quite honest, the views revealed to his gaze through this little hole weren't exactly breathtaking, but it was better than having no eyes at all. He could turn it this way and that way – it was like looking through a spyglass, or the optical tube on a submarine, what they called a periscope.

Just how good his luck was became clear when the wagon finally arrived at its destination and stopped. Then Yakov Mikhaiovich discovered that Ginger, whom he had eyed all the way along the road through his spyglass, was standing right there beside him. She had got out of her boneshaker and stood behind a rose bush that was within arm's reach of Yakov Mikhkailovich's observation post.

The nun had sighed and wailed, wondering how she would get into the town now. Her Arab (he was called Salakh) hadn't shown her any sympathy.

You ought to have dressed up as a boy, you brainless nanny-goat, the secret observer reproached her. It might still not be too late – think.

But she just kept hopping from one foot to the other and sighing.

He wasn't actually worried about her, though. He knew from experience that she was far from brainless and was bound to think of something, she wouldn't give up. They'd done right when they put their money on Ginger. They were no fools.

He was a little anxious about something else: what if she slipped away again, like the times before? She was far too spry and unpredictable. And God couldn't keep on being so generous with miracles for Yakov Mikhailovich.

Suddenly he heard steps. And a voice – high and slightly squeaky, halfway between a man's and a woman's: '*Madame, vous n'avez pas le droit de rester ici.*' And then in Russian, with a note of surprise: 'You?'

Yakov Mikhailovich turned his spyglass in the direction of the strange voice. In his circle of vision he saw an aging, painted woman wearing a wig, a light dress and sandals (she looked a bit broad in the feet). Clear enough: a sodomite dressed up as a woman.

The nun was as pleased to see the old pederast as if he was her own dear mother. 'Ah, what good luck to meet you here! Hello, dear Iraida!'

'Irodiada,' the man-woman corrected her, then threw her hands up in the air and started gabbling. 'How did you get here, my dear? And why aren't you in your habit? What are you doing here?'

Ginger didn't answer straight away, and Yakov Mikhailovich turned his spyglass on her. She wrinkled up her forehead, as if she couldn't make up her mind whether to tell the truth or make up some lie.

She told the truth. 'Well, you see ... There's a man I really need to find.'

'Who?'

'He's a rather strange man. He dresses strangely and speaks strangely ... In Bet-Kerim they told me that he was there yesterday morning and he came towards Sodom. He didn't go back. So I thought he must have stayed here ... He's skinny, with a tangled beard, in a white robe with a blue belt ...'

'Manuila? You're looking for the man who calls himself Manuila?' the pervert asked in a changed voice.

'Yes! Have you seen him? Tell me, have you seen him? I absolutely have to talk to him! If you could get him to come here ...'

'He's not here any more.'

'What?' the nun gasped. 'What have you done with him?'

Yakov Mikhailovich quickly took aim on the man in fancy

dress and saw him wave his hand in the direction of the sea. 'He took the launch to go to Ani-Jidi. At dawn, before it got really hot.'

'Thank God!' the nun exclaimed for some reason. 'Isn't Ani-Jidi the oasis to the north of Bet-Kerim? We drove past it.'

'Yes, the road to Jerusalem runs from there.'

'So he's on his way to Jerusalem?'

The pederast shrugged. 'I've no idea ... He said something about a garden.'

'For God's sake, remember!' the nun exclaimed. 'It's very important!'

Yakov was very keen to hear this too – he even put the tube to his ear instead of his eye.

Iriodiada said hesitantly: 'I think what he said was: "On Thursday night I have to be in a certain garden."'

Come on now, come on now, Yakov Mikhailovich thought to himself, egging her on. Come on, remember.

'That's all. He didn't say anything else about it.'

'A-ah!' Ginger exclaimed.

The observer quickly put the neck of the jug to his eye again. The nun had put one hand over her mouth and her eyebrows had risen almost to the middle of her forehead. Was she surprised at something? Or had she figured something out?

Naturally, there was no way that Yakov Mikhkailovich could know what garden it was, but that wasn't important. The important thing, he whispered to Ginger, is that you've guessed. And he spat out a worm that had clung to his lip.

Thursday night – was that tomorrow or the day after? What with all this wandering around Palestine, he'd lost track of the days of the week. And it seemed he wasn't the only one.

'What day is it today? Wednesday?' the nun asked.

'I don't know, my dear; we live by the ancient calendar here. Today is the day of the Moon, tomorrow will be the day of Mars, the day after tomorrow ...'

'Yes, yes, it's Wednesday!' Ginger interrupted her. 'Tell me, is it possible for me to use your launch?'

'What *are* you thinking of? You need to get away from here as quickly as you can, or you'll be arrested. They've already gone to get the sentry. This is private property; it's guarded very strictly.'

'How far is it from here to Jerusalem?' the nun asked, paying no attention to the man's words.

'I really don't know. A hundred or a hundred and fifty versts.'

'Salakh, can you get me there by tomorrow evening?'

'I'll spoil the horses,' the Arab grumbled. 'They won't work again for a week.'

'How much does a week of your work cost?'

'Two hundred francs.'

'You bandit!'

'For wife it's free,' the Arab replied mysteriously.

'All right, let's go!'

'What all right?' Salakh asked. 'Two hundred francs all right or wife all right?'

'We'll see when we get there. Let's go!' And the nun ran out of his field of vision. Half a minute later he heard hooves clattering and wheels creaking. They were off to Jerusalem.

It was time for him to climb out of this damned cart. Oho, so now it would be a hundred and fifty versts through the desert on his own two feet . . . Never mind, we can do it.

But then, he could buy a gig in Bet-Kerim. With a canvas top, like a tent. And take along another couple of tents in different colours. Change them every now and then, so they wouldn't notice they were being followed.

Well come on then, go away, Yakov Maikhailovich thought, trying to hurry the pederast. But he still dawdled, as if on purpose.

A couple of minutes later, he heard a tramping of boots and jangling of swords as two Turkish soldiers came running up with the driver of the wagon that had given Yakov Mikhailovich his free ride to Sodom.

They started jabbering in their own language. The sodomite replied hesitantly, in a reassuring tone of voice. He must have lied and said there wasn't any woman there, because one of the soldiers swung his hand back and gave the driver a slap round the ear and then started swearing. Yakov Mikhailovich didn't understand their language, of course, but it wasn't hard to guess what he said: Ah you devil, you and your stupid lies, making me run around in the heat.

The soldiers went away, and so did the sobbing Arab, but the damned sodomite was still hanging about beside the bush. For some reason he touched the flowers and the leaves and shook his head sorrowfully.

Come on, damn you, time's too precious. In his impatience Yakov Mikhkailovich moved slightly and a little soil spilled out of the wagon.

The man-woman looked round in puzzlement at the wagon – he seemed to be looking straight down the tube into Yakov Mikhailovich's eye. In his mind he gave the pervert a friendly warning: Turn away, you blockhead, it will be better for your health. But no, he walked right up to the wagon.

He stood so close that the only thing Yakov Mikhailovich could make out through the hole was one side of his bust (just look at all that padding stuffed in there) and a hand with all the little hairs shaved smooth.

The hairless hand opened out into a palm, completely obscuring his view.

'What's this rag doing here?' a voice muttered, and a moment later there was a tug on Yakov Mikhailovich's sleeve.

All right, it's your own fault. He grabbed the stupid fool by the wrist and straightened up sharply.

The old pervert's eyes almost started out of his head when he saw the black shape of a man rising out of the soil. Then they rolled up and he gently collapsed.

Just like a real woman. He's fainted. Yakov Mikhailovich leaned down over the motionless body, trying to make up his mind.

Break his neck and stick the body in that big heap of earth over there. The day's coming to an end, nobody will dig her up before tomorrow morning, and by morning we'll be far away, halfway to Jerusalem. But what if someone does dig her up? They have a heliograph installed on that tower over there. They'll signal the guard post.

Why risk it?

Yakov Mikhailovich jumped up and down, shaking off the lumps of soil that had stuck to him. He carefully picked them up and tipped them back into the wagon. Then he shaped the earth back into a cone and smoothed it down with his hands. From a standing start, he took a big jump over on to the lawn, so that he wouldn't leave any tracks in the dust.

He looked round.

The sodomite was still lying there in a heap.

All right, let him live. What can he say? That a big black figure climbed out from under the soil and then disappeared without trace? Who will ever believe him? He won't even believe it himself. He'll think he got too much sun.

Yakob Mikhailovich hitched up his loose *shalwars* and set off down the road at a springy, muscular trot in pursuit of the setting sun.

To help keep his breathing regular, he murmured to himself: 'One-two, one-two, in the garden I'll meet you. One-two, one-two, in the garden I'll meet you . . .'

Instead of air, his mouth gulped in hot dust, and he started spitting it out. Oh, this dratted place.

Never mind. It looks like tomorrow evening it will all be over.

XIV

The Berdichevsky Étude

An old acquaintance

'FSC Dolinin, Council, Min. Int.' – that was what was written in an irregular, almost illegible hand in the column head 'Visitor'.

'Full State Counsellor Dolinin?' Matvei Bentsionovich muttered, ruffling up his head of golden-reddish hair. 'Dolinin?'

'Yes sir,' the warder confirmed. 'His Excellency was here on a tour of inspection. He deigned to honour me with a conversation. He said that we needed to divide up our prisons: one for subjects under investigation, one for hardened criminals and one for petty offenders. He was also pleased to enquire after the kinds of prisoners we have here. Well, I told him about the gendarmes officer, and the threat from bandits and nihilists. And I said as that was what came of intemperate habits. His Excellency expressed a desire to take a look in person. He was pleased to talk with Mr Ratsevich for at least an hour.'

There was no need for any more theories, Berdichevsky realised with absolute certainty. Everything fitted together perfectly, although exactly how wasn't entirely clear as yet.

After leaving the prison, he walked round the streets for a long time, completely blind to his surroundings. The confusion gradually cleared and the facts arranged themselves in an orderly sequence.

Not so fast, not so fast, the public prosecutor rebuked himself every now and then. No hasty conclusions, nothing but the bare sequence of events. The bare sequence of events was as follows:

Six months earlier the bankrupt debtor Ratsevich had been visited by 'a very important individual' to all appearances without any premeditation, entirely by chance. Or perhaps not entirely by chance? No, no – conjecture must be left for later.

For some reason the high-ranking inspector and reformer of the criminal investigative system had taken an interest in a social outcast with the practical skills of a wolfhound. Why exactly? Was Dolinin perhaps also a pederast? But then, the prisoner would hardly have confessed his preferences to an important St Petersburg official straight away. It was not very likely. Quite improbable, in fact.

But it was an indubitable fact: an interest had been taken. Such a great interest, in fact, that three days later a sum to cover the prisoner's entire debt had arrived from the Russian Trade, Industry and Commerce Bank, which, by the way, had its head office in St Petersburg. Ratsevich had gone free and soon disappeared from Zhitomir – for ever.

Questions: why did Dolinin do this and where did he get so much money? Pelagia had said that he was not from an aristocratic background, he had risen to the top through his talent. If that was so, there was nowhere he could have acquired great wealth.

The facts, nothing but the facts, Berdichevsky reminded himself. Very well then. The five months after Ratsevich's release are a blank. We know nothing about the dashing gendarme's whereabouts and activities during this period. But we do know that on the evening of 1 April he was on the steamer *Sturgeon* and he killed the peasant Shelukhin, having taken him for the 'prophet' Manuila.

That very night Dolinin arrives on the steamer. By coincidence he happens to be in the nearest district town on one of his tours of inspection. A remarkable coincidence, especially in view of the meeting in the prison in Zhitomir.

The full State Counsellor leads the investigation in person, the killer disappears from the ship in some mysterious fashion. And who, one asks led the search for him? Dolinin again. Matvei Bentsionovich remembered what Pelagia had said: he himself went to investigate the cabin of the fake Mr Ostrolyzhensky, after which he announced that it was empty, ordered a guard to be posted at the door and no one to be allowed in. Perhaps the cunning investigator's acquaintance from Zhitomir was inside all the time? All very simple. And afterwards Dolinin secretly let him go ashore – while the guard was being changed or some other way. Not very difficult for the head of the investigation, who is everybody's boss and trusted by everybody.

What happened after that?

The big man from St Petersburg decided that he had to accompany the body of a cheap villain to an isolated village, in person. How strange! At the time, of course, Sister Pelagia and everybody else involved in the investigation thought that the investigator was bored with bureaucratic office work and in any case, being a conscientious man, he was used to seeing every job through to the end. Meanwhile the killer, who was linked to Dolinin in certain mysterious ways, set out to follow the expedition. It was even possible that while they travelled on the barge, Ratsevich was hiding on it, down in the hold. Then he made his own way through the forest, keeping close all the time. When Pelagia stumbled across the spy by chance, Dolinin fed her a lot of nonsense about evil spirits, and did, it so deftly that the highly intelligent nun did not suspect a thing.

Next comes the most important part.

Having established the identity of the dead man, Dolinin left the village, but Ratsevich did not follow. He stayed behind. Why?

That is clear. In order to kill Pelagia. But why did he not do it sooner – for instance during that encounter in the forest?

After a moment's thought, Matvei Bentsionovich found the answer to this question. Because he had not yet been ordered to do it. So he only received orders to kill the nun after the investigator left.

From whom? Naturally, from Dolinin; it could not have been anyone else.

Berdichevsky forgot that he had set aside the drawing of conclusions for later and became completely engrossed in his hypotheses which did seem, however, rather well founded.

Perhaps the investigator had wanted Pelagia to be killed when he, Dolinin, was not anywhere nearby? So that he would have an alibi, or possibly out of a sense of delicacy – he did not want to see it. But there was another, more plausible explanation. In Stroganovka Pelagia must have done or said something from which Dolinin realised that she was close to solving the murder on the steamer. That was most probably the reason why the investigator had invited her to go on the expedition with him: in order to find out how dangerous she was. And he decided that she was dangerous and could not be left alive.

Following these deductions through incidentally threw up the answer to the first of Matvei Bentsionovich's deferred questions. Mr Dolinin needed the social outcast with skills of a wolfhound precisely because he *was*, firstly, an outcast and, secondly, a wolfhound, i.e. a specialist in secret operations. And homosexuality most likely had nothing at all to do with it. The official from St Petersburg might very well never have discovered this circumstance. And was it really of any importance in any case?

Now the other unanswered question: did Dolinin find his way into the 'noble' cell number eleven of the provincial prison by chance? What if he deliberately used his tours of inspection across the Empire for spotting people who could be useful for his as yet unclear goals? It was a supposition – no more than supposition – but it was certainly highly plausible.

A dam suddenly seemed to burst in Matvei Bentsionovich's brain: thoughts, suppositions and flashes of insight suddenly came pouring in so fast that the public prosecutor felt as if he was choking in a mighty flood.

But up ahead he could see another barrier, mightier than the first, and the water there was seething and foaming furiously. Just who was Full State Counsellor Dolinin?

Berdichevsky began recalling everything he had heard about this man from Pelagia and other sources.

Dolinin worked for many years as an investigator of criminal cases. There was a family drama – his wife left him. Pelagia had told this story with compassion; she evidently knew some of the details, but she had not divulged them to Matvei Bentsionovich. She had only told him that the abandoned husband was on the brink of despair, but he met some wise, kind man who turned him to God and liberated him from his thoughts of self-destruction. And that was precisely when the breakthrough in Dolinin's career came – he took wing and forgot his sorrows, immersing himself in important state business.

Well now. All of this raised questions.

Firstly, who was this wise man who saved the investigator's tormented soul?

Secondly, how remarkable that the 'saved soul' began recruiting professional killers.

Thirdly, was it a coincidence that Dolinin's 'enlightenment' and his professional elevation occurred at the same time?

Finally, the fourth and most important point: what determined Dolinin's actions? Or *who*? And what was the purpose of these actions?

Berdichevsky's head was spinning. But one thing was clear: there was nothing more to be done in Zhitomir. As Prince Hamlet said, there was a more powerful magnet.

An American spy

When Matvei Bentsionovich got off the train at the Tsarskoe Selo Station, the very first place he went was the Central Post Office of St Petersburg, in order to see if there was any news from His Eminence. The public prosecutor had sent the Bishop a short report from Zhitomir without, however, going into the details – they were not for the telegraph service. For instance, he had decided not to explain about Dolinin. All he had said was that in 'the case known to Your Eminence' the trail led to the capital of the Empire.

There were no letters from Zavolzhsk, but the State Counsellor did receive a money order for five hundred roubles, with a note in the accompanying form: 'May the Lord preserve you.'

Ah, His Wonderful Eminence! Nothing superfluous, only what Berdichevsky needed most of all just at the moment: money and a blessing.

From a university friend who now worked in the Ministry of the Interior the public prosecutor learned that Sergei Sergeevich Dolinin was returning that evening from his tour of inspection in the Nizhni Novgorod province and was expected in the office the following day. This was most opportune. Now we shall see who he visits immediately after his arrival, thought Matvei Bentsionovich. He went to the Nikolaevsky Station and learned from the timetable that the train arrived at half past eleven in the evening. And so he found himself free for almost the whole day.

Berdichevsky had spent several years in St Petersburg as a student and he knew this beautiful, cold city well. From the point of view of a provincial, the city was spoiled by its abundance of official state buildings – their yellow and white colouring deadened and drowned out the city's true colours of grey and blue. If you took away all the ministries and public offices, Matvei Bentsionovich pondered, Peter would be a mellower and more agreeable place, much cosier for the people who live here. In any case, what sort of place was this for a capital city – right on the very edge of a gigantic empire? It was this abscess that skewed Russia's face out of shape. The seat of power ought be moved to the east, and not to Moscow, which would always survive in any case, but to somewhere like Ufa or Ekaterinburg. Then the ship of state might finally straighten up and stop taking on water over the side.

However, we cannot say that Matvei Bentsionovich devoted the whole of his walk to thoughts on such a monumental scale. He spent the middle part of the day in the Gostiny Dvor, choosing presents for his wife and children. This took him several hours, because it was a fussy job that had to be got right. God forbid that he should forget that Anechka could not stand green, that Vaniusha was only interested in toy locomotives, that woollen fabrics made Magenka sneeze, and so on and so forth.

Having dealt with this pleasant but wearying task, the public prosecutor gave himself a little holiday: he walked round the shops, imagining what present he would buy for Pelagia, if she were not a nun and if their relationship were such as to allow him to give her presents. Impossible dreams led the State Counsellor into the perfumery row, and from there they made him turn into the haberdashery row, and he only came to his senses in the lacy *dessous* section. He blushed right red up to the roots of his hair and walked quickly out into the street, to cool off in the damp Baltic breeze.

Day was giving way to evening. It was time to prepare for Dolinin's arrival.

According to the address book, the member of the ministerial council resided at Sholtz's House on Zagorodny Prospect. Matvei Bentsionovich took a look at the house (an ordinary four-storey apartment building – General Dolinin's apartment was on the first floor) and located the right windows.

He took a room in the Helsingfors lodging house, which was located most conveniently – almost directly opposite. And now darkness had stealthily fallen. It would soon be time to go to the Nikolaevsky Station.

★

Berdichevsky had an exceptional stroke of luck with his cabby. Number 48-36 proved to be a young lad, very quick on the uptake. When he found out what was required, his eyes began blazing so brightly that he even forgot to bargain over the price.

The Moscow train arrived on time. The public prosecutor had met Dolinin and even spoken with him in Zavolzhsk, so he avoided making himself conspicuous, waiting behind a news-paper kiosk until Sergei Sergeevich walked by and then falling in behind.

Nobody met the Full State Counsellor – unfortunately. Berd-ichevsky had been imagining a mysterious carriage and a hand that would open the door for the inspector as he approached. Not just an ordinary hand, but one with a special kind of ring, and there had to be a uniform sleeve with gilt embroidery. But there was none of this – no hand and no carriage. Dolinin modestly got into a cab, set his plain travelling bag down beside him and rode off.

There was no need to explain everything twice to number 48-36 – he had started moving even before Berdichevsky ran up to him. The public prosecutor jumped on board and whispered: 'Don't crowd him, don't crowd him.'

The cabby maintained an ideal distance – about a hundred paces – allowing two or three carriages to get in front of him, but no more, so that they would not block his view.

Dolinin's cab did not go to Nevsky Prospect, but turned off on to Ligovskaya Street. He seems to be going home, Matvei Bentsionovich thought, disappointed. That proved to be right: Dolinin turned on to Zvenigorodskaya Street.

They had to wait for some time at Sholtz's house. The lights went on in the windows of Dolinin's apartment, and then went out again in all but one. Was he preparing for bed, writing a report? Or getting changed to go somewhere else in the middle of the night?

The public prosecutor was not sure what to do. Was he going to hang about here until the morning?

Well, at least for as long as the light was burning. What if Dolinin was expecting a late visitor? But the light in the final window burned for forty-two minutes and then went out. He must have gone to bed after all.

'Who is he, a spy?' the cabby asked in a low voice.

Berdichevsky nodded absent-mindedly, wondering whether he ought to settle down for the night in the cab.

''Merican?' number 48-36 enquired.

'Why American?' the public prosecutor asked in surprise.

The lad just sniffed. The devil only knew what was going on in his head and why he chose to grant the supposed enemy of society such an exotic citizenship.

'No, Austro-Hungarian,' said Matvei Bentsionovich, naming a more plausible country.

The cabby nodded. 'Your honour, do you want me to keep watch on the windows here? At least till morning? I'm well used to it, I won't fall asleep. How about it? I've got oats in the nosebag. And I won't charge dear. Three roubles, that's all. Two and a half, eh?'

He was clearly desperately keen to keep watch on the Austrian spy. But more importantly, it was actually quite a good idea. And the price was reasonable.

'All right. I'll be over there in that lodging house. You see that window? On the corner, the ground floor. If he goes anywhere or anyone comes to him – even if the light just goes on – you let me know immediately?' Then Berdichevsky started thinking: The only thing is, how?

'I'll whistle,' suggested 48-36. 'I can do a special whistle, like a real bandit.'

He folded his fingers together and gave a deafening whistle – horses squatted down on their hindquarters, the doorman stuck his head out of the Helsingfors, and police constables' whistles answered in the distance from two directions.

'No, don't whistle,' said the public prosecutor, huddling down on his seat and looking up anxiously at Dolinin's windows in case the curtain trembled. 'Better run across and throw a few stones.'

He went to bed without taking off his clothes or shoes. He took a swig of the Moselle he had bought in the Gostiny Dvor – straight from the bottle, but not too much. The last thing he needed at his age was to turn into a drunk.

He lay there with his hands behind his head, taking a sip from the bottle every now and then. Sometimes he thought about Masha, sometimes about Pelagia. In some incomprehensible fashion these two women, so entirely unlike each other, had fused into a single being for whom Matvei Bentsionovich felt such a tender affection that it brought tears to his eyes.

Berdichevsky was woken by a crystalline, ethereal sound, and at first he didn't realise what it was. It was not until the second stone struck the window – with a force that cracked the glass – that the public prosecutor scrambled hastily to his feet and started dashing around the room, still half-asleep.

The room was bright. Morning. Matvei Bentsionovich jerked up the window frame and stuck his head out.

The cab was waiting at the pavement. 'Quick, mister, quick,' said number 48-36, waving his hand. 'Lep it, or he'll get away.'

So the State Counsellor did – he grabbed his frock coat and hat and 'lepped it' straight over the windowsill. He bruised his leg on the way, but that immediately woke him up.

'Where?' he gasped.

'He's turned the corner!' The cabby lashed his horse. 'That's all right; we'll catch him in a flash!'

Berdichevsky tugged his watch out of his pocket. Half past seven. Sergei Sergeevich had set out for work rather early. The public prosecutor's somnolence had disappeared as if by magic; he could feel the excitement of the chase bubbling up into his chest.

The closed carriage driving ahead of them was black, of the kind that usually transport officials with a general's rank to their offices. It turned on to Zabalkansky Prospect and drove along the embankment for a while, but went past the turn on to Izmailovsky Prospect.

Aha, he's not going to work! The Ministry's offices are on Morskaya Street!

'What happened during the night?' Berdichevsky asked abruptly.

'Nothing, Your Honour. I didn't sleep a single minute, don't you worry about that.'

'Here.' The public prosecutor handed him, not two and a half roubles, or even three, but four, for his diligence. But the cabby didn't even look at how much he was being given – he just put the money in his pocket. You ought to join the detective department, brother, Matvei Bentsionovich thought. You'd make an excellent agent.

The carriage drove along the Fontanka Embankment, across the bridge on to Ekaterinhof Prospect, and stopped soon afterwards in front of a building with large windows.

'What's that?'

'A grammar school, Your Honour.'

But Matvei Bentsionovich had already recognised it himself. Yes, a grammar school. Boys' school number five, wasn't it? What could Dolinin want here?

Sergei Sergeevich did not get out of his carriage, and he even drew the curtains together.

Curious.

Nothing of any note took place in front of the grammar school. The tall door opened every now and then to admit pupils and teachers. The attendant doffed his cap and bowed deeply in greeting to some pompous gentleman – possibly the headmaster or an inspector. Just once Berdichevsky thought he saw the curtain twitch slightly, but thirty seconds later it was drawn closed again, and a second after that the carriage set off.

What was all that about? Why did Dolinin come to this place at such an early hour? Not to look at the children, surely?

Ah yes, precisely to look at the children, Matvei Bentsionovich suddenly realised. Or rather, at one of them. Pelagia had said that when they separated, Sergei Sergeevich's wife took their son.

Absolutely nothing mysterious at all. A father who has been away and has missed his child. He didn't show himself to his son – either he had promised not to, or he was too proud, or perhaps he did not want to torment the boy, who had grown accustomed to a new father.

It seemed like nothing out of the ordinary, a perfectly normal human thing to do, but Berdichevsky was perplexed. Somehow one did not expect perfectly normal human actions from a fiend who hired murderers and spilled innocent blood.

Or was Dolinin not a fiend after all?

The public prosecutor was no longer a boy of eighteen, after all, and his life and work should surely have taught him that not all fiends are as black as Count Charnokutsky; but even so Matvei Bentsionovich felt confused – he had never imagined that there might be anything human about the monster who had planned to have Pelagia killed.

Well, I suppose even a viper loves its baby vipers, the State Counsellor muttered to himself, driving away his inappropriate incongruous doubts.

The city had completely woken up now. The street filled up with carriages and an industrious morning crowd strode briskly along the pavements. The distance from the object of pursuit had to be reduced, otherwise they might lose him.

And just before the Mariinsky Palace they did lose him. The policeman on duty waved one hand to halt the traffic and the black carriage went rolling on in the direction of the equestrian statue of Nicholas the First, leaving Berdichevsky stuck on the bridge. He very nearly went running after it on foot, but that would have attracted attention: a respectable middle-aged gentleman racing along the embankment, holding his hat down on his head.

The cabby stood up on his box, and then climbed right up on to the seat.

'Well did he turn on to Morskaya Street?'

'No, he went straight on, towards St Isaac's!'

Not going to work in the ministry this time, either!

Eventually the traffic started moving again. Number 48-36 lashed the horse, deftly overtook a fiacre, cut in right in front of a four-horse omnibus, and a minute later he was already rumbling across Senate Square.

Suddenly he pulled hard on the reins and shouted, 'Whoa!'

'What are you doing?

The lad jerked his head to one side. There was the familiar black carriage, driving towards them. The curtains at the window were open. There was no one inside.

He had got out. But where?

On the right was the square with the statue of Peter the Great. Straight ahead was the Neva. There wouldn't have been enough time for the carriage to set down its passenger on the Anlgiiskoe Embankment and drive back.

So Dolinin must have gone into one of the massive public buildings located on the left, between the boulevard and the embankment: either the Ruling Senate or the Holy Synod. Most likely the Senate, the country's supreme court of law. What business would an investigator have in the Synod?

'Where to now, Your Honour?' the cabby asked.

'Wait over there,' said Berdichevsky, pointing to the railings of the square small park.

Who had Dolinin gone to see in the Senate when he was only just back from his official tour of inspection? A man whom he visited before his own superiors must surely be a key figure in all this most sinister conspiracy.

What he ought to do was this: go up to the duty clerk keeping the record of visitors and say: 'Full State Counsellor Dolinin of the Ministry of the Interior is due to arrive here any moment. He has forgotten some important documents; I'll wait here, to give them to him.' The clerk would say: 'His Excellency has already arrived, he is with such-and-such.' And if he didn't say who Dolinin had gone to see, Berdichevsky could ask. It was impudent, of course, but it would clear everything up straight away.

Or would it be better to wait and continue the surveillance? The public prosecutor was roused from his torment of indecision by the sound of someone delicately clearing his throat.

Matvei Bentsionovich started and looked round. Standing beside him was a doorman, wearing a three-pointed hat, a uniform with braid trimming and white stockings. Not just a doorman, a veritable field marshal. While Berdichevsky was examining the building of the Senate, he had completely failed to notice this stuffed dummy approaching.

'Your Honour, you are requested kindly to step this way,' the field marshal-doorman said respectfully, but at the same time strictly, speaking in the way that only servants who are employed at the highest peaks of power can do.

Berdichevsky was taken aback. 'Requested by whom?'

'You are requested,' the doorman declared so forcefully that the public prosecutor asked no more questions.

'Shall I wait, mister?' number 48-36 shouted.

'Yes.'

Matvei Bentsionovich had made up his mind so firmly to go into the Senate, the building closest to the embankment, that he did not immediately understand what was wrong when his escort tactfully touched him on the sleeve.

'Step this way, please,' he said, pointing to the entrance of the Holy Synod.

Inside the doorway, the doorman remarked casually to the duty clerk who was sitting there, lazily driving away the flies: 'To Konstantin Petrovich. He is expected.'

Ah . . . ah, you blockhead! Matvei Bentsionovich stopped and slapped himself very painfully on the forehead – as a punishment for being so blind and dim-witted.

The doorman swung round at the sound. 'Swatted a fly? They're a terrible nuisance. Multiplied like wildfire, they have.'

Co-thinkers and soulmates

Matvei Bentsionovich's guide handed him over to an elderly clerk who was waiting on the bottom step of the stairs. The clerk bowed politely without introducing himself and gestured for Berdichevsky to follow him.

In the reception room of the great man who was regarded as the most powerful individual in the Empire – not so much because of his official position as because of his spiritual influence on the Emperor – there were about fifteen visitors: these included generals in full-dress uniform and two senior churchmen with medals; but there were also simpler people there: a lady with red, tearful eyes, an agitated student, a young junior officer.

The clerk approached the secretary and pronounced those magic words: 'For Konstantin Petrovich. He is expected.'

The secretary looked closely at Berdichevsky, darted out from behind his desk and disappeared through a tall white door. Thirty seconds later he reappeared.

'You are requested to step this way . . .'

Unable to think of where to put his hat, Matvei Bentsionovich resolutely set it down on the secretary's desk. If they were according him the honour of skipping the queue, they could respect his hat too.

He bit his lower lip and the fingers of his right hand involuntarily clenched into a fist. He went in.

There were two men sitting beside the absolutely gigantic desk at the far end of the vast study. One was facing Berdichevsky, and although the public prosecutor had never seen the Chief Procurator in person before, he immediately recognised those ascetic features, sternly knitted eyebrows and rather prominent ears from all the portraits.

The second man, dressed in a gold-embroidered civil uniform, was seated in an armchair and he did not turn to glance at the new arrival straight away. When he did look round, it was for no more than an instant. Then he turned his face back to Pobedin.

Konstantin Petrovich, famous for his old-fashioned St Petersburg courtesy, got to his feet. At close quarters the Chief Procurator proved to be tall and erect, with a wizened face and sunken eyes that glowed with intelligence and strength. Looking into those remarkable eyes, Berdichevsky remembered that the Chief Procurator's ill-wishers called him the Great Inquisitor. It was not surprising: he looked the part.

Dolinin (naturally, it was he sitting in the armchair) did not get up. On the contrary, he gazed demonstratively off to one side, as if trying to show that what was going on had nothing to do with him.

Speaking in a gentle, resonant voice, Konstantin Petrovich asked: 'Are you surprised, Matvei Bentsionovich? I see you are surprised. You should not be. Sergei Sergeevich is far too valuable to Russia for him to be left without protection and supervision. I know, I know everything. I have had reports. About the surveillance yesterday and the surveillance today. Yesterday no one bothered you – we had to find out just what kind of bird you were. But today, when we found out, we decided to have a word with you. Quite openly, heart to heart.' Pobedin shaped his thin dry lips into a smile of good will, even sympathy. 'Sergei Sergeevich and I understand the reason that has impelled you to undertake a spontaneous investigation. You are an intelligent, energetic, brave man – you would have got to the bottom of things anyway, if not today, then tomorrow. And so I decided to invite you in myself. For a meeting with the visors up, so to speak. It is unseemly for me to hide. I suppose you have imagined Mr Dolinin to be some appalling evil-doer or conspirator?'

Matvei Bentsionovich did not reply to that, he merely lowered his head; but he did not lower his gaze, so that the effect was that of a scowl.

'Please sit here, opposite Sergei Sergeevich,' the Chief Procurator invited him. 'Do not be afraid; he is no evil-doer, and I, who am his mentor and leader, do not wish anyone ill, no matter what the liberal gentlemen might say about me. Do you know who I am, Matvei Bentsionovich? I am the people's servant and sympathiser. And as for the monstrous conspiracy that you no doubt believe you have uncovered, I confess quite honestly: yes, there is a conspiracy, but it is very far from monstrous – it is sacred: its goal is the salvation of Russia, Faith and the Throne. One of those conspiracies, you know, in which all good, honest men of faith should participate.'

Berdichevsky opened his mouth to say that most conspiracies, including the monstrous ones, pursued some sacred goal such as the salvation of the Motherland, but Konstantin Petrovich raised an imperious palm.

'Wait, do not say anything yet and do not ask any questions. There are many things I must explain to you first. I require helpers in the great task that I have mentioned. I have been gathering them, year by year – one grain and one crumb at a time – for many years now. They are true men, my soulmates. And they also choose helpers for themselves, men who are useful. It has been reported to me that your investigation has followed the trail of precisely one such *useful man*. What was his name now?'

'Ratsevich,' Sergei Sergeevich said, opening his mouth for the first time.

Although he was sitting directly opposite the man from Zavolzhsk, in some miraculous way he contrived not to look at him. Dolinin's face was sullen and blank.

'Yes, yes, thank you. Following this Ratsevich's trail has led you, Mr Berdichevsky, to Sergei Sergeevich, one of my helpers – only recently acquired, but already he has demonstrated quite excellent qualities. And do you know what I have to say to you?'

Matvei Bentsionovich did not attempt to answer this rhetorical question, especially since he had no idea whatever of the direction that this astounding conversation might take.

'I believe in Providence,' Pobedin declared solemnly. 'It is what has led you to us. I told Sergei Sergeevich: "Of course, we could exterminate this public prosecutor, so that he will not harm our cause. But take a look at his actions. This Berdichevsky acts like a man who is purposeful, intelligent, selfless. Is this not the very set of qualities that you and I value in men? Let me have a word with him, as a good shepherd. He will look into my eyes, and I into his, and it might very well be that we shall find ourselves a new co-thinker."'

Berdichevsky started slightly at the word 'exterminate' and failed to listen very attentively to the remainder of the Chief Procurator's speech – there was only a single, panicky thought left twitching in his mind: your fate is being decided right now, this very minute.

Konstantin Petrovich apparently failed to understand the real reason for the other man's reserve. 'You have no doubt heard that I am an anti-Semite, an enemy of the Jews. It is not true. To classify people according to their nationality is something I would never do. I am not an enemy of the Jews, but of the Jewish faith, because it is a poisonous tare that springs from the same root as Christianity and is a hundred times more dangerous than Islam, Buddhism or paganism. The worst enemy is not he who is alien to you, but he who is your own kin! And therefore the Jew who, like unto you, has abjured the false faith of his fathers and accepted Christ, is dearer to me than the Russian who abides in the bosom of the true faith through the grace of birth. However, I can see that you wish to ask me about something. You may do so now. Ask.'

'Your Excellency . . .' Matvei Bentsionovich began, trying to control the trembling of his voice.

'Please – Konstantin Petrovich,' the Chief Procurator corrected him gently.

'Very well . . . Konstantin Petrovich, I did not entirely understand about the conspiracy. Do you mean that in a figurative sense, or . . .'

'In the most direct sense possible. Only a conspiracy is usually arranged in order to overthrow the existing order, while my conspiracy exists in order to save it. Our country, yours and mine, is teetering on the brink of a precipice. If it fails to hold and plunges into the abyss, it is the end of everything. Our long-suffering homeland is being dragged to its doom by a mighty satanic power, and those trying to avert this catastrophe are few in number. Disunity, a decline in morality and, worst of all, a lack of faith – this is the Gogolesque troika that is bearing Russia towards the edge of the chasm that is already close, verily it is close! And the pit breathes fire and brimstone!'

Konstantin Petrovich made the transition from soft-spoken rationality to prophetic pathos quite naturally, without the slightest strain. The Chief Procurator was certainly exceptionally gifted as a public speaker. But when the passionate frenzy of those eyes and the entire charge of spiritual energy were directed at a single, solitary listener, the pressure was quite impossible to resist. And he has no need to address crowds, thought Berdichevsky. An audience of one man is sufficient for him, because that man is the autocratic ruler of all Russia. Despite himself, Matvei Bentsionovich began feeling flattered. Here was the great Pobedin, expending all the fervour and zeal of his statesman's soul on a minnow like him.

Trying not to submit to the Chief Procurator's magnetism, the State Counsellor said: 'I beg your pardon, but there is something I don't understand . . .' He lost the thread and started all over again – he had to choose his words very carefully here. 'If the theory that I developed is correct, then the cause of everything that has happened . . . of Mr Dolinin's actions, was the determination to kill the sectarian prophet Manuila, at no matter what cost. In order to achieve this goal and also to cover his tracks, the Full State Counsellor stopped at nothing. If a perfectly innocent nun had to be eliminated – then by all means. He did not even take pity on a little peasant girl.'

'What girl is that?' Pobedin interrupted him, with a glance of annoyance at Sergei Sergeevich. 'I know about the nun, but nothing about the girl.'

Dolinin replied abruptly: 'It was Ratsevich. A professional, but he got carried away, and he turned out to be rotten. I have already said that I was mistaken to recruit him to our cause.'

'Anyone can make mistakes,' the Chief Procurator sighed. 'The Lord will forgive, if the error was genuine. Continue, Matvei Bentsionovich.'

'Well then . . . I wanted to ask . . . What is so special about him, this swindler Manuila? Why was all this necessary for his sake . . . all *this*?'

Konstantin Petrovich nodded and answered very seriously, indeed solemnly: 'You truly are a highly intelligent man. You have seen through to the very essence. Then you should know that the individual whom you have mentioned represents a terrible danger to Russia, and even more than that – to the entire Christian world.'

'Who – Manuila?' Berdichevsky asked, amazed. 'Come now, Your Excellency! Surely you are exaggerating?'

The Chief Procurator smiled sadly. 'You have not yet learned to trust me as my soulmates trust me. I can commit errors of the mind or the heart, but never of both at the same time. This is a gift vouchsafed to me by the Lord. It is my predestined role. Believe me, Matvei Bentsionovich: I see further than other people, and much is revealed to me that is hidden from them.'

Pobedin looked Berdichevsky straight in the eyes, hammering home every word. The public prosecutor from Zavolzhsk listened as if he were in a trance.

'Everyone who comes into contact with Manuila is infected with the fatal disease of disbelief. I myself have spoken with him and felt this seductive power, and only rescued myself through prayer. Do you know who he is?' asked Konstantin Petrovich, suddenly speaking in a terrible whisper.

'No.'

'Antichrist.' The word was pronounced with quiet solemnity.

Berdichevsky blinked in fright. Well, how about that! The most influential man in the state, the Chief Procurator of the Holy Synod, is insane. Poor Russia!

'I am not insane, and I am not a religious fanatic,' the Chief Procurator said, as if he had read Berdichevsky's thoughts. 'But I do believe in God. I have known that the Evil One was on his way for a long time. I have been expecting him. And it turns out that he is already here. He has appeared out of nowhere and wanders around Russia, getting a feel for things, taking stock, for he has no need no hurry – he has been granted three and a half years. For it is said in the Revelation of St John: "*And he was given lips that spoke proudly and blasphemously, and he was given the power to act for forty-two months. And he opened his lips to blaspheme against God, to blaspheme against His name, and His dwelling, and those living in heaven. And it was granted to him to wage war against the saints and defeat them; and power was granted to him over every tribe and tongue and race. And all those living on earth shall bow to him, those whose names are not written in the book of life of the Lamb, sacrificed from the creation of the world."*'

These terrible and obscure words alarmed Matvei Bentsiono-vich. Pobedin no longer seemed like a madman to him but even so, it was quite impossible to believe that the pitiful rogue Manuila was the Beast of the Apocalypse.

'I know,' Konstantin Petrovich sighed. 'It is hard for a practical man such as yourself to believe in such things. It is one thing to read about the Antichrist in the sacred literature and quite another to imagine him among real people in our age of steam and electricity, and here in Russia! But let me tell you this,' said the Chief Procurator, waxing passionate once again: 'Russia is precisely the place! The very meaning and destined purpose of our country lies in this, that it is appointed to be the battlefield between Light and Darkness! The Beast chose Russia because she is a special country – she is an unfortunate country, furthest of all away from God, but at the same time closer to Him than any other! And also because we have suffered vacillation here for a long time in both the social order and in faith. Our country is the weakest link in the chain of Christian states. The Antichrist has seen this and prepared his blow. I know what that blow will be – he confessed it to me himself. You and Sergei Sergeevich have no need to know it; let the burden of knowledge remain mine alone. I will say only this: it is a blow from which our faith will not recover. And what is Russia without faith? An oak with no roots. A tower with no foundations. It will collapse and be scattered as dust.'

'Antichrist?' Berdichevsky repeated hesitantly.

'Yes. And not in metaphorical terms, like Napoleon Bon-aparte, but absolutely, completely real. Only without any horns or tail, with a quiet, heartfelt manner of speaking and an endear-ing gaze. I can feel people, I know them. Well, *Manuila is not human.*'

The simple, everyday manner in which these words were spoken sent a chilly shiver running down Matvei Bentsionovich's spine. 'What about Sister Pelagia?' he asked in a feeble voice. Of what is she guilty?'

The Chief Procurator replied sternly: 'The institution of capital punishment exists in every state. In the Christian coun-tries it is employed in two cases: when someone has committed a serious offence against humanity or represents a serious danger to society. The first case applies to hardened criminals, the second to those who undermine the foundations of morality.'

'But Pelagia is not a murderer and not a revolutionary!'

'Even so, she represents an immense danger to our cause, and that is far worse than any offence committed against humanity. An offence can be forgiven; Christ himself has told us to do that.' At this point Pobedin's face convulsed for some reason, but he instantly recovered control of himself. 'We can, we even should, show mercy to a cruel murderer who has repented. However, not to eliminate a person who may be full of good intentions, but nonetheless represents a danger to the entire world order, is a crime. It is just like a doctor who fails to amputate a gangrenous limb from which deadly poison will flood throughout the body. Such is the higher law of the community: to sacrifice one for the good of the many.'

'But you could have talked to her, just as you are talking to me now,' Matvei Bentsionovich exclaimed. 'She is an extremely intelligent woman and a true believer, she would have understood you!'

The Chief Procurator glanced at Dolinin, who raised his stiff, gloomy face and shook his head: 'I could tell straight away that she was dangerous. I kept her close by, to get a better look at her. I had already realised that she was too clever, she was bound to get to the bottom of things, but I kept putting it off . . . I know her kind, they won't let go of a puzzle until they have solved it. And she was already getting close to the solution.'

Konstantin Petrovich took up the conversation again. 'I can talk to you, Matvei Bentsionovich, because you are a man, and you can see past particular cases to what is truly important. A woman will never understand me, because for her the particular case is more important than the Whole. You and I will sacrifice one person in order to save thousands or millions, even if that person is infinitely dear to us and it makes our hearts bleed. But a woman will never do that, and millions will die together with the unfortunate individual on whom she has taken pity. I have seen this Pelagia of yours, and I know what I am saying. She would not wish to remain silent and she would not be able to. The sword has already been raised above her head. I grieve for this extraordinary woman, and Sergei Sergeevich grieves even more, because he has managed to fall in love with her.'

Berdichevsky looked at Dolinin in horror, but not a single muscle twitched in the investigator's face.

'We shall mourn her together,' the Chief Procurator concluded. 'And let our consolation be that her final resting place will be in the Holy Land.'

Matvei Bentsionovich almost groaned out loud in his despair. *They know, they know everything!*

'Yes, we know,' said Konstantin Petrovich, with a nod that confirmed his ability to read the other man's thoughts. 'She is still alive, because that is how we need it to be. But soon, very soon, she will be no more. Alas, there is no other way. The assembly of soul-brothers sometimes has to take such bitter and painful decisions – even when it is not just a matter of a simple nun but of far more distinguished individuals.'

Berdichevsky suddenly recalled the old rumours about the sudden demise of young General Skobelev, who had supposedly been condemned to death by a secret monarchical organisation called the Sacred Militia.

'The Sacred Militia?' he said uncertainly.

Pobedin frowned. 'We have no name. And the Sacred Militia was the stupid, infantile initiative of ambitious courtiers. We are not men of ambition, although each of my helpers is appointed to a high position in which he can be of maximum use to the motherland. I shall find you a job too, you may be sure of that; but I want you to join us, not out of careerist considerations, but out of conviction ... Now listen to this.' The Chief Procurator looked hard at the State Counsellor, and Berdichevsky cringed under that piercing glance. 'I am going to tell you something that is known only to the very closest circle of my friends. We have developed a plan of emergency measures in case the danger of a revolutionary eruption becomes too great. The problem is that the authorities and society remain childishly unconcerned. People are inclined to underestimate the threat contained in theories and ideas – until such time as blood is spilled. Well then, we shall open society's eyes! We shall seize the initiative! At the moment the ulcer of revolution in Russia has been cauterised with red-hot iron, but that is merely temporary relief. When a further wave of revolutionary violence becomes inescapable, we shall act first. We shall start the terror ourselves.'

'You are going to kill the revolutionaries?'

'There is no point in that. We should only arouse sympathy for them. No, we shall kill a revered dignitary of high standing. If necessary, more than one. And we shall spread the word that it is the beginning of revolutionary terror. We shall choose a worthy, respected individual, so that everyone will be horrified ... Wait, Matvei Bentsionovich, do not shudder so. I have not yet told you everything. The murder of a minister or a governor general will not be enough; we shall arrange explosions at railway stations, in apartment buildings. With large numbers of innocent victims. Monstrous provocation, you will say. But have you read Nechaev's *Revolutionary Catechism*? Our enemies are willing to commit acts of provocation and cruelty. And so we have the right to use the same weapons. I pray to God that it will not come to that.' Pobedin crossed himself fervently. 'And so that you will not think me the Devil incarnate, let me tell you one more thing: before the explosions begin, another highly placed dignitary will be killed, one whom the sovereign himself respects, to whom he pays close attention. Unfortunately, not close enough ...'

'You?' Berdichevsky gasped.

'Yes. And that is not the greatest of the sacrifices that I am willing to make for the sake of mankind!' Konstantin Petrovich exclaimed with anguish, and tears began to flow from his eyes. 'What is it to give one's life? A mere trifle. But I shall sacrifice something far more valuable: my own immortal soul! That is the very highest price that a human leader is obliged to pay for the happiness of human beings if it is necessary! Do you think I do not understand what a curse I am taking on myself? There is no ministry more sacrificial than mine. I will say a terrible, even blasphemous thing: my sacrifice is greater than that of Jesus, for He kept His soul. Jesus called on us to love our neighbours as ourselves, but I love my neighbours *more* than myself. I shall not even begrudge my immortal soul for their sake ... Yes, in ordering the killing of those who are innocent but dangerous for our cause, I doom my own soul! But it is for the sake of love, the sake of truth, the sake of my neighbour!'

At this moment the Chief Procurator's eyes were no longer looking at Berdichevsky, but upwards, at the ceiling, at the centre of which a magnificent crystal chandelier gleamed brightly.

He is not speaking to me, but to the Lord God, Matvei

355

Bentsionovich realised. So he must still be hoping for His forgiveness.

Konstantin Petrovich wiped away his tears with a handkerchief and spoke to Berdichevsky in a tone that was intimate, yet also stern and uncompromising.

'If you are willing to walk this road to Calvary with me, then set your shoulder to the Cross and let us go. If you are not, then move aside; do not get in the way! Well then? Are you staying or leaving?'

His Excellency takes a stroll

Matvei Bentsionovich left the building of the Holy Synod an hour later, no longer a state counsellor, but the owner of a higher title – a full state counsellor, with the rank of a general. The promotion had been effected with quiet fantastic ease and rapidity. Konstantin Petrovich telephoned the Ministry of Justice and spoke for no more than three minutes, then called the Palace, where he spoke with Another Person so important that Berdichevsky's palms began to sweat. 'An absolutely invaluable individual to the state, entirely at my own responsibility' – such were the words spoken about the unknown man from Zavolzhsk. And to such a person!

Other officials waited months for their promotions to be confirmed, even after they had completed the full term of service, but in this case everything was resolved in the blinking of an eye, and even the decree was due to follow immediately, with today's date.

Matvei had been promised an appointment to a responsible position in the immediate future. And while the Chief Procurator was selecting a worthy field of endeavour for his new co-thinker (it would take a week or two), Berdichevsky was instructed to remain in the capital. Konstantin Petrovich advised him not to return to Zavolzhsk. 'Why get involved in pointless explanations with your spiritual father?' he said, demonstrating yet again the absolutely exhaustive extent of his knowledge. 'The Governor of Zavolzhie will be informed by telegram, your family will be brought on. In a day or two the Ministry will provide you with a state apartment, fully furnished, so you need have no concerns about domestic arrangements.'

But His Brand-New Excellency had no concerns about settling in.

Berdichevsky emerged from the Synod building on to the square. He screwed his eyes up against the bright sunshine and put on his hat. The cab was waiting by the railings. Number 48-36 was staring at the fighter against Austro-Hungarian espionage, waiting for a sign. Matvei Bentsionovich hesitated for a moment, then went across to him and said casually: 'Take me for a ride, brother.'

'Where do you want to go?'

'I don't really know; I suppose the embankment will do.'

The ride along beside the Neva was simply remarkable. The sun had hidden behind the clouds, and there was a fine drizzle sprinkling down from the sky, but the passenger raised the leather top and screened himself off from the outside world. Then it turned bright, and the top was lowered again.

His Excellency rode along, smiling at the sky, the river, the glimmers of sunlight flitting across the walls of the buildings.

'Turn on to the Moika,' he ordered. 'No, wait – I think – I'll take a walk. What's your name? This is the second day we've been driving around, and I never asked.'

'Matvei,' said the cabby.

Berdichevsky was surprised, but not greatly so, because during the morning his capacity for surprise had been significantly diminished.

'Can you read and write?'

'Yes, sir.'

'Well done. Take this for your pains.' He slipped several pieces of paper into the pocket of the cabby's caftan. The driver did not even thank him, he was so upset. 'Is that all, Your Honour; don't you need anything else?' His voice was actually trembling.

'Not "Your Honour"; it's "Your Excellency", Matvei Bentsionovich told him grandly. 'I'll find you when I need you, number 48-36.' He clapped the beaming lad on the shoulder and went further on foot.

His mood was a little sad, but it was calm. Goodness knows what the former public prosecutor of Zavolzhsk was thinking as he stepped out along Blagoveshchenskaya Street at a relaxed stroll. Once, on the bank of the Admiralty Canal, his eye was caught by a maid taking two little girls for a walk, and he muttered mysteriously: 'And will they really be better off if their father's a scoundrel?'

Another time, on Post Office Square, he whispered in reply to some thoughts of his own: 'Simple, but at the same time elegant. The Berdichevsky Étude.' He chuckled merrily.

As he walked up the steps of the Central Post Office, he even started singing in an entirely tuneless voice, but without any words, so that the melody was quite impossible to recognise.

He scrawled rapidly on a telegram form: 'Find P urgently. Her life in danger. Berdichevsky.' He handed it through the window to the telegraph operator and dictated the address: 'His Eminence Mitrofanii, the Episcopal Conventuary, Zavolzhsk, "blitz".'

He paid one rouble and eleven kopecks for the telegram.

When he went back out into the street, His Excellency stood on the steps for a while. He said in a quiet voice: 'Well it was a life. It could have been lived more worthily, but that was how it turned out . . .'

It seemed clear that Matvei Bentsionovich wanted very much to talk to someone, and for lack of such a person he had struck up a dialogue with himself. But he was not saying everything out loud – only a few fragments of thought, without any obvious logical connection.

For instance, he muttered: 'A rouble and eleven kopecks. What a price.' And he laughed quietly.

He looked to the left and the right. The street was full of people walking along. 'Right here, is it?' Berdichevsky asked someone invisible. He shuddered, but then immediately smiled shamefacedly. He turned to the right.

The next phrase he uttered was even stranger: 'I wonder if I'll get as far as the square?'

He walked at a leisurely pace towards St Isaac's Cathedral. He crossed his arms and gazed admiringly at the glistening pavement, the copper gleam of the dome, a flock of pigeons circling in the sky.

He whispered: '*Merci*. It's beautiful.'

Matve Bentsionovich appeared to be waiting for something, expecting someone. The next phrase he uttered supported this assumption. 'Come on, how much longer? This is impolite, to say the least.'

What exactly he found so impolite remained unknown, because at that very instant a solidly built young man who was in a hurry to get somewhere ran smack into the new Full State Counsellor. However, the sturdy fellow (he was wearing a striped jacket) apologised politely and even supported Matvei Bentsionovich by the shoulder when the Full State Counsellor gasped out loud. Then he raised his straw hat and jogged on his way.

Berdichevsky swayed on the spot for a moment, with a smile on his lips, then suddenly collapsed on to the pavement. The smile widened even further and froze; the brown eyes gazed calmly sideways at a rainbow-coloured puddle.

A crowd gathered round the man who had fallen – they fussed and gasped, rubbed his temples and so forth, and meanwhile the sturdy young man strode down the street and into the Post Office through the service door.

An official of the postal service was waiting for him at the telegraph station.

'Where is it?' asked the man in stripes.

He was handed a sheet of paper, a telegram addressed to Zavolzhsk.

The man in stripes was apparently already familiar with its contents – he did not bother to read the message but simply folded the sheet of paper carefully and put it in his pocket.

XV

Full Moon

Near the garden and in the garden

In front of the Jaffa Gate, Pelagia gave the order to turn right.
They skirted the old town from the south along the Kedron
Ravine. To their right in the distance the white headstones of
the Jewish cemetery on the Mount of Olives were like an
immense stone city, but Polina Andreevna scarcely spared a
glance for the famous necropolis, whose inhabitants would be
the first to rise on the Day of Judgement. The exhausted traveller
had no time now for holy places and tourist sites. The round
moon was already quite high in the sky and she was very afraid
of being too late.

'If we're not where I told you to go in five minutes, you won't
get your two hundred francs,' she said, prodding her driver in
the back.

'And marry?' Salakh asked, turning round. 'You say "all right".'

'I told you, I already have a Bridegroom, I don't need another
one. Get a move on, or you won't get the money either.'

The Palestinian sulked, but he lashed the horses anyway. The
hantur rumbled across a bridge and turned right on to a small
street that ran steeply uphill.

'There, that's your garden,' Salakh muttered, pointing to a
fence and a gate. 'Five minutes not over yet.' Polina Andreevna's
pulse raced as she looked at the entrance to the most holy of all
gardens on Earth. At first glance there was nothing exceptional
about it: just the dark crowns of trees, with the dome of a church
rising up behind them.

Was Emmanuel here or had he gone already? Or perhaps she
was mistaken?

'Wait here,' Pelagia whispered and went in through the gate.

360

How small it was! Fifty paces from one side to the other, certainly no more. In the centre an abandoned well, with ten or so crooked, knotty trees standing around it. They said olive trees were immortal, or at least they could live for two or three thousand years. Did that mean some of these trees had heard Jesus pray for this cup to pass him by? The nun's heart faltered at the thought of it. But Pelagia's chest felt even tighter when she saw that there was no one in the garden apart from her. The moon was shining so brightly that it impossible to hide.

No need to despair, Polina Andreevna told herself. Perhaps I have arrived too early. She went back out into the street and said to Salakh: 'Let's go down that way. We'll wait.'

He led the horses down to the road, where there was a gap that had formed in a tumbledown wall and it was overhung by the thick branches of trees, so that the cart could only be spotted if you knew where it was.

Salakh asked in a whisper: 'Who we wait for, eh?'

She did not answer, merely waved her hand for him to be quiet.

Strangely enough, during those minutes of waiting Pelagia did not have the slightest doubt that Emmanuel would come. But this did not lessen her agitation; on the contrary, it intensified it.

The nun's lips moved as she silently recited a prayer: 'How beloved is Thy dwelling place, Lord of power! My soul hungers and thirsts to see the courts of the Lord, my heart and my flesh delight in the living God . . .' The act of prayer simply arose of its own accord, without any involvement of her reason. She reached the words: 'For one day in Your courts is better than thousands . . .' before she realised that she was reciting the prayer for the transition from the earthly life to the Eternal Dwelling.

The realisation set her trembling. Why had her soul suddenly thrown up the psalm that was prescribed for those standing on the threshold of eternity? But before Pelagia could recite another, less frightening prayer, a man wearing a long robe and carrying a staff turned off the road into the steep little street.

That was all the nun had time to make out, because the next instant the moon was hidden behind a small cloud and it went completely dark. The wayfarer walked by very close, only about five paces away, but the nun still could not tell if he was the one she was waiting for.

She watched him to see if he would turn into the garden.

He did. So it *was* him!

Then the moon escaped from its brief imprisonment and Pelagia was able to see tousled shoulder-length hair and the white robe with a dark belt.

'It is he!' she exclaimed aloud and was about to go rushing after the man who had gone into the park when something absolutely unexpected happened. Someone grabbed hold of her hand and swung her sharply back round. Pelagia and Salakh had been so absorbed in watching the back of the man with the staff that they hadn't noticed someone else creeping up on them.

The man's appearance was terrifying: a fierce face with flat features and a beard, broad shoulders, the butt of a carbine sticking up from behind his back. He had an Arab scarf wound round his head.

The stranger held Salakh by the scruff of the neck with one hand and gripped Pelagia's elbow with the other. 'Who are you people?' he hissed in Russian. 'Why are you hiding? Are you plotting something against *him*?'

As if he had only just noticed that she was a woman, he released her elbow, but seized the Palestinian by the collar with both hands, and so fiercely that he almost lifted him off the ground.

'Russians, we Russians,' Salakh babbled, terrified.

'And what if you are Russians?' the terrifying man growled. 'All sorts of people want to kill *him* – Russians too! Why are you here? Were you lying in wait for *him*. Tell me the truth, or ...' He brandished a massive fist and the poor Palestinian squeezed his eyes tight shut. The mighty hero easily held him suspended with just one huge hand.

Recovering from the initial shock, Pelagia said quickly: 'Yes, we were waiting for Emmanuel. I need to talk to him, I have some important news for him. And you ... who are you? Are you one of the "foundlings"?'

'The "foundlings" are busy saving their own souls,' the bearded man said with gentle derision. 'But I have to save *him*. Never mind about my soul ... Just as long as *he* is alive. And who are you?'

'Sister Pelagia, a nun.'

The reaction to this seemingly inoffensive introduction was unexpected. The stranger flung Salakh to the ground and grabbed hold of the nun's neck.

'A nun! A black raven! Was it him, that walking skeleton, who sent you? It was him, him, who else! Tell me, or I'll rip your throat out!' Pelagia watched numbly as the blade of a knife glittered in front of her face.

'Who is "he"?' the half-strangled woman asked, struggling to understand what was going on.

'Don't give me that, you snake! I mean him – the one in charge of all you black-robed vermin! You all spy for him, all you weasels work for him.'

The one in charge of the black-robed vermin – that is, the head of the order of clergy?

'You mean Chief Procurator Pobedin?'

'Aha!' the bearded man cried triumphantly. 'You confessed! Lie down!' he said, kicking Salakh, who was attempting to sit up. 'I saved Manuila from the old vampire once, and I'll save him again!' His broad mouth spread out into a crooked-toothed smile. 'I expect Kistyantin Petrovich hasn't forgotten the servant of God Trofim Dubenko?'

'Who?' Pelagia asked hoarsely.

'What – didn't he tell you how he falsely accused the holy man of stealing and clapped him in jail? And he put me there to guard him. All those years I served Kistyantin Petrovich like a dog on a chain! And I'd have died as a dog, if I hadn't risen to the dignity of a human being! "Trofimushka," he says to me, "keep an eye on this thief and troublemaker, he's a dangerous man. I don't trust the police guards. Watch him in the station until tomorrow, don't let him do any talking to anyone, and in the morning I'll get a warrant to move him to the Schlisselburg Fortress."'

Pelagia remembered Sergei Sergeevich's story about the gold clock stolen from the Chief Procurator. So this was what really happened! There never was any theft, and Konstantin Petrovich had not magnanimously released the alleged thief – quite the opposite, in fact. The highly intelligent Chief Procurator had perceived some serious danger for himself in the wandering prophet. He had begun by locking him in a cell in a police station and setting his underling to guard him, and then taken measures to shut him away him more securely – Pobedin's resources in this regard were well known.

'You didn't allow Emmanuel to talk to the other guards, but you talked to him yourself, didn't you?' the holy sister said, more as a statement than a question. 'Please let go of me; I'm not your enemy.'

'Yes I spoke to him. In all my life nobody had ever spoken to me like. Kistyantin Petrovich is a great master at the tongue-wagging, but everything he says against Manuila is a load of chaff.'

Trofim Dubenko's fingers were still round the nun's throat, but they were squeezing less tightly now and the hand holding the knife had been lowered.

'And you took the prisoner out of the police cell? But how did you manage that?'

'Simple. At night they only had one man in uniform sitting at the door. I gave him a tap on the back of the neck with my fist and that was that. And then I said to Manuila: I'll go with you to the end of the earth, because you can't take care of yourself. You'll get yourself killed on your own, but you have to live for a long time and talk to people. Only he didn't take me. No need, he said, and I'm not supposed to. I have to go alone. And don't you be afraid for me, he says – God will take care of me. Well, he didn't want to take me, so I didn't try to force him. I didn't go with him, I went *after* him. Wherever he goes, I go. God might protect him and he might not, but Trofim Dubenko certainly won't let him come to any harm. Months and months I've been following Manuila. Across Mother Russia, right across the wide ocean, across the Holy Land. He's one of God's fools – there's no suspicion in him. Would you believe I've followed him almost halfway round the world and he doesn't realise it? Just don't let him see you – that's the whole secret of it. Do you know he walks? He never looks back. Just walks on, waving his stick. Doesn't even look down at his feet. Just straight ahead or up at the sky. And he likes to turn his head to the sides as well, that's true. Like I said – a holy fool.'

Manuila's bodyguard spoke in a voice full of tenderness and admiration, and Pelagia suddenly remembered the 'miracle of the Lord' that Malke had told her about.

'Tell me, was it you who killed the Bedouin bandit in the mountains of Judaea?'

'The one with the sword? That was me. Look, I've got a carbine. I swapped for it in the city of Jaffa. I had this engraved watch – Kistyantin Petrovich gave me it for serving him so well. A curse on that service and on that skeleton and his lousy watch. The bandit was nothing special. Manuila calls down disaster on himself almost every day. If it wasn't for Trofim Dubenko, bad people would have buried him in the ground a long time ago,' the bearded man boasted, then suddenly stopped short. 'Ah, you're a cunning one, you are! Hah, you loosened my tongue. Haven't spoken our language for a long time, so I couldn't stop myself. Tell me: are you from Pobedin or not?' He flourished the knife again.

'No, I'm here on my own account. And I wish Emmanuel . . . Manuila no harm. On the contrary, I want to warn him.'

Trofim Dubenko looked at her intently. He said: 'Come on, then.' And he ran his massive paws all over her, searching to see if she had a concealed weapon.

Pelagia held her hands up and endured it.

'All right,' he said. 'Go. Only on your own. Your friend can stay here. But there's one condition: not a word about me. Or else he'll send me away, and he can't be left without someone to look after him.'

'I promise,' the nun said with a nod.

For a minute or so the garden seemed to be empty again.

Pelagia walked from one end of it to the other, gazing around her without seeing anyone. But when she stopped in bewilderment, she heard a voice from the very centre of the garden, asking something in a language that she did not know.

Then at last she made out the figure sitting in the grass by the old well.

'What?' the nun asked with a shudder.

'Are you Wussian?' the voice asked, with a child-like lisp on the letter 'r'. 'I asked what you're wooking for? Or who?'

'What are you doing there?' she babbled.

The man was sitting absolutely still on the ground, bathed in the white moonlight. It was his stillness that had prevented her from noticing him, although she had walked past him very close.

Approaching him hesitantly, Pelagia saw a thin face with wide-open eyes, a clumpy beard (it seemed to be streaked with grey) a protruding Adam's apple and a pair of eyebrows that seemed to be permanently raised in readiness for joyful amazement. The prophet's hair had been cut in the Russian peasant style, but a long time ago, at least six months, so that the hair had grown and hung almost down to his shoulders.

'I'm waiting,' Manuila–Emmanuel replied. 'The moon's not quite in the middle of the sky yet. That's called "at its zenith". I have to wait a wittle bit.'

'And . . . and what will happen when the moon is at its zenith?'

'I'll get up and go that way.' He pointed to the far corner of the garden.

'But there's a fence over there.'

The prophet glanced round, as if someone might overhear them, and whispered conspiratorially: 'I made a hole in it. When I was here earwier. One plank opens, and then you can go up the hill thwough the monastewy.'

'But why don't you go by the street? It goes up the hill too,' said Pelagia, also lowering her voice.

He sighed. 'I know. I twied; it doesn't work. Probabwy evwy-thing has to be exactwy like it was then. But the main thing is the full moon, of course. I compwetewy forgot about it, but now I've wemembewed, Passover awways used to be at full moon, onwy now the Jews have got evewything confused.'

'What have they got confused?' Pelagia asked, wrinkling up her forehead as she tried to make sense of his words. 'Why do you need the full moon?'

'I can see you came here to speak to me,' Emmanuel said unexpectedly. 'Speak.' Pelagia started. How did he know? But the prophet got to his feet, proving to be a whole head taller than the nun, and looked into her face. There were sparks of moonlight glittering in his eyes.

'You want to warn me about something,' he said, screwing up his eyes as if he was reading aloud in the dark and had to strain to see.

'What?'

'You've been wooking for me for a wong time because you want to warn me about something bad. It would intewesting to talk to you. But it's alweady time for me to go. Come with me, if you wike. We can talk on the way.' He beckoned to her and set off towards the fence.

One of the planks really was secured only by a single nail at the top. Emmanuel swung it aside and squeezed through the narrow gap. Feeling strangely numb, Pelagia did the same.

Moving uphill, they walked through the dark courtyard of some monastery, then out through a wicket gate into a side street. There were Arab shanties on both sides, without a single light burning in any of them. Once, at a bend, the nun glanced back and found herself facing the Temple Hill, crowned by the round cap of the Mosque of Omar. In the moonlight Jerusalem looked as dead as the Jewish cemetery across from it.

Pelagia suddenly realised that she had not introduced herself and said: 'I'm Pelagia, a nun . . .'

'Ah, a bwide of Chwist,' Emmanuel laughed. 'The son of God has so many bwides! More than the Sultan of Turkey. And not one of them ever asked him if he wanted to mawwy them.' The blasphemous joke shattered Pelagia's special, almost mystical mood, created by the moonlit atmosphere in the Garden of Gethsemane.

For a while they walked uphill in silence. It's time I explained everything to him, the nun thought, and she began guardedly and dryly, the quip about the brides of Christ still in her mind.

'I have bad news for you. You are in mortal danger. You have very powerful enemies who wish to kill you and will stop at nothing. Your enemies will not be stopped because you have left Russia—'

'Enmity is a mutual substance,' the leader of the foundlings interrupted her flippantly. 'And since I'm nobody's enemy, I can't have any enemies of my own. That seems weasonable to me. The people you mention are mistaken; they think I can cause them harm. I just need to talk to them, then evewything will be cweared up. I will definitewy talk to them, if it doesn't work again today. And if it does work, I won't be here any more, and they'll cool down.'

'If what works?' asked Pelagia, baffled.

'I could expwain, but you wouldn't bewieve me anyway.'

'Ah, they won't talk to you! They want to see you dead. Your enemies simply kill anyone who gets in their way, without the slightest hesitation! That means that eliminating you is very, very important for them.'

At this point the prophet squinted sideways at Pelagia – not in fright, but with a bemused expression, as if he didn't really understand why she was so very agitated. 'Sh-sh-sh!' he whispered, putting one finger to his lips. 'We're here. And the moon's exactwy at its zenith.' He pushed open a half-rotten gate, and they went into a yard overgrown with dry grass. Pelagia could just make out a shack with a collapsed roof at the back of it.

'Whose house is that?'

'I don't know. No one wesides there any more. I'm afraid some disaster happened here. I can sense these things ...' Emmanuel gave a chill shudder and put his arms round his own shoulders.

Pelagia was not at all interested in the abandoned hovel. She was burning up with frustration and annoyance. She had spent so long searching for this man, and he wouldn't even listen to her!

'Perhaps you think that you're out of danger because you left Russia?' the nun said angrily. 'But that's not so! They'll find you, even here. I think I know where the threat comes from, but it seems so unlikely ... And then, why would he be so furious with you? That is, I have a supposition, but it's not so very—' Pelagia broke off. As she looked at the ludicrous figure of the leader of the foundlings standing on one leg and scratching his ankle with the other foot, the holy sister felt quite ready to admit that her 'supposition' was a monstrous absurdity.

'No, Pobedin is simply insane ...' she muttered.

'What you say is incompwehensible,' Emmanuel said. He put down his staff, lifted a wooden board up off the ground and started scraping away a heap of rubbish, sending branches, potsherds and lumps of earth flying in all directions. 'And you're not tewwing me the most important thing.'

'What most important thing?' Pelagia asked in astonishment as she watched this strange performance.

He tugged some planks out from under the rubbish, exposing a pit, and in the bottom of the pit there was a black hole.

'Is that an underground passage?'

'No, it's a buwiaw chamber. A cave. There are people buwied here who wived a long time ago – two thousand years or even

368

much more than that. Do you know what Eneowithic is? And Chalcowithic?' he asked, pronouncing the high-sounding words with great pomp.

Pelagia had read about ancient Jewish burial sites. The Jerusalem hills were riddled with caves that had once been used for burying the dead. It was not really surprising to find one of these chambers in the yard of an abandoned peasant hovel. But what did Emmanuel want with it?

He struck a match and lit a tightly twisted rag soaked in oil. His bearded face gazed up at Pelagia out of the pit, illuminated by the crimson flame. The night around her instantly seemed blacker.

'It's time for me to go,' Emmanuel said. 'But I can see you want to ask me about something and you don't dare. Don't be afwaid: ask. If I know the answer, I'll tell you the twuth.'

Down there, below me, there's a cave, Pelagia thought, transfixed. *A cave!*

The nun completely forgot that she had sworn never to venture underground again. 'Can I go down there with you? Please!'

He looked up at the moon hanging at the precise centre of the sky. 'If you pwomise you'll come out soon and you won't wait for me outside.'

Pelagia nodded, and he gave her his hand.

At first the passage was very narrow. She felt stone steps under her feet, crumbling with age in places, but not worn at all. How could they possibly have been worn?

When the stairway ended, Emmanuel lifted up the hand holding the rag torch and it became clear that the burial chamber was quite extensive. There were dark niches in the walls, but the light was too dim for her to make them out clearly.

The prophet turned his face to Pelagia and said: 'Have you had a wook? Now ask your question and go.'

Suddenly his eyebrows, which were set very high in any case, lifted even closer to the roots of his hair. Emmanuel was not looking at his companion; he was looking over her head, as if he had suddenly seen something very interesting there.

But Pelagia was not watching where he was looking. Feeling desperately anxious, she took a deep breath, raised one hand to her temple in an involuntary gesture and asked her question.

No matter how the string twists and turns

When the *hantur* reached the Jaffa Gate and turned to the right, Yakov Mikhailovich immediately realised that they were intending to skirt round the wall. In that case, they wouldn't get far; he could send off a telegram to Peter. It was more than a week since he had been in contact – that wasn't good. And the twenty-four four telegraph was right here – that was what had given him the idea.

He worked a veritable miracle of efficiency: it took him only two minutes to thrust the telegram, written in advance, in through the little window and to pay.

The content of the telegram was as follows: 'Will take delivery of both loads today. Nifontov'. That was the code name for him to use until the assignment was completed. When it was completed he could write anything he liked in the telegram, but the signature had to be 'Ksenofontov'. Those it was meant for would understand.

Yakov Mikhailovich (still acting under the name of Nifontov) had managed everything excellently: sent off the message, and caught up with the *hantur* – not far from the gorge that was called Gehenna, that same fiery ravine where, as the holy wrote, 'the worm did not die and the fire did not die down'. The inhabitants of ancient Jerusalem used to throw the bodies of people who had been executed into the ravine and cover them over with excrement, and to prevent the plague creeping out of the cursed pit, fires burned there by day and by night.

There you have it, the whole of human life, Yakov Mikhailovich sighed as he lashed his horse on. We live in a privy and shit on everyone else, and when you croak, they'll pile shit on top of you and set you on fire, so you don't stink. Such were the sombre philosophical thoughts that came to his mind.

It was simply splendid that the moon was full and there weren't many clouds – an exceptional stroke of luck. And he had to admit that this entire mission, so long and troublesome, seemed throughout to have enjoyed a certain Supreme patronage and protection. He could have lost the thread in Jerusalem, and beside Mount Megiddo, and in Sodom; but every time diligence and luck had seen him through. Yakov Mikhailovich himself had not set a foot wrong, and God had not forgotten about him either.

Now there was almost nothing left to do. If Ginger had figured right (and she was a smart woman), then we ought to get everything settled up today, and then we'd change our name from the fumbling Nifontov to the triumphant Ksenofontov.

What might the reward be for such a tough assignment? he wondered.

He didn't usually allow himself to dwell on such pleasant matters until the job was done, but the moonlit evening had put him in a pensive mood. And the end was very close now – Yakov Mikhailovich could sense that in his gut.

That certain *little business* would be completely forgotten, and all the relevant documentation held by the investigator would be destroyed – that had been promised unconditionally. He had served his time, wiped the slate clean. He wouldn't have that Sword of Damocles hanging over his head any longer. Today dost Thou release, O Lord. But he could probably ask for something over and above that, a little something for himself in the form of a few crisp pieces of paper that rustled pleasantly in the fingers. His intuition told him that they were certain to pay him a bonus. His bosses had really been infuriated with this Manuila. He must have done something special to get them so fired up. God knows what, but it's none of our business.

He tried to figure out how much money they might give him and what he ought to do with it. Buy himself a little house somewhere on the Okhta? Or should he invest it in interest-bearing bonds? And it was too early to retire. Now that the *little business* would be completely forgotten, he could work for the pleasure of it – meaning for proper compensation. If they got stingy, then he could always show them the door. A high-class specialist in delicate matters would never be short of clients. For instance, if he charged for his efforts in Palestine at the full rate, including all that sailing across the sea, roaming around in the desert and other adventures – how much could he take them for then?

The zeroes began crowding into Yakov Mikhailovich's brain, but before they could arrange themselves into a single long row, the nun's *hantur* turned off the wide road, crossed a bridge and disappeared into a narrow side street.

He had to get a bit closer.

Once again Yakov Mikhailovich didn't put a foot wrong – he didn't go barging into the side street, but drove on a bit further along the road. He guessed that this was the end of the horse-drawn excursion and all further movements would be on foot.

He jumped down on to the ground and slapped the mare from Bet-Kebir on the crupper: Off you go now, equinus, wherever your fancy takes you. Thanks for your help, you're no longer needed.

He took a cautious peep round the corner.

The Arab was standing with the horses; the nun wasn't there. But a minute or two later she appeared too, coming out of a small gate and heading towards that Salakh of hers. They exchanged a few words about something, went down the slope and put the *hantur* in a shadow where it was almost invisible.

Aha, Yakov Mikhailovich twigged. Now this looks like an ambush!

Come on now, come on now. His hand was itching – he really needed to crack his joints, but he couldn't afford to make a sound right now.

He spotted the wayfarer before the other two did. The tall, gaunt man was walking along the moonlit roadway, tapping with his staff.

It's him, Yakov Mikhailovich realised, and that very moment he was transformed from Nifontov into Ksenofontov. Now everything that still had to happen was a purely technical matter – in other words, no problem at all.

He pressed back against the fence, waiting for Manuila to turn into the side street.

But then another circumstance emerged, one that could really only be categorised as an unpleasant surprise. There was someone stealthily pursuing the main mark, at a distance of about fifty paces. Unfortunately the moon hid behind a cloud, so he couldn't get a good look at this second individual straight away. All he could see was that he was a real bear of a man and he walked like a bear too, waddling along without a sound.

So what kind of news was this? A competitor?

Yakov Mikhailovich could creep along just as quietly as the Bear. He fell in behind him and inched along close to the wall.

He couldn't hear what Ginger and the Bear talked about, but

it was a heated conversation. The Arab and the nun both came in for rough treatment. But then all they seemed to come to some understanding. Ginger slipped away through a small gate, while the hulk stayed with the driver and the two of them talked about something or other.

Yakov Mikhailovich crept a bit closer. They were talking Russian! Would you believe it!

'He'd be done for without someone to protect him,' said a muffled voice. 'He's just like a little child! How can you let someone like that wander around on his own?'

'I guard too,' the Arab replied grandly. 'I take care of her. Woman! Without me she done for a hundred times.'

'That's for sure. A woman's a woman,' the Bear agreed.

Ah, so that's who we are. Yakov Mihailovich had not been informed that Manuila had a bodyguard, and that made him feel a little offended with his bosses. This is no joking matter, gentlemen, you ought to warn me.

He crept right up close and huddled right down. The technical problem was more complicated than he had thought at first. He peered into the darkness, trying to assess his opponent's strength.

The opponent looked very strong and rather dangerous. Yakov Mikhailovich was well acquainted with this solid, thickset breed; you couldn't put them away with a single blow – they had too much life in them. And you had to deal with this one precisely, without making any noise.

The Arab didn't need to be taken into account. A feeble kind of man, a bit of a coward – all you had to do was hiss at him. During his wanderings Yakov Mikhailovich had grown quite accustomed to this Salakh. You might even say he had grown attached to him. So cheerful, with that white-toothed smile always stretching right back to his ears. When they stopped and camped for the night, Yakov Mikhailovich had sometimes crept closer to the *hantur* in order to hear the Arab singing his songs.

He had decided in advance that he wouldn't do away with Salakh. He felt sorry for him. Of course, if the job required it, he would polish him off without even thinking about it. But the science of psychology said that this trembling hare would never snitch, and Yakov Mikhailovich had a great respect for psychology.

The only thing he needed from the Arab was for him not to yell. But that was already tricky enough. That was the question. A problem with two unknowns: how to shut the Arab's mouth and fell this big Bruin at the same time – naturally, without making a sound. He thought hard for half a minute and came up with the answer.

He backed away to the corner. On the road there he picked up a stick – it looked like a spoke from a large wagon wheel, one and a half arshins long. The end had split, so it had been thrown away. Just the job.

Yakov Mikhailovich limped back into the side street, with his shoulders rounded, muttering something incomprehensible to himself. He barely crept along, leaning on the stick. Who would ever be scared of a cripple like that?

But even so, Bruin and the Arab turned and looked suspiciously at this wanderer in the night.

Yakov Mikhailovich hobbled closer and pretended that he had only just noticed them. He gasped in fright, as if to say: I hope these are not wicked people!

He limped right up close to them and bowed, supporting himself on the stick with his left hand and pressing his right hand to his heart and his forehead in the appropriate manner.

He spoke to the Arab in a squeaky, pitiful voice: '*Djamal li vallakhi ibn khurtum?*'

He himself had no idea what he was asking about, because the words meant absolutely nothing; they were simply meant to sound like Arabic to the great Russian Bear.

Hearing this gibberish, the massive man let his shoulders slump – he didn't see any threat or danger in this local invalid wandering in the night.

But Salakh was astounded by the nonsense. '*Eish?*'

Yakov Mikhailovich bowed to him again, slowly, and then sprang erect briskly and hit the Arab with his knuckles under the base of the nose – crunch! He struck hard, but not too hard, otherwise the nose bone would penetrate the brain and the man would be done for.

The blood spurted out of Salakh's nose in a fountain and he fell flat on his back, out cold. Silently, without a single sound, just the way it should be.

Without halting his corkscrew movement for a moment, Yakov Mikhailovich turned to face the Bear.

The Russian's jaw was still dropping. Mother Nature had endowed the Bruins with heroic stature, but they were a little slow on the uptake – the scientific term for it was retarded reactions. But that was only for the first split second, so it was best not to rely too much on their retardation. Once, during his days in settled exile, after the hard labour, Yakov Mikhailovich had seen a bear catching fish by the river. A fisherman with a spear was no match at all. You couldn't afford to dawdle with a Bruin. He wouldn't give you time to sneeze.

But Yakov Mikhailovich didn't dawdle. He thrust the end of the stick into that mouth hanging wide open in astonishment – drove it in so hard that he could hear the teeth crunch. That was so he wouldn't yell.

In his left hand Yakov Mikhailovich had a handy little knife, Finnish-made, with a special spring mechanism. He clicked out the blade and struck, not at the heart, because a stab to the heart wouldn't settle a big brute like this, and not at the throat, because he would just bubble and gurgle. He struck at the ileum, the point in the belly where a shout is born.

He did the job and jumped back five paces, to avoid the death grip of those massive outstretched arms.

Bruin pulled the stick out of his mouth and blood gushed out over his beard.

He opened his mouth, but he couldn't shout – the blade stuck in his ileum wouldn't let him. Then what was supposed to happen happened. The Bear finished himself off. Every hunter knows that a bear stuck with a fork will pull it out of himself and open up the wound. And this Bear did the same. If he'd left the knife sticking into him, then his life wouldn't have drained away so quickly. But the great fool grabbed hold of the handle, grunted and tugged it out. Then he came at Yakov Mikhailovich, swaying on his feet as he moved. Yakov Mikhailovich took a step backwards, a second, a third, and that was all that was needed. The Bruin's legs folded underneath him and he collapsed on to his knees. He knelt there, swaying backwards and forwards, as if he was praying to his bear god – and then fell flat on his face.

Ooph!

Meanwhile the Arab had come round. He was trying to lift

himself up on one elbow, feeling at his smashed and bloody nose with his hand, sniffing.

Yakov Mikhailovich, feeling mellow after a job so well done, leaned down over him and told him in a quiet voice: 'I'm going to go and kill the other two now. How about you – do you want to live?'

Salakh nodded, and the whites of his goggling eyes glowed in the dark.

'Live, then, I don't mind,' Yakov Mikhailovich said magnanimously. 'Clear out while the going's good. And not a word to a soul. Understand?'

The Arab quickly scrambled up on to his hands and knees.

'Come on, then,' the magnanimous man said, slapping him on the shoulder.

'She my bride!' the Arab suddenly said.

'What?' Yakov Mikhailovich thought he must have misheard.

But the Arab whined quietly and hugged his benefactor round the knees, trying to knock him over. It was so absolutely unexpected that Yakov Mikhailovich very nearly did go tumbling to the ground.

So he had been mistaken about the man. The psychological definition had been inaccurate. If he was such a great hero, he would have done better to yell at the top of his voice – that might really have caused a problem; but what good was a grab round the knees?

Yakov Mikhailovich punched the ungrateful fool on the top of his head, and when the Arab slumped over and buried his nose in the ground, he stamped on his neck just below the back of his head, and there was a loud crunch.

He made himself a promise for the future: no more charitable psychology. He was no Dr Gaaz.

The gate led into a kind of waste lot with a few crooked trees growing in it. Whose stupid idea was that, to waste a good fence on closing off such a useless piece of land?

Yakov Mikhailovich could see straight away that there was no one there, but he wasn't discouraged. He ran round the edge, looking for another way out. He didn't find another gate or a door, but he did find a plank that had been moved aside. This had to be where the little darlings had climbed through – there wasn't anywhere else.

He ran through the monastery courtyard and found himself on a little street that ran up the hill. He dropped down and pressed his ear to the ground.

The sound of steps was coming from the right. He dashed after it.

There they were, the precious sweethearts. A tall shadow – that was Manuila, and the other one beside him was a woman, with her hem brushing the ground.

And here am I, my dear marks, your Ksenofontor.

His hand drew the revolver out of his pocket . . . No point in getting too fancy, this was an ideal spot – not a soul around, not a single light. And there was no need to take too much care. Who was going to launch an investigation round here?

Catch up with them, bang! in the back of his head, and then hers. Then one more time, just to make sure. Yet Yakov Mikhailovich did not hurry. Firstly, this long moment was beautiful, as the great writer put it. And secondly, he suddenly felt curious about where they were climbing to. What were they after on the top of the Mount of Olives?

The prophet and the nun turned into some kind of yard. Watching through the fence, Yakov Mikhailovich saw Manuila rake away the heap of rubbish, and he started getting excited: could it be buried treasure? He actually broke into a sweat at the thought.

Then the Scatty and Ginger went down into the pit.

Very kind of you, Yakov Mikhailovich thought approvingly. Just cover over the pit with rubbish afterwards, and everything's tied up very neatly.

He went down into the hole, following the light burning inside it. He had his gun at the ready.

Manuila spotted Yakov Mikhailovich emerging from the darkness and stared at him over Ginger's shoulder. But the nun just carried on standing with her back to him, the same as before.

She ran her fingers nervously below her ear and asked in a trembling voice: 'Were you . . . *there*?'

PART THREE

There

XVI

The Gospel according to Pelagia

A letter from the next world

Notification arrived first by telegram, and then the letter came.

The official message, sent to the chancellery of the Governor of Zavolzhie from the Ministry of Justice stated with true telegraphic laconicism that Full State Counsellor Berdichevsky had died suddenly of a heart attack in St Petersburg.

For a brief moment there remained a faint hope that this was a misunderstanding, for Matvei Bentsionovich was only a state counsellor, and not yet 'full'; but the first telegram was followed by a second, which said that the body had been forwarded on such-and-such a train at state expense and would arrive at the railway station nearest to Zavolzhsk at such-and-such a time.

Well there were groans of horror and dismay, and many people even cried, because the deceased had had a great many well-wishers in Zavolzhsk, not to mention his extensive family.

Marya Gavrilovna, who did not cry, but simply repeated over and over again: 'No, it's not true, no, no, no!' and shook her head like a clockwork doll, was given the very best doctor to care for her. The Governor's wife took the orphans into her temporary care and the town began preparing for the formal reception of the body and the even more formal farewell to it.

His Eminence Mitrofanii seemed numbed by grief. At first, like the widow, he was not granted the release of tears by the Lord. The Bishop strode around his study with his hands clasped behind his back, the knuckles white from being grasped so tight. Any servants who peered in through crack in the door immediately backed away at the sight of the expression on his face. The grief-stricken prelate strode on for half the night, and just before dawn he sat down at his desk, laid his head on his crossed hands and finally broke into sobs. It was the right time, dark and desolate, so there was no one to see this weakness of his.

In the morning His Eminence felt unwell. He gasped for breath and clutched at his heart. They were frightened that he might suffer the same fate as his favourite godson: a ruptured cardiac muscle. His secretary, Father Userdov, went running to consult the vicar on whether they ought to administer the last sacraments, but that evening a letter arrived from the steamer, and when Miotrofanii read it he stopped panting for breath, sat up on the bed and put his feet down on the floor.

He read it again. And then again.

The crooked scrawl on the envelope, full of mistakes, said: 'To Bishop Mitrofanii, City of Zavolsk in Zavolzhie provins, urjent, for him to reed and no one els'. Inside there was a crumpled sheet of paper with Berdichevsky's handwriting on it: '48-36, send this note by post, at the extra-urgent rate, to: His Eminence Bishop Mitrofanii, Zvolzhsk, Zavolzhie province, for personal delivery.' What the meaning of this mysterious missive could be, why it was traced out in capital letters, and what the figures '48-36' meant Mitrofanii did not understand, but it was clear that the message was of extreme import and might possibly contain the key to the disaster in St Petersburg.

The Bishop studied the uninformative note so intently that he didn't immediately realise that he should turn the sheet of paper over.

When he did, there was the actual message – not written in capitals but in feverish, higgledy-piggledy running script:

The letters are jumping about I'm writing this in a cab. It's a good thing it's raining – I've put up the top and no one can see, Pelagia is in danger. Save her. I know who the culprit is, but you must not know, and do not try to find out. Go to her and take her as far away as possible, to the ends of the Earth. I myself will not be able to do any more. They are following me and of course they will keep following me. Let them. I have thought up an excellent manoeuvre – 'The Berdichevsky Étude' – to sacrifice one figure in the hope of saving a hopeless game.

I do not ask anything for my family. I know you will not abandon them. Goodbye.

Your son Matvei.

This time one reading was enough for the Bishop. He did not construct any hypotheses or try to analyse the meaning of this rather incomprehensible letter, but accepted it as a clear and direct instruction to act. The former cavalry officer awoke within His Eminence: when the bugle is sounding charge and the sabre-slashing has begun, there is no time to think? – you have to follow your instincts and the wild rush of your blood.

The Bishop's weakness had disappeared as if by magic. He leapt off the bed and roared for the lay servants and his secretary.

A minute later the episcopal residence had been transformed into a newly active volcano. One servant was already galloping off to the quayside to book a steam launch to Nizhni. Another was running pell-mell to the telegraph office to book a railway ticket from Nizhni to Odessa and a cabin in a fast maritime steamship. A third had been despatched to the Governor with a hastily written note in which Mitrofanii informed him that he had to leave urgently and the vicar would conduct Berdichevsky's funeral. God only knew what His Excellency and the whole of Zavolzhsk society would think, but that did not concern His Excellency in the least.

Having issued the instructions indicated above, the Bishop began dressing and packing hastily for a journey. But Userdov, choosing a moment when Mitrofanii had withdrawn into the dressing room, gave rein to his irrepressible curiosity and snaffled the letter that had effected such a miraculous change in the Bishop off the desk. Father Serafim was extremely interested in this note from a dead man – so interested, in fact, that he actually decided to make a copy for himself in his notebook. Absorbed in this occupation, the Bishop's secretary did not hear His Eminence, already wearing his travelling cassock and stockings but not yet his shoes, come back into the study.

When Userdov realised that he had been discovered, his face contorted in a pale grimace of terror. He backed away from the Bishop, who was silently advancing on him, and shook his head, but was unable to utter a single word.

'Ah, so that's it,' Mitrofanii drawled ominously. 'Matiusha and I used to rack our brains, wondering how all our secrets were known to our enemies, and all the time it was you, you Judas. It was you who reported about the boot print, and about Palestine. Who is your master? Well!'

The Bishop barked out that 'Well!' so fiercely that the chandelier started jangling and the secretary went down on his knees with a thud. At that moment his remarkably handsome face was not at its best.

'Tell me, you vile creature!'

The secretary jabbed one finger up towards the ceiling without speaking.

'Higher authorities? Out of careerist considerations? I know you want to be a bishop – that's why you haven't married. Who do you report to? The Okhranka? The Synod?'

His Eminence grabbed the trembling Userdov by the scruff of the neck. The secretary squeezed his eyes tight shut and would certainly have given away his secret, but Mitrofanii opened his fingers.

'Very well. Matiusha told me not to try to find out, so I won't. He has the brains of a minister of state – he wouldn't forbid me for no reason. And this is my final pastor's blessing for you in parting.'

He took a short swing – exactly as he used to do many years ago during the Junkers' brawls, and smashed Father Serafim in the face, not in any merely symbolic sense but in a most convincing manner, so that the secretary's nose crunched and shifted sideways.

The poor wretch tumbled backwards on to the carpet, with blood streaming from his face.

He'll be a bishop all right, Mitrofanii thought fleetingly as he walked towards the door. He definitely will. But with a crooked nose.

In the hallway a lay servant was waiting with a hastily packed suitcase. His Eminence crossed himself with broad sweeps of the hand in front of the icon hanging opposite the entrance door – an image of his favourite saint, the apostle, Judas Thaddaus, comforter of the despairing and patron of hopeless causes. He took his mitre and wide-brimmed travelling hat and ran out into the courtyard, where a team of four was already champing at the bit.

It was less than half an hour since the letter had arrived.

The bishop reads another letter and has two dreams

Two days later, before boarding the steamship in Odessa, Mitrofanii sent off a telegram to the father archimandrite at the mission in Jerusalem, enquiring whether His Reverence had any knowledge of the whereabouts and health of the pilgrim Lisitsyna.

The reply arrived in time to catch him. The archimandrite said that a pilgrim by that name had stayed at the hotel, but she had left eight days earlier for an unknown destination and had not since returned, although her things were still in her room.

Mitrofanii ground his teeth, but forbade himself to despair.

Throughout the five days of the sailing to Jaffa, he prayed. Never before, it seemed, had he devoted himself to this activity for such a long period of time, with almost no respite.

The pilgrims crowded round the window of his cabin, gaping respectfully at the Bishop bowing repeatedly to the floor. They even agreed among themselves not to pester the holy man with requests for blessings – let him bless all of them at once, before they went ashore.

Eight days after leaving Zavolzhsk, His Eminence was in the Orthodox Mission in Jerusalem. He went straight to the chancellery, to enquire whether his spiritual daughter had returned yet.

'Why, yes', they told him, 'the very day after we received Your Eminence's enquiry. We sent another telegram to Odessa immediately, but obviously it missed you.'

'Thank you, Lord! Where is Pelagia?' Mitrofanii exclaimed, so relieved that his legs almost buckled under him. 'Is she safe and well?'

'We can't say', they replied. 'None of our people have actually seen her. But last Saturday the messenger boy from Mrs Lisitsyna's hotel arrived with a delivery for Your Eminence. The next day the father archimandrite had sent a message to the guest, saying that Bishop Mitrofanii was concerned about her welfare, but Lisitsyna was not in her room. And since then they had not been able to find her in even once, despite trying many times.'

Realising that there was nothing to be achieved here, the Bishop, citing weariness after his long journey, withdrew to the chambers reserved for especially distinguished guests. Without even taking off his hat he sat down at the table and opened the envelope with trembling fingers.

He saw an entire stack of sheets of paper covered with familiar handwriting. In his agitation he dropped his pince-nez and broke the right lens. He read the letter through the crucifix of the cracks.

To His Eminence Mitrofanii, light, strength and joy.

I hope that you will never read this letter. Or do I really hope that you will? I do not know; but if you do read it, that will mean that everything was true, and that is absolutely impossible.

I have begun badly and only confused you. Forgive me.

And forgive me also for my deception, for exploiting your trust. You sent me on a distant pilgrimage, wishing to protect me from danger, but I concealed the reason why I chose the Holy Land of all possible places. I did not set out to Palestine for the sake of peace and quiet, but in order to see something that I had started through to the end. You spoke the truth when you said that I do not have the nun's talent of praying to God for people. Of all Christ's brides I am the most wayward. But I shall write about brides at the end; now is not the right moment.

As you recall, they tried to kill me three times: once in Stroganovka and twice in Zavolzhsk. And when I thought about this, it became clear that such powerful killers coud not possibly find me so abhorrent in my own right. There was no possible reason. So the reason did not lie in me. In what then? Or in whom?

How did it all begin? With the killing of a certain sham prophet – and the subsequent events were also connected in one way or another with the ill-famed Manuila. I did not understand what sort of man he was, although I had seen that some people wished to kill him, and others to protect him, and that the former were more powerful and sooner or later they would achieve their goal. As for my place in this business, I was like the unfortunate Durka: I had simply been in the wrong place at the wrong time and somehow got in their way. So they decided to remove me, as one removes a stone from the road, in order not to stumble over it again. That was the only reason I could be of any interest to the enemies of Manuila.

As you know, I have investigated murders on numerous occasions, but surely it is a hundred times more important *to prevent a murder from happening*? And if you think that this is within your power, surely it is a mortal sin to do nothing? If I have lied to you by default it was only out of fear that if you knew the whole truth, you would never have let me go.

And there was another reason, apart from saving Emmanuel (I prefer to call him that now). He and I are connected by the remarkable event that occurred in the cave, of which you already know – an event for which I was unable to find any explanation, and which I could not get out of my mind. Emmanuel had been in the same cave – indeed, according to the village people, *that was where he came from.* So I thought that perhaps he might explain this mystery to me.

Two things were clear.

In the first place this prophet or false prophet (that was not for me to judge) had to be sought in the Holy Land. He was either there already or would arrive there some time very soon – the 'foundlings' talked about that, and it was no accident that Shelukhin, the pseudo-Emmanuel, was on his way to Palestine.

And, in the second place, Emmanuel's enemies had to be sought among those who travelled on the steamer *Sturgeon* with us. (Let me say straight away that this conclusion proved not to be entirely correct, but I only realised that after travelling round Judaea, Samaria, Galilee and Edom.)

My list of suspects was assembled as follows.

Who could the former gendarme Ratsevich have been working for? I wondered.

The 'Warsaw bandits' that Matvei Bentsionovich mentioned were excluded. Even the most fastidious of robbers would not have tried to eliminate me so ingeniously and persistently. And the idea that some mere preacher could have caused them such great inconvenience was even more incredible.

But to the misanthropic lunatics who call themselves the

'Oprichniks of Christ' might well see a preacher who led people away from the Orthodox faith into 'Yiddishness' as a fierce and dangerous enemy.

The same also applied to the opposite camp – the fanatical supporters of an insular Judaism, who regarded Emmanuel as an evil jester who mocked their faith.

Also on the steamer was a group of Zionists, extremely determined young people who suspected Emmanuel of being connected with the Department of Security, the Okhranka. It is well known that the supporters of the idea of a Jewish state include some fanatics who are willing to go to extremes in order to achieve their goal as soon as possible.

Subsequently, when I was already here in Palestine, I also developed another theory, but I will not acquaint you with it, in order not to confuse you, especially since, like the preceding ones, it proved to be incorrect.

On the basis of my list of suspects, I devised a plan of action and set about implementing it immediately on disembarkation from the ship. I was driven on by the fear that Emmanuel's powerful enemies would find him first and I would be too late.

First of all I went to Jerusalem ...

The Bishop read about how Pelagia had tested and discarded her theories one by one, while at the same time constantly drawing closer to the restless prophet, who would simply not stay in one place.

Something strange was happening to Mitrofanii. From the very beginning he had been in a state of extreme agitation, and with every page it grew more intense. The trembling of his hands grew ever more powerful, so that eventually he was obliged to lay the sheets of paper on the table and weigh them down with his spectacle case. The sweat was streaming down His Eminence's face, but he did not notice it. He merely took off his hat absent-mindedly and put it beside him. But when he accidentally knocked it on to the floor with his elbow, he did not notice that either.

Eventually the nervous stress reached its extreme limit and was transformed into its opposite. The Bishop's head began spinning and he felt an irresistible urge to sleep.

Many years earlier, at the Battle of Balaclava, the future bishop, then a cavalry squadron commander, had seen the general commanding the Russian forces fall asleep at the observation point. The general was sitting at a folding table, concentrating intensely as he looked through a telescope and gave orders, and suddenly, at the very height of the battle, he nodded off – simply lowered his head on to his folded arms and fell asleep. Frightened adjutants went dashing across to him, but the chief of staff, an old and experienced solder said: 'Leave him alone, it will soon pass.' And indeed, five minutes later the general woke up in good form and carried on directing the battle as if nothing at all had happened.

The same thing happened to Mitrofanii now. The lines of writing unwound into a single long, knotty thread, and the thread led the Bishop down into darkness. One moment he was reading, and the next his head drooped over the table, his right cheek sank down on to his folded elbows and he instantly fell into a deep sleep.

His Eminence had two dreams, one after the other.

The first dream was a sweet one.

Mitrofanii saw the Lord God before him in the shape of a radiant cloud, and the cloud spoke to him in a ringing voice: 'What good to me are your sombre prayers, Bishop? What good are monasticism and monks to Me? They are mere foolishness and aggravation. Love each other, my people, husband love wife and wife love husband, and I shall ask no better prayer from you.'

And immediately Mitrofanii found himself in a house. The house was on the shore of a lake and in the distance he could see mountains, blue at the bottom and white at the top. The sun was shining, there were heavy apples hanging on the branches of the trees in the garden, and a gentle woman's voice was singing a lullaby. Mitrofanii looked round and saw a child's bed, and Pelagia was sitting beside it, but not in her habit and wimple – she was wearing a morning dress, and her bronze-coloured hair was hanging loose down to her shoulders. Pelagia glanced at Mitrofanii and smiled affectionately, and he thought: All these years I have wasted. If only the Cloud had spoken to me earlier, when I was younger! But never mind, I am still strong, we will be happy for a long time yet.

The he turned over from his right cheek on to his left, and that started a quite different dream.

It was as if he had woken up and carried on reading his spiritual daughter's letter, although in fact he had not woken up at all. At first he read with his eyes and then, instead of reading, he seemed to be listening, and Pelagia herself took the place of the sheet of paper in front of him.

'I am no longer among the living,' her voice whispered. 'You will see me no more on the Earth, because now I dwell in Eternal Life. Ah, how good everything is here! If only you, the living, knew this, you would not be afraid of death at all; you would look forward to death with joy, as a child looks forward to Christmas or his birthday. God is nothing like the Church's teachings about him: he is kind and understands absolutely everything. You foolish people pity us and weep for us, but we pity you. You suffer so very much – you are so afraid of everything.'

Now the sleeper could not only hear Pelagia's voice, but see her too. She was surrounded with a radiant glow – not as bright as the God-Cloud, but a shimmering rainbow that was a delight to the eye. 'What must I do?' Mitrofanii cried eagerly. 'I want to come to you! If I must die, I will do so gladly – that is nothing. Only take me to you!' She laughed quietly, like a mother laughing at a little child's babbling: 'What a great hurry you are in. Live for as long as you are destined, and do not be afraid: I will wait. For after all where I am there is no time.'

These words comforted the Bishop, and he woke. He rubbed his eyes and put on the pince-nez that had fallen off his nose. He carried on reading.

The red rooster

'...were you there?' I asked Emmanuel, and was about to add, 'in that cave', but just at that moment there was a rustling sound behind me. I turned round and saw a man standing there. He was dressed as an Arab and for a second I thought he was one of the local people who had happened to see us go down into the burial chamber. But the stranger's round, thick-lipped face broke into a mocking smile and he said in perfect Russian: 'Now then, what have you got here, my little babes in the wood? Treasure? That's for me, if you please. You won't have any more use for it.'

'What treasure?' I babbled, and suddenly noticed that he had something in his hand – something black, with a dull gleam.

I realised that this was the very thing I had been so afraid of. I was too late. They had found him, and now they would kill him. Strangely enough, at that moment I didn't think at all that they would kill me, I felt so annoyed with myself. All those days I had wasted, although I felt, I knew, that precious time was passing!

Then the round-faced killer struck another blow at my self-esteem. 'Thank you, sister, you have a nose like a bloodhound. You led the hunter straight to the prey.' When he said that, I felt really terrible. So they had found Emmanuel thanks to me! I was to blame for everything! And worst of all, at that appalling moment I behaved shamefully, just like a woman: I burst into tears. I was completely crushed by the pain and shame of it all; I felt like the most pitiful creature in the entire world.

'What, no treasure? That's a pity. But I'm still glad to meet you like this. Extremely glad,' the villain joked. 'I'd love to banter a bit more with you, but there's a job to be done.' And he raised his gun, about to shoot; but Emmanuel suddenly shoved me aside and took a step towards the killer.

'You earn money by killing people? Is that your trade?' he asked without a trace of anger or condemnation – his tone sounded more like curiosity or joyful amazement to me.

'At your service,' said the round-faced man, bowing as if he were accepting a well-deserved compliment. He clearly felt completely in control of the situation and had no objection to deferring the execution of his evil intent for a little longer.

'How good that we have met like this!' Emmanuel exclaimed. 'You are the man I need!' He took another step forward and threw his arms open wide, as if he was about to embrace the murderer.

The round-faced man stepped back and lifted the gun barrel higher, so that it was aimed directly at the prophet's forehead. The expression on his face changed from mockery to wary suspicion.

'Ah-ah ...' he began, but Emmanuel interrupted him.

'I need you, and you need me! I came to see you, for you!'

'In what sense?' the killer asked, completely baffled.

I waited, terrified, quite certain that he would shoot now, this very moment. But Emmanuel did not even look at the gun; I do not think that he was afraid at all. Now, with hindsight, I realise what an absolutely incredible sight it was: an unarmed man stepping towards a man with a gun, and the armed man backing away with tiny little steps.

'There is no one in the world more unhappy than you. Your soul is crying out for help because the Devil has completely crushed the God in it. The good in the soul – that is God; and the bad is the Devil. Surely you were told that when you were a child?'

'Ah,' said the killer, baring his teeth in a scowl. 'So that's it. A sermon. Well, you've got the wrong man there ...'

I heard the click of the hammer being raised and cried out in terror.

Emmanuel turned to me and spoke as if everything was quite normal: 'Watch, now I'll show you his child's face.'

I did not understand what he meant. Neither did the assassin.

'What are you going to show her?' he asked. He lowered the gun slightly and his small eyes blinked in confusion.

'Your child's face,' the prophet said enthusiastically. 'You know, at any age every man still has his first face, the one with which he came into the world. Only this face is hard to see. Well, how can I explain it to you? Two old school friends, who haven't seen each other for thirty or even fifty years, meet by chance. They look at each other, they recognise each other, they call each other by their old funny nicknames. For an instant their old faces become the same as they were many years before. The child's face is the most genuine one. It doesn't go anywhere; over the years it is hidden under wrinkles, creases, beards ...'

'Any other time I'd be glad to chat with such an interesting talker,' the murderer said, gathering his wits and interrupting Emmanuel. 'But now turn around.'

I realised that something had happened to this terrible man. He was no longer able to shoot the prophet while looking him in the eye. And in my mind I cried out to Emmanuel: 'Don't stop, keep talking!'

But he did stop. He slowly raised his hand with the palm outwards, moved it from left to right, and a miracle happened.

The killer suddenly froze, the hand holding the pistol sank down and his gaze followed the hand, spellbound.

I have read about hypnosis and I do not think it is miraculous, but this was a genuine miracle that took place before my very eyes. The man's face began to change. The puffy cheeks became tauter, the nose became a little more pert, the wrinkles smoothed out, and I saw the face of a boy – the round, funny, trusting face of a seven-year-old mummy's boy with a sweet tooth.

'Yasha, Yashechka, what have you done to yourself?' Emmanuel asked in a high voice, like a woman's.

A tremor ran across the killer's face, and the strange vision disappeared. There once again was the face of a man who had lived a hard and sinful life, but the eyes remained wide open, like a child's.

He waved at Emmanuel with the hand still holding the gun. He waved the other hand too, as if he was trying to drive away some ghost or phantom. Then he turned round and dashed headlong out of the tomb.

'Won't he come back to kill you?' I asked, shaken by what I had seen.

'No,' Emmanuel replied. 'He will be too busy with other things now to bother about us.'

'How do you know his name?' I asked. 'Is he really called Yasha?'

'That was what I heard. When I look into a man's face, I hear and see many things, because I am ready to hear and see. He is a very interesting man. Absolutely black, but still with a white spot. Everybody always has at least a tiny little white speck.

And it's the same with those who are the whitest of white: only a tiny drop of black, but it's still there. That's more advantageous for God.'

That was what he said – 'advantageous'.

I am not able to convey his distinctive manner of expressing himself and so I smooth it out, but Emmanuel's speech is extremely colourful. In the first place, he lisps in a very funny way. He speaks smoothly, but he likes to put in bookish words at appropriate and inappropriate points – you know, like a self-taught peasant, who devours books one after another and understands what he has read after his own fashion.

For a few minutes after the terrible man ran away I was not myself and I babbled all sorts of womanish nonsense. For instance, I asked him: 'Weren't you afraid to walk towards a gun like that?'

His answer was funny: 'I'm used to it. Such is my occupation, talking to the *misérables*.'

Strangely enough, I understood him perfectly well. He must have come across the French word *misérables* in some eighteenth-century book and been captivated by its lovely sound.

'Good people do not need me,' he said, 'but bad people (*misérables*) do. They're dangerous and they can hurt you, but what's to be done about that? You go in to them like a lion-tamer entering the lion's cage.' And then Emmanuel's eyes suddenly lit up. 'I saw that in Perm, in the Ciniselli Circus. What a brave man the lion-tamer is! The lion opens its jaws wide, its teeth are like knives, but the lion-tamer just twirls his moustache and cracks his whip!'

He forgot all about the *misérables* and started excitedly telling me about an animal-trainer in a circus, and as I looked at him I did not know what to think; I was overcome by doubt once again.

Now that I have told you how Emmanuel dealt with the murderer, and you have understood that he is a truly exceptional man, the time has come to broach a subject that I have avoided so far, in order not to provoke your indignation.

You remember that when I was telling you about my trip to

Sodom, I wrote: 'As soon as heard I the words "Friday" and "garden" together, everything fell into place.' I realised where and when I would find Emmanuel. My hypothesis proved correct.

Well then, now I will tell you this hypothesis, which is so absurd that I only dare to state it now.

One moment. One moment. Let me gather my courage.

Very well.

WHAT IF THIS IS THE SECOND COMING?

I can just see your bushy eyebrows raised in anger, and so I hasten to correct myself.

No, of course I did not think that the 'prophet Manuila' was Jesus, sent to man again after two thousand years. But what if this individual genuinely believed that he was Christ.

His entire way of life, all his words and deeds, his very name (you remember, of course, that the Saviour's given name was Emmanuel) prompted this thought. Not a preacher inspired by the truth of Jesus, but a man who *felt himself to be the Messiah* and therefore reshaped the laws and basic principles of Christianity in the same way as Jesus would have done, for He is His own maker and transformer of laws.

During the days spent wandering round the Holy Land I grew so accustomed to this fantastic hypothesis, that there were times when a blasphemous thought would creep into my mind: What if he really *is* Jesus?

Where had he come from this 'wild Tartar'? How was it possible for a peasant from Vyatka or Zavolzhie to know ancient Greek and Aramaic?

Completely confusing reality and fantasy, I told myself: If he is a man from ancient Palestine, transported to our time by some miracle, he could not have mastered Russian so well in three years. And then I shuddered: did I mean that He could not have? If it were He, then He could do far, far more amazing things than that!

When I heard that Emmanuel had to be in a certain garden on the night before Friday, I immediately remembered the Friday night when the Saviour was betrayed and seized in the Garden of Gethsemane.

So that was where I had to go. And that was where I found him: in the Garden of Gethsemane!

When I had recovered slightly from my fear, I took a grip on myself. I interrupted the story about the lion and the lion-tamer and asked him point-blank: 'Are you Jesus Christ?'

I trembled inside as I asked the question, afraid that now my companion's face would be distorted into a mask of insanity and I would hear the feverish ranting of a madman whose mind can be tripped into a maniacal fit by a single word – in this case the name of the Saviour.

This is what he said to me (I repeat that I am only conveying the content, for I cannot reproduce the full originality of his speech):

'My parents named me Emmanuel, which means "God with us". The name Yehoshua was given to me by my *shelukhin* – in Russian it means "the help of Jehovah", but I heard the word "Christ" for the first time here, in this world, and for a long time I could not understand who he was, this crucified god to whom everybody prayed. But when I learned Russian and read the New Testament, it was like being struck by a bolt of lightning. Many things in that book are confused and distorted, there are a lot of tall stories; but the more I read, the clearer it became that it was about me, that I am the Crucified One. I am the Crucified One!'

When I heard how angrily he repeated: 'I am the Cwucified One, I am the Cwucified One,' I was certain that the man in front of me was mentally ill. But even if he was psychologically damaged, I liked him and found him interesting. In an attempt to restore clarity to his clouded reason, I asked cautiously: 'But how can you be Jesus? Were you crucified?'

But this question only agitated him even more. 'I was not, I was not! I didn't realise straight away, but then I understood! It's all a terrible mistake that has lasted two thousand years.'

'Who did they crucify?' I asked even more gently.

'I don't know. Perhaps Didim, or perhaps Yehua Taddai. Ever since I realised what happened I've been trying to guess who they killed. Didim looks exactly like me – that's why he was called that: in Greek the word means "twin". And Yehuda Taddai looks like me too; he's my cousin. (*I remembered that the disciple Judas Thaddaeus was indeed the cousin of Jesus.*) Didim is so reckless! And stubborn ... But no, it wasn't him. I laughed a lot when I read in the Gospel about him putting his fingers in the holes from the nails. That's exactly what Foma-Didim would have done, so it means it wasn't him they crucified. It must have been Yehuda, my mother's half-nephew. Or perhaps Nafanail? He has blue eyes too. Not many people in Jerusalem knew me to look at, so any of the *shelukhin* could have pretended to be me ... No, I can't guess which of them was executed. But I do know for certain who thought the whole thing up: the other Yehuda, the one from Keriot. He's a Judaean and they're more cunning than we Galileans. Yehuda, son of Shimon, persuaded Kifa, and he convinced all the others. They always listened to him! You knew, they were the ones who brought me here and shut me in: Kifa and Yehuda.' He gestured round the cave.

I will tell you the rest of what he said in brief, omitting my questions, his exclamations, and also my thoughts concerning the events described. It will be best if you form your own opinion of the plausibility of this story.

And so, if the narrator of the story is to be believed, he (that is, the wandering preacher Emmanuel-Yohoshua, who lived in Palestine nineteen centuries ago) came to the city of Jerusalem on the eve of the great festival of Passover. He was accompanied by twelve disciples who had attached themselves to him in the course of his travels. Most of them were fishermen from the Sea of Galilee, and the others could be categorised as *misérables* – Emmanuel obviously always had a weak spot for 'dark people'.

In Jerusalem, where Emmanuel had never been heard of before, he followed his usual habit of talking to various people, and some abused him while others listened attentively. Eventually someone reported the heretic to the municipal authorities for undermining the principles of the Jewish faith and the preacher was forced to go into hiding. On Thursday night he and his disciples gathered outside the city, in the Garden of Gethsemane, and consulted on what to do next. Flee from the city? But all the roads were covered; the mounted guards would easily overtake the fugitives.

Then the senior member of the *shelukhin*, Kifa, said 'Teacher, there is a place nearby where you can hide. You can stay there for two or three days, until those who seek you cease their searching.' Kifa and another *sheluahk* called Yehuda, son of Shimon, whom Emmanuel called 'very clever and cunning', took their leader to the summit of the Mount of Olives, into the yard of a certain poor widow, where an ancient cave had recently been uncovered. It had once been used to bury the dead, until there was no more room left in the chamber.

The disciples left Emmanuel a lamp, water and bread, and went away. After a little while, however, he was overcome with remorse (how could he wait for things to pass over in a safe sanctuary while his *shelukhin* exposed themselves to danger?) and he tried to go back to the garden, but it turned out that his disciples had blocked the way out with rocks.

And then something like an earthquake happened. Emmanuel lost consciousness for a moment and when he came round he heard a little girl's voice repeating a strange word: '*Pe-tya! Pe-tya!* It was Durka, the girl from Stroganovka, looking for her rooster.

'At first I thought that I had died in the earthquake and gone to the world of the dead,' he told me. 'Everything there is different from in the land of the living: different nature, different people, a different language, different customs. But I just couldn't work out if it was heaven or hell. It seemed different to me at different times. Sometimes I thought it must be heaven: so many trees, so much water, no heat. But sometimes I thought: No, this is hell. It's only in hell that it gets so cold and the earth turns as white and hard as a dead body. Then I decided that it wasn't hell or heaven, but a different world where you go after death and you have to live the same way as in the previous one – do what is pleasing to God and overcome the Evil One in yourself. Afterwards, I thought, you probably died again, and then there would be another world, and then another, and so on until the soul reached the end of the journey destined for it by the Lord.'

I told you that I experienced something similar in the Stroganovka cave. The ground shook there too, and something strange happened to time. As an old treatise that I discovered in your library says: 'And there are also caves that are called Special, in which there is no passage of time, and a man who enters into them may disappear for centuries or be cast out into a different time, or even into another Special Cave.'

I recall I was absolutely fascinated by these 'Special Caves'. According to the treatise, in them there is no passage of time. But Emmanuel, being an individual of a completely different temperament, was not at all surprised by the supernatural quality of what had happened, and not even particularly interested in it. 'God has many marvels,' he remarked in passing, and then went on to talk about something else – how unjust the Gospel was to his beloved *shelukhin*. This subject was much closer to his heart.

'Yehuda from Keriot did not betray me! Nobody ever betrayed me! He invented this whole adventure' (that was the word Emmanuel used) 'in order to save me. He went to the high priest and said: "I will show you where Yohoshua from Nazareth is hiding, give me the promised reward." He did that deliberately, so that they would crucify someone else and be satisfied. And he deliberately hanged himself afterwards, so that no one would doubt his betrayal. Oh, you have no idea how cunning he was, my Yehuda. And how noble! And now everybody curses him and spits on his remains! It's insufferable!

'Yehuda showed them one of my *shelukhin* – either Didim or the other Yehuda, or someone else – and he said "Yes, I am Yohoshua from Nazareth," and the others confirmed it. It was probably Taddai after all: both of us were like our grandfather – the same features, the same height. Did they really crucify him? That is the most terrible form of execution. Even death on a stake is less painful; life drains away with the blood then. But in a crucifixion you keep trying, over and again, to lift yourself up with your feet so that you can get a breath of air, and the sun pierces straight into your brain, and the executioner holds up a damp sponge on his spear. You know that you must not drink – it will only prolong your agony – but your parched lips reach out of their own accord ... And it lasts so many hours, until the crowd and the guard get bored. Then they break your shin-bones, so you can't lift yourself up any more, and soon you suffocate ...'

Then he started to cry, and I had to comfort him. He smeared the tears across his face and kept repeating: 'I have to go back. I have to go back to my own people. But the cursed cave will not let me! Three years I wandered round the land of Russia. At fist I didn't understand a thing about what had happened. Then I realised, only I didn't know what I ought to do. But just recently I heard a voice. That happens sometimes: I hear a Voice. His Voice.' (Emmanuel pointed up at the ceiling of the cave.) 'The voice said to me: "Go back. They have crucified the wrong person, and so the people have failed to understand anything. Even worse than that, they have understood everything wrongly! And for almost two thousand years they have been tormenting each other, tormenting each other." And I realised that had to go back and put everything right.

'I left Russia, hurrying to get here in time for the festival of Passover. I managed to find the cave. It was fortunate that the house was abandoned and nobody lived there. I dug for long time before I found the entrance – in two thousand years it had had sunk seven cubits under the ground. On Thursday night I went down into the cave to wait for Friday and stayed there until the morning, but nothing happened.

'The next Thursday I decided to follow my exact route from the garden – perhaps that was the important thing? But again nothing happened. I tried again several times, but my own time would not take me back again; its gates were closed. Then I set off to walk round my native land – to look and think and talk to people.

'And after two days I suddenly remembered that there was a full moon then! In my time Passover was always celebrated on the fifteenth day, at the full moon. I entered the cave on the night before the fifteenth day of Nisan.'

Then Emmanuel recollected where he was, fluttered his hands and said: 'Ah, woman, I have been talking with you too long!

Where is the moon?' He dashed out into the open. And I dashed after him

The moon had already set and Emmanuel groaned in frustration. 'I missed it. That always the way when I get talking with anyone.'

There was a cock-crow in the distance: dawn was near.'

Emmanuel started speaking again, angrily: 'And they have slandered Kifa too. He could not have denied me three times before the cock crowed. I believe that Kifa went to the house of the high priest. He must have wanted to make sure my pursuers had not noticed my substitution. But I don't believe that he "went forth and did weep bitter tears". I can't believe that Kifa wept when he heard a rooster crow!'

Then I suddenly remembered and said: 'What does the rooster mean? Not the one in the Gospel, but the other one – the red one? What is its significance?'

He gasped at me, from which I concluded that he did not know anything about the magical properties of the red rooster, and I had been wasting my time racking my brains over ancient treatises and absurd hypotheses. What could a rooster have to do with anything?

But Emmanuel suddenly slapped his hands against his sides and cried out so loudly that some bird of the night flapped its wings and took flight: 'The rooster! Why, of course!' And he added something in Hebrew or Aramaic.

'What? What?' I cried out in fright.

'It's not the full moon that's important, he explained, stumbling over his words. 'It's the rooster. I completely forgot about him! That's why the cave won't let me through! Ah, I'm so grateful to you, woman! But how did you find out about the rooster?'

I was terribly agitated – an unfathomable secret that could change my entire view of the world was about to be revealed to me. I told him: 'From a book in which it is written that if a red rooster crows at the hour of dawn in a Special Cave, the soul and body of a man will be suspended between worlds, and he can be cast out into a different time and place. Is that really true?' I trembled inwardly as I asked.

But he shrugged and said, 'I don't know anything about that. But I have to find myself a rooster!'

'A red one?'

'Yes, yes, he was red. Do you have any money?'

I started at the unexpected question, and answered: 'Yes.'

'Will you buy me a red rooster at the market? I haven't got any money at all.'

'Of course I will. So the red rooster must be very important, then?'

'Of course it is!' he exclaimed. 'Without it old Miriam won't be able to survive.'

I was afraid that he was raving. 'Who?' I asked.

'Miriam, the poor widow that this plot of land belongs to, or used to belong to in my time. Miriam keeps chickens there and lives by selling the eggs. And her rooster followed me into the burial chamber. Roosters are so inquisitive. I only found him after Kifa and Yehuda had already gone. The old woman can't manage without a rooster! Who's going to mate her chickens? Now I understand why God would not let me back through! He is so just and merciful!'

I asked him: 'So there was a rooster in the cave with you, and he crowed before the earth shook?'

'Yes, I think so.'

I paused for a moment, trying to comprehend the significance of this incredible phenomenon. But I failed. I asked: 'A red rooster, why that's absurd! How could that possibly be?'

Emmanuel smiled. 'Is there any wise man who knows all the laws on which the world is founded? Then why be surprised if God teaches us a new lesson or reveals a new parable to us?'

'What could be the sense of such a strange parable?'

He thought for a moment and asked: 'Tell me, is it stupid to believe in miracles?'

'No,' I replied. 'That is, yes. I don't know. It is stupid to hope that a miracle will intervene in your life and remove all your sorrow.'

'Yes, to hope for a miracle is stupid,' he agreed. 'And senseless. As senseless as a red rooster crowing in a Special Cave.'

We did not talk about anything else, because I suddenly felt incredibly tired and could hardly stay on my feet. No doubt it was a reaction to all the shocks of that remarkable night.

We went back down into the chamber and slept there until morning. The ground was hard, but I have never slept so soundly and peacefully. And when the first rays of sunlight peeped in through the opening, we went to the city market to buy a red rooster.

We found a bird of the right colour without any trouble. The breed is very widespread here; it must have been established thousands of years ago.

We took the first red rooster that we came across. We bought it without haggling or examining it, and it turned out to be a bad bargain – the bird had a cantankerous character. Emmanuel had to hug it close the whole day long, and the nasty bird scratched his arms all over with its beak and spurs. But my companion bore it all without complaining and merely remonstrated with the red-feathered bandit. Alas, the bird proved less susceptible to the prophet's wonder-working speech than hardened villains.

By the way, on the question of villains. Once I felt someone's gaze on me in the crowded street. Swinging round sharply, I saw the round-faced bandit who was called Yasha. He hid round a corner, but not before I got a look at him.

I wanted to grab Emmanuel by the sleeve and run, drag him away from the danger, but the round-faced man suddenly stuck his head back out and put one finger to his lips.

Then I remembered Trofim Dubenko and felt reassured. All right, I thought, let Emmanuel have two bodyguards instead of one.

Ah, Your Eminence, what a wonderful day that was. If only it weren't for that dratted rooster, driving us crazy with its tricks! We ought to have bought a bird in the evening, not early in the morning, and we ought to have picked one with a more peaceable character.

We talked about all sorts of things – far too much to put into a letter. I can tell you just a few of the things he said that stuck in my memory

Emmanuel is exceptionally interesting to listen to; many of his thoughts are interesting and even paradoxical. Amazingly enough for a prophet, he does not have a shred of sanctimonious hypocrisy. For instance, when he saw the street women who came out to ply their trade at the Zion Gate, he started talking to me about physical love, although he knew that I was a nun. He said: 'There is no sin in affections of the flesh, and on the contrary, those who wither their flesh by abstinence commit a sin against God. The one thing you must not do is to debase and insult this joyful mystery by exchanging it for common coin. That is as bad as mocking the other two great mysteries – birth and death.' And he went dashing over to convince the harlots of Jerusalem not to defile God's joy. It cost me an effort to drag him away from the furious girls, who were ready to give him a good slapping.

The one subject that I tried to avoid, in order not to provoke another maniacal fit, was Jesus Christ. But we happened to stop for a drink of water on the Via Dolorosa, beside a wooden sculpture of the Lord, bowed under the weight of the cross. Emmanuel looked at the statue for a long time, as if he were measuring himself against some task, then suddenly turned round and said: 'You know, you are not the first one to recognise me. There was someone else, a procurator.'

It has started again, I thought with a helpless sigh and asked: 'Two thousand years ago?'

'No,' he said, 'three months ago, in St Petersburg.'

I shall try to relate what he told me after that as accurately as possible, because you will undoubtedly recognise the person concerned.

'The Procurator summoned me to see him and spoke to me for a long time about God, the Church and various other things.

'The Procurator was an intelligent man and he knew how to

listen. It was pleasant and interesting to talk to him. I didn't identify myself in order not to upset him – his entire room (and it was a very large, beautiful room) was hung with images of the Crucified One.

'Concerning the Church, I told him that it was quite unnecessary. Everyone should follow his or her own path, and any good person can be the guide, or even a bad person – that happens too. But what sort of trade is it to be a priest? How can you tell if a priest is a good person himself or not? And why can only men be priests? Are not women kinder and more self-sacrificing than men?

'And concerning God, I told the Procurator that He had been necessary before, in earlier times, in order to instil the fear of God into people. It's like in a family: when a child is little and cannot tell good from bad for himself, the parent has to influence him with the threat of punishment. But in two thousand years mankind has grown and is no longer afraid of God's wrath, and now something else is needed – not glancing over your shoulder at the wrathful Almighty, but listening to your own soul. That is where God is, in the soul, not in heaven, and not on a cloud. I told the Procurator: I walk over the Earth, look at people and see how much better they have become than they used to be – wiser, kinder and more compassionate. Still not grown up, but no longer foolish infants, as they were in the times of Moses or John the Baptist. Another covenant between God and man is needed now, a completely different one.

'Suddenly the old man waved his hand to shut me up. He knitted his thick, grey eyebrows and looked into my face for a long time – one or two minutes – and then he asked in a shrill voice: "Is it you? You?" And he answered himself: "It is you ... " and I realised that he had understood.

'"Why have you come to hinder me?" he asked. "It is hard enough for me without you. You are mistaken about people. You do not understand a single thing about them. They are still foolish little infants, they cannot manage without a strict shepherd; they will perish. I swear to you than man is weaker and lower than you thought. He is weak and mean. You have come too soon."

'I tried to explain to him that it had just happened, but he did not believe me. He went down on his knees, folded his hands like this and wept. "Go back from whence you came. In the name of Christ the Lord ... no, in the name of Your Heavenly Father, I implore you!"

'I replied honestly that I would be glad to go back, but I could not.

'"Yes, yes, I know," he said with a sigh.

'He got up and started walking round the room, talking to himself bitterly: "Ah, my soul, my soul ... but not for own sake, for my neighbour ..." Then he suddenly rang a bell and ordered me to be taken away. Although I still had a lot of things to say to him.'

There you have it, Your Eminence, the complete solution to our 'puzzle', as Sergei Sergeevich Dolinin used to say. Only what are we to do with this solution, now that we have it?

I already regret having written about this. With your fearless character, you will set about exposing the criminal; but you will get nowhere – you will merely earn a reputation as a madman.

I implore you, none of that is necessary. The Procurator thinks that he has struck a blow against the Son of God, and he is willing to pay for that with the immortality of his very soul. Let him pay. He will not pay to you and me, but to Him.

Ah, it is evening already. It is dark outside. I have sat over this letter the whole day long, and there is still so much I have not written!

Before I explain to you the most difficult part, which I hardly even understand myself, let me tell a few more of the things that Emmanuel said, because I keep remembering them all the time.

He astounded me when he said that he did not know whether God existed or not and that *it is not important*. 'What if there is no God?' he said; 'does that mean that man can act like a beast? We are not children who only behave properly in the presence of adults.'

And he also said: 'Do not strive to love the whole world; that way not many people will get much love. When you wish to build a tall tower, first sit down and work out if you have the funds to complete the building. But there are many who promise to love the whole world and all people, although they have no idea what love is. They cannot even love themselves. Do not dilute your love, do not spread it in a thin layer, like a drop of oil on a large pancake. Rather love your family and friends, but with all your heart. If your strength is very little, love yourself, but truly and faithfully. Do not betray yourself. That is, do not betray God, for he is your true self. And if you are true to yourself, that will be your salvation.'

But we did not finish talking about the most interesting thing of all. I asked him if he believed in life beyond the grave. Is there anything after death or not? He was surprised and said: 'How should I know? I'll find out when I die. While you are living here, you should think about this life, not the next one. Although, of course, it is interesting to dream. It seems to me that there must be another life and that the death of the body is not the end of a man, but a kind of new birth.' Then he became embarrassed and said: 'I even have an entire hypothesis about that ...'

'A hypothesis?' I said, realising that he had confused some learned words. 'Please tell me about it; it's very important for me to know!'

Emmanuel started to answer: 'I think – that is, I am almost certain, that at the moment of death every soul ...' Just then the wretched rooster broke free off his grasp and set off across an empty plot of land! We had to chase him and catch him. Just imagine it: the strident crowing, the idle onlookers whistling and hooting, feathers flying in all directions. So I never did learn what Emmanuel wanted to reveal to me about the afterlife.

Now that I am alone, I can see that I wasted the precious hours when we were together far too thoughtlessly. I chattered a lot myself, instead of listening. Sometimes I started talking about unimportant trivial matters, and there were times when we simply said nothing.

How different today is from yesterday. How *unnecessary* all the things that my gaze falls on have become! How lonely the world is! How empty.

Why did I let him go? Why did I not stop him?

I thought he would come to my hotel in the morning, embarrassed and, perhaps, wiser. And we would laugh at that stupid rooster together.

I did not sleep at all last night. I smiled as I imagined how I would make fun of him. I thought what I would ask him about when he came back.

But, of course, he did not come back.

Lord, Lord, what have I done?

What if it is all true?

Then he is the One; then they will seize Him, and scourge Him and put a crown of thorns on His head, and break Him on the cross!

And I let him go!

But could I really have stopped him? He is gentle, kind, awkward, but it is impossible to stop him. The intelligent 'Procurator' realised that only too well.

Last night Emmanuel went into the cave with a red rooster under his arm. And he did not come back.

Today is Saturday.

At first I waited for him, then I realised that he would not come and I sat down to write this letter. I have only taken a single break – to go to the market and buy a red rooster.

I am more experienced now. The new rooster is calm and even redder than yesterday's. He is here, ogling with his round eye and pecking millet out of a saucer.

I shall leave this letter at the mission, although I am sure that tomorrow morning I shall have to collect it again. And now I shall send all the money that I have left to Salakh. I never went back to the poor man that night. He must think me an ungrateful creature, hiding from him because I do not wish to pay.

*

If you do read this letter, please do not think of me as a fugitive nun who has betrayed her vows. After all, I am a bride of Christ – who else should I follow, if not Him?

I shall be *there* one day after Him. And if He is crucified, I shall wash His body with my tears and anoint it with myrrh and bitter aloe.

Do not frown so, do not frown! I have not lost my mind. It is just that after a sleepless night and an anxious wait, I am prone to exaltation.

I understand everything very well. And I know what really happened.

Three years ago an eccentric peasant, a tramp, crept into a cave in the Urals to spend the night, and the cave was a strange one, where people are visited by grotesque visions, and the tramp dreamed of something that took away his ability to speak and his memory, and he imagined that he was Jesus Christ. Certainly, this is a kind of insanity, only it is not malevolent, but benevolent, like the insanity of holy fools.

Am I right?

And the most astounding thing is that it is impossible to prove or verify anything in this story, as is always the case in matters of faith. As a certain novel says, the entire world is built on absurdities, they are too necessary here on earth. If you wish and are able to believe in a miracle, then believe; if you do not wish and you are not able, then choose a rational explanation. And it is well known that there are many phenomena in the world which at first seem supernatural to us, but later are explained by science. Do you remember the Black Monk?

And I also know what happened last night.

Emmanuel-Manuila deceived me. He decided to rid himself of this clinging woman, because he likes to walk round the world on his own. He did not want simply to say: 'Leave me alone, woman' – for, after all, he is kind. He left me the possibility of a miracle as a souvenir and went to travel round the world.

Of course, nothing will happen to me. There will not be any displacement in time and space. What raving nonsense.

But nonetheless, I shall go into the cave tonight, and I shall have a red rooster under my arm.

THE END